CONNIE MANN

THE LIAR'S TREASURE

A SPERANZA TEAM NOVEL

Tyndale House Publishers
Carol Stream, Illinois

Visit Tyndale online at tyndale.com.

Visit Connie Mann's website at conniemann.com.

The Liar's Treasure

Cover design by Dean H. Renninger

The Liar's Treasure is a work of fiction. Where real people, events, establishments, organizations, or locales appear, they are used fictitiously. All other elements of the novel are drawn from the author's imagination.

For information about special discounts for bulk purchases, please contact Tyndale House Publishers at csresponse@tyndale.com, or call 1-855-277-9400.

Library of Congress Cataloging-in-Publication Data

A catalog record for this book is available from the Library of Congress.

ISBN 978-1-4964-8744-5

Printed in the United States of America

32 31 30 29 28 27 26
7 6 5 4 3 2 1

Praise for the Speranza Team Series

Buckle up for a page-turning novel reminiscent of *National Treasure* and Indiana Jones. This story has it all: mystery, layers of suspense, and the lightest touch of romance. I enjoyed every page and wanted time and responsibilities to pause so I could get lost in the story. Highly recommended!

> **CARA PUTMAN,** award-winning and bestselling author of *The Vanished* and *Flight Risk*, on *The Liar's Treasure*

A pulse-pounding mix of danger, secrets, and globe-trotting fun. *The Liar's Treasure* is pure storytelling gold. Connie Mann's books always move to the top of my to-read list.

> **CHRISTY BARRITT,** award-winning author of *Pressure Point*

Get ready for a wild ride with Sophie, Mac, and the Speranza team. One can hope there is more to come from this dynamic group. Mann's latest is perfect for readers of Susan May Warren and those who love a good conspiracy read.

> ***LIBRARY JOURNAL*** starred review of *The Crown Conspiracy*

The Crown Conspiracy took me on a breath-stealing, heart-stopping adventure through castles, Venice, and the Alps. Connie Mann's terrific novel is chock-full of fascinating layers of romance and intrigue amid a backdrop of art forgery that segues into a treasure hunt. Highly recommended!

> **COLLEEN COBLE,** *USA Today* bestselling author

The story grips you with the first words and doesn't let go until the last page. I highly recommend this exciting thriller!

> **CARRIE STUART PARKS,** Christy Award–winning author of *Fallout*, on *The Crown Conspiracy*

This novel will take you deep into a world of dangerous deception and a high-stakes conspiracy, where one woman must decide how far she will go to protect those she loves. The fast-paced action left me breathless!

DIANN MILLS, bestselling author of *Facing the Enemy*, on *The Crown Conspiracy*

Mann spins an intriguing action adventure with the kind of twists and turns that take the reader on an exciting ride. A delightful read.

RACHEL HAUCK, *New York Times* bestselling author, on *The Crown Conspiracy*

Connie Mann had me on the edge of my seat with her latest heart-pounding romantic suspense, *The Crown Conspiracy*! From page one, her clever blend of intrigue and action kept me glued to the page.

SUSAN MAY WARREN, *USA Today* bestselling and RITA Award–winning author

In loving memory of Captain Virginia Ferguson, who blazed a trail for countless women to follow and whose life embodied the Speranza spirit of women helping women. You not only taught me to handle a boat, your example and encouragement to "do it like I taught you" forever inspire me to be the best captain, mother, woman of faith, mentor, and friend I can be. Thank you, Ginny. For everything.

Hope is an anchor for the soul.

PROLOGUE

OFF THE COAST OF AVILÉS, SPAIN—1728

Cira tried to keep her balance on the rocking wooden deck of the *Bartholomew*, head down in seeming defeat, watching through hanks of her wet hair as the pirates pawed through the passengers' trunks, flinging belongings overboard. They were getting closer, ever closer, to the one thing she prayed they'd never find.

Rain poured down in sheets and plastered her silk gown to her skin. The way the sailors' eyes flicked over her had her heart pounding from a new kind of fear.

They were going to kill her if they found it.

Worse, they'd enjoy it.

She shivered, despite the balmy air, then took a deep breath so she could focus on the knots binding her hands behind her back. She didn't dare glance Maura's way again. She'd seen her fifteen-year-old sister peek from the companionway several minutes ago, still in her cabin-boy disguise.

Barely an hour ago, there had been a loud thump, followed by the sound of running feet. Before anyone had time to whisper the word *pirates*, the door to the captain's dining room had burst open and several sailors had stormed into the room, all well armed.

Cira had frozen, a spoonful of turtle soup halfway to her mouth.

A tall man wearing a finely tailored crimson coat with bold brass buttons entered behind his men. When Captain Arnaud muttered, "You!" the pirate captain shot him point-blank.

Cira managed to bite back her scream, though the matron beside her let loose a deafening shriek. The woman paid dearly for her lack of self-control as the pirates hauled her and the other five passengers up on deck. Cira would forever cringe at the memory of the two bodies being tossed overboard as though they had no more worth than their belongings.

Her wet fingers slipped off the knot—again—as she struggled to free her hands.

The *Maria Claire* had left the port at Avilés mere hours ago. How had no one noticed their vessel being chased, then boarded by this gang of thieves? She blinked rainwater out of her eyes and felt another trail of water slide down the neck of her sodden gown. Thunder cracked overhead. *How indeed?*

At least their feet weren't bound. The pirates had forced the passengers across the planks they'd placed between the two vessels. Now they stood, huddled in the rain, as the pirates looted the *Maria Claire*, carting supplies, belongings, and provisions onto their own ship.

The *Bartholomew* flew no flag, so Cira was uncertain whether the dark-eyed captain was a pirate or a privateer, though she supposed the distinction didn't matter at this point.

She yanked her wayward thoughts sharply under control. If she didn't find a way to escape, she'd be dead in minutes. She had to save Maura. And the box their parents died protecting.

They were only four hours from shore. She wouldn't fail in her sworn duty to protect their heritage, at least not without a fight.

One of the pirates, who wore a large gold hoop in one ear, used his machete to slide another trunk to the center of the deck.

"Who owns this?" The pirate captain nodded at the trunk. He

leaned against the mast, arms folded across a solid chest, watching from under his hat brim as though the rain meant nothing.

Beside Cira, an older man lifted his chin. "That belongs to me." He sent a reassuring nod to his wife, then eased in front of her, effectively blocking her from view. She cried silent tears.

The sailor pried the latch off the trunk with his machete and rooted around inside, cackling when he came up with a small sack that clinked as he picked it up. He hefted the weight. "Bit of gold in there, I'm thinking, Captain."

The captain caught the bag in one hand, then bowed to the passenger. "Thank you for your contribution to our cause." He raised his flintlock pistol.

Cira squeezed her eyes closed, but she couldn't block out the horror. Or the wife's screams.

Head down, she focused on her bindings.

Another sailor slid her trunk to the center of the deck, and Cira froze as his comrade pried off the lock, then plunged his hands inside. *Dear God in heaven, help us.*

He pulled out the oilskin case and grinned, showing off his three remaining teeth. "Oh, ho, what have we here?"

Her heart sprinted like a jackrabbit as she waited, choosing her moment.

"Don't open that bag in the rain, you fool." Cira shouted to be heard above the downpour. "It's a book. You'll ruin it."

The captain straightened away from the mast and approached, eyes narrowed. He waved the sailor under an overhang, out of the rain.

This was her one and only chance to save the book.

And possibly herself and her sister.

She risked a sideways glance. Maura had vanished. Cira could only hope and pray she was safely hidden until Cira could find her.

Eyes locked on the sailor glaring at her, she worked faster, almost sagging with relief when the knot finally gave.

The sailor opened the case's strap and reached in for the Book of Days.

"Don't you dare touch that with your filthy hands!" Cira kept her hands behind her back and straightened her spine. "Put the gloves on. They're in the case."

Both men turned to glare at her, but she didn't flinch.

The captain nodded at the sailor, who reached for the gloves and pulled them on.

"You won't get away with stealing it, you know. That book is powerful."

"How so?"

Cira almost smiled at the captain's intrigued expression. "The book judges motives. If you try to steal it or use it for selfish reasons, you'll die."

The captain's laughter rang out. "And how, pray tell, does it know anyone's intentions?"

Cira shrugged. "I'm not sure, exactly. But I know it does."

The captain nodded at the sailor again. "Show me."

The crewman's eyes went round as saucers. "B-but—" He bit back the protest when the captain reached a hand toward his pistol.

As carefully as if he were handling a keg of lit powder, the crewman slid the book out of the case and showed the captain. He slowly turned the pages, waiting while the captain studied each one. Even in the gloom, the gilt edging and exquisitely rendered paintings fairly glowed from within.

Cira bided her time, internally counting off the minutes.

"Return the book to me at once. It does not belong to you. If you do not, you will suffer the consequences."

The captain chuckled, then his eyes went hard. "You, mademoiselle, have a lively imagination, but I grow weary of the game."

A sudden crash sounded as a nearby sailor dropped his machete and rushed toward them. "Captain! Toothless don't look so good."

Even as he said the words, Toothless slumped to the deck, motionless, the book beside him. His friend dropped to his knees and tossed the book aside as he patted the man's cheeks, trying to rouse him.

Cira didn't hesitate. She snatched the gloves from Toothless's hands, then scooped up the case and book as she ran to the side of the ship. She shoved the book and gloves into the case and hoped the oilskin could survive a dip in the ocean.

She had one leg over the side of the vessel when she heard the telltale click of a pistol being cocked behind her.

"There is nowhere to go." The captain's weapon was pointed straight at her, never wavering as the ship rode the swells.

Cira glanced down, way down, and grinned. Maura motioned from a small rowboat far below.

"I don't take kindly to anyone killing my crew."

She turned back to the captain. "I didn't kill him. The book did. You should have listened to me."

Cira tossed the case over the side and launched herself after it.

She hit the water with a mighty splash, then fought with all her strength to reach the surface. Her waterlogged dress kept trying to drag her under.

Cira was frantically dodging the captain's bullets when a strong arm wrapped around her waist and hauled her into the rowboat. She thumped her elbow as she landed in the bottom. Her rescuer tossed the oilskin case at her, then grabbed the oars and rowed around the stern toward the *Maria Claire* while lead balls hit the water all around them.

One explosion rang out, then another as flames shot out of the *Maria Claire*. They hid behind the hull, out of sight. It wouldn't buy them much time, but they had no other options.

She glanced at Maura, who slumped beside her, equally soaked, blood oozing from a gash on her forehead. Maura's hand lay atop the wooden box next to her.

"Maura!"

Her sister opened her eyes, grimaced in pain, then closed them again.

The book clutched to her chest, Cira grabbed her sister's hand and sobbed with relief.

Until she spotted the pistol tucked into their rescuer's waistband.

1

NEW ORLEANS, LOUISIANA—PRESENT DAY

Octavia Tucker Benoit was not a woman smart people crossed. Not even if you were the formidable New Orleans society matron's granddaughter. Which was how Camille Abernathy found herself in an upstairs bedroom of an ornate mansion-turned-private-library in the French Quarter, trussed up like a beauty-pageant queen yet again this year, arguing with her almost-eighteen-year-old daughter. She'd so much rather be home with a good book on this blustery December evening.

She kept her tone light. "Come on, Cass, really? Combat boots? You know Gran will have kittens if you go downstairs wearing those."

"Yes, but she'll be mad at you, not me, so it all works out." Cassandra winked, her cheeky grin an exact replica of Camille's cousin Marcel, the inveterate charmer who was Cass's favorite grown-up and the source of her newly acquired sass.

Despite her exasperation, Camille smiled and shook her head. She'd deal with Cass's cheekiness and Marcel's influence another day. A quick check of her watch made her wince. The fundraiser had officially begun five minutes ago. "Time to go, baby girl. You know your gran."

"On time is late," Cass said, mimicking her grandmother's firm tone. Before Camille could get her moving toward the door, Cass propped her fists on her hips and scowled into the cheval mirror. "I hate this stupid dress. I look like a freaking twelve-year-old playing Disney Princess." She slapped her hands against the blue satin gown that belled out over several petticoats and flipped an indignant hand toward the tiara perched atop her dark hair.

Camille met her daughter's eyes in the mirror, shocked anew by the beautiful young woman scowling back at her. She ignored the flicker of panic and sorrow Cass's upcoming graduation inspired and kept her tone light.

"I understand. I do. I didn't get to pick my outfit, either." Camille quirked an eyebrow and indicated her own poufy dress, also complete with tiara. "But you know the literacy fundraiser is Gran's favorite charity event of the year. She wants us here as a show of solidarity."

Cass rolled her eyes. "I get why she wants *you* here. But why me? Only old people come to these things."

"Hey! Who you callin' old?" Camille grinned.

Cass's cell phone buzzed. She read the text, then plopped on the couch, crossing her arms. "I'm not going."

And just like that, her daughter was twelve again. Camille pinched the bridge of her nose. Let out a sigh. "Take it up with Gran—some other time. Right now, it's time to suck it up, buttercup. You know the drill. We smile, talk to all those old people about supporting literacy. I'll take a bunch of pictures for the sponsors of tonight's event, then we'll grab pizza on the way home."

"I'm never doing this again." Cass stood and flounced toward the door. Camille stopped her with a hand on her arm and held the blue satin ballet slippers aloft. "Just be glad they don't have spike heels like mine."

One corner of Cass's mouth quirked up as she took the ballet flats from Camille. "True."

As they approached the sweeping staircase that led downstairs, Camille straightened her spine, pulled out her best pageant smile, and took her daughter's hand, holding her camera in the other. "The things we do for family—and pepperoni pizza."

Cass rolled her eyes and met her grin, then adopted the same serene demeanor as they descended the stairs together, ready to perform their duty.

Camille smiled. *That's my girl.*

Lucien Broussard strode into the stately French Quarter residence as though he belonged there, despite the jet lag still fogging his brain and the slightly too-tight fit of his hastily rented tux. But Pops had been insistent, and Lucien didn't have the heart to deny him.

He paused to scan the elegantly dressed crowd, saw a few people glance his way and whisper. How long would it take before somebody came to kick him out? Most likely Octavia Benoit herself. Like she had when he had the temerity to show up at her Garden District mansion years ago to offer Camille his condolences after J. T.'s death. Octavia had coldly dismissed him as one of those "no-good Broussards."

He wandered the luxurious room, then plucked a glass of champagne from a passing waiter's tray. He had just taken a sip when he glanced up and sucked in a breath. Coughed into his fist. He stepped behind a potted palm to avoid drawing attention to himself while he tried to catch his breath.

Camille Abernathy and her daughter, Cassandra, had just started down the stairs, and the sight hit him like a mule kick to the chest. Camille was even more beautiful than she'd been the last time he laid eyes on her two years ago. And Cass, wow. All grown up. She was the spitting image of Camille when she was in high school. No wonder his best friend J. T. had instantly fallen madly, hopelessly in love with Camille. Both women had the same tall, willowy build. Same striking dark eyes, same shoulder-length, coal-black hair. He'd assumed they'd be here tonight, but he hadn't been prepared. Not really.

Certainly not for the guilt that reared up and slapped him, hard. *I'm sorry, J. T.*

"What do you think you're doing here?" an imperious voice inquired from behind him.

Right on cue. Lucien turned slowly, grinning as he reached for her gloved hand and pressed a quick kiss to the back before releasing her. Octavia delivered an icy glare, clearly annoyed that a mere stable boy had breached her castle. Lucien widened his smile. He wasn't so easily cowed these days.

"You look positively regal tonight, Mrs. Benoit, as always," he drawled. "Lovely shindig." He indicated the mansion with his champagne glass.

Irritation pinched her mouth. "I asked what you're doing here."

"Attending the fundraiser, of course. Pops asked me to deliver his donation. In person."

A flicker of . . . something passed through her eyes at the mention of his grandfather, then instantly disappeared. "There was no need for you to travel *all* this way across town, as donations can be made electronically these days."

He raised an eyebrow at her implied reference to the poorer side of town. "No trouble. He also asked me to deliver this." He pulled the white envelope from his breast pocket and held it out.

She regarded it like she would a coiled rattler. "What is it?"

"A request."

Her sudden hesitation surprised him. Though Mrs. Benoit had to be in her seventies, like Pops, she'd always been a remarkably confident woman, elegant and self-possessed. Her gaze bounced from him to the envelope and back before she snatched it from his hand and tore it open.

All the color drained from her face as she read, and he reached out to catch her in case she fell. She shook off his hand and stepped away, then tucked the letter into a pocket in her skirt with a hand that trembled just the slightest bit. When she spoke, her voice dripped ice. "Kindly remind Claude that the diary has *never* belonged to his family, despite his delusions, nor will it ever. It is Benoit property and so it will remain. It is not for sale. At any price. Please show yourself out."

She spun on her heel and strode away.

He smiled as he lifted his glass in toast to her retreating back.

That went pretty much exactly as Lucien had expected.

Let the games begin.

"Who is that?" Cass murmured as they descended the stairs. "He reminds me of Chris Hemsworth in *Thor*, well, without the shaggy blond hair." She jutted her chin toward the back of the room.

Camille followed her daughter's gaze and stumbled on the thickly carpeted runner. She gripped the banister to steady herself and called upon her years of unwanted pageant participation to remain calm and unruffled. Never mind the urge to bolt from the room.

"More like Pirate Jack Sparrow," she muttered.

What was Lucien Broussard doing here? She'd seen him watching her from the fringes at Gramps's funeral two years ago, but he hadn't approached. Beyond that, she hadn't laid eyes on him since before J. T.'s death. She'd heard he'd gone to Africa or someplace after he left the Army, doing heaven only knew what. Local rumors ranged from mercenary to private security to outright piracy. Given his family's long history of pirate ancestors, anything was possible. Not that she followed the gossip.

Camille steered them toward the opposite side of the room, but they hadn't gone far before Lucien stepped into their path. He bowed formally. "Good evening, Camille." He raised her hand to his lips and brushed a kiss over her knuckles, a familiar hint of mischief in his deep-blue eyes. "You're as lovely as ever. A veritable fairy-tale princess come to life."

She stiffened at his veiled reference to the hated moniker he'd given her in high school. But it was his husky drawl and unmistakable cologne that sent a remembered—and most unwelcome—shiver of awareness down her back. She snatched her hand back, annoyed that after nearly two decades, the man could still throw her off balance. Before her flustered brain could come up with anything coherent to say, he turned to Cass.

"You must be Cassandra." He reached a hand toward her ear and withdrew a lovely white paper flower, which he presented to her with a flourish. "I'm Lucien Broussard."

"How did you do that?" Cass asked, smiling.

"A bit of magic." He smiled and pointed to her hair. "May I?" At her nod, he tucked the bloom behind her ear.

Irritation spiked at how easily he charmed her daughter with the same ridiculous trick that had captured her attention so long ago. "What are you doing here, Lucien? I thought you were . . . somewhere far away."

He cocked his head and those piercing blue eyes dared her to run away. "Did you now? You know better than to believe everything you hear."

"You guys know each other?" Cass's eyes bounced from one to the other.

"A long time ago," Camille said, just as Lucien said, "We went to high school together. Your dad and I were tight."

Curiosity bubbled out of Cass. "Really? Why haven't I met you before? Were you in the Army with my dad?"

When Camille saw Lucien's subtle flinch at Cass's question about the military, she relaxed slightly. He wasn't as unaffected as he pretended to be.

"I was. Your dad was one of the good guys. The best, actually." He turned to Camille. "I'm just in town to take care of some family business."

"Will you tell me more about him?"

Cass's eagerness pierced Camille. She'd always told her daughter all she could about the father who'd died before she was born, but somehow, hearing about him from Lucien had hit her daughter differently.

The smile he sent Cass was tender, gentle. "Anytime." His eyes darted over Camille's shoulder and he stiffened. "But for now, if you ladies will excuse me." He sent them a blinding smile before he turned and strode away.

"Wow." Cass pulled out her phone, no doubt texting her best friend Lindsey as she wandered over to the refreshment table, her annoyance over the dress forgotten in the wake of Lucien's smile.

Or maybe that was just Camille. *Wow, indeed.* How could the man still affect her so? She took slow breaths to calm her speeding pulse as she raised her camera and scanned the room, relieved when she confirmed that Lucien had disappeared. Thankfully.

Do your job. Then you can get out of here.

She strolled around the room snapping pictures of the well-heeled guests while mentally shoring up her defenses for when she had to face Lucien again. It would be too much to hope his presence was a one-time thing.

Several hours later, the last guests had finally departed, leaving large donations behind. Gran thanked Camille and Cass for doing their part, and Cass graciously claimed she'd been glad to help. Camille gave herself points for not snorting at that. Now, bundled against the cold in heavy coats and scarves, they headed toward Camille's car, parked much farther away than she wanted to walk in heels, but such was parking in the Quarter.

"How come you've never told me about Lucien? Does he live around here?" Cass shifted her backpack more comfortably as they walked.

So many possible answers. Camille settled for, "We knew each other a long time ago. Like he said, he and your dad were close friends. I'm not sure where he lives these days."

Cass kept her head buried in her phone as they walked. "Have you talked to Uncle Marcel lately?"

"Not since I got back from my last job, why?" Though not for lack of trying. Marcel had been dodging her calls, well aware that she was angry that he'd taken Cass to some pirate museum he'd just discovered—on a school day—without checking with her. To make matters worse, some idiot had run them off the road!

"Just wondering."

Camille waited until Cass finally peered up from her phone before she asked, "Is there something wrong? You can talk to me, you know. About whatever it is."

Cass snorted, then rolled her eyes again, a gesture Camille had come to hate. "Sure, Mom. 'Cause you always listen and take my needs into account. Like when you moved us out of Gran's house to the back of beyond without giving me any choice."

"I thought you love Gramps's farm!"

Cass didn't respond.

"Okay, maybe we should have talked about it. But I know you, Cass. And hopefully you know me well enough to know I can help. Whatever it is."

"Stop hounding me, Mom, geez. You do this after every trip."

Because you're sneaking around and spending too much time with Marcel. I'm afraid for you. But she bit her tongue, searched for words her daughter would hear.

Someday she wanted to tell Cass about her work with Speranza, the centuries-old secret society and the amazing team of women Camille worked with. She wanted to give Cass a Speranza medallion, invite her to join the network and pledge her loyalty to helping women in trouble around the world, the same way Gran, and then Willa, had invited Camille. But her daughter had some growing up to do first.

"Cass, I—"

Cass stopped in the middle of the sidewalk, hands on her hips. "I'm not involved with the wrong crowd, I'm not doing drugs, I'm not pregnant. Just stop already. I can't breathe when you get like this."

With that, Cass spun on her heel, grabbed her skirts, and took off, darting across the street and down an alley.

Momentarily stunned, Camille blinked as she gripped her camera bag in one hand, her skirts in the other, and raced after her daughter, stumbling in her ridiculous heels. "Cass!"

A cold wind whipped down the narrow street. Lucien picked up his pace as he hurried toward his rental car. He'd forgotten how cold and damp it got in New Orleans in December.

He'd left the fundraiser and its prissy appetizers and headed to an old friend's bar for a thick burger and fries. The lively conversation had been almost enough to distract him from the gut punch any encounter with Camille Abernathy produced.

He blinked gritty eyes, rubbed a hand over his face. He could have used a few hours of shut-eye before embarking on tonight's fool's errand. The endless delays during the trip from Kinshasa, Democratic Republic of the Congo, to NOLA had taken almost forty-eight hours and gnawed at what little patience he had left.

Which was why he'd gone straight from the airport to the hospital to lay eyes on Pops, confirm what the doctors had said about his grandfather's injury—and his recovery.

Pops was also the reason he'd shown up at the fundraiser tonight. Pops had insisted this couldn't wait, and Lucien didn't have it in him to disappoint him. Again.

He rounded a corner and spotted Cass Abernathy darting out of an alley and running across the street, still in her ball gown. She glanced over her shoulder, eyes wide with fear, as a man raced out of another alley and followed her, a determined expression on his face. He was gaining on her.

Where was Camille?

Lucien was halfway across the street before he decided to move. He intercepted the guy like he was still playing high school football, bodychecking him just as the guy reached out to grab the backpack Cass was wearing.

Dressed in black from head to toe, including the hoodie hiding his face, the guy stumbled but didn't fall. He spun and made another lunge for Cass.

Lucien stepped between them, grabbed Cass by the shoulders, and shoved her toward Camille, who had followed Cass from the alley and raced toward them, poufy skirts clutched in her hand, panic etched in her face.

"Run!"

2

Camille barely registered Lucien's husky voice before she grabbed Cass's hand and they sprinted down the block and around the corner, fighting their gowns with every step.

Lucien had bought them a few seconds, but no more.

Camille glanced over her shoulder. The guy in black turned the corner and growled as he barreled toward them.

She saw Lucien a few steps behind him, quickly closing the gap.

Beside her, Cass wheezed and tried to slow their pace. "I. Can't. Breathe."

Camille tightened her grip, tugging Cass along. "We can't slow down right now, baby. We have to keep moving." She'd made her share of enemies in her work with Speranza, and until she knew exactly who was after them, they needed to get out of here, quick.

Cass nodded and did her best to keep up, muttering, "Stupid dress," as she stumbled.

A quick peek confirmed that the man was gaining on them.

Camille checked the streets around them. "Stay with me. I have a plan."

"Trying," Cass panted.

"You can do this. You're tough." Still running full-out, Camille kept one hand on her dress, let go of Cass's hand, and rooted around in her camera bag until her fingers found what she wanted.

She hung a quick left, then pulled them into an alley, ducking behind a dumpster. She pushed Cass farther into the shadows, then fished her lighter from the bag's side pocket. Camille lit the fuse and rolled the smoke bomb toward the mouth of the alley.

As soon as the smoke started to swirl, she grabbed Cass's hand and turned in the opposite direction. "Let's get out of here."

Cass glanced over her shoulder as they ran, pink smoke billowing, obscuring the alley behind them. "What is that?"

"A distraction. Left over from my last photo shoot. It's a girl!"

Cass snorted and almost tripped again. "I can't laugh and run!"

At least it kept Cass's mind off her terror. Camille slowed slightly, then squeezed her daughter's hand. "I've got you. Keep going."

They raced to the end of the alley, turned down another.

"Mom!"

Camille checked behind them, turned back, and plowed right into Cass, who'd stopped short.

They'd hit a dead end. An eight-foot-high chain-link fence blocked the exit. Running feet sounded nearby.

"We have to climb. Grab your dress with one hand." Camille toed off her shoes, jumped onto the fence, and started climbing. "At least you're not in heels."

Cass mumbled something about small favors, grabbed her dress, and climbed after her.

"That's my girl. You've got this."

They scaled the fence in record time, jumped down, and were racing toward the street when the man in black slammed into the fence from the other side, cursing up a storm.

They'd almost cleared the alley when a bullet whizzed by their heads and struck the building.

Cass shrieked.

"Don't look back!"

Lucien watched Camille and Cass take off across busy Canal Street, still teeming with traffic this late in the evening, the guy in the hoodie hot on their heels, a pistol gripped in his hand. Lucien picked up his pace.

He lost sight of them for a moment but spotted a cloud of pink smoke around the next corner. He ran that way. Had to be Camille's handiwork, the kind of thing she'd use for photo shoots. He kept running, searching every alley and checking behind dumpsters and in doorways.

What kind of trouble had they gotten into? This didn't seem like a typical snatch-and-grab. This guy was too persistent.

Lucien rounded another corner and saw mother and daughter racing across the street, right in front of a city bus. The guy in the hoodie wasn't far behind. Lucien lengthened his stride and tackled the would-be mugger before he reached the curb.

They went down hard, Lucien slamming an elbow on the concrete as he landed on him. Before he could get a good grip, the guy twisted out from under him and came up swinging.

Lucien dodged the blow and returned one that snapped the man's head back. Blood spurted from his nose.

The guy howled in pain as he stumbled backward and took off in the opposite direction, Lucien hot on his heels.

Lucien chased him around another corner and skidded to a stop as a black car screeched to the curb. The guy hopped in and the car sped away.

He doubted Hoodie Guy would come back, but just in case, he ran back the way he'd come. He'd find Camille and Cass, make sure they got home safe.

Something felt really wrong about this situation. Your typical mugger didn't have an accomplice in a fancy car.

A quick check of the alley where he'd seen the smoke confirmed they weren't there. But he spotted the ridiculously high heels Camille had been wearing. He picked them up, then eyed the eight-foot-high chain-link fence. Impressive.

He'd walked several more blocks with no sign of them when his phone rang. "Broussard."

A nurse from the hospital told him his grandfather had fallen out of bed. "What? How is that possible? Doesn't it have rails?"

"He tried to get to the bathroom on his own," the nurse said.

"Is he all right?"

"They're taking him to X-ray to make sure he didn't do any further damage. Or break his other hip."

Lucien scrubbed a hand over the back of his neck and muttered, "Stubborn old man. I'll be there as soon as I can."

When Camille spotted a city bus lumbering toward them, she towed Cass around the corner and they slipped behind it, then kept pace and used the bus as cover until she found the entrance to a small park.

They ducked inside, ran past the fountain in the middle and out the other side.

They zigzagged down half a dozen more alleys before Camille slowed to a walk, then stopped, hands on her hips, slowing her breathing. Behind her, Cass leaned against the brick wall of a decaying building, trying to catch her breath.

"Do you think he's gone?"

Camille blew out a relieved breath. "I think so."

Before she finished speaking, something hard jabbed her in the back and a male voice growled, "Hand over the backpack and no one gets hurt."

3

OUTSIDE NEW ORLEANS—TWO DAYS EARLIER

Cassandra maneuvered Gramps's old Toyota pickup next to the mailbox, scooped out the mail, and tossed it onto the passenger seat before she barreled up the gravel drive to the farmhouse.

She dumped her keys, backpack, and the mail on the ancient kitchen table, then rooted around in the pantry for cookies. Munching on one, she stared out the wide kitchen windows toward the dock on the Mississippi, wishing Gramps were here to take her fishing. She missed him.

Until three months ago, she and Mom had lived in Gran and Gramps's ginormous old mansion in town. Cass loved the cool old architecture, and Mrs. H. always had fresh-baked cookies in the jar, plus a whole staff to take care of the place, which Cass had never really thought about until they moved here. Now she had to do gross chores like cleaning bathrooms and doing laundry and cooking. None of her friends had to do stuff like that.

Well, except maybe Lindsey.

Cass could hear her friend's voice in her head. *"Entitled, much?"* Lindsey attended St. Thomas Preparatory Academy on a scholarship and constantly ribbed Cass about her "poor, deprived life."

Yeah, okay. Cass was spoiled. But was it wrong to like nice things? It wasn't like Gran didn't have money.

Still, part of her was glad they lived here now, though she'd never tell her mother that. Gramps's farm was on River Road, but it wasn't anything like Destrehan or the other well-known plantations the tourists came to gawk over. Their farm had been in Gramps's family for, like, over a hundred years, and Gramps had worked here every day until the horrible heart attack two years ago that had taken him away from them. Cass stood, combat boots thumping the wooden floor as she grabbed milk from the ancient fridge. She didn't like to think about that day.

At least she didn't have any homework tonight. Mom would be back from her trip to Munich for some friend's art show tomorrow. Cass didn't understand why she couldn't just stay here by herself when Mom was traveling, instead of going back to Gran's every night. She was almost eighteen. Geez.

She grabbed another cookie and sorted through the stack of mail, smiling at the familiar handwriting.

"Oooh, what did you send me this time, Uncle Marcel?" She ripped open the padded manila envelope, and an old book fell out. It was tied with a strip of leather, and she worried it would fall apart if she even breathed on it.

Last time Uncle Marcel was in town, she'd skipped school and they'd driven two hours outside New Orleans and poked around an old house museum that was rumored to have been owned by a pirate back in the day. They had "official" captain's logs like this for sale in the dusty little gift shop. Total replicas but still cool. He must have bought one when she wasn't watching.

Slowly, carefully, she untied the string, then opened to the first page. Huh. That was different. Good thing she'd aced her French classes or she wouldn't be able to read it. As it was, the fancy, half-smudged writing was hard to decipher.

She read aloud in French. "Ship's log, the *Bartholomew,* Captain Talon in command."

She slowly turned the brittle pages, taking her time, trying to get the rhythm of the entries. There were lists of crew names, supplies, cargo.

Boring. She flipped ahead a few pages. Descriptions of the weather. *Yawn.*

But then things got a little more interesting. She read about two crewmen getting into a knife fight and the captain making the loser walk the plank. *Nice.*

More stuff about the trip across the Atlantic. Boring days on end and then terrible storms where they all thought they were going to die. *No thank you.* Cass got seasick in the bathtub. She always made up some excuse not to go out on the family boat, and Lindsey ribbed her about it. "Boat? Don't you mean the Benoit family yacht?" *Boat, yacht, whatever.* Cass was a landlubber.

She kept reading. Toward the end of the diary, she stopped, reread the words, flipped back a few pages, and read them again. Now they were getting somewhere.

Oooh, they were pirates and they'd kidnapped a girl and her sister. They took everyone prisoner, moving them to their pirate ship, then set the other ship on fire.

The girl, Cira Fontana, was super feisty. She straight up told the sailor trying to rob her that if he took her book away from her, if he stole it for selfish reasons, he would die.

Cass laughed as she turned the page. This girl was smart, buying time, making up a story. Cass could picture it: Cira keeping them distracted while she tried to free herself. At least that's what Cass would have done.

The captain laughed at her, told the crewman to show him the book, but Cira stopped them again, said to get out of the rain and put on gloves so they didn't ruin the pages.

Surprisingly, the captain did what she asked, then stood over the book as the crewman showed him every page.

Minutes later, the crewman keeled over and that was it. Like, straight up died on the spot.

Just like Cira said he would.

Whoa. Whoever wrote this should be writing novels. They were really good. They sure had her going. What a great story.

She kept reading.

In the panic after the crewman fell to the ground, Cira grabbed the book and case and took off running. She leaped over the side of the pirate ship and into the water.

The captain sent his men to get her—and the book—but they disappeared.

Cass was grinning as she carefully closed the diary. She examined the cover again, then studied the pages. If they really wanted to sell a bunch of these, they'd have to make them out of thicker paper. This thing seemed too flimsy. But it was still really cool.

She pulled out her phone and snapped a couple pictures, then opened her Instagram account and started typing:

According to Pirate Captain Talon, if you try to steal the Fontana family's Book of Days for nefarious reasons, you will die. Just ask his crewman, who croaked minutes after taking the book from one of the Fontanas' great-granddaughters. #piratediary #coolreplica #piratelegends #fontanafamilybookofdays

Cass hit Share, still grinning. This should get her lots of likes. Even from her friends at school who thought she was a total history nerd.

She sent Uncle Marcel a quick text.

Hey, thanks for the diary. Did you buy it the day we went to that museum? Loved the story at the end about the guy dying after touching the book. When will you be in town again? Love you.

He didn't respond, but that wasn't weird. Sometimes she didn't hear from him for a couple of weeks and then he'd pop up in town. He worked for Gran in the family import/export business and traveled all over, making deals and stuff. He was Mom's cousin, but he and Mom had been raised by Gran and Gramps after his parents died. He was definitely the fun relative. Mom took everything way too seriously.

Cass flopped on the couch and surfed Netflix for a while. She had a little time before Gran freaked out that she wasn't home yet. She finally settled on an old movie with Cary Grant, her favorite. She hadn't slept well the night before, so she must have dozed off because she jolted awake when her phone rang.

"Hey, Lindsey. What's up?" She blinked, surprised it was dark outside.

"Girl, your nerdy pirate post has gone viral. Well, viral for you anyway." She snorted.

Cass sat up and checked her phone. She hadn't turned her notifications on after she left school. Which never happened. She opened the Instagram app. "Holy cow." There were hundreds of likes and dozens of comments.

"You're going to be an influencer yet," Lindsey teased. "Maybe you should change your handle to @historynerdgirl."

Marcel Davis sat hunched over his bourbon at a small out-of-the-way bar in Grand Isle, Louisiana, and considered his options. There weren't many.

Payment was due today and he didn't have it.

Not yet, anyway.

His stomach churned. He just needed a bit more time. The same lie every gambler told himself. But it was true. Unfortunately, the people he owed money weren't big on granting extensions. He rubbed his knee, which still throbbed from the reminder they'd issued a week ago. How could he have known that the insider info a friend had given him was wrong?

At least he wasn't in jail like his so-called friend. Though that might be safer.

His mind raced, scrambling to come up with the money some other way.

He could go to Gran and confess all. Ask her for help. He shuddered. Not while he drew breath. Her "not another penny" declaration, the responsibility lecture, and her disappointed expression last time still made him cringe in shame.

He just needed to find the right buyer for the diary. Quietly. He would pay his debt and then figure out a way to put the money back into the business coffers so Gran would never be the wiser.

He pulled out his phone, read the text from Cass, and grinned for the first time in days.

Hey kiddo, do me a favor, tuck that diary away and let's not mention it to your mom or anyone else for now, ok? I'll grab it next time I'm in town.

After he hit Send, he started a text to a fence he knew. A hand clapped onto the back of his neck as a large bald man slid onto the stool beside him.

Marcel stilled, a greasy sense of foreboding humming through him. He rubbed his sore knee. It was never a good omen when the enforcer showed up.

"Nice place." Johnny Four-Fingers eyed the dark room, barely visible through the haze of cigarette smoke. "Little far from your place in town, isn't it?"

"Two hours is just about far enough to clear my head a bit, you know?"

"Not far enough to avoid paying your debts." Johnny raised an eyebrow and signaled the bartender for a drink, his missing pinkie finger obvious through the haze.

"The boss will get his money." Marcel picked up his drink, then set it down quickly when he realized his hand was shaking.

"It's due today."

"I just need a little more time. I have a lead on something that'll get me paid up with the boss quick-like." He forced a smile, hoping his friendly, casual tone would keep his limbs intact.

"That so?"

"Absolutely. It's a rare find and I know a few discreet buyers that'll pay a pretty penny for it."

Johnny nodded and pulled out his phone. "Discreet, huh? We talking about the pirate's diary?"

When Johnny turned the phone around, Marcel's heart stopped for a beat before jump-starting like a mouse trapped by a determined cat.

"What's that?" He kept his tone curious, showing none of the panic coursing through his veins.

"That's the picture of the diary your, ah, niece—Cassandra, right?—posted on Instagram a while ago. Gotten quite a bit of attention, too." He held the phone closer in case Marcel had missed the thousands of views the picture had already garnered.

Without thought, Marcel spun off the chair and leaped for the door. He slammed into a mountain of a man standing behind him. He'd been so focused on Johnny Four-Fingers, he hadn't even noticed him.

"Now don't be in such a hurry, Marcel. Boss wants to talk to you."

Burly Guy grabbed his arm and frog-marched Marcel out the door, Johnny bringing up the rear.

The black SUV was parked in the back lot, hidden from the road. Marcel had one foot in the back seat when the blow came from behind and hit him in the back of the head.

In that split second, he realized what he'd done.

Oh, dear God. Keep Cass safe.

The world went dark.

4

PRESENT DAY

Camille saw Cass's eyes widen right before something hard poked Camille in the back.

"Hand over the backpack and no one gets hurt."

Without conscious thought, Camille reached behind her, grabbed the man's wrist, and flung him sideways into the wall, breaking his grip on the gun. He grunted in pain and shook himself as though to clear his head.

Cass stood frozen in shock as Camille scooped up the gun, grabbed Cass's hand, and they took off running again.

They didn't slow as they wound their way back through the side streets, both panting heavily. Finally, Camille slackened their pace, her bare feet ice cold and aching. She had a stitch in her side and Cass's face was beet red. They couldn't run much farther. She had to believe they'd gone far enough.

She scanned the area, and a jolt of panic hit her, hard. Nothing seemed familiar. Should they head left? Or right? The never-ending frustration of her directional dyslexia normally just made her feel stupid, the butt of endless childhood jokes, but this was something else entirely. Cass's life was in danger. She tugged them under the overhang of a closed shop. She had to think. Figure this out.

"Want me to call us an Uber? I remember where we parked." Cass's chest heaved, her voice shaky.

Camille's breath came out in a whoosh. "Good idea. Thanks." She pulled Cass in for a hug, trying not to grip too tightly. "You did good tonight. You okay?"

Cass nodded, slipped out of her grasp, and went back to her phone, typing like mad.

Camille paced as they waited, trying to burn off the adrenaline. And the panic. Once the Uber driver took them to where she'd parked, to be on the safe side, she asked the driver to wait while they climbed into her car, to ensure that scary guy wasn't lurking nearby.

They sat in silence for a moment.

Camille blew out a breath. "Okay then. That was terrifying."

Cass met her eyes. Grimaced. "Yeah."

"Sure you're okay?"

Cass nodded. "I think so."

Camille started the car, pulled away from the curb. "I'm starved."

"I'm really not hungry." Cass sent her a smug little smile. "I ate so many of those little quiche things that Gran gave me the evil eye."

Camille chuckled, the tension in her shoulders slowly uncoiling as they wound through the city. After twenty minutes, when she was sure they weren't being followed, she plugged Gran's address into the GPS.

Cass had been texting, again, still, always, and finally lifted her head when Camille turned onto Jackson Avenue. She'd been remarkably calm—and quiet—after what they just went through. "We're not going to the farm?"

"I think we'll be better off at Gran's tonight." The Tucker-Benoit mansion might be showing its age in places, but Gran's security system was state of the art.

Cass nodded and went back to her phone, but her shoulders relaxed some.

Once they reached Gran's home in the heart of the Garden District, Camille turned onto the brick driveway. She punched in the security code, and the imposing metal gate swung inward. Thick hedges around the perimeter kept the tourists from glimpsing more than the house's white-brick exterior and black-scrollwork balconies.

When the gate swung closed behind them, she finally let out a slow, relieved breath.

Lucien sat in his nondescript rental car across the street from the Tucker-Benoit mansion and waited. He tapped a finger on the steering wheel. Last he heard, Camille and Cass still lived here with their grandmother. But what if they'd moved?

He should have walked them to their car, then followed them home, but fear of an awkward conversation had made him hesitate. *Stupid.* Though this wasn't the dangerous corner of the developing world where he worked, he knew what could happen to two women alone, anywhere.

He checked his phone. Waited some more.

When Camille's car finally pulled up to the gate and glided through, he let out a breath and headed for the hospital.

Camille and Cass tiptoed into the marble foyer, hoping to slip in unnoticed. They were halfway to the stairs when Gran emerged from her study, heels clicking on the stone. "I didn't expect you tonight. I thought you were going to the farm."

Camille stepped forward to give the requisite kisses on each cheek. Cass did the same.

"We thought we'd stay one more night, with your permission."

Gran eyed them. "Is there an issue with your cell phone?" Displeasure slid through her rich Southern drawl. Gran didn't like surprises. "And why are you sweating, Cassandra?"

Cass's head snapped up and she sent Camille a frantic look.

Camille answered. "It was cold, so we ran for the car after the event ended."

Gran's raised eyebrow said she didn't believe that for a second. "Run along then. Your rooms are prepared for you, as always."

"Thanks, Gran. Good night." Camille shepherded her daughter up a sweeping ironwork staircase that could have come straight off a movie set. She ushered Cass into her room and closed the door behind them, then crossed her arms.

"What do you know about what happened tonight?"

Cass hung her coat in the closet. "Nothing."

Nope. Not buying it.

Camille appreciated Cass's aversion to outright lying, but that didn't mean her daughter always told the whole truth, either. Cass should have been asking a thousand questions, but she'd stayed silent. She knew something. Camille tried a different tack. "Do you know why someone tried to grab you?"

Cass slithered out of the dress, pulled on sweats. "I have no idea."

Still no eye contact.

Camille pushed a little harder. "What was in your backpack that someone wanted?"

Cass's jaw clenched like she was biting back words.

"Talk to me, Cass. Someone tried to grab you tonight!"

"I know that! But there's nothing in my backpack besides school stuff."

Camille narrowed her eyes. "What does Uncle Marcel have to do with any of this?" Some might call that a logic leap, but not Camille. The concern on Cass's face earlier when she'd asked about Marcel was all she needed to convince her he was somehow involved. When she got her hands on him, Camille would wring his neck.

Cass kept shaking her head, arms wrapped around her middle. "I don't know. I don't know."

Camille took a step closer. "You don't know? Or you won't say?" Trouble seemed to follow Marcel, but he usually slithered right out from under it with a smile and a wave. What if this time, though, whatever he'd gotten himself into had spilled onto Cass? Camille clenched her jaw. That worry was one of the main reasons they'd moved to the farm.

Instead of answering, Cass flung herself into Camille's arms. "I was so scared."

"I know, baby. Me, too." Camille held her tight, rubbing her back, relief gradually loosening the knot in her belly. Finally, she drew back. "Even if you don't know for sure, tell me what you *think* this might be about."

Cass kept shaking her head, then shrugged helplessly. Finally, she stepped away and swiped at her tears. "Those crazy moves tonight were sick, Mom. Where'd you learn all that self-defense stuff?"

Camille let her change the subject. For now. She'd get to the bottom of it in the morning. "Couple of classes. Came in handy."

"Will you teach me, too?"

She cocked her head, surprised. "Of course. Or better yet, we'll take a class together."

Cass nodded, then picked up the photo of J. T. in his dress uniform that sat on her dresser. "I wish I'd known him."

"Me, too, baby. He loved you from the minute he knew you were coming." Camille waited, braced for more questions.

Cass set down the photo. "Love you, Mom."

"Love you, too, baby girl." Camille kissed her on the forehead, then slowly stepped away. "We'll talk more in the morning. Try to get some sleep."

As soon as she pulled the door closed behind her, Camille pulled out her phone and called Marcel. It went right to voicemail. "Call me, Marcel. Now. Something's going on and I need to know what. Someone put a target on Cass's back and it better not be you."

When he hadn't responded by the time she got to her room, she sent a follow-up text. **Don't you dare try to hide out from me right now, Marcel. What's going on? Someone went after Cass tonight.**

Just the thought of it was enough to give her nightmares.

She didn't think she'd sleep a wink, so when she woke several hours later, it took a minute to get her bearings.

A quick check of her phone had her wide awake. No response from Marcel.

She hurried down the hall to Cass's room, needing to lay eyes on her daughter, make sure she was sleeping soundly.

Cass was gone.

5

Pulse pounding, Camille flipped on the light in Cass's room, took in the rumpled blankets and last night's clothes piled on the floor. She stepped into the adjoining bath, found a wet towel on the floor. She took a deep breath. *Think, Camille. Be logical.*

There was no sign of forced entry at the second-floor balcony doors. If someone had tried to open them without disarming the system, the shrieking alarm would have woken the entire household. Which Cass had learned the hard way one night when she tried to sneak out. Camille would never forget the guilty expression on her daughter's face.

Camille took another breath. Okay, Cass hadn't been snatched from her bedroom. Maybe she couldn't sleep and had gone downstairs to hang out with Mrs. H., Gran's longtime cook and head housekeeper, who regularly rose well before dawn to bake.

Sure enough, when Camille entered the kitchen, Mrs. H. had just pulled a tray of biscuits from the oven.

"Good morning, Camille. You ready for breakfast?"

Camille kept her growing worry out of her voice. No sense panicking everyone without cause. "Have you seen Cass this morning?"

"Not yet, no. I expect she'll be sleeping in after last night." Mrs. H. had been working for Gran for over forty years and somehow always knew what was happening. She put a biscuit on a plate, added bacon and sliced melon, and handed it to Camille.

Gran marched into the kitchen, already dressed for work in a trim lavender suit, heels, not a gray hair out of place, never mind that dawn was still an hour away. "Good morning, Camille." She poured coffee. "Did you sleep well?"

"Not too bad, thank you." She'd get quicker answers if she followed a few social niceties. "Have you seen Cass this morning?"

Gran paused with the cup halfway to her mouth. "Isn't she still in bed? I assumed we wouldn't see her before noon today."

"So did I." Camille set down her cup, her anxiety ratcheting back up. "Neither of you have seen her this morning?" When both women shook their heads, she dialed Cass, frustrated when it went straight to voicemail. She left a "call me right away" message, then sent the same via text, fingers drumming the table as she waited. Cass didn't respond. On a hunch, Camille logged into the security system. "Did either of you open the back door this morning at two thirty?"

Gran and Mrs. H. exchanged concerned glances.

"No." Gran set her china cup down with a click. "What's going on here, Camille?" Worry glimmered in Gran's eyes.

"I'm not sure yet, but I'm going to find out. Call me right away if you see or hear from her." She spun and ran for her car.

Camille raced toward the farm, the note from Cass she'd found on her windshield crumpled on the seat beside her.

I got a ride home with a friend. Didn't want to wake you.

She'd added a heart as though that made everything okay.

The note helped Camille's panic, but not much. This wasn't like Cass at all. She often asked to stay at the mansion rather than go to the farmhouse. Said she liked it better in town. What was going on with her?

The note was definitely in her handwriting, but had someone forced her to write it?

Camille pulled up in the parking area behind the farmhouse, and her fear ramped up again. Gramps's old Toyota wasn't in its usual spot.

She raced up the back steps with her key in hand, then stopped. The door wasn't closed all the way. She pushed it open with one finger. "Cass?"

No answer.

Even in the early morning light, the destruction was clearly visible.

Someone had completely trashed their kitchen.

"Cass?" she called again.

Camille stepped into the room, her tennis shoes crunching on the broken white ceramic canisters she'd bought when they moved in. Every cupboard door stood open, the contents tossed on the floor. Larger bags and boxes had been upended and strewn around the room.

Still no answer.

The living room was no better. The couch cushions were slashed, and the stuffing from the throw pillows lay in drifts like mounds of snow.

This wasn't random destruction.

Someone had clearly been searching for something.

Camille pictured the guy who tried to grab Cass last night, and all her fear rushed back in.

She raced up the narrow stairs and found all three bedrooms equally destroyed. Same with the bathrooms.

But still no sign of Cass.

She ran back down the stairs, suddenly terrified that her daughter had been lured here and then snatched.

Think, Camille. Don't let panic scramble your brain. Was there any evidence that whoever trashed the house took Cass?

She spun in a slow circle, looking for anything that could help. She pounded back up the stairs and into Cass's room. The mattress had been pulled off the bed and slashed, so there was no way to tell if the bed had been slept in. She rushed to the closet, saw a gap in the clothes, a few empty hangers. Had Cass grabbed a few outfits? Given that most of her wardrobe lived on the floor of her room, Camille wasn't sure. Why hadn't she paid more attention?

Wait. She dropped to her knees and reached under the bed. Where was Cass's other backpack, the flowered one she used on weekends or for sleepovers? Camille turned on her phone's flashlight but couldn't find the pack.

She sat back on her heels. Okay, if she was right about the weekend backpack, that meant Cass had come back here and packed some clothes.

But had she done that on her own? Or had someone forced her?

Why had Cass been targeted? Because she clearly had been. Camille shuddered and squeezed her eyes shut against the image of that guy trying to grab her.

Why had he taken her backpack? What was he after?

Logic said since the house had been trashed, he hadn't found it yet.

Had they grabbed Cass this morning to try to force her into giving them whatever it was?

Camille's blood pounded in her ears. She needed to rein in her panic enough to form coherent thoughts. Because none of her wild speculation told her where Cass was now. She needed a direction, a place to start searching.

She hurried back downstairs, scanning the wreckage again.

A flash of yellow near the kitchen trash can caught her eye. She plucked a padded mailer out of the mess and wiped stale coffee grounds from it. Anger spurted when she saw Marcel's slanted scrawl on the return address.

Cass's incessant texting during last night's event and her question about Marcel suddenly made a frightening kind of sense. All the hair on the back of her neck stood at attention. What had he sent Cass? Dang it, he must have pulled her into some crazy scheme. Camille pulled out her phone and dialed, frustrated at leaving yet another voicemail.

"Call me now, Marcel. What did you send Cass? Where is she?"

He still wouldn't respond, which had her worry digging deeper. Marcel doted on Cass. He wouldn't ignore her. Not intentionally.

What now?

She could call Picasso in New York, the tech wizard of their Speranza team, to do her magic and figure out who had been chasing them, but Camille didn't want to involve the team, not yet, if this turned out to be a family matter involving Marcel. Who was going to pay, and pay dearly, if he had in fact put Cass in danger.

Don't jump to conclusions.

She grabbed her phone and called Lindsey. She didn't answer, so Camille left a message asking her to call immediately.

She took a deep breath, let it out slowly. Then another. But it didn't stop the gooseflesh from pebbling her arms as another thought occurred to her.

What if this had nothing to do with Marcel?

Then who wanted to kidnap her daughter? For what purpose?

What did Cass have that someone wanted badly enough to kidnap her to obtain?

Camille turned and ran back to her car and sped out of the driveway. She could think of only one place her daughter might go.

Please, God, help me find my girl.

6

ROME, ITALY

He stood in the shadows across the street from the small restaurant, impatience gnawing at him. He'd spent all day following the woman around the city, waiting for the right opportunity. She'd spent an inordinate amount of time at the Pantheon, ogling the ancient building, scribbling in her notebook. Speaking of which, he made a mental note to take it with him when they finished their . . . encounter.

Then she'd gone to Trevi Fountain before heading over to explore the Colosseum. Idiot woman had turned from serious historian to tacky tourist in one day. The professor claimed that visiting all these musty old buildings and collecting ancient manuscripts helped her make history come alive for her college students.

His jaw clenched. Her so-called altruistic work with the Foundation was another smoke screen to hide her sins from the light of day. It was all a lie to cover her real motives. Right now she wanted that book, for the power contained within it.

It would not stand.

Earlier, when she'd emerged from a dusty museum and two men had chased her down the block, annoyance had shot through him. He didn't like to change his plans. But the police had showed up, the men had disappeared, and after she answered the officer's questions, she'd continued her trek around the city, stopping at every ridiculous, trinket-filled souvenir shop on the block.

Though she had stopped and peered over her shoulder more often than before.

Finally, long past nightfall, she emerged from the restaurant, blessedly alone. He expected her to hail a taxi, but instead, she glanced around again, then started walking back toward her hotel.

Perfect. Surely God smiled down on his work by providing the opportunities he required.

He watched her cross the street to an ATM that was set back in the shadows. He tsked. They really should have better lighting at these things.

But they did have cameras, so he stepped farther into the shadows and waited.

As though she could sense his eyes on her, she nervously checked both directions before she stepped away and headed in the opposite direction.

All that vigilance wouldn't do a bit of good, of course.

He picked up his pace. When he grasped her arm and pulled her into an alley, she spun and twisted, trying to break his hold. "What are you—?"

His grip tightened. He had no time for questions. "You have been deemed a liar, Tara Jameson. You proclaim your desire to do good in this world, yet you sin under cover of darkness. The price for your transgressions is death."

She froze in horror as he pulled the knife from his sleeve.

In one practiced move, he spun her in front of him, her back to his front, and neatly sliced her throat.

He pulled her deeper into the alley so she wouldn't be discovered too soon, then hurried away, tossing his gloves and bloody coat into a trash can as he went.

Justice had been served, punishment exacted.

For now.

A sense of satisfaction filled him, and he savored the moment as he walked, drawing out the feeling as long as he possibly could. Because, unfortunately, the exquisite euphoria wouldn't last.

The book was still out there.

And there were always more evildoers to punish.

7

NEW ORLEANS

Camille made the thirty-minute drive from River Road to Lakeside in twenty. It was still dark on a Saturday morning, so traffic wasn't too bad. She drove into the parking lot of Gentilly Marina, parked, then used her key to access Pier 3, where Marcel kept his thirty-four-foot cabin cruiser. Gramps's beloved 1947 Chris-Craft, a forty-foot wooden cruiser he'd christened *Easy Does It* years ago, was moored five slips down the row.

Gramps used to take the boat—or yacht, as Gran called it—out to the dock at the farm regularly. He'd sit on the aft deck with a drink, then toss a line in the water while enjoying a nice afternoon with friends or family. Nobody in the family had taken her out since Gramps died two years ago, which was a shame. The boat held such great memories.

Camille shoved nostalgia aside as she hurried to Marcel's boat. She chucked boating protocol and hopped aboard without checking to see if he was there. "Marcel! Get out here!"

No response.

The door that led to the tiny galley and sleeping quarters below was closed. If he had a woman in there . . . well, too bad. She yanked the compartment door open and stopped.

The inside had been as thoroughly searched and trashed as the farmhouse. No evidence of a struggle, thank goodness, but no sign of Marcel—or Cass—either.

She hurried up the three steps into the cockpit, annoyed that she'd been right. Marcel was obviously involved.

As she scanned the marina, she saw movement on Gramps's boat.

Cass!

Camille hopped onto the dock and raced toward the *Easy Does It.* Just as she reached the boat, a tall, broad-shouldered man wearing a ball cap stepped out of the salon and onto the aft deck, his back to her, hands on hips as he scanned the marina. The glow from a far-off security light told her his silhouette was all wrong to be Marcel. Was this the guy from last night?

She didn't stop, just planted her palms on the gunwale, swung her legs over the side, and landed behind him. As he turned, she shoved him, hard. Once. Twice. Forcing him backward. "What are you doing here?"

The backs of his knees hit the gunwale and he pinwheeled his arms, trying to regain his balance. At the last second, he grabbed her arms and took her with him over the side.

Camille hit the water with a splash. And came up sputtering and furious.

"What were you doing on my boat?" Camille swam to the ladder attached to the dock and glared over her shoulder.

He said nothing as he climbed up behind her. He swiped the water from his face, then wrung out his ball cap. She stepped well out of reach and studied him in the predawn gloom.

"Tell me why you were on *Easy Does It* or I'm calling the police right now."

"I saw movement on board and went to investigate." He slipped the cap back on and she glimpsed a military dog tag tattooed on his right bicep. "Pops's boat is one row over. I'm staying aboard while I'm in town."

Lucien. His deep voice scraped across her nerve endings and goose bumps raced over her wet skin. She wrapped her arms around her middle, fighting the urge to run. Or stammer like a schoolgirl, the way she had last night. She hadn't recognized him in the ball cap. Just acted on instinct.

He still carried himself like a soldier. Or like his pirate ancestors. Short dark hair, hardened physique visible through his wet clothes, that air of supreme confidence, like he was captain of a sailing ship.

She tilted her chin up, fought to keep her tone casual as she studied him, still barely visible in the shadows. "Did you find anyone?"

"No." He met her gaze. "Cass okay after last night?"

Camille debated how much to say. They were, for all intents and purposes, strangers. "She will be." She paused. "Thanks for the assist, by the way."

He shrugged dismissively, rubbed a hand over a darkening bruise on his jawline. "It's all good."

"Sorry I didn't, ah, recognize you earlier." She waved a hand to indicate Gramps's boat.

"No worries, Princess. It's been a while." He'd alluded to it last night, but now he drawled the nickname, one side of his mouth curved up in a half smile.

She refused to take the bait, unnerved at the way he quietly watched her. "Have you seen Cass since last night?"

When he looked away, jaw clenched, Camille stepped forward and grabbed the front of his soggy T-shirt. "Tell me."

He raised an eyebrow but otherwise didn't react, and Camille realized she'd plastered herself against his chest. Her cheeks heated as she took a hasty step back.

"I think she spent the night on your gramps's boat."

"What aren't you saying?"

In answer, he turned back to *Easy Does It,* stepped aboard, and slid the door to the salon open. She followed.

It looked worse than Marcel's.

She studied him over her shoulder. "You're sure it was her?"

"No. It was dark. I took off after her, wanted to make sure she was okay, but I lost her." He scrubbed a hand over the back of his neck. "Maybe she had a car nearby?"

"Very possible." She'd forgotten about Lucien's protective streak, the football hero who'd sit with the nerdy kids to keep the bullies away, who'd split his sandwich with the kid who had no lunch. Of course he'd go after Cass. "Marcel wasn't with her?"

"Not that I saw."

Camille's worry gripped tighter. She'd convinced herself that Cass was with Marcel. But if she wasn't, where was she?

"Do you have any idea what this is all about?" She waved her hand toward the mess. It was a long shot, but she asked anyway.

He scanned the marina, then sighed before he turned to her. "I think it's because of the pirate's diary."

Camille leaned back against the gunwale. Had worry and lack of sleep completely scrambled her brain? "I don't know what you're talking about."

"Have you checked her Instagram lately?"

"No. I was out of town and just got—wait. Why would *you* be checking her Instagram?"

He pulled his phone out of his shorts pocket, wiped the screen with his soggy shirt, and turned it to face her. "Check her latest post."

Camille read the post once, twice, then gasped at the number of likes and comments. "Oh, sweet mercy." She sagged, afraid her knees were going to buckle.

"Yeah. Pretty much every treasure hunter who's seen the post wants that diary, thinking it'll lead them to the Fontana family's Book of Days."

"Is this some kind of joke?"

"No. This sort of discovery brings out all the crazies, though. There have been rumors about that Book of Days for years. Centuries, actually."

Camille's mind raced. "You think whoever tried to grab her backpack last night is after the diary?"

"That'd be my guess." He paused, as though debating saying more.

Fear for Cass threatened to swallow her whole. But her voice was steady. "What do you know about it?"

He shrugged, not quite meeting her eyes. "Listen, about the diary. Pops asked me to—"

Her phone rang and she grabbed it with shaking hands. "Lindsey! Is Cass with you?"

"I'm sorry, Ms. Abernathy. She's not. Is she okay?"

Camille forced a calm she didn't feel. "I'm sure she is. If you hear from her, please call me right away."

Just as she hung up, her phone buzzed with a text: **Urgent. Team Zoom call in an hour.**

"I have to go." She hadn't wanted to involve the Speranza team in a personal matter, but she suddenly changed her mind. This was Cass. Camille would take whatever help she could get.

Lucien's voice sounded far away. "Camille. Wait. I need to talk to you about—"

Camille wasn't listening. She was running for her car, water squishing in her shoes.

She had to find Cassandra. Make sure she was all right.

8

OUTSIDE NEW ORLEANS

Camille pulled around behind the farmhouse and froze, eyeing the newer beige sedan parked under a live oak tree. She slowly walked up the back steps, the roar of a vacuum getting louder with every step. She entered the kitchen and her jaw dropped. She pulled the plug on the vacuum, and sudden silence filled the room.

"What are you guys doing here?"

"Hello, Camille. Good to see you." Sister Mercy Garcia, one of the newer Speranza team members, glanced over her shoulder and smiled. The petite, dark-haired, dark-eyed Filipina stood on a step stool, wiping down canned goods and placing them back in the cupboards. When they didn't have a mission, the trained nurse and bullwhip expert worked in medical clinics for the poor in Paris. She had traded her nun's habit for jeans and a T-shirt today.

"Where else would we be?" Henrietta "Hank" Barrett shoved her ball cap back over her short dark hair. Last Camille heard, the former military pilot turned freelancer and ace engine mechanic was working in Germany. Now she scooped flour and cereal from the floor into a black trash bag.

Camille blinked back tears at Hank's matter-of-fact statement. "That your rental car?"

"Yep, though I made a few adjustments." She grinned, gray eyes twinkling, then wiped her dusty hands on her coveralls. They'd almost finished putting the place back to normal.

When Camille got the text from Picasso, their tech wizard, telling her to get to the farmhouse for a Speranza team Zoom call ASAP, Picasso hadn't mentioned that the team had flown in from Europe. After their last mission ended, Camille had flown straight home to Cass, while the others had taken a few days in Europe to unwind before heading back to their regular jobs.

"Hey, Camille." Sophie Williams waved from the living room, where she stood coiling the vacuum cord. In addition to her Speranza work, Sophie ran the Fortier art gallery in Munich with her friend Lise and also copied stolen paintings and returned the originals to their rightful owners. Blonde hair loose, the team's Robin Hood art forger wasn't in disguise today. "Gang's all ready. We were just waiting for you."

"How did you know I needed hel—" Her phone buzzed. Relief hit hard when she pulled it from her tote and saw Cass's number. "Cass! Where are you?"

"They're following me! I don't know what to do!" Cass panted like she was running.

Camille was already in motion, grabbing keys and her bag. "I'm coming. Where are you, baby? Are you in Gramps's truck?"

Hank stepped in front of Camille. "Put it on speaker." She turned and made a "gimme" motion to Mercy. "Keys." Mercy ran to the living room, fished keys out of her large bag, and tossed them to Hank.

"Yes, Gramps's truck. I stopped at Lindsey's and saw the same truck go by twice. He slowed down every time, like he was, I don't know, searching for me. I didn't know what to do, so I left. But now he's behind me."

"Where are you right now?" Camille stabbed at the phone and finally got it on speaker. She slung her tote over her shoulder and flung the back door open. She'd deal with Lindsey lying to her later.

"He's getting closer, Mom!"

"Don't slow down. Keep driving, baby—you can do this." Camille raced down the back steps, opened the door to her vehicle, but Hank blocked her from getting in.

"Where is she?"

She glared at Hank, made a "just wait" motion. "Are you headed here?" It took everything she had to keep the panic from her voice.

"Yes! Near Destrehan Plantation."

"You head her way. I'll cut them off." Hank muttered the words, then took off toward the rental.

Camille hopped into her car. "Good, keep coming, Cass. I'm heading toward you. Go past the farm. I'll find you!"

There was a thump. Cass shrieked.

"Mom! They just rammed the truck!"

"Are you okay?"

"I think so. What do I do?"

"You're doing everything right. Just keep driving this way." Camille slammed the door as she started the car. *Sweet Jesus, please protect my girl.*

Ahead of Camille, Hank, with Mercy riding shotgun, hooked a right at the end of the drive and disappeared in a cloud of dust.

Camille spun the wheel hard left, tires spinning as she fishtailed onto the road toward Cass. "Hang on, baby! I'm coming."

ZURICH, SWITZERLAND

Jolie Ward paced her office at the Becker Foundation's international headquarters and tried to ignore the worry building inside her. It wasn't like Tara to ignore her calls. Certainly not three of them. They weren't just colleagues. They'd become good friends through their work at the large, internationally known NGO. Jolie—with help from Tara—vetted and approved all the Foundation's project requests, but Tara was also a history professor and lectured all over the world. She specialized in ancient documents and was forever on the hunt for rare manuscripts to share with her students. A passion she shared with Nelson Becker, the president of the Foundation, who, like Jolie, originally hailed from New Orleans.

Tara was searching for another old book and had gone to Rome to chase down clues before they were to meet in Romania for the water-project dedication. But even when Tara was deeply involved in hunting some obscure piece of history, she was a professional.

Jolie's phone buzzed and she snatched it up on the first ring. "Tara?"

"Ah, no. Good afternoon, Ms. Ward. I am sorry to bother you. But we have a situation."

Jolie straightened in her chair, all senses on alert. Irina, the local Romanian woman heading up their water project, was a lot like Tara. Neither got rattled easily. "Tell me what's wrong."

"Everyone in the village knew they were supposed to keep boiling their water and using the portable filters until the new well and community filtration system was dedicated after you and Professor Tara arrived. We were all eager to have you and the professor here for the ceremony."

A knot formed in Jolie's stomach. "But . . . ?"

"But some of the villagers apparently couldn't wait. A small group of them turned it on last night, got water, and took it home."

Jolie's mind raced. Why would Irina call about something like this? "That isn't what we planned, but I understand their excitement. It's okay. Not a problem."

"It shouldn't have been, no. But it is." The older woman took a deep breath, then heaved out a sigh. "Three out of those four women are being transported to the hospital as we speak. One of them is elderly. They are very concerned."

Jolie tried to process what she was hearing. "What's wrong with the women?"

"They will run more tests at the hospital, but the paramedics think there is something wrong with the water."

Jolie stiffened, pulse pounding. "Have you already shut down the system and made sure no one can use it?"

"Yes, of course. I have also asked one of the village women to keep watch."

Jolie's thoughts jumped to logistics, next steps. She would think about those poor women and the ramifications to their project on the plane later. "Let me get hold of Tara and we'll be on the next flight. I'll let you know as soon as we arrive."

"Ah, well, about Ms. Tara . . ."

Jolie stilled at the tone. "What about Tara?"

"This is difficult to say. But three of the local women say Tara was near the well yesterday."

Not possible. Tara was in Rome yesterday. She'd texted Jolie a selfie taken in front of the Pantheon. "You can't possibly think Tara poisoned the well?"

A long pause followed. "At this point no one knows what to think."

"How do they know it was Tara? Could they be mistaken?"

"All three of them said Tara was wearing her usual straw hat, large sunglasses, and carrying her canvas messenger bag."

Which was definitely Tara's fieldwork uniform. This didn't make sense. At all. "Thank you for letting me know. I will get back to you as soon as possible." Jolie disconnected, then immediately dialed Tara's cell number again. It rang five times before going to voicemail. "There's a problem in Romania. Call me as soon as you get this."

She was trying to wrap her head around what was happening when Dot Becker asked Jolie to come to her office immediately.

"I'm afraid I have sad news," Dot said the moment Jolie sat opposite the woman's large desk. Tall and thin, with short gray hair and a steely gaze, Dot ran the organization, never mind that her husband's name appeared on the letterhead as both president and CEO.

Nelson Becker sat in the other guest chair wearing an

immaculately tailored suit, as always. His engaging demeanor and genuine concern for people were what made donors open their wallets wherever he spoke on behalf of the Foundation. But seeing his normally jovial expression replaced with deadly seriousness made Jolie's unease deepen.

"Irina just called me about the well problem. As soon as I get hold of Tara, we'll figure out what's happening."

"I don't know anything about the well." Dot waved a dismissive hand, then leaned forward and folded her hands on the desk, her expression solemn.

Before she could say anything, Nelson interrupted in his thick New Orleans drawl. "Did you talk to Tara yesterday? Any news on her search?" He'd been asking Jolie for an update every time he saw her. When he wasn't speaking at fundraising events or leading special projects, Nelson spent his free time chasing ancient manuscripts all over the world. Though while Nelson kept his finds, Tara made sure hers were added to her university's collection.

"I didn't speak to her, but she did text a selfie from the Pantheon."

When Nelson opened his mouth to ask more questions, Dot shot him a glare, then turned to Jolie. "We just got a call from the carabinieri in Rome."

She paused, and Jolie froze.

"I'm sorry to tell you that the police found Tara deceased in Rome."

"What? No. That can't be right. Irina said several women saw her at the village in Romania yesterday." Where she poisoned a well? Absolutely not.

"They said her body was found late at night, near an ATM. They believe it was a robbery gone wrong."

"This doesn't make sense," Jolie whispered.

"I agree," Dot said. "Tara wouldn't have foolishly gone to an ATM late at night and then flashed cash around. She knew better."

"Especially if she felt she was getting close to the Book of Days," Nelson added.

Jolie blinked at the change of subject, tried to keep up. She knew

Nelson and Tara shared a fascination with this ancient book, but what did that have to do with anything?

Her confusion must have shown. "I guess you haven't seen the latest," Nelson said. "An old pirate's diary, said to contain clues to the Book of Days, just turned up in New Orleans. Apparently, your friend Camille Abernathy's daughter somehow got her hands on it." He turned his phone so Jolie could see an Instagram post and the thousands of likes and comments.

"I don't understand." Jolie looked from Nelson to Dot, who shrugged.

"That diary is the key to finding the Book of Days. Camille's grandfather snatched it out from under me at an auction years ago, then told everyone it had been destroyed." His jaw clenched. "Obviously, he lied."

At the mention of Camille and her grandmother, memories, good and bad, flashed through Jolie's mind like an old flip-book. Of Octavia, who'd been Jolie's mentor during high school, pitting her and Camille against each other in beauty pageants. Of that last pageant, when Camille saw the bruises on Jolie's back and threatened to expose her family secrets. Of Jolie's deliberate sabotage, costing Camille the crown—and the college scholarship. And of Octavia, helping Jolie escape her family and then more recently, helping her get this job with the Beckers, giving her a chance to make a difference in the world.

"Jolie?"

Her gaze bounced from one to the other and she realized they were staring at her. She tried to focus but couldn't seem to wrap her head around the fact that her friend was gone. "You think this diary had something to do with Tara's death?"

"We can't discount the possibility. Or that it's connected to the Book of Days," Nelson said. "Contact Camille Abernathy and have her courier the pirate's diary to us. We'll pay whatever it costs, of course."

Jolie struggled to make her brain function, to understand what the diary could possibly have to do with Tara's death.

"The police also said they found several large deposits in Tara's bank account, with no paper trail to indicate where they came from."

"They think she was what, taking bribes? None of this makes any sense."

Nelson patted her hand. "We absolutely agree. We need you to investigate, find out why Tara died. Starting with getting us that diary."

"But the police—"

Dot softened her voice. "Tara was one of us. We owe her this."

Jolie nodded and walked back to her office as if in a trance. She sank into her chair and let the tears come.

A while later, she dried her eyes, picked up the phone, and found Camille's number. She started to tap the number, remembered the time difference, and decided to try again a bit later.

Jolie propped her elbows on her desk, rubbing her temples as she tried to make sense of everything. First money showed up in Tara's account. And now it appeared she'd been impersonated? And murdered?

Someone had gone to an awful lot of trouble to make her friend appear guilty.

The question was why? Who had something to gain?

And Nelson's barrage of questions about the pirate's diary had raised the hair on the back of Jolie's neck.

Could this diary have something to do with Tara's death? Or was this about the wells somehow?

Before she could change her mind, Jolie hurried down the hall to Tara's office, sat at her friend's messy desk, and turned on the computer. She typed in Tara's last name and birth date, then the standard log-in, betting Tara hadn't changed it. She was right.

Jolie scrolled through Tara's e-mail, feeling like a snoop, searching for anything that seemed out of place, anything that might give her a clue where to begin.

She found a folder named *Diary* and started scrolling. The last file included a phone number. With a New Orleans area code.

Jolie dialed and waited through three rings. Just before the call went to voicemail, a vaguely familiar voice answered. "Professor Jameson. Good to hear from you. I was beginning to think you'd changed your mind. As I said before, as soon as the money clears—"

"Marcel Davis?" Jolie's onetime classmate and Camille's cousin had a thick Cajun drawl that was unmistakable.

A stunned silence followed. "Who is this?"

"Jolie Ward. How do you know my friend?"

"Put Professor Jameson on the phone. Let me talk to her."

"First, tell me how you know her. This is important, Marcel."

"We were doing a bit of business together. But then she stopped answering my texts and calls."

"When was this?"

"Yesterday. Why? Put her on the phone, will you?"

"I wish I could." Jolie took a deep breath, then forced the words out. "She, uh, she's dead. Apparent robbery."

Marcel muttered a curse. "Tell me everything."

Jolie heard the near panic in his voice. She'd been gone from New Orleans for years, but according to local friends, Marcel had been skirting the edges of the law for a while. "If you know something about what happened to her and why, you'd better spit it out, Marcel. Right now."

Several seconds ticked by.

"I had an old diary that I put up for sale online in a, uh, private forum. Professor Jameson contacted me and we made a deal. I told her I would get the diary to her the minute the funds cleared my bank. She said I'd have the money today." He sighed. "And that's the last I heard from her. I thought she'd changed her mind."

"How much money are we talking about?"

"There were quite a few interested parties. She won the bid at just under thirty-five thousand dollars, US."

"This diary wouldn't have anything to do with an illuminated Book of Days from the 1500s, would it?"

A moment of stunned silence stretched out. "How did you know that?"

"Tara was my friend and coworker at the Becker Foundation. She told me she was researching it. Something about a legend."

Marcel's sigh came through the line. "Yeah, the Book of Days is part of the Liar's Treasure, but if even half of what they say about the collection is true, it's not only worth a fortune, it's pretty scary stuff. People connected to it have died. And now this."

Jolie didn't have time for old legends and speculation. "You still have the diary, is that right? And you never got Tara's money?" When he mumbled confirmation, she said, "Send me that diary. As soon as we hang up. You'll get your money."

"Ah, I don't think I can—"

"My friend is dead, Marcel. I need to figure out what happened to her. Don't mess with me right now."

She heard footsteps in the hall, but they stopped outside her office. She hung up on Marcel's verbal tap-dancing and yanked the door open. As she stepped into the hall, she caught a glimpse of someone turning the corner. She sprinted after them, rounded the corner, and saw the elevator start down.

She spun in the opposite direction and raced down the stairs to ground level.

But when she burst into the lobby and scanned the area, whoever it was had disappeared.

9

OUTSIDE NEW ORLEANS

Camille's chest hurt from how hard her heart pounded, and her sweaty hands kept sliding off the steering wheel. She wedged her phone halfway under her thigh so she could keep the line open without the phone sliding onto the floor.

"Mom!" Cass's voice was high and tight. "They just rammed me again. Why are they doing this?"

Dollars to donuts, as Gramps would say, it had everything to do with Marcel's pirate diary. She gritted her teeth. "We'll talk about that later, baby. Right now, just focus on staying on the road." *And staying alive*, but Camille wouldn't utter the words aloud. Her hands cramped on the wheel. *Please, Jesus, please. Protect my girl.*

Camille was gasping for breath, afraid she would hyperventilate, when Gramps's ancient Toyota pickup came into view half a second before the hulking shadow of a jacked-up black pickup appeared behind it.

She gripped the wheel tighter. Forced her voice to stay calm. "I see you. Just keep coming toward me."

Off to her right, Camille spotted Hank's rental flying toward River Road from a side street, a cloud of dust in its wake. The little car resembled a toy compared to the black pickup. Camille knew Hank planned to cut off the truck. Which meant Cass had to get out of the way.

"Turn left, baby! Turn left!" Camille shouted.

"Left? Are you sure?"

As soon as Cass turned the wheel, Camille knew. "No! No! Right! Turn right!" She shouted at the top of her lungs, but it was too little, too late.

Cass had done exactly what Camille told her. Which was exactly the opposite of what she should have done.

The black pickup crossed the double yellow line into oncoming traffic just as Hank slid into the intersection in front of it. At that moment, Cass jerked the wheel left as Camille had told her to and clipped Hank's left front bumper.

Time seemed to stretch and slow as the huge pickup rammed Hank from behind. Cass's little truck glanced off Hank's bumper and rolled. It bounced once and rolled again.

Another bounce and it landed on its roof in the ditch.

Brakes squealed as Hank's rental slid across the road and careened into the ditch on the opposite side of the highway.

"Cass!" Camille screamed, her foot jamming the accelerator all the way to the floor.

The huge pickup raced past in a cloud of exhaust.

Hank and Mercy burst out of the rental and sprinted across the road to the upside-down Toyota.

When Camille reached Cass's truck, she stomped on the brakes, her car fishtailing as she brought it to a rocking stop on the shoulder. She launched herself out of the car, sliding down the embankment shouting her daughter's name.

"Cass! Can you hear me? Cass!"

Hank spun toward Camille and intercepted her before she reached the Toyota, gripping her arms to stop her, ignoring Camille's struggles. "Easy, Eagle Eye. Your girl's okay, just a little banged up. Help us get her out. And maybe bury the panic a bit, yeah?"

It took a second for Hank's words to register. Camille stopped, drew in a breath, and met the former helo pilot's calm, steady expression. "Okay, okay." She swallowed the panicked screams in her head, blew out a harsh breath. Hank let her go.

It took every bit of Camille's long-ago beauty-pageant skills to hide her horror at the blood running down her daughter's face as she hung upside down by her seat belt. But she was alive and conscious and the most beautiful sight Camille had ever seen. She forced a smile and stepped closer, reaching in to stroke her daughter's arm. "You're okay, baby. Hang on. We'll get you out in a second."

Mercy stepped closer. "Does anything hurt anywhere, Cass? Your neck? Back?"

Cass took a deep breath, and Camille's panic eased further at Mercy's calm, clinical questions. "No. Just my head."

"Okay. Did you lose consciousness? Black out for a bit?" Mercy kept her voice low, taking Cass's pulse, running her trained nurse's eye over her, assessing injuries.

"I don't think so."

"That's good." Mercy smiled. "Can you move your arms and legs?" After Cass demonstrated, Mercy patted her arm and stepped back. "We'll have you out of here in no time."

Mercy nodded at Camille and Hank, and Camille's breath whooshed out of her lungs. Cass was okay. *Thank You, Jesus.*

It took some time and a good bit of finagling, but they got Cass untangled and pulled her through the broken window and onto the grass.

Cass immediately tried to climb to her feet.

Mercy stepped up beside her and grabbed one arm while Camille steadied her other side. "Easy, sweetheart. Let's just give it a minute."

"Mommy," Cass whispered, and Camille's heart cracked. When was the last time her feisty teen had called her that?

Camille stroked her arm. "I'm right here, baby. I'm not going anywhere."

Cass tipped her face up. "I don't feel so goo . . ." The words trailed off and Cass's eyes rolled back in her head.

"Cass!" She went limp in Camille's arms.

10

NEW ORLEANS

Lucien stepped into his grandfather's hospital room that afternoon and propped a shoulder against the doorjamb. Thankfully, Pops hadn't broken his other hip, but he had some pretty ugly bruises from his latest escapade. Claude dozed in the bed and Lucien's jaw clenched as he studied him. Pops seemed so . . . old. And frail. Completely opposite the larger-than-life character he'd always been.

Pops's eyes blinked open and his smile lit up the room as he raised the head of the bed.

"Hey, Pops, how's it going?" Lucien kept his tone deliberately upbeat as he gave Pops's whiskery cheek a kiss. He hated how the place smelled. Hated the implications of his grandfather's presence here.

"Lucien, my boy. Good to see you." Pops shoved his hands through the white fringe rimming his ears, reached to slide his ever-present captain's hat over his bald pate, pulled out an unlit cigar, and clamped it between his teeth as he scrutinized Lucien. "What took you so long to get here?"

Lucien raised a brow. "Can't spend all my time with you, Pops, tempted though I might be." He grinned. "Though you'll be happy to know I spent some time at the warehouse and the shop, checking on things." Broussard's Pirate Emporium & Antiques had been in the family for several generations, complete with rumors of ill-gotten gains passing through the warehouse by the waterfront to the shop in the Quarter.

"'Bout time you showed a little interest in the family business."

Lucien let that go. "What's so all-fired important that you texted me—" he checked his phone—"five times in three hours?"

Pops waved that away. "I wanted you to know it was urgent, is all."

"I'm listening." Lucien crossed his arms over his chest and waited, unease growing at the familiar gleam in his grandfather's eye. Pops had gotten it every time he stumbled onto the next, "sure bet." The next, "We'll find it, son, easy-peasy." Pops's treasure fever had never waned.

"Did you get the diary?" Pops demanded.

"I told you what Octavia said last night. I haven't had a chance to talk to Camille about it yet." He decided not to mention their early morning encounter at the marina. Having her plastered against his chest for that brief moment had churned up all kinds of memories he'd worked hard to forget.

"Well, what are you waiting for? If you don't jump on this, somebody else will snatch it up right out from under our noses. Again."

"What do you mean, again?" Lucien decided not to mention the guy chasing Cass last night, either. Pops needed to focus on healing.

Pops rubbed a hand over the back of his neck. "Back when I was young, long before you were born, that pirate diary came up for auction at a big, fancy auction house here in town. I went, hoping to get my hands on it."

"I take it you got outbid."

"Darn tootin'. By that uppity Robert Benoit, who bought it for Octavia Tucker." A faraway gaze came into Pops's eyes. "That Octavia sure was a looker back then. Still is."

Lucien thought *formidable* was a better description of the older woman, but he hid a grin. "Did you try to buy it from her afterward?"

"Tried. Got shot down." He sighed. "Next thing I know, Octavia and Robert got married and a couple years after that, there's some cockamamie story in the paper about a flood at the Benoit farm. The diary was supposedly 'unsalvageable.'" He made air quotes.

"And now Cassandra Abernathy—Octavia Benoit's great-granddaughter—posted about it on Instagram."

"Right. Flood-schmood. We need to get our hands on that diary. It's the only way to find the Book of Days." Pops's eyes glinted, once again alight with treasure-hunt fever.

"Octavia said it's not for sale. My guess is Camille will say the same."

Pops merely shrugged. "There are other ways to get it."

Lucien rubbed the back of his neck. Pops had never understood that Lucien's sense of right and wrong had always been far more rigid than his own. Sure, things could get a little dicey in his work in Africa as he and his team smuggled food and medical supplies past the rebels and safely into the hands of those who needed them. But that was something entirely different than stealing the diary from Camille, of all people.

He studied his grandfather's excited expression. In his gut, Lucien had known that's what this was about. How could it not be? It was all anyone in treasure-hunting circles had been talking about since Cass's post went viral. But some naïve part of him had been hoping he was wrong. "Is this the same Book of Days you and I spent every childhood summer hunting?"

Pops fingered the unlit cigar, nodded. "Right." Then he sat up straighter. "But think of it, Lucien. We could finally find it."

When Lucien merely nodded toward the wheelchair beside the bed, Pops's grin got wider. "And by *we*, I mean *you*. With my help. I think we could find the whole shooting match, the entire Liar's Treasure."

Lucien threw his head back and laughed. He couldn't help it. "I think you hit your head when you broke that hip, Pops. 'Cause there is no way we're going to find that treasure. People have been searching for it since the 1500s." He knew, because okay, when jet lag refused to let him sleep last night—or maybe that was Camille—he'd researched the treasure he'd known very little about as a child and learned all about the crazy legend that surrounded it.

Pops held up his palm when Lucien started to interrupt. "Hear me out before you start telling me all the namby-pamby reasons it can't be done. Not sure how you survived the Army with that attitude."

Lucien refused to engage. Not about this. "What makes you think we can find it when nobody else has in all these years?" He narrowed his eyes, studied Pops's face. "Do you know something I don't?"

Pops shifted, winced. Then he smiled broadly. "Only that if anyone can find it, you can, Son. I believe in you."

Lucien quirked an eyebrow. "Laying it on a little thick, aren't you?"

Pops huffed out a breath and leaned back, deflated. "I need to do this, Lucien." Then he grinned, the same excited, confident grin he got before every treasure hunt. "This old man needs one last adventure, even if I can't go along." He paused. "Say you'll do it."

Lucien opened his mouth, closed it. He couldn't deny he was tempted. But the NGO he worked for depended on him. He'd only planned to be here until Pops was back on his feet and could get back to work. That didn't leave time for treasure hunting, which was expensive and never came with a guarantee. Their best finds over the years had ultimately barely made enough to break even.

But Pops had never asked for anything from him before, not in all these years. Lucien was twelve when an elaborate con his parents had set up went south and they took off in the middle of the night and never came back. Pops took him in and that was that. It hadn't taken long for Lucien to figure out that some shady deals went down in the warehouse, but he'd never asked. And Pops never said. Just loved his grandson.

Lucien didn't have it in him to completely shut down this man who'd always been there for him. "Why don't I see if I can come up with the diary and we'll go from there," he finally said.

Pops's grin said it all.

11

NEW ORLEANS

Cass had just been returned to the curtained ER cubicle after another scan when Gran arrived that afternoon, heels clicking on the linoleum floor. Camille sat beside the bed, holding her daughter's hand.

"Hey, Gran." Cass smiled briefly, then her eyes slid closed again.

"Hello, darling." Gran leaned over the bed, kissed Cass's pale cheek. "We'll talk about proper greetings another day."

Cass's lips curved in a smile, but she didn't open her eyes.

Gran indicated the hall, a steely expression in her eyes, and Camille decided she couldn't cope with a lecture right now on either etiquette or protecting her daughter, no matter how much she deserved it.

"Sit with Cass for a few minutes, would you?" Camille squeezed Gran's shoulder and slipped out before she could say anything.

Camille hurried down the hallway, not sure where she was going except that she had to get out of here and get her emotions under control, preferably away from prying eyes.

Her baby could have died today.

She walked out the doors to the emergency room and didn't

stop until she reached her car, leaning back against it, her mind a churning mass of guilt and recriminations.

It was all her fault. She'd told Cass to turn the wrong way. *"You're so stupid." "Dumb as a rock." "What an idiot." "No wonder you're never picked for a team."* Taunting voices from her childhood, from every dance class and PE game she'd messed up with her directional dyslexia, shouted in her ear, condemning her.

They weren't wrong. The pageants Gran had forced her into had helped her confidence, helped her find ways to hide and manage her dyslexia, but when Camille got stressed, all of that vanished.

And her daughter almost died.

A chill raced over her and she wrapped shaking hands around her middle, wishing she'd grabbed a jacket. The wind off Lake Pontchartrain had attitude today. She gritted her teeth, trying to keep the tears at bay.

"The adrenaline crash can pack a wallop," a deep voice drawled, and Camille's head snapped up.

Lucien stood in front of her, hands in the pockets of a well-worn leather bomber jacket that reminded her of the one he'd worn in high school. "I hear she's going to be okay."

Camille huffed out a soggy laugh. "That's what everyone keeps saying."

He paused, studied her. "Sometimes it takes a while for the mind and body to process that the danger is past."

A memory of Lucien and J. T. grinning proudly, arms draped around each other's shoulders, both in their crisp dress uniforms, flashed across her memory, followed instantly by an image of J. T.'s flag-draped coffin. She supposed Lucien would know all about that, more than most.

Her chin came up, ready to tell him she was fine, when suddenly the dam broke and tears burst out, all the terror and panic she'd been holding back let loose like a hurricane.

Embarrassed, she turned her back and tried to pull herself together as emotions pounded her from all sides.

Lucien stepped over without a word and pulled her against his hard chest, drew his jacket around her, and held her close.

For a second she froze, her mind shouting that she should protest, step away, insist she was okay. But she couldn't remember the last time anyone had offered a shoulder to cry on. And Lucien still smelled the same, and somehow, in his arms she felt . . . safe. She found herself burrowing closer, inhaling his scent and absorbing the warmth of his embrace, her tears soaking his shirt.

"She's okay, and so are you. It's all okay." He repeated the words over and over in time to the soothing rhythm of his warm hand on her back.

Camille cried until the storm petered out and all that remained was mortification at the way she clung to him. She stepped back and swiped a hand down her cheeks, wiped her nose with a crumpled napkin from her pants pocket. "Sorry to fall apart like that." She straightened, forced herself to meet his gaze. "Thank you."

"Any port in a storm, right?" He winked, and the concern in his eyes nearly undid her.

She rubbed her arms. "I need to get back to Cass."

"Before you go, I have something for you." He walked over to a black Harley, pulled out a grocery sack, and held it out to her with a smile. "You lost your slippers last night, Cinderella."

His slow Cajun drawl again shot Camille eighteen years back in time, to the memory she'd spent years trying to forget. To prom night with its fairy-tale theme and that one reckless, forbidden kiss that still haunted her dreams. What if she hadn't taunted him into kissing her that night? What if she hadn't run back to J. T. and let her guilt take the two of them too far?

She slammed the door on all the what-ifs. The past was gone. She was a mother now. "Thank you. But you could have pitched them." A small smile stole across her face. "They're wicked uncomfortable."

"I know a way to keep Cass safe."

Camille blinked at the abrupt change in topic. Right. Cass. "How?"

"Sell me the pirate diary. Pops asked me to buy it from your family."

She turned to face him more fully. "You think it will lead to the Book of Days?"

"I do. I told Pops I'd try to get it for him. He dragged me all over creation on treasure hunts as a kid, trying to find that doggone book."

Hank appeared from between the cars. "Doctor is getting ready to sign Cass's discharge papers."

"I need to go."

Lucien didn't speak until Hank turned back toward the hospital. "Sell it to me, Camille. Protect your daughter. You've already seen what people are willing to do to get it. I'll make sure everyone knows I have it." The words were spoken calmly enough, but Camille heard the tone of command behind them just the same.

She'd stopped blindly following anyone's orders years ago. "I'll think about it."

"Don't wait too long. Others may not ask so nicely." He turned and walked away.

12

When Camille's phone buzzed just before eight the next morning, waking her from a restless sleep, she groaned and rolled over, letting the call go to voicemail. She'd been up every hour throughout the night, checking on Cass, and had finally fallen asleep.

Instead of leaving a message, the caller tried again. And a third time.

Camille snatched up the phone and barked, "Who are you and why are you calling me this early?"

She heard nothing, but she knew the call had connected. "Speak, or I'm hanging up." She listened for a few more seconds. "Too late. Don't call again."

"Wait. Don't hang up."

Camille's hand tightened on the phone. "Jolie?"

She exhaled a sigh. "Yes. Hi, Camille."

"Why are you calling me? Especially at this hour?"

"Um, sorry. I wouldn't have called at all. Except . . . I think Cass may have put herself into a situation." There was a pause. "And I may need your help."

"That's new. You sure didn't need or want my help years ago." The words burst out as Camille remembered the ugly bruises on Jolie's back when they were in high school, the fury in her friend's voice when Camille offered to help.

The silence seemed to go on forever before Jolie finally spoke.

"I was afraid of the consequences of your help."

Camille sat up in bed, shoved a pillow behind her back. "What does that even mean, Jolie?" What Camille remembered was Jolie calling her names and rattling her so badly during their final pageant that she flubbed her speech, turned the wrong direction getting off stage, tripped, fell, and lost the pageant. And the college scholarship. To Jolie. Winning had never been about the money for Camille, but about proving that her directional dyslexia didn't define her, that she was smart and capable. Instead, she'd been publicly humiliated.

"You've heard the saying about the devil you know?"

Camille pushed the past aside, focused. "Yes. So?"

"I was afraid that if you outed my father for his abuse, my siblings and I would be split up and sent to foster care. I was terrified and lashed out at you. Not my finest moment. I know you were only trying to help. I'm sorry."

Camille froze as the words sank in and shame washed over her. Why had she never considered it from Jolie's perspective, never asked? Because she'd been a spoiled brat, that's why. Only concerned with herself. Regret swamped her. "I'm so sorry you had to go through all that. And that I wasn't a better friend. I really am sorry. . . . You're doing well now?"

Another long pause followed. "I am. It's taken a while, but I'm good. So are my sisters."

"I'm glad to hear it. Truly. But why are you calling me? And more importantly, what does it have to do with Cass?"

"Right. I don't know if Gran told you, but I work in Zurich, at the headquarters for the Becker Foundation, a huge nonprofit with humanitarian projects all over the world. One of our current projects is in a small town in Romania, mostly women artisans.

There are weavers and women who paint these amazing eggs and also embroider traditional folk costumes. It's really cool."

She stopped, took a breath. "Anyway, the water had too many nitrates, so we built a new well and filtration system. Before my friend and coworker Professor Tara Jameson and I could dedicate it, several women drank the water and were poisoned." She told Camille about the accusations that Tara sabotaged the well.

"What did Tara say when you confronted her about it?" Camille asked.

"I couldn't. Tara was killed in Rome yesterday."

"What? You should have led with that. Geez, Jolie. I'm so sorry. What do the police say?"

"They're calling it a robbery gone wrong. But they also found several recent deposits in Tara's bank account. Now they're thinking bribery."

"Do you think she poisoned the well?"

"Absolutely not. She was as excited about helping these women as I was."

"You still haven't told me how this connects to Cass."

"Right." She told Camille about her friend's background and love of old books and manuscripts and the phone number she found in Tara's e-mail. "When I called the number, Marcel answered. He said Tara was going to buy the diary."

Camille stared at the phone in shock. "Are you kidding me?"

"No. And one of my bosses, Nelson Becker—you remember him?—asked me to get him the diary Cass posted about. He wants to buy it. He's into old books, too. I asked Marcel to send it to me, but the way he hemmed and hawed, I'm not holding my breath."

Camille bet her cousin was even now frantically trying to sell it to the highest bidder.

Jolie paused. "There are thousands of likes and shares on that post, Camille. I wanted to warn you, let you know Cass might garner unwanted attention."

Camille rubbed the tightness in her chest. "Too late. Someone tried to kidnap Cass and also tried to run her off the road."

"Oh, wow. Then I'm glad I called. At least if you know why someone is after her, you can keep her safe."

Unless you have directional dyslexia and you send your daughter straight into danger instead of away from it.

Camille shoved the thought away, cleared her throat. "I appreciate you telling me this."

"Gran said you work for an organization that helps women. Is this the kind of thing you do? Can you help me figure out who poisoned the well? And why Tara was killed?"

Camille was shocked Gran would mention Speranza to an outsider. But that could wait. Someone had poisoned a well. And killed a woman.

More important, they'd put a target on Cass's back.

"I'll talk to the team and get back to you."

13

When Camille came downstairs, Sophie, Hank, and Mercy were sitting at the big pine table in the farmhouse's kitchen, laptops open.

"Everything okay?" Mercy asked when Camille appeared in the doorway.

Camille sighed, plopped into a chair. "Not even close. I just got a call from a childhood friend. Jolie works for an NGO based in Zurich." Camille filled them in, watching the worry build in their faces as she talked.

Hank narrowed her eyes. "You didn't tell her you'd send the diary, did you?"

"Of course not. I'm not that dumb."

"Nobody said you were." Mercy's voice was kind.

A flush spread over Camille's face. She'd spent years telling herself that her dyslexia didn't mean she was stupid. If she took her time, she could—if not control it—then at least manage it. Yesterday's accident, and her conversation with Jolie, had thrown her.

"Jolie and I go way back, and I was not the friend I should have been." She sighed. "But she's doing well now, for which I'm grateful."

Picasso suddenly appeared on their laptops, surrounded by walls of monitors, her usual ball cap in place, hiding her face, the scars barely visible around the edges. Mercy angled her screen so Camille could see, too.

"Hey, guys. I've been doing some digging about this diary. Thanks to Cass and her Instagram post, I had some idea where to start. Especially the names." Keys clicked as she talked. "According to what I found, the name Fontana is real and the two sisters mentioned in the diary were descendants of the original owner of something called an Illuminated Book of Days."

"What is that, exactly?" Hank wanted to know.

Picasso pulled up a picture and a collective gasp went around the room.

The book was exquisite, with an intricate painting on the cover and gilt along the edges.

"There are no pictures anywhere of the Fontana family's actual book, since from what I can tell, no one knows where it is and it's never been on public display. But"—she clicked to another picture—"this is a similar one, based on what I've been able to find online. I have more digging to do, though."

Hank whistled appreciatively. "Wow. That one's even fancier."

Picasso chuckled. "And that's just the cover. They usually had individual pages painted, too, each one also a work of art." Her fingers clicked her keyboard and soon more images filled their screens.

Camille drummed her fingers on the table. "Why is it called a Book of Days, though? Is it like a calendar?"

"Of a sort." Mercy clicked a few keys on her own laptop. "We used a Book of Hours when I lived in the convent for a while. It lists the prayer times throughout the day. A Book of Days was a bit different, almost like a family diary. Or the precursor to the journals people keep today. Here is a less ornate one."

"How much does one of these books sell for?" Hank had her own laptop, of course, but her research was generally limited to YouTube how-to-repair-stuff videos.

More clicking as Picasso's fingers flew over the keys. "Here's the info from a fairly recent sale at Sotheby's auction house in New York."

Camille's jaw dropped. "Thirteen million? Oh my. I had no idea."

"But not all are worth anywhere near that much. It has to do with the quality of the artwork. Here's one that sold for a mere forty-five thousand dollars."

"Still not chump change. How big is it?" Hank held out her hands like she was holding a shoebox. "Like this? The diary said it was in some kind of case. It's easily transported then." She thought for a moment. "So, this Book of Days is why everyone is so all-fired determined to get their hands on the diary?"

"The Book of Days is certainly a valuable piece of art," Sophie agreed.

"Yes to both, Hank. I spoke with Lucien Broussard, a guy I went to high school with, at the hospital yesterday, and he offered to buy the diary. He said he and his grandfather spent summers trying to find the Book of Days. Lucien wants to try again." Camille picked up her phone. "I've been trying to get in touch with Marcel since this all started. He won't call me back."

Hank leaned her chair back on two legs, arms crossed. "Is it like him to blow you off?"

"No." Camille paused. "Well, not when it concerns Cass anyway. Those two are tight." She drummed her fingers on the table, her worry growing. At least one person was dead and Cass had been hurt because of this diary. She hoped Marcel was okay, even though she wanted to wring his neck for getting Cass tangled up in whatever mess he'd made.

"Guys." Picasso's voice went high with excitement. "This is why everyone's after the diary. Check out what I just found on a treasure-hunting website." She split her screen and an article appeared.

Renewed Interest in a Centuries-Old Legend

Rumors have circulated for centuries about the Fontana family's Illuminated Book of Days, supposedly created in Italy in the 1500s. Its pages are said to contain clues to other pieces in what is known as the Liar's Treasure, which includes Countess Alonza's Portable Altar. Neither of these incredible pieces of art have been seen since the early eighteenth century, when a ship's captain supposedly ignored a young girl's warning that trying to steal her family's Book of Days would bring certain death. The crew member holding the book died several minutes later, apparently proving the truth of the statement. The girl escaped with the book, and no one has seen or heard any more about the pieces since.

Still, rumors persist about the Liar's Treasure and its similarity to the biblical story of Ananias and Sapphira, whose deceitfulness earned them instant death. It is said that when all the pieces of the treasure are together—and no one knows exactly how many there are—the set is able to judge motives. If you are found worthy, you will gain untold riches. But it comes with a warning: If you are not worthy, if your motives for obtaining the treasure are impure, you, like the unfortunate crew member, will die instantly.

The rumors resurfaced when a post appeared on Instagram referencing that same ship captain's diary and the Book of Days.

"Sounds like Cass and Marcel inadvertently opened Pandora's box." Mercy's quiet voice was thick with worry.

"Right, but we still don't know where the diary is now," Hank said.

Camille jumped to her feet. "I'm an idiot. I keep calling Marcel. But Cass posted about the diary on Insta—"

"I know where it is."

All heads swiveled toward Cass, who stood in the doorway, pale but determined.

The farm encompassed more than five hundred acres and had several outbuildings. When Camille inherited the property from Gramps, she leased the fields to their nearest neighbor, along with the two barns closest to the river, since the property had a deep-water dock. Most of the crops had been transported to New Orleans by water.

They followed Cass out the back door and across the farmyard to the third barn, closest to the farmhouse, where Gramps once housed his dairy cows. The animals were gone now, but the neighbor still stored hay in the hayloft. Cass bypassed the large wooden door and stepped through a smaller one next to it. The team followed. Once inside, the smell of hay made Camille sneeze.

Without breaking stride, Cass walked down the center aisle of the cavernous space and started up one of two ladders to the hayloft. The other was on the far side.

As Camille climbed up behind her daughter, she heard a noise from the loft above. "Cass, wait," she whispered.

Cass froze and peeked over her shoulder. Camille put her index finger to her lips. Behind her, Hank and Mercy were silently backing down the ladder. Sophie was already halfway across the barn to the door.

Another footfall sounded. Camille stepped up behind Cass and whispered in her ear, "Let me slip past you. Then head back to the house."

"But I can help—" Cass started.

"Just do it, please." Camille didn't wait for a response. She maneuvered past Cass on the narrow wooden ladder and quietly swung up into the loft. Hay bales were piled everywhere, in stacks of varying heights. She moved quickly and quietly up and over them, memories of hide-and-seek with Marcel when she was a child playing in her mind.

Ahead of her, Camille heard the loft door squeal open on rusty hinges and felt the outside air rush in. She grinned. They wouldn't be able to get away now. It was a long way to the ground from here.

A muffled curse, a thump, then the other door swung open.

Camille didn't hesitate. She leaped over the nearest bale and landed behind the man standing in the open doorway, dressed all in black, a hoodie shadowing his face.

"Stop!"

He ignored her and spun in the opposite direction, grabbed the hook at the end of the heavy cable, and swung out of the open loft door.

14

Camille lunged for him but missed by inches. She stood in the open doorway and watched him slide down the cable to the muddy barnyard below.

He'd taken less than five steps when Mercy's bullwhip cracked the air and wrapped around his ankle, yanking him off his feet. He landed in the mud with a frustrated curse.

Camille rushed down the ladder to intercept him, but she was too late. He had scrambled to his feet and taken off in the opposite direction, Hank hot on his heels.

"Uncle Marcel!" Cass cried as she sprinted past Camille, following Hank.

Really? Camille caught up with her daughter and squinted at the man dodging and weaving through the thick stand of trees separating their farm from the neighbor's. The build was the same, but her cousin didn't have a limp. Usually.

They ran full-out, but he had a head start.

A car engine started and they ran toward the sound. But he'd disappeared.

Up ahead, Hank stopped, hands on her knees, trying to catch her breath as she scanned the trees.

Camille studied Cass. "What makes you think it was Marcel?"

She shrugged, wouldn't meet her eyes. "That's where he asked me to hide the diary. No one else would know to check there."

Camille clamped down on all the words crowding her tongue, starting with her fury that Marcel had involved Cass in the mess he'd gotten himself into. She'd take that up with him as soon as she got her hands on him. Camille drew a deep breath, let it out. "I say we head back. Figure out plan B."

Hank swatted a mosquito. "Makes sense to me."

15

Once they got back to the farmhouse, Camille checked her phone and found two voicemails from Gran, the second one decidedly snippy. *"I would appreciate an update on my great-granddaughter, if you can spare a moment out of your busy day, Camille."*

Camille caught herself rolling her eyes, smiled, and then dialed. "Good morning, Gran." She updated her on Cass, debated for a moment, then said, "We just came in from the barn. I don't know if you've kept up on Internet news lately—"

"Is this about Cassandra's Instagram post about the diary?"

Camille's jaw dropped open. Her grandmother followed Cass's Instagram account? Since when? Did she know anyone in her family anymore? "Um, yes. Cass took us out to the barn to retrieve it from where Marcel told her to hide it, but someone was there and escaped with it."

Gran paused. "That someone being Marcel, I take it."

How did Gran know all this? "We think so, yes."

Another long silence followed. "I'll be there in thirty minutes. We have much to discuss."

She wasn't kidding. Gran arrived and by the time she finished talking, Camille didn't know what to ask first. "So let me make sure I understand. The diary was handed down through the females in your family, until your grandmother had to sell it during the Great Depression to put food on the table."

Gran nodded, took a sip of her coffee. "She did what she had to do."

"Does this mean you have pirates in the family tree?" Hank asked, grinning.

Gran's cup hit the saucer with a snap. "People, women especially, in my family have always done whatever it takes to survive."

"We'll take that as a yes, then." Hank raised one eyebrow.

"How did Marcel get it?" Mercy asked. "Did he buy it from someone?"

Gran snorted, a wholly unladylike sound that made Cass snicker. She got a sharp glance in return.

Finally, Gran stood, pulled a faded newspaper from her briefcase, and set it in front of Camille. Everyone crowded around, reading over her shoulder.

Camille tapped a finger on the page. "According to this, the diary came up for auction and Gramps bought it for you."

"Yes, well, he wanted to get my attention." She patted her hair. "It worked."

Mercy pointed several paragraphs into the article. "Camille, is this Nelson Becker the same guy your friend Jolie works for?"

"Yes. Do you know him, Gran?"

The older woman nodded briskly. "Yes, he's always been fascinated with old books and legends, even when we were young."

Hank indicated a grainy photo beside the article. "What about this Claude Broussard? Says he was in the bidding war, too, but dropped out."

Gran scowled. "He should never have been allowed into the auction at all. He couldn't afford it."

"Says here he claimed the diary belonged to his wife's family," Hank pressed.

"I could say I was related to Queen Elizabeth, but that wouldn't make it so."

Camille studied Gran's face. "The same Claude Broussard who is Lucien's granddad, right?"

A flush crept up Gran's cheeks, and she lifted her chin. "He is. And he's still the scoundrel he was all those years ago. His grandson is no better."

Cass piped up. "If Gramps bought you the diary, why did Uncle Marcel send it to me? How did he get it?"

It was a very good question.

The silence stretched. Finally, Gran said, "Several years after we were married, there was a flood in one of our storage buildings. Robert told me the diary was destroyed along with many of our old records."

"Except it wasn't," Sophie said.

"No. We were doing some remodeling at the office recently, and workers brought me several boxes of Robert's paperwork they'd found in a back closet. The diary was hidden amongst those papers." Gran paused. "Marcel was at the mansion that day."

"You mean he stole it from you?" Cass's voice was quiet, shocked.

Gran turned to Cass, voice gentle. "I imagine he thought he could use it to get out of his most recent debts and then put it back before I noticed, but things didn't turn out quite the way he planned."

"So what do we do now?" Camille asked.

Gran went to her briefcase once more and laid a sheaf of papers on the table. "Perhaps we should start with this."

Camille scooped up the pages, flipped through them. "You copied the whole diary?"

"Every page. Years ago. Just in case something happened to the original." Her cell phone rang, her voice clipped as she answered. "I'll be there shortly. Thank you." She picked up her briefcase. "I have a meeting, but I assume you ladies will do whatever you have to do to make sure Cassandra is safe from any unsavory interest in this diary." She kissed Cass on the forehead. "Rest, my girl, and do let me know if you hear from Marcel."

The thread of steel behind the words echoed in the room.

Once the door closed behind Gran, Hank asked, "Now what?"

"Did Jolie give any indication of exactly how good this Nelson Becker is at identifying old manuscripts?" Sophie asked.

Hank fist-bumped Sophie. "Yes! You're going to copy it, aren't you?"

Sophie tapped a finger against her lip. "No, not me. All of us." When everyone protested at once, Sophie held her hands up for quiet. "I know how to make paper look and feel old. Ink, too. Are you game to help me?"

Heads bobbed all around.

Sophie's skill with forgeries of all kinds, especially artwork, was epic.

Mercy's brow furrowed. "But how does sending Nelson a copy of the diary help us?"

Camille pursed her lips, considered. "It would put Jolie in his good graces, for sure—help keep her in the loop so she can feed us information about what he's up to regarding the treasure search while she's also investigating the poisoning and the deaths."

Cass grinned at Sophie. "I'm down."

"It will actually be pretty tedious, but it's important we get it right." Sophie eyed Camille. "While Cass and I run out for supplies, I need you to take photos of each page, then crop and save them as png files so we can print them on the aged paper."

Sophie nodded to Hank and Mercy. "You two work on ideas for creating a, shall we say, distraction page."

"What should we tell Jolie if she calls?" Mercy asked.

Hank spoke first. "Just tell her we'll send it as soon as possible."

"Actually, no." Camille drummed her fingers on the table. "We'll have Jolie let the Beckers know we have a lead on it, but we're not sure if it will pan out. See how they react." Camille pushed back from the table. "That may also buy us some more time to figure out what's happening over there and how much is connected."

The idea had been colossally stupid, and Marcel knew it. Worse, it would ruin his life and the only relationships that mattered. Actually, it would destroy the only relationships he had. Cass's trusting brown eyes flashed in his mind. And Gran's stern expression. He squeezed his eyes shut and took another sip of bourbon for courage.

He hadn't seen any other choice.

Not if he hoped to stay alive. He rubbed his aching knee, opened his laptop, and checked the bids. As the clock ran out, the bidding jumped significantly higher, ending on a nice number that would help get him out of his current troubles. Cass's Instagram post had actually boosted the numbers quite a bit.

He watched the screen until the money showed up in his account, made the necessary transfers to one of his offshore accounts, then tossed back the last swallow, closed the laptop, and grabbed his phone. The absolute mess someone had made of his boat confirmed his decision. He'd find the Book of Days, then finish cleaning up his financial mess—hopefully before Gran realized he'd taken money from the business accounts in the first place.

He buttoned everything up, threw his go bag over his shoulder, and headed out.

This late at night, there weren't many people around, so no one to pay much attention. Once he'd walked several blocks from the marina, he utilized skills he'd never admit to and hot-wired an old beater and wound his way around the city. He finally found a copy machine at an obscure convenience store in a sketchy part of town and spent an hour copying the diary, thankful there were no security cameras.

He spent what was left of the night huddled in an alley, waiting for the local package-delivery store to open. Wearing sunglasses and a hat pulled low, he overnighted the diary, then headed out of the city.

Sophie, with the team's help, worked her magic and made the pages appear hundreds of years old. After they spent hours drying them with hair dryers and in the oven, Camille printed the pages with ink Sophie had mixed herself, and once it dried, Hank and Mercy meticulously bound them together. Dawn wasn't far away when they finally finished.

Cass had fallen asleep on the couch several hours before, and Camille couldn't bring herself to wake her.

"Great job, everyone." Sophie showed them the finished book.

"You don't think this Nelson guy will know the difference?" Hank peered over her shoulder as she washed her hands at the sink.

Sophie yawned, tucked her blonde hair behind her ears. "He shouldn't, no. Not unless he's a lot better than we were led to believe. I think it'll work. We did good."

"While you guys were binding the pages, I started reading more of the diary," Camille said, stifling a yawn. "That handwriting is tough to decipher, and my high school French could be better, but I think the young pirate who helped Cira and Maura escape was actually Captain Talon's nephew. He eventually married Cira and took over as captain of the *Bartholomew*."

"Interesting. You have to wonder how that love story happened. But I'll wonder later. Sophie, this was a great idea, but I'm beat." Mercy blinked rapidly, then rolled her shoulders.

"Camille, before I forget, did Cass ever say why she went to the marina?" Hank dried her hands on a towel. "Was she trying to find Marcel?"

Camille sighed. "Yes. I should have realized that immediately."

"Oh, quit beating yourself up, Camille." Sophie pulled out what appeared to be another page of the diary. "So before we go get a few hours of shut-eye, I took Hank's and Mercy's ideas and did one more thing."

Camille picked it up. "What is this?"

"The best way I could think of to protect Cass."

16

The team gathered in the farmhouse kitchen several hours later, ready to hammer out a plan. Camille had given up trying to sleep after an hour, worried about Cass, so she'd caught up on e-mails, including postponing a freelance assignment to photograph an orphanage in Nigeria. Once Cass entered high school, Camille had started to accept assignments farther afield. In the two years since Willa recruited her for the Speranza team, she'd become proficient at juggling her photojournalistic work and occasional modeling assignments around Speranza missions.

Now she stood at the stove, holding her second cup of coffee in one hand, scrambling eggs with the other, while Mercy stirred a delicious-smelling Filipino chicken-and-rice dish in a large frying pan.

Sophie wandered in, yawning, and poured coffee. "Morning. Mercy, that smells great." She picked up her phone and almost spewed her coffee. She coughed, took a steadying breath. "Wow. I can't believe how many likes there are already. Have you seen this?" She turned the phone so Camille could see Cass's Instagram account.

There were thousands of likes on the fake diary page. Camille's stomach clenched as she read the caption aloud:

"**From Captain Talon's diary—'Despite the delays caused by an unexpected storm, we navigated safely south of the city, unloading our cargo under cover of darkness before indulging in the comforts of women and whiskey. This small isle has much to recommend it, including the company of fellow captains, comfortable beds, and convenient shell middens.' #piratediary #coolreplica #piratelegends #fontanafamilybookofdays #historynerdgirl**"

Mercy set the chicken and rice on the table. "You did good, Sophie. This is exactly what we were hoping for."

Never one to sit still, Hank was scrolling through channels on the small TV in the corner. "Nice. We've hit the big time now, ladies. Check it out." A reporter was standing in front of a small museum in the French Quarter talking about the diary and long-ago auction Gran had told them about, as well as the diary's connection to the Book of Days.

"We spoke with several avid treasure hunters who, interestingly enough, felt that because of the Abernathy and Benoit families' connection to the diary—and the recent posts on Instagram by Cassandra Abernathy—the families might know more about the whereabouts of the highly-sought-after Fontana family's Book of Days than they are letting on."

The reporter turned to a young man with a scruffy beard who insisted that Camille's family definitely knew more than they were saying.

Camille tuned them out, concern for Cass's safety foremost, until Hank exclaimed, "That's the guy! The one in the jacked-up pickup."

All eyes turned that way as Hank cranked up the volume.

Fury propelled Camille closer to the screen. That was definitely the bearded guy who'd run Cass off the road. "He's not the same one who chased us after Gran's event, though. That guy was clean-shaven."

"I'm guessing both are local treasure-hunter wannabes." Hank crossed her arms. "More enthusiasm for the chase than any actual skill."

"Doesn't make them any less dangerous." Camille dropped into a chair and rubbed her arms against a sudden chill. When her phone rang, she took a deep breath before she answered. "Good morning, Willa. Let me put you on speaker. The team is all here."

"Great. Good morning, everyone," the Speranza team leader said. "I wanted to give you a quick update and also let you know that Picasso is going to be out of commission for a bit."

"Is she okay?" Camille shared a worried look with the other women.

Their tech wizard, who'd worked with Willa the longest, was a genius with a computer but also something of a mystery. Picasso worked out of an underground office in New York City and always kept her skin covered, hiding serious scarring nobody talked about.

"She will be. She has to have surgery related to a previous injury, but she should be fine. She just won't be able to work for a couple weeks."

The team swapped another round of concerned glances.

"Also, Scoop and I are headed to Kenya on another mission. He's helping me track missing medical supplies and the woman delivering them."

From what Camille had gathered when she was recruited for the Speranza team two years ago, Willa Campos lived on a small island somewhere in the Mediterranean but had a contact list to rival heads of state. She always had her finger on the world's pulse and was an absolute genius at connecting women who were trying to make the world a better place—and who needed help because of it—with Speranza.

Camille had also learned that Willa never went anywhere without Scoop, a tough-as-nails former Spec Ops leader and possibly a bit more than Willa's friend.

"We'll say a prayer for everyone's safety." Mercy made the sign of the cross. The petite nun's quiet calm had been invaluable since Willa recruited her just over a year ago.

"Thanks. We'll be out in the bush with limited communication, but we'll touch base as often as we can."

"Any idea how long you'll be gone?" Hank had muted the TV and stood by the table, arms folded, fiddling with the leather band that kept her Speranza medallion hidden behind her battered Timex. She'd been recruited around the same time as Camille and, like MacGyver, could fix or jury-rig anything.

"Hard to say. We're thinking a week, maybe two. How are things on your end?"

Camille updated her on the legend of the Liar's Treasure and the fake diary page Sophie had created. And the most recent news report.

"Smart thinking, buying a little time. When are you leaving?"

Hank said, "Tonight," at the same time Camille said, "I'm not going."

Silence filled the room.

"Why not?" Willa's voice was calm, curious.

"Isn't it obvious? Someone is after Cass because of that diary. I can't leave her alone."

"Sophie's misdirection should send everyone off in another direction."

Camille shot out of her chair and started pacing, arms wrapped around her waist. "Or they'll come after her even harder because of that reporter." She shook her head. "It's too dangerous. I need to stay here."

"What about Jolie and her request for help?"

Camille's head snapped up. Gran stood in the kitchen doorway, dressed in another of her severely tailored business suits and sensible heels, her expression implacable. The small Speranza emblem camouflaged in an intricate brooch caught the light as she set a cardboard box on the table.

"The team will help her figure out what happened to her friend." Camille scanned the room. "I need to take care of Cass."

"Willa told me about Picasso." Gran poured herself a cup of coffee, took a sip. "Leave Cass with me and go help Jolie. Cass is good with a computer, so she can do research for us while Picasso is on the mend. After she gets her schoolwork done, of course."

"You make it sound so easy."

"It is easy. Jolie needs help and you're very good at what you do." Gran's gaze encompassed the whole group. "All of you. So go do what you do."

Gran had been part of Speranza for decades, but two years ago, she'd told Camille about the secret organization and bequeathed her responsibilities to her, moving into a support role.

Camille shook her head. "Cass is my responsibility. Always has been. I can't just leave her. What if something happens to her?"

Gran set her cup down and met Camille's eyes. "You know as well as I do that something can happen to us at any time, anywhere. But not unless it has first passed through God's hands."

In one smooth move, Gran reached behind her suit jacket, pulled out a pistol, and laid it on the table, eliciting a shocked gasp from Camille. "Also, anyone who tries to get near Cass will have to go through me."

Hank barked out a laugh, then quickly smothered it.

Camille just stared from the gun to Gran and back again, mouth open in shock. "Do you know how to use that thing?"

"I wouldn't carry it if I didn't. I am not a fool. Your gramps didn't just teach you to shoot. He taught me years ago and we went to the range every week for all of our marriage. I still go. It certainly came in handy on more than one Speranza mission."

In an uncharacteristic gesture, she reached up and cupped Camille's cheek. "Go do what you were created to do and let me do the same. Your girl will be safe with me. Besides, Jolie is like family, and she needs help figuring out who killed her friend."

"I agree," Sophie said. "We need you with us, Camille."

"You do know Jolie better than anyone," Mercy added.

"I don't know if you've realized it yet, but the vultures are already circling." Gran tucked the gun into the holster at the small of her back. "There are already three news vans parked at the end of the drive."

Worry and responsibility warred for control. Camille's throat went dry as she studied each of them in turn. "Hank, what do you say?"

The other woman chewed the inside of her lip, and Camille could see her thinking through and discarding various scenarios. "The post Sophie created will help, but after that news report, I don't think Cass will be completely safe until we find this Book of Days and let the world know it's somewhere far away from wherever she is and she no longer has anything to do with it."

Hank propped her hands on her hips and speared Camille with a hard stare. "Until then, I think every kook and treasure hunter will be after you and Cass, thinking you'll lead them to the book, and after that, the treasure. So the quicker we find the Book of Days, the better."

Silence filled the room, but all Camille could hear was Cass's scared voice calling her "Mommy."

Finally, Sophie nodded slowly. "I think Hank's right."

At that moment, Cass wandered into the room, still in her pj's. She kissed Camille's cheek as she walked to the coffee maker, poured coffee, and took a sip. When she turned around, she almost sloshed her coffee. "Gran! What are you doing here so early?"

"Good morning, dear." She patted Cass's cheek, then stepped to the table and opened the cardboard box. In one smooth move, she pulled out a pair of well-worn combat boots and thumped them on the table.

Camille walked over and ran a hand over the cracked leather, smiling as memories rushed through her. "These were Gramps's."

"For real? From when he was in the Army?" Cass picked one up, inspected it.

Gran nodded. "He served in Vietnam. The boots were found in the same storage room as the diary."

The last time Camille had seen them, she'd been about ten. She'd found them in the back of Gramps's closet and clumped around the farmhouse for days. When she'd asked why he kept them, Gramps said, *"They're to remind me that we have to put feet to our faith."*

When the room went silent, Camille realized she'd said the words aloud. She walked over and gathered Cass in her arms. "I know, baby girl. I miss him, too."

Cass wiped the tears from her cheeks. "That was one of his favorite sayings."

"It was." Camille smiled, glanced at the team. "Sometimes I got tired of him saying it. Because he always added, 'Faith is easy when you're standing on familiar ground.'"

Cass slipped out of her arms and stroked one of the boots, then eyed Gran. "Can I have one of the shoelaces?"

"Of course."

Cass pulled it out, then immediately started twisting and turning it, weaving the strands together, lightning fast. "There." She tied the ends of the bracelet she'd made around her wrist, then held it up for everyone to see. "Now it's my reminder, too." She pulled out the other shoelace and handed it to Camille. "You should have one, too." She met Camille's eyes. "I know you guys are getting ready to leave soon."

Camille opened her mouth, closed it. Though Cass knew the team traveled all over the world helping women in trouble, Camille again stopped before sharing details about Speranza's centuries-old legacy. Still not the right time.

Instead, she pulled Cass into her arms again and met Gran's eyes over her daughter's head. The other woman gave a slight nod.

"We have to put feet to our faith."

"Faith is easy when you're standing on familiar ground."

Her stomach churned and her hands wanted to shake, but Gramps—and Gran—were right. If she believed the things she'd tried to teach Cass, it was time to put her money where her mouth was. Though Camille had absolutely no doubt that Gran would protect Cass with her life if it came to that, Cass's safety was ultimately in God's more-than-capable hands. It was Camille's fear, her need to be in control, that was keeping her in New Orleans.

She eased away from her daughter, took a deep breath, and tied the shoelace to the handle of her camera bag. Time to trust God to do what only He could do—and go do her part to find the Book of Days.

Give me courage, Lord.

She smiled at Cass, then turned to the team. "We leave tonight."

"Excellent. Camille, I want you to take point on this mission." Willa's voice came from Camille's phone and everyone startled. They'd forgotten she was still on the line. "Octavia, is there someplace you and Cass can hole up for a little while?"

Gran's chin came up. "You know the Tucker-Benoit mansion has state-of-the-art security."

"What about when you're at work? Will Cass be there alone with Mrs. H. after school?" Camille asked.

Gran propped one hand on her chin, thought for a moment. "A friend of mine has a vacation home in a small town a few hours from here. One that has great Internet. Cass can do her schoolwork online, and I'll keep up with the office from there."

Sophie studied Gran for a moment. "You'll have to stay inside, out of view. No offense, Ms. Benoit, but there's no way you'll be able to blend in."

Gran appeared ready to argue, then she gave a sharp nod. "Of course. I'll do whatever it takes to keep Cassandra safe."

Hank clapped her hands together. "All right, people, let's move. We need to find this book and help Jolie figure out why her friend was killed."

17

GRAND ISLE, SOUTH OF NEW ORLEANS

Lucien parked his pickup on the grass at the edge of the overcrowded marina parking lot and elbowed his way through the crowd. The two-hour drive to Grand Isle from New Orleans had taken three hours today due to traffic.

An old Army buddy kept a small center-console fishing boat there and had told Lucien he was welcome to use it anytime. He'd never taken him up on his offer. Until today.

Lucien threaded the boat around the throng of vessels headed for the smaller Isle Grand Terre just to the northeast of Grand Isle. Apparently he wasn't the only one who thought Cass's latest IG post from Captain Talon's diary pointed the way here.

Isle Grand Terre was said to have been a favorite hangout and treasure-burial site for French pirates in the past. Of course, the reference to handy Native American shell middens on the island wasn't exactly a giant "*X* marks the spot."

He avoided the crowded marina and beached the boat in the sand. After he set the anchor and waded ashore, he studied the area, spotting several people walking along the shoreline toting shovels. He heaved out a sigh. Were they planning to dig up the entire island?

He'd known this trip would be a waste of time. He should be at the warehouse updating inventory for Pops and researching the Book of Days.

He stepped around several deep holes in the sand and shook his head. There was no way on God's green earth the Book of Days was lying around anywhere near here. He'd need to spend a lot more time and do tons more research before he put a shovel in the ground.

Time he didn't have to waste.

Before he gave up, he pulled out his phone and checked Cass's Instagram post again, but nothing new jumped out at him. He figured Cass or, more probably, Camille had sent all the treasure hunters on a wild-goose chase away from the city to take the spotlight off Cass. At least, that's what he would have done. He'd just needed to make sure.

There was one person who might know the real scoop. He grabbed his phone.

Before he could dial, a commotion broke out behind him. He spun around in time to see two guys grab another man and start dragging him toward a boat anchored just offshore.

The man shouted and fought to get free.

Lucien took off running in that direction, elbowing his way through the onlookers. When the man tried to jerk away again, Lucien realized why the voice sounded familiar.

"Marcel! What's happening, man?"

One of the two guys holding Marcel glanced over his shoulder and muttered something to the other.

Lucien didn't slow down. He ran full tilt, grabbed the guy on the left by the arm, and spun him into the surrounding gawkers. As he did, Marcel used his free hand to send an uppercut into the other's jaw, sending him to the ground.

"Let's get out of here!" Lucien took off the way he'd come, Marcel hard on his heels as they ran down the beach. Lucien didn't slow until he neared his boat. "Get in!"

They slogged through thigh-deep water. Lucien pulled the anchor, hopped in, and fired it up, then took off, weaving his way around the other boats, headed back toward Grand Isle.

When there was no sign of the thugs by the time they reached the marina, Marcel's panting finally slowed. He turned his head, sent Lucien that trademark impish grin. "Thanks for the assist."

Lucien scanned the other man. The bruise around Marcel's eye was purple and green, he had another bruise along his jaw, and his knuckles were scraped and bloody. There was also a barely healed cut along his temple. None of it was new. "You look like you've been keelhauled, man."

Marcel shrugged, then winced. "Ran into a bit of trouble recently. Nothing I can't handle."

"And the two guys trying to drag you away just now?"

"Part of the trouble."

"Let me guess. This is about the diary. Are you trying to find it?" When Marcel didn't answer, realization dawned. "No, you're trying to sell it. You have it. You're after the rest of the treasure."

Marcel wrung out the hem of his soggy T-shirt.

"I need to see that diary, man."

Still nothing.

"I just saved your bacon. You owe me."

Marcel slowly focused on him. "Don't tell me you're after it, too?"

Lucien cocked an eyebrow. Waited.

Finally, Marcel grinned, the telltale gleam in his eye that Lucien remembered from high school. The one that said a scheme was underway. "Maybe we can help each other."

A SMALL VILLAGE IN ESWATINI

"Welcome, welcome, sir. It is so good of you to come, to visit our country and see our work here." Motsa Sanele smiled broadly at his pale-skinned visitor. He waved a hand. "Please, let me show you our latest project."

His visitor nodded, his hat pulled low over his face against the burning midday sun. He wore lightweight khaki clothing to combat the desert heat. "Thank you."

"After Miss Jolie was here only last month, I will admit I had not expected another visit from anyone on the Becker Foundation staff for quite some time."

His guest shrugged. "We have found spot checks to be good practice for everyone, to be sure things are always done correctly."

"But of course, sir. Surely you are not implying some wrongdoing on our part?" Alarm filled Motsa and a trickle of sweat slid down his collar.

His visitor stopped and stared at him. "For a worldwide organization like the Becker Foundation to do the good work we do, our reputation must be spotless, our staff above reproach."

Motsa stumbled. "But of course."

They walked along the dusty path to a small cistern.

"This is our newest well, and it has made all the difference for our women and children in this area particularly." Motsa kept talking, his nerves rising with every minute that passed without his visitor saying a word.

Finally, the man bent to tie his shoe, then rose. "Thank you for the tour." He mopped his face with a handkerchief. "I admit the heat is getting to me. Perhaps we can continue the tour later." He turned and waved Motsa ahead of him on the return path.

There was no shade out here, just a few straggly bushes fighting to survive.

Motsa turned to head back. He hadn't taken three steps when his guest suddenly wrapped an arm around his neck. He whispered in Motsa's ear, "Did you think no one would find out about the ways you betrayed your countrymen? About the bribes you accepted to let gunrunners and militants store their weapons of destruction in your village?"

Motsa felt the point of a knife in the middle of his back. "Please. No. You don't understand. It was for protection. If they store the weapons here, our people will remain safe."

"And you pocket a fortune. All in the name of doing good. Of making the world a better place."

"But I am—we are—our village is—"

"You have been judged and found guilty of greed and selfish ambition, Motsa Sanele. And the penalty is death."

It took a moment for the searing pain to register, another for Motsa to realize he would die out here, alone.

The man dragged him to the bushes and shoved him out of sight. Tears leaked out of Motsa's dark eyes as his lifeblood drained onto the sandy soil.

18

MĂRGĂU, ROMANIA—TWO DAYS LATER

After more than twenty-four hours of travel, plus the eight-hour time difference between here and New Orleans, Camille was exhausted and figured the rest of the team was equally tired.

The Speranza team stood on a low hill above the town, where the new well had been installed. Quaint little cottages lined both sides of the single street. In the distance, the Apuseni Mountains rose into a crisp blue sky.

"I feel like this was a waste of time," Hank muttered.

"You may be right," Camille said. "Besides confirming that the poison was an overdose of sodium fluoride, the project director couldn't tell us anything we didn't already know, and neither could anyone else."

They'd interviewed all of the artisans, one at a time, but there didn't seem to be any new information to be had.

Camille paced the area, praying she'd made the right choice by coming. She had checked in with Cass and Gran at least a half-dozen times before Cass told her to quit already. They were fine.

"This has setup written all over it." Hank rubbed the back of her neck.

"But was the professor killed because of the well or because of the diary?" Sophie asked.

"For what reason, though?" Mercy had her arms wrapped around her middle, eyes narrowed. "There has to be a motive."

"Right. We know Tara was buying the diary from Marcel. She was found near an ATM, but there is no record of her withdrawing money. So a random robbery seems unlikely." Camille paced as she talked.

"Plus the police told Jolie that Tara's hotel room was searched. To me, that says diary connection," Hank added.

Sophie tapped a finger against her lips. "What about the extra money in her account? If she'd paid Marcel, there should be less money."

"We're asking the right questions," Camille said, "but I don't think we'll find the answers here."

The team started down the hill toward their rental car.

Halfway down the street, a young woman named Elisabeth whom they'd interviewed earlier beckoned Camille to her cottage, making a hurry-up motion. She herded the team inside the small space, looked both ways, then closed the door behind them.

A crowded worktable stood under the window. Hank took up position next to it so she could watch the street and Elisabeth at the same time.

Sophie approached the table. "Wow. These are incredible."

"Are those eggs?"

Hank reached out and Sophie barked, "Don't touch!"

Hank snatched her hand back and shot Sophie a glare.

"Sorry. They're made of actual eggshells and can break if you so much as sneeze on them."

"Why would you make them out of eggshells, then? Why not something sturdier?"

Elisabeth smiled. "It is tradition here in Romania, especially for Easter. I paint all year to have enough inventory to sell."

The eggs were exquisite, the colors vibrant and the designs incredibly intricate.

Hank indicated a magnifying glass on a stand. "I bet this makes it easier."

"It would be impossible without it." Elisabeth grimaced. "Though my beloved grandmother would say I was cheating." She turned to Camille. "I wanted to tell you that I do not believe what others are saying about Professor Tara. She wanted good things for us. She said she was going to Rome to do some research. Did she find what she was searching for?"

Interesting question. "We don't think so, no. But we're not sure."

"I made this for her." Elisabeth handed one of the painted eggs to Camille, smiling sadly. "It is—how do you Americans say? A bonus. I think you should have it now."

Camille cupped the egg in her palms. "It's beautiful."

At the same time, Hank barked, "Bonus for what?"

The harsh tone earned her a glare from Mercy.

Camille turned the egg over and studied the building on the back side. "Is this a particular church?"

"Yes. It is the Moon Church in Oradea," Elisabeth said.

"What made you paint this particular church for Tara?" Camille asked.

Elisabeth glanced out the window, suddenly nervous. "You must go. I am very sorry that your friend is gone." She ushered them out the door and closed and locked it behind them.

"That was weird." Hank nodded to the egg in Camille's hands. "But could be we just got our first clue."

Maybe Tara had come here for more than the water project. Maybe it was connected to the treasure everyone was after, too.

Camille spied Elisabeth peering through the lace curtains at the window. "Very possibly. Next stop, Moon Church."

19

After two hours in the car and a late lunch, the team parked in front of the Moon Church in Oradea. They stood on the sidewalk and took in the Byzantine architecture.

"It's bigger than I expected." Hank craned her neck.

"Cathedrals usually are," Mercy drawled and ignored Hank's eye roll.

"Check out the spire." Sophie pointed to a moon with a clock-face above it. "The moon does a rotation around its axis every twenty-eight days to indicate the moon phases, and that is linked to the clock mechanism above it. A local mechanic named Georg Rueppe designed it back in 1793." She stopped, shrugged. "I think the fact that it still works is pretty fascinating."

"Pretty cool." Hank pulled the door open and they filed in, stopped. "Wow."

"Are we looking for another egg?" Mercy scanned the area around her.

"Let's split up, see if anything catches our eye." Camille started toward the right side while the others went left.

She cradled the painted egg in her palm, checking it against the brightly colored frescoes covering every inch of wall space. She dodged the tourists wandering around on this weekday afternoon, focused on the walls to see if anything jumped out at her.

She heard footsteps and turned as two men came toward her: early thirties maybe, dressed like European travelers in creased jeans and button-down shirts, nice shoes. One wore his blondish hair in a ponytail, the other had a wicked scar along his cheek. Both appeared riveted by the artwork. As they approached, Scarface plowed into her, mumbled an apology, yanked her camera bag off her shoulder, and started to take off.

"Hey!" Camille gripped her bag with one hand and tried to keep the egg from hitting the floor with the other, but he tugged harder and the strap slid through her grip.

She turned to give chase, but Ponytail blocked her with his arm. The egg slipped from her fingers and hit the stone floor with an unmistakable crack.

"Stop them! They stole my bag."

Sophie stuck her foot into the aisle and Scarface stumbled and flailed, trying to find his footing.

Mercy yanked the makeshift belt from around her waist and snapped the whip. The sound reverberated through the cathedral as it wrapped around his ankles. She snapped her wrist again and Scarface sprawled headlong on the slippery floor, the bag sliding from his grasp.

Ponytail reached for it, but Hank shoved him aside and Sophie snatched the bag before he could scoop it up.

Camille yanked her phone from her back pocket and snapped a couple pics of their faces just as a security guard galloped into the room shouting for them to stop.

Hank raced after them, Sophie right behind her. Mercy casually retied the belt at her waist, while Camille tried to explain what happened to the guard, who spoke almost no English.

After assuring him they were fine, she went back up the aisle and carefully picked up the egg. It had cracked but was still intact. As she turned it this way and that, she saw something that surprised her.

Mercy hurried toward her. "Did you find something?"

"Maybe. I need a flashlight."

Mercy pulled out her phone.

Hank and Sophie returned, both breathing hard. "We lost them. They had a little white Fiat waiting around the corner."

"They obviously know their way around the city," Sophie added. "What are you doing?"

"I think . . . yes . . . this egg has been opened before. See the glue? I think there's something inside it."

As carefully as possible, Camille put her fingernail in one of the cracks and tried to widen it without breaking the rest of the shell.

"Wait. Let's get some pics of the outside first, in case it doesn't work." Sophie snapped pictures from all angles. "Okay, now open it."

Barely breathing and trying to keep her hand steady, Camille eased the crack open. But at the last second it gave way and one side of the egg collapsed.

"Wait." Camille carefully removed a folded piece of paper inside. She read the address aloud.

Sophie already had her phone out. "It's in Tuscany, near Florence."

Camille held up the crushed egg, smiled. "I think Elisabeth was telling Tara—and now us—to go there."

"Why not just hand over the address?" Hank crossed her arms, scowling. "And why send us to this church first?"

Mercy studied the parishioners and tourists milling around. "Maybe someone was supposed to meet her here?"

"We may never know. But"—Camille hitched her chin at the camera bag Sophie had set down on a pew—"both Jolie and the director of the water project said Tara always carried a messenger bag. Mine is a similar design."

"So this may not have been a random purse snatching," Mercy said.

Camille saw the security guard approaching them, an official-looking man in tow. "Let's continue this another time."

They hurried outside. Hank took the wheel, Camille riding shotgun, with Sophie and Mercy in the backseat.

Two blocks from the church, Hank said, "Hang on. Our friends in the white Fiat are back."

She spun the car in a tight U-turn and hit the gas.

Camille fingered the shoelace and whispered a prayer for Cass.

"Faith is easy when you're standing on familiar ground."

20

NEW ORLEANS

Lucien sat in Pops's ancient leather desk chair, trying to get comfortable despite the springs poking his backside. The massive wooden desk in the office at the waterfront warehouse, cluttered with piles of paper and random antiques, had always been the old man's domain. Lucien had done his homework on the other side of the desk for years. But nobody sat in Pops's chair except him. A half-smoked cigar sat in the ashtray, a whiskey decanter beside it, the whole place reeking of Claude's favorite Cubans.

Lucien shifted in the seat and examined the familiar room. It still felt wrong to sit in Pops's chair. Floor-to-ceiling shelves lined every wall, and more books were piled on the floor in front of some of them.

He opened the copy of the pirate's diary he'd purchased from Marcel and started reading, glad his French was up to snuff due to his work in Africa. Pops would rather Lucien had purchased the actual diary from Camille, but she had left him a snippy little voicemail repeating what Octavia had said: The diary belonged to her family and was not for sale.

Good thing Marcel felt differently. Well, differently enough to sell him a copy.

Lucien pored over every page, slowly, made a few notes, but nothing jumped out at him. And even if something did, he wasn't sure that would be enough to find the Book of Days. If it had been hidden this long, clues wouldn't be scattered around in a neat little trail.

He pulled over the stack of research books Pops had told him to check and sifted through them until he found the worn leather journal that had belonged to Pops's beloved wife, Nadine, the grandmother who died before Lucien was born. He laughed at some of the entries. She sounded like a real spitfire and had been strong enough to stand up to a rascal like Claude. Their love for each other was also apparent.

Lucien read more entries here and there as he flipped through the pages of her neat script. Finally he found the section in the middle where Pops had said she talked about the pirate's diary. Sure enough, Nadine's grandmother had also claimed that the diary belonged to her family, but she gave no evidence to support that claim. And even if it was true, was her family descended from the Talon family of pirates—which seemed the most likely—or from the Fontana family, whom the treasure belonged to? He could research Nadine's genealogy, he supposed, or just ask Pops, but Lucien wasn't sure that effort would net the results he wanted.

He was about to set the journal aside when he noticed a small symbol drawn in the bottom corner of one of the pages: an anchor with a feather across it. He couldn't find any explanation given. A quick online search on his laptop didn't yield any results either.

"What are you doing in Claude's chair?"

Lucien eased his head up and slid his hand to the knife sheathed at his waist. "Who wants to know?" He'd never seen the man before, but he knew the type. About Pops's age, he had mean eyes, a superior attitude, and unless Lucien missed his guess, that bulge under his suit jacket was a gun.

"Remy Landry, Claude's business partner." He extended a meaty hand over the desk.

Lucien ignored the hand and leaned back in the chair, folded his arms. "Since when?"

Remy sat in the chair opposite, crossed one leg over his other knee, pointed a finger at Lucien. "You must be Claude's grandson. The one usually in Africa or somewhere. You have his eyes."

"What kind of business are you and Pops doing together?"

The man shrugged. "A little of this and that for our mutual benefit." He hitched his chin toward the books on the desk. "Claude said you were going to help him find that old book everyone's hot to get their hands on. He said it's worth a fortune." He raised an eyebrow.

"How much does he owe you?" Lucien sat forward in the chair, leaned his hands on the desk, eyes steady on the other man's.

"Let's just say that book would go a long way to putting him back in the black."

Lucien slowly unfolded himself from the chair and leaned over the desk. "Thanks for dropping by." He indicated the door. "Don't come back."

"Be careful with that attitude, boy. Claude still lives in this town, even when you're not here."

FLORENCE, ITALY

After Hank finally lost the Fiat, they had crashed at a nearby hotel before catching an early flight from Romania to Italy. By early afternoon, they'd checked into a small hotel on the outskirts of Florence and were gathered in Sophie and Mercy's room to map out their next steps.

The band around Camille's heart had loosened a smidge when Gran reported that they were safely settled into their little hideout and all was well—despite Cass's whining about being kidnapped and dragged to the back of beyond for no reason. Camille smiled. If Cass was being dramatic, she was fine.

Hank spread a local map out on one of the twin beds. "So, I think we—"

Sophie walked out of the bathroom and Hank did a double take. "Wow. No matter how many times I see you do that, I'm always amazed."

"Thanks. I think it'll work." Instead of her usual blonde hair, Sophie wore a dark wig and had styled it to mimic Tara's hairstyle. Camille's camera bag, which according to Jolie resembled Tara's messenger bag, was slung over her shoulder, and Sophie wore an Oradea T-shirt and the ball cap with the Becker Foundation logo Irina had given her in Romania.

Mercy gave her a critical once-over. "Unless someone knows Tara, they won't be able to tell the difference."

"That's the idea," Sophie said with a grin.

If whoever killed the professor saw her, they would know something was up, but the team had decided it was worth the risk.

Camille sat on the bed opposite Hank, scrolling through the photos she'd taken of Ponytail and Scarface at the Moon Church yesterday.

"I wish Picasso could run them through facial recognition for us." Mercy was wearing her habit again today in case they ended up in another church. And also because it rendered her invisible. Nobody noticed a nun, especially one wearing a veil.

"Me, too. Though I did read more of the diary on the plane." Camille grinned, then quickly sobered. "Apparently poor Cira was as unlucky in love as her ancestors, and Captain Talon's nephew was as much of a pirate as his uncle. According to Jacques's entries, after his uncle died, he purchased the *Bartholomew* with funds he obtained by selling his sick wife's 'fancy book.'"

"He stole the Book of Days from his sick wife?" Mercy propped her hands on her hips. "What a scoundrel."

"Exactly. But I did a search on the *Bartholomew*, and it was owned by a guy from Florence. So maybe that's why Tara told Jolie she was headed here after the well dedication."

"We won't know until we check." Hank tapped the map.

"You sure I shouldn't go back and talk to the woman who made the egg for Tara?"

Mercy's question had merit. Her ability to get people to talk never ceased to amaze Camille.

"Not just now, but we may need to revisit that." Camille picked up her copy of the diary and flipped pages. She pointed. "Here. Check this out. After the entry about selling his wife's 'fancy book,' there is a small notation in the margin. It says, *I libri illuminano*, which I think means 'Books illuminate' in Italian."

"That is correct," Mercy confirmed. She spoke Italian and French and her English was flawless, though when she was tired, her cadence sometimes slid back to her native Filipino accent.

"May I see that?" Sophie asked. She held the diary under a table lamp so she could see it better. "I think this is in different handwriting."

"You think someone else added it?" Mercy asked.

"That's my guess." She passed the diary around.

Camille squinted at the words. "I hadn't noticed that, but I think you're right."

"But why?" Hank asked. "And how does that help us find the Book of Days?"

"Could be a descendant added it, or a family member," Sophie said. "It may not help us at all, but in my experience, anything unusual could lead to a clue."

Camille nodded agreement with the rest of the team. Since Sophie's expertise was forgeries and retrieving stolen items, nobody doubted her opinion.

She turned back to the map Hank was pointing at. "I think Elisabeth was sending Tara to another church. Let's get over there."

They hadn't driven more than three blocks from the hotel when Hank said, "Well, doggone it, here we go again."

Camille glanced in the side mirror. Sure enough, another

vehicle was following them, only this one was a nondescript beige sedan. The surprise was the fierce-looking woman who gripped the wheel.

NEW ORLEANS

The sun had yet to rise when Lucien marched into the rehab facility. "I'm here to see Claude Broussard. I'm his grandson."

The young woman stepped back uncertainly and flicked her eyes toward a sign on the wall proclaiming that visiting hours were between 9:00 a.m. and 9:00 p.m. A long moment passed before she nodded warily and checked her computer. "He's in room 112."

"Yes, I know." He turned away, then back, and managed a smile. "Sorry. Not enough caffeine." Or sleep.

Halfway to Pops's room, Lucien veered into the restroom, braced his hands on the sink, and pushed his emotions down. If he stormed into Pops's room like this, he'd make things worse.

Lucien paused before he stepped inside and forced a smile. "Hey, Pops." He gave his grandfather a hug, then backed up and propped a shoulder against the doorframe.

Always an early riser, Claude sat up in bed, reading the newspaper. "I sure hope you're here to spring me from this place." Pops slapped his hand on the arm of the wheelchair beside the bed. "Doreen in PT is likely to kill me."

Lucien couldn't help but smile. "Guess she's doing her job, then."

Pops was improving all the time. His pallor was fading, and he seemed stronger and clearer now that he was off most of the pain meds.

"What are you doing here this early, son? Did you find something useful in all those books?"

"Remy Landry came to see me. Says you two are in business together."

Something flickered in Pops's eyes before he crossed his arms over his chest and raised his chin. "And?"

"What business, Pops? From what I read, the Feds have been trying to bust him for racketeering for years."

Pops ran a hand over his fringe of hair, wouldn't meet Lucien's eyes. "Nothing you need to concern yourself with."

"This guy is bad news. The kind you don't want getting their hooks into you. Though it sounds like it's already too late for that."

"He offered me a way out of a bad spot a while back. Don't worry, I have it all under control."

"By having me try to find that Book of Days? Why didn't you tell me if you needed help?"

"Because you're not here, are you, boyo!"

Pops had never been a yeller, so the shout hit Lucien like a slap. "You know I would have—"

"I tried to call you. You didn't call back."

"What?" The betrayal in Pops's eyes made him feel like pond scum. "Pops, I never got a message from you, or I would have found a way to call right away." Cell service was always spotty, but he had a satellite phone for his supply runs.

Pops had never asked for help. Not once. If he had, Lucien would have moved heaven and earth to provide what he needed.

Claude waved that away. "It doesn't matter. Like I said, I have it all under control."

"What kind of deal did you make with him?"

Pops studied his hands, then finally looked Lucien in the eye. "Let's just say that finding the Book of Days is our best shot at getting rid of him for good."

"That's what Remy said last night. You going to tell me the rest of it?"

They faced off across the room.

Pops clenched his jaw. "Just find that Book of Days, son."

"I'll do my best. I came to tell you I'm headed to Florence." Lucien had been too angry—and okay, worried—after Remy left last night to sleep, so he'd done a deep-research dive and found an interesting tidbit tying the Talon family of the diary to the Gallo family of Florence.

"You think it's there?"

"Only one way to find out." He leaned in and hugged Pops's too-thin frame. "Stay out of trouble, all right? I'll keep you posted."

Lucien was halfway down the hall when someone called his name. "Hey, Doc. What's up?"

"I'm glad I caught you. I'm pleased with Claude's progress so far. We should be able to increase his PT within a day or two. But I'm hoping you can impress upon him the need to take his prescriptions regularly once he's released."

"Which prescriptions are we talking about, exactly? I thought he was off the major pain meds."

"I'm talking about his heart medication."

The doctor must have seen his confusion. "He didn't tell you." He sighed. "Your grandfather had a heart attack several months ago. He fell off that ladder because he hadn't been taking his meds like he's supposed to."

The more the doctor talked, the more Lucien felt the ground shift under his feet. His life had just been spun off its axis.

First, he'd find the Book of Days. And then he'd figure out how to be here for the man who'd raised him.

21

ZURICH, SWITZERLAND

Jolie sat in her office at the Becker Foundation and tried to focus. Unsure how to figure out if Tara's death was connected to the well project, she'd spent all night poring over the accounting, acquisitions, and purchase-order records for every single item connected to it. The numbers weren't adding up. What she didn't know was why.

What was she missing?

A knock sounded and the receptionist delivered a box and an overnight package with the diary from Camille. Jolie opened the package first and flipped through the diary, amazed that it had caused so much heartache.

She forced emotion aside as she opened the box containing Tara's carry-on. Jolie had asked the carabinieri to send it to her, and then she'd forward it to a distant family member she'd located.

Jolie set it on the desk and blinked back tears at the sight of Tara's hat, sunglasses, and the ratty messenger bag she was never without. Jolie went through the carry-on, but nothing unusual caught her eye. But then she picked up the messenger bag, surprised to find it empty.

Where was the little notebook Tara was forever scribbling in?

Throat thick, Jolie ran her hand over the worn fabric. *Wait.* She ran her hand back again and felt something hard and rectangular in the bottom.

She cut the seam and found Tara's notebook sewn inside. For safekeeping, obviously, but what was in it that she wanted to hide? Jolie flipped through Tara's messy script. Half of the notebook talked about the Book of Days and the pirate diary. No surprise. But the second half contained much of the same well-project data Jolie had spent the night studying. But Tara had this on her laptop. Why write it down and hide it?

Before she could make sense of it, the receptionist buzzed her, notifying her of an impromptu staff meeting.

Jolie's unease grew. The last unscheduled staff meeting had not yielded good news.

She walked into the conference room and poured a cup of coffee, selected a pastry. "Good morning, Nelson."

He was again dressed in an immaculately tailored suit, every white hair perfectly in place, powdered sugar coating his lips. He licked them and took a sip of coffee before responding. "Good morning. You turn up anything useful yet?"

Several other staffers filed in as Jolie debated what to say. The conference-room door closed with an authoritative click.

"If everyone would have a seat, we'll get started."

At his wife's strident tone, Nelson winked. "I guess social time is over. We'll talk later."

Jolie's stomach churned as she took her seat and nodded to her fellow staff members across the antique mahogany table.

Payne Martin lifted his teacup in greeting. "Good day, Miss Ward. I just read your e-mail," he said in his crisp British accent. "Thank you for reminding us, always, of our calling to continue to make the world a better place, even in times of great sorrow." Quiet and shy, the tall, thin British expat had financial contacts all over the world that helped keep the Foundation moving forward.

"Thank you." Jolie kept her voice steady.

"I'm that sorry to hear about poor Tara," Jamie Lawson said from across the table, his Scottish brogue thicker than usual. "She was a fine lass."

"Thank you." Jolie blinked back tears as she tried to smile.

Joseph Garcia, a retired doctor from Spain and head of Quality Control, turned to her. "My condolences, as well. I know you were friends. Has there been any further word on what poisoned the water?"

"Overdose of sodium fluoride, unfortunately."

Dot had taken her usual seat at the head of the table, Nelson to her right, beside Jolie. "Of course we are all devastated by the news of Tara's death. And of the well poisoning in Romania. We're working with the police and doing everything we can to figure out what happened."

Dot's brisk tone rubbed her the wrong way, but Jolie updated everyone on what had taken place in both Italy and Romania.

"Thank you, Jolie." Dot paused, scanning the room. "I'm afraid I have some more upsetting news. Motsa Sanele from Eswatini passed away three nights ago. We just got word."

Shocked silence filled the elegantly appointed conference room, and Jolie's unease turned to a hard knot in her stomach. She eyed the shocked expressions of the other staff members. Another committee member dead? In the same week?

"How did he die?" Jolie's outburst earned her a sharp look from Dot.

"We don't know yet. But I'll e-mail everyone when I learn more. We'll of course send the appropriate condolences to his family." She scanned the staff. "Now, on to other business. Despite the sadness of recent events, Nelson and I are committed to making our annual summit in two weeks our best yet. It's important to have that time with our staff, committee members, major donors, and program recipients, in addition to the general public."

"We never want the organization to grow so large that we lose our connection to each other," Nelson added. "The retreat center we've reserved just outside of Florence should be perfect. It's a nice change from the impersonal convention centers of previous summits."

Dot continued talking, asking the other staffers for updates, but Jolie's mind was on the deceased Foundation representative. She'd met Motsa Sanele last month on her trip to Africa and found him to be both hardworking and passionate about creative ways to meet the needs of his countrymen.

Was there a connection between his death and Tara's? Maybe it was just a coincidence, but Jolie wouldn't be able to let it go until she learned the details.

"Thank you all." Dot stood, signaling the end of the meeting. "A word before you go, Jolie?"

She sat back down. "Of course."

Dot waited until the other staff members left, then closed the conference-room door.

Nelson leaned forward, hands clasped on the conference table, anticipation all over his handsome features. "Do you have the diary?"

Jolie pulled the padded envelope from her briefcase and handed it over. "It was just delivered. The invoice is in there as well."

Nelson waved that last away. "Did Tara say anything else about the Book of Days?"

Jolie thought of the notebook and kept her expression bland. "Like what?"

Dot picked up her iPad and turned it so Jolie could read the article from a treasure-hunting website.

Renewed Interest in a Centuries-Old Legend

Jolie skimmed the article, cataloging the key points from previous conversations with Tara. The Fontana family's Illuminated Book of Days . . . contained clues to other pieces of the Liar's Treasure, including Countess Alonza's Portable Altar. . . . Ship's captain ignored young girl's warning that stealing her family's Book of Days would bring certain death. Crew member died and girl escaped with book. . . . Nothing about the pieces since.

Speculation about the treasure's similarity to the biblical story of Ananias and Sapphira . . . When set was all together, it could judge motives. . . . Worthy meant untold riches. Unworthy got you instant death.

Jolie kept scrolling. Mention of Cass's post about the diary . . . and another post pointing to Isle Grand Terre, a popular hideout of French pirates in the 1700s. Jolie set the iPad on the table. "That sounds about right."

"Tara didn't tell you anything more? Any details about how the treasure judges motives?" Nelson's eyes bored into her, expression intense.

Jolie flicked her eyes from him to Dot and back. "No, that's all I know." She hadn't known about the second Instagram post, but that wasn't what Nelson was asking. Shock hit her like a blow. "Wait a minute. You actually believe this legend? You think Tara found this treasure and what, it killed her?"

"We can't discount the treasure's power." Nelson's fist banged the table.

Jolie jumped, but Dot ignored her husband. "We don't know what to think."

Stunned, Jolie tried to take it all in.

"Keep working with the police in Rome," Dot continued. "And also see what you can find out about Motsa's death. We need to know why he died."

"But more important, we want you to find the Book of Days, Jolie."

She snapped her attention back to Nelson, to the fevered gleam in his blue eyes. Had he lost his mind? "People have been searching for that book forever, and even more will be now that this article is out there. Old manuscripts are your expertise. What help could I possibly offer?"

"If you got that diary from Octavia's family, then you can bet she made a copy." His tone hardened. "Her people will be going after the Book of Days next. Guaranteed. I want you to keep tabs on their progress and report back to me immediately. I want that book. Do you understand?"

Jolie kept all her worry and frustration carefully hidden. "I understand."

She returned to her office and locked the door before reading every page of Tara's notebook. Should she ask Nelson about Tara's notes on the Book of Days? She hesitated, then decided to gauge his reaction. His door stood slightly ajar, and she lifted her hand to knock when she realized he was talking to someone. She peeked through the opening. He was on the phone.

"Do what you need to do to get it for me. I don't trust Octavia Benoit any farther than I can throw her. But dollars to donuts she's sent people to find it. I want it first." He paused. "Good, keep me updated."

Jolie spun and sprinted back to her office, breathing hard. She had to warn Camille.

22

FLORENCE

Thanks to Hank's expert driving, they lost the woman tailing them. Eventually. Camille figured she gained a few gray hairs as Hank sped down narrow, single-car lanes between crumbling buildings, side mirrors tucked in so they didn't get torn off, but it worked. She didn't know if the woman and the two guys were working together, but the good news was if they were being followed, it kept the attention off Cass.

Hank pulled to a stop at the curb, and Camille led the way for the two-block walk to the small church whose address had been in the egg.

Sophie readjusted Camille's camera bag across her chest as they walked. "When I grow up, I want to drive like you, Hank."

One side of Hank's mouth slid up in a half smile. "Watch and learn, grasshopper."

At the church, a massive wooden door led into a dim interior, lit only by a few stained-glass windows and some flickering candles. The room carried the hushed feel of a place of worship, but on a much smaller scale than the Moon Church they'd visited yesterday.

Once they reached the front, with its surprisingly ornate altar, Camille leaned close, voice low. "Any ideas?"

Mercy scanned the room behind them. "This might be a good time to catch up on your prayers." She nodded to a nearby pew. "Let me have the egg. I'll be right back."

Camille handed her the little box containing the crushed remains of the egg. Then she and Hank and Sophie slid into the pew and took their places on the wooden kneeling bench. Camille cast a quick peek over her shoulder, turned back around, and smiled as she bowed her head. "Mercy is talking to the cleaning lady."

Mercy slipped back up the aisle and sidled over to the older woman, who wore a kerchief over her hair, apron around her ample middle, and pushed a broom over the stone floor. She smiled at the woman. This was where she felt most comfortable. Not necessarily in a church, but when she was talking with people. "*Mi scusi. Conosci una donna di nome* Tara Jameson?" *Do you know a woman named Tara Jameson?*

The woman eyed Mercy's habit. She regarded the painted egg inside the little box, and something like fear flashed across her face as her attention landed on the rest of the team, then returned to Mercy. *"Chi vuole saperlo?" Who wants to know?*

"I'm here on behalf of Tara's good friend Jolie." Mercy slid her Speranza medallion out from under her collar and got a blank stare. Not Speranza, then. She tucked it away again. "Do you know Tara?"

"I know of her," the woman said, eyes still on the area behind Mercy.

Interesting. Mercy kept her focus on the other woman's face. "I'm afraid I have sad news. Tara has died."

The woman reared back in shock, gripping her broom. "What happened?"

"That's what we're trying to find out," Mercy said in Italian. "What is your connection to Tara?"

She studied Mercy before she said, "One of my niece's cousins works with Tara for the water people. She said Tara was trying to find a book."

"Would that book happen to be the Fontana family's Book of Days?"

The woman stilled, peered around again, then tilted her head toward a back corner of the church. Mercy followed.

"Wait here." The woman suddenly slipped through a hidden door in the paneling. She returned several minutes later with an elderly nun in tow.

The woman was tiny and frail, leaning heavily on her cane, and for a moment Mercy froze, seeing her favorite auntie, her mother's sister, who had been killed along with Mercy's parents that terrible day. She shoved the memories away.

"This is Sister Maria-Anna." The cleaning woman hitched her chin toward Mercy. "Show her."

Mercy pulled out her Speranza medallion, then tucked it away again.

The sister's eyes followed the medallion. "We've waited so long," she whispered.

The cleaning woman nodded to the nun, then turned and started pushing her broom again, giving them privacy.

"What have you been waiting for?" Mercy asked.

Sister Maria-Anna gave her a thorough once-over. "How did Tara die?"

Interesting that both women knew Tara, or had heard of her. "We don't know, not for sure. The police say it was a robbery gone wrong."

Eyes sharp, the sister leaned farther on her cane. "You don't believe it."

"We don't."

"Who are those women with you?" She nodded toward the rest of the team. "Also Speranza?"

Mercy relaxed slightly. The sister clearly knew the meaning of the medallion. "Yes, we're helping Tara's friend Jolie figure out what happened."

"You think it has to do with the book," Sister Maria-Anna said.

"Yes. Don't you?"

Sister Maria-Anna said nothing, and Mercy kept her gaze steady, sure she was being tested somehow.

"Has anyone else been here asking about the Book of Days?" Mercy finally asked.

The sister huffed out a laugh, her voice stronger now. "There is always someone here looking for the Book of Days."

"Why do they come here, specifically?"

"Because one of the descendants of the original Fontana family lived in this town for most of her life. People think the book is hidden somewhere nearby."

Excitement slid over Mercy's skin, but she kept her expression neutral. "Is that true? And if so, do you know where it might be?"

The sister merely raised a brow. "If I knew, why would I tell you?"

Mercy met her eyes. "Because one woman is dead and another has been threatened. We're trying to keep the Liar's Treasure out of the wrong hands."

Sister Maria-Anna said nothing.

Mercy tried a different tack. "Who else has been asking about the book *recently*?"

"Enforcers who work for Caesar Gallo, a wealthy man from Milan. He claims the book belongs to him, as he is descended from the no-good husband of Countess Alonza: Antonio Gallo." Her chin came up. "Some say he already has the book and now wants the entire Liar's Treasure."

Something in her expression made Mercy ask, "Will he—or his men—try to hurt you for more information?"

The woman spat. "I would tell them nothing."

Mercy noted that she didn't deny having knowledge. "Could you tell me where this female descendant lived?"

"The property has been abandoned for decades. There is nothing left. Though foolish people still come with their shovels and try to dig up the past."

Two burly men dressed in well-cut black suits entered the building, their shoulder holsters obvious under their jackets. They could have come straight from central casting as Mafia enforcers.

Camille hurried toward Mercy. "Time to go. Hank's getting the car."

Sister Maria-Anna paled as she spotted the men. She turned to leave.

They were out of time and out of options.

Inspiration struck. Mercy gently put a hand on the aging sister's arm, met her eyes, and blurted, *"I libri illuminano."*

The woman froze, eyes round as saucers before they filled with sudden tears. She quickly pulled herself together and whispered an address, repeating it twice. Then she reached into her habit and pressed something into Mercy's hands. "You must hurry, but be careful. Go with God, Sister."

The nun turned and slipped through the hidden panel. Mercy waited until it clicked shut.

The men split up, one heading down the center aisle toward Sophie, the other toward Camille and Mercy.

At that moment, a priest stepped into the sanctuary from a side door. Mercy spun toward him, waving her arms. "Good day, Father." When she reached him, Mercy whispered, "Sister Maria-Anna is already out of harm's way, but please escort the cleaning lady to safety as well."

When he spotted the two men, he nodded sharply and called out, "Signora Caterina," as he headed toward the woman, put an arm around her shoulders, and led her away.

The two enforcers started toward them.

Camille hitched her chin at the camera bag and made a "gimme" motion. Sophie nodded and then darted between the pews, pulling off the bag as she went.

Once she reached the side aisle, she tossed it to Camille, then spun and landed a sharp kick to the taller guy's midsection, propelling him backward between two pews.

"Go!" Sophie shouted to Mercy. They raced out the side door.

Camille eyed the shorter, stockier of the two men marching toward her, his gaze fixed on the bag.

She barely hid a smile as she repositioned it in front of her, counting down the seconds.

"Come on, you thug, let's see what you've got," she muttered.

When he made a grab for the bag, Camille spun in a tight circle and swept his legs out from under him.

Before he crumpled in a heap, she'd turned and was halfway up the aisle and out the side door, racing for the street out front.

As she rounded the building, she spotted Mercy sliding into the backseat of the rental car. "Go, go." Camille motioned.

Mercy peeked out the back window, then leaned over and swung the door open.

Hank started to pull away from the curb.

Camille put on a burst of speed, leaped into the car, and slammed the door.

The taller guy behind her wasn't quite quick enough. He gripped the door handle just as Hank hit the gas. The car dragged him a few feet before he let go and bounced into the road.

"Ouch," Sophie murmured, peering over her shoulder. "That's gonna hurt."

"Look out!" Camille shouted as the little white Fiat from yesterday in Romania shot out of a side street.

Hank swerved, but the car clipped their back bumper and spun them farther into the street. Muttering, Hank brought the car back under control and they raced away, the Fiat gaining with every passing second, Ponytail at the wheel.

23

OUTSIDE NEW ORLEANS—MORNING

Gran's friend's "hideaway" was actually an antebellum mansion. There were four huge upstairs bedrooms. Cass paced the one that faced the back of the house. She nearly stepped out of the French doors onto the balcony but stopped and peeked around the curtains instead. Gran would have a cow if she broke the don't-go-outside-for-any-reason rule on the second day.

But she was tempted. Her whole life felt like some crazy reality show.

She was hiding outside some little no-name town with her grandmother. Who carried a gun. And claimed she knew how to use it. Un-freakin'-believable. Why hadn't she known that? Apparently nobody trusted her enough to tell her anything. Geez, if she hadn't been listening outside the kitchen door, she wouldn't even know that much. What else didn't she know?

And more important, when was her mother—and Gran—going to accept that she wasn't a little kid anymore and stop treating her like one?

She paced back to the bed, rubbing her arms. She brushed the bracelet she'd made from Gramps's shoelace and sighed. She knew why she had to be here, but she still felt like a prisoner, and it was making her twitchy.

At least the house was cool, the kind of place she'd love to live in one day. The renovated mid-1800s plantation home had huge Doric columns in front and was painted white with black shutters. It could have been a movie set. She'd snapped a few pics when they got here and now sent them to Lindsey, who was a sucker for old houses, too.

Cass aimed her phone camera at the creaky, polished-wood floors, crown moldings, and ornate medallions in the middle of each ceiling. The antiques and Persian rugs were threadbare but comfy, so she sent pics of those to Lindsey, too, with the caption: **Bored. But at least the house is cool.**

She probably wouldn't be so antsy if Gran hadn't told her she couldn't leave the house for any reason. Something about being told she couldn't made her want to do it even more. Now she sounded like Uncle Marcel.

Which brought up a whole other worry. She grabbed her cell, but her call went straight to voicemail. Again. "Hey, Uncle Marcel. You haven't called me back and it's freaking me out a little. Call me and tell me you're okay." She paused. "Please? Love you."

She flopped into the worn club chair by the window with her laptop. She'd finished her school assignments an hour ago. Maybe some online research would distract her. At least this prison had great Internet.

Her phone buzzed with a text. She grabbed it, disappointed that it wasn't Uncle Marcel. But Lindsey's message made her grin.

Girlfriend, have you seen the # of shares and likes on your last IG post? Great hashtags, too. Why aren't you at school, btw? And where are you? This place looks really cool.

Cass opened the Instagram app. She'd been getting ahead on her reading for English, so she hadn't checked since last night. Sure, she liked IG, but the girls at school who posted pictures of their lunch and made reels about stupid stuff all day long made her want to gag. She just posted when she had something to say.

"Wow." She'd have to tell Sophie the diary page she created was getting as many eyeballs as the first one. More, actually. Maybe she and Gran could go home since they'd clearly sent whoever was after Cass away from the city.

Cass wasn't sure what to think about her mom's work friends. They were nice and all, but the looks they sent each other when they thought Cass wasn't paying attention bothered her. What weren't they telling her?

She typed in the hashtags #captaintalonsdiary, #fontanafamilybookofdays, and #countessalonza and then sat up straight as serious excitement shot through her. This was crazy. More and more people were losing their minds over this diary every day.

Several websites had posted the picture of the diary page Sophie had created and quoted the clue she'd made up. Several sites added the hashtags #islegrandterre, #grandislepirates, and #piratehideout.

She grabbed her laptop and spent a while researching the small islands south of New Orleans that had been French pirate hideouts back in the day. But she didn't discover anything she didn't already know.

When her phone buzzed sometime later, she snatched it up. "Uncle Marcel! Where are you?"

"Hey, squirt. How you doing? Why aren't you in school? Playing hooky without me? Shame on you."

"I wouldn't dare sneak out without you." She paused. "Can you tell me what's really going on with this diary? Everyone is treating me like I'm a little kid."

The pause grew long and Cass checked to be sure the call hadn't dropped. "Uncle Marcel?"

"What does your mama say?"

"She hasn't told me anything. But I overheard her say you put a bull's-eye on my back because of that stupid diary. So her friend made another fake page and posted it online to get the attention off me."

"I wondered about that. That's why I called, actually. So that's nothing but a fake clue?"

"Yep. Just a way to get people to stop following me."

"Maybe you and your mom should lay low until this all blows over."

"We are. Don't worry. Actually, I'm hanging with Gran."

"Good. She'll keep you safe. Listen, kiddo, I have to—"

Cass wanted to ask if he knew about Gran's gun, but instead she said, "What kind of trouble are you in, Uncle Marcel? I'm worried about you."

"Ah, my girl, that's my line. I worry about you. I'll be fine, okay? Don't wor—"

A voice started shouting, there was a thud, a cry of pain, and then . . . nothing.

"Uncle Marcel!" Cass screamed his name over and over, but there was no response.

24

FLORENCE

Camille's cell phone rang as Hank raced around the city, trying to lose their tail. "Hey, Cass."

"Something's happened to Uncle Marcel! I don't know what to do. You have to help him."

"Whoa, baby, slow down. Take a breath and tell me what's happening."

"Uncle Marcel called me and we were talking and then there was a thud and what sounded like someone getting hurt and then the call dropped. What if that was him? What if he's hurt?"

"Easy, sweet girl. Take a breath. Do you know where he was when he called you?"

"No. I told him I was worried about him. He asked about the fake post we put up on Instagram."

"I just bet he did," Camille muttered, gripping the dash as Hank took a left with a screech of tires. "Listen, Cass, I'm sure he's fine. You know your uncle—"

"This is different and you know it. Somebody already beat him up. What if they really hurt him bad this time?"

Camille chose her words with care. "Cass, your uncle is a tough, smart man. He's always gotten himself out of trouble. If you're right about what you heard, he'll do it again this time, too."

"I need to find him, make sure he's okay."

Alarm shot through Camille. "No, ma'am. You need to stay right where you are, with Gran. Uncle Marcel would be furious—and so disappointed in you—if he thought you doubted he could take care of himself. Let him deal with whatever he has going on. He'd want to know you were safe, Cass, just like I do."

"I can't just sit here doing nothing. I'm not a little kid."

"You are a very smart young woman." Camille paused. "Actually, I have a really important job for you, if you think you're up for the challenge."

"It's not something stupid just to keep me busy, is it? That only worked when I was, like, twelve."

Camille smiled as she braced for another corner. "No, seriously, I need your help."

Cass paused. "What is it?"

The tiny glimmer of interest in Cass's tone loosened a bit of the band around Camille's chest. "I need you to put those research skills of yours to use and find out everything you can about a guy named Caesar Gallo from Milan. He's supposedly here in Florence to get his hands on the Book of Days. Claims it's his since he's descended from Countess Alonza's husband."

"No way. It belongs to the women in the family. Didn't her husband try to steal it?"

"Yep, and he died trying, or so the legend goes. Do your thing, Cass, and tell us where this guy lives and anything else you can dig up about him. Will you do that for me?"

Another pause stretched out. "Okay. But only if you promise to try to find out where Uncle Marcel is."

"Deal. Let me know what you find ASAP, okay?"

As soon as they hung up, Camille dialed Gran, told her about Cass's call.

"You leave Marcel to me." Gran's clipped tones softened as she said, "And I'll make sure Cassandra doesn't attempt to chase after him."

"Thank you, Gran." Camille hung up, then leaned her head against the back of the seat and let out a breath.

Hank checked the rearview mirror again. "I think we finally lost them."

"Good," Sophie said, looking at her phone's GPS, "because we're not far from the old farmhouse. Hang a left here."

"So as we were leaving—" Mercy began just as Camille's phone buzzed again.

"Hold that thought." She answered the call. "Hi, Jolie. What's up? You find anything?" Camille put it on speaker.

"Yes. No. Maybe." Jolie huffed out a breath. "I don't know."

"Slow down and tell me what's happening."

"So the carabinieri delivered Tara's things, and I found her messenger bag. I couldn't find the notebook she always carried, but then I found it sewn inside the bottom of the bag."

"Interesting that she hid it. Did you read it? What did it say?"

"A lot about the Book of Days. And she also included the same data about the well project we keep on our laptops. Which doesn't make sense."

"Have you noticed differences?"

"I haven't had a chance to examine it closely." She heaved a breath. "At the staff meeting we learned that another committee member, Motsa Sanele, died a few days ago. In Eswatini. He was a good man."

"Do they know how?"

"Dot said she'd find out." Jolie drew an unsteady breath. "But there's more. I went to Nelson's office and heard him on the phone, telling someone to find the book before Octavia's people do, no matter what."

Camille's eyes narrowed. "Good to know. See what you can find out about Mr. Sanele's death. And go over that notebook with a fine-tooth comb and let me know if anything jumps out at you. But be careful."

"You, too."

They left the city proper, the landscape spreading out into the rolling hills and vineyards depicted on postcards.

The team discussed Jolie's call, but Camille couldn't focus past the worry for Cass churning in her gut. She was also furious with—and okay, worried about—Marcel. But that was nothing compared to the fear that Cass would do something stupid like try to find him—by sneaking out on Gran. And if she did, would whoever was following "Octavia's people" find Cass and put her in more danger?

When Camille realized she was panting like a Chihuahua in August, she deliberately did a few breath prayers, something she'd learned from a Sunday school teacher during her pageant years. *"Just say God's name,"* Mrs. Brown had taught them. *"Breathe in, 'Yah,' and out, 'Weh.' Again. And again, until you're calm."*

Please, God, keep my girl safe. And Gran. And even Marcel. "Yah-Weh."

By the time they turned onto a dirt track near the abandoned farm, Camille felt steadier. Ready. Hank pulled behind a stand of trees, out of view of anyone passing by on the narrow road. Though the fact that they hadn't seen another car for the last ten minutes was a good sign.

"So as I started to say earlier, we should see if we can figure out what this opens," Mercy said as they climbed out of the car. She held a rusty skeleton key in the palm of her hand.

All eyes snapped in her direction.

"Where did you get that?" Camille asked.

"Sister Maria-Anna pressed it into my hand as we took off." Mercy paused. "After I said, *'I libri illuminano.'*"

"And you're just telling us now?" Hank raised an eyebrow.

"I tried. There were a few other things happening, if you recall." Mercy relayed her conversation with Sister Maria-Anna.

"Did she say anything else when she gave it to you?" Sophie wanted to know.

"Just that we should hurry and go with God. But earlier, after

I showed her my Speranza medallion, she said, 'We've waited so long.'"

"Waited so long for what?" Hank asked.

"Maybe she meant they've been waiting for someone from Speranza to show up and ask about the Book of Days," Camille said.

Sophie nodded. "That makes perfect sense."

Mercy rubbed her arms. "I just got goose bumps. What if we're it?"

"But why give it to Speranza and not someone else?" This from Hank.

"I told Sister Maria-Anna we wanted to keep the Liar's Treasure out of the wrong hands."

"Maybe that's why she gave you the clue," Sophie said.

They fell silent as they absorbed the ramifications of such a responsibility. This had become bigger than they had ever imagined.

Camille shaded her eyes with her hand as they studied the stone farmhouse. There were holes in the roof, and the heavy timbers supporting it sagged. Several nearby outbuildings had collapsed over the years. A large stone patio with a rotting pergola spread out from beside the house, with an overgrown, weed-covered garden beyond it.

"Seems like an unlikely place to stash a valuable illuminated manuscript," Camille said.

"How old do you think this place is? Would there still be books here?" Hank had pulled on a ball cap to shield her eyes.

"This type of architecture is usually from the 1700s or so. But it's pretty run-down," Mercy ventured.

"Maybe we'll get lucky." Camille followed Hank toward the front steps. "Watch for rotting boards, ladies."

"Yes, Mother." Hank shot a grin over her shoulder.

They walked inside and stopped. The large space was completely empty. No books. Or cabinets with handy secret compartments. No desks that might contain hidden drawers, no hidden rooms behind bookshelves.

"Well, this is disappointing." Mercy propped her hands on her hips as she surveyed the living area.

They checked the rest of the farmhouse but found nothing.

Outside, Sophie crouched down, one hand holding her Tara wig in place in case their pursuers found them again. "There's a basement."

Fresh piles of dirt sat beside a half-rotted door. Camille grimaced. "The sister wasn't kidding. We're obviously not the first people here."

Unfortunately, the basement didn't offer up anything but more piles of dirt. No books.

Neither did a check of the outbuildings.

They were running out of places to look.

"Found something," Hank called from the patio at the side of the house.

They found her hunched over a medium-sized sundial that had once been set into the stone. Someone had dug it up and then tossed it aside. They checked the area below it, but nothing was hidden there.

Beyond the patio, concealed by shrubs and waist-high weeds, several statues, some of them broken, circled what had once been a small fountain. A few depicted angels; the others were children.

Mercy and Hank pulled the weeds back while Camille and Sophie checked every statue, eyes peeled for a keyhole or anyplace that might lead to a keyhole.

"Should have brought a machete," Hank grumbled, trying to avoid stickers and thorns.

They found nothing.

Suddenly Mercy turned and rushed over to a statue of a young girl reading a book. *"I libri illuminano."* She bent down and started to brush dirt from the statue.

The team hurried over and helped, finally exposing two barely visible seams at the base of the statue.

Camille turned on her phone flashlight. "Yes!" she whispered. She pulled out her pocketknife and pried the section of stone out.

Underneath was a keyhole.

She turned to Mercy. "Want to do the honors?"

Mercy had to lie flat on her stomach to insert the skeleton key and open a little wooden door. Camille shone her light in as Mercy reached a hand into the opening.

Excitement shimmered in the air as she pulled out a flat leather pouch, covered in dust and debris, that had obviously not been removed in a very long time.

Mercy opened the flap. She scooped out the pile of papers and flipped through them, murmuring in Italian as she scanned them. "Huh. Not what we were hoping for. These are farm records. Crops, supplies, harvest counts"—she unfolded another document—"and something like property records maybe."

"Another wild-goose chase," Hank muttered.

"I don't think so," Sophie said. "Someone wouldn't have gone to that much trouble to hide those papers if they weren't important."

"You're right." Mercy slid the papers back into the pouch. "Sister Maria-Anna wouldn't have said, 'We've waited so long,' if this was just household records."

"We'll have to study it later." Camille slid the piece of stone back into the statue and locked it. "Tuck everything under your habit and let's go." She hitched a thumb over her shoulder toward the dirt road, where a large black SUV slowly cruised past.

"Apparently our two Mafia types found us," Hank said as they started walking toward their rental.

When the black SUV suddenly backed up and swerved toward them, the team started running.

25

OUTSIDE NEW ORLEANS—LATER THAT DAY

Cass was surfing the Internet, doing more research on pirates and treasure, when Gran burst into her room without knocking. Cass froze in surprise.

"Collect your things, Cassandra. We're leaving in two minutes." Gran was out of breath, her always-calm demeanor gone.

"What's wrong? Is it Uncle Marcel?"

Gran muttered something. "This better not be about Marcel." She stopped and took a calming breath. "Our location has obviously been discovered. We need to leave. Now."

"But how? I don't understand—"

"If you don't pack your things right this minute, we're leaving without them. And give me that ridiculous phone." Gran snatched it out of Cass's hand.

That, more than anything, galvanized Cass into motion. "Okay, okay. Geez. Chill."

"I will chill, as you call it, when I know you're safe. Two minutes." Gran spun toward the door, and Cass heard her heels clicking down the stairs.

Something bad was happening.

Cass automatically reached for her phone to text Lindsey and then remembered that Gran had taken it. She scooped up her backpack, tossed in her few changes of clothes, added her laptop and phone charger, then raced into the bathroom, where she dumped her cosmetics bag on top.

"Thirty seconds," Gran shouted.

Cass shoved her feet into her tennis shoes and took the stairs two at a time.

Gran stood by the front door, peering through the curtains on the sidelight. She grabbed Cass's arm, which was very unlike her—Gran wasn't a touchy kind of person—and led Cass out to the garage, her eyes darting this way and that the whole time.

"What's happ—?"

Before she got the question out, Gran clapped a hand over her mouth. "Quiet, Cassandra. Please."

Cass nodded once and Gran released her and hurried into the garage.

"Get into the back seat and duck down so you can't be seen."

A thousand questions crowded Cass's tongue, but one look at Gran's face and she simply nodded and did as she was told.

Gran slid behind the wheel of the dark SUV she'd rented and casually backed out of the garage. She drove down the long drive, paused at the edge of the road, then turned toward the tiny town. At least, that's where Cass thought they were going since she couldn't see. She'd never, in all her life, seen Gran this rattled.

After a few minutes, she heard Gran on her cell phone. "I'm headed there now. Thank you again. I won't forget this."

Cass's legs had fallen asleep by the time Gran stopped the SUV. Cass opened her mouth to ask where they were, but Gran stopped her. "Do not say a single word until we are inside, Cassandra. Do you understand?"

Cass nodded, knowing Gran couldn't see her, but she wouldn't risk saying anything.

Gran opened the passenger door and motioned her out. "Stay low and follow me."

They dashed to the front door of a small cabin hidden deep in a stand of trees. It smelled musty inside, like no one had been there in a long time.

Gran made sure all the curtains were tightly closed around the combination living-dining room, then she checked the two bedrooms before motioning Cass to the plaid sofa by the stone fireplace.

"Who did you talk to, Cassandra? Who did you tell where we were?"

Cass drew back in shock. "I didn't tell anyone."

"What about Marcel?" Gran sat beside Cass.

Cass shook her head. "No! I didn't. But he's in trouble, Gran. He called and then I heard a crash and what sounded like somebody getting hurt and then nothing."

Gran closed her eyes and hung her head. She let out a huge breath, then met Cass's eyes. "You're sure you didn't tell him? No hint? No little clue?"

"No! We need to help him, Gran. He's in trouble."

"His trouble is of his own making." Gran's voice was stern, its usual no-nonsense tone. "It's you I'm worried about."

In a surprising move, Gran reached over and cupped Cass's cheek. And Cass could have sworn the glimmer of tears flashed in her eyes. But then it was gone.

"If not Marcel, then someone else. Who?"

"The only person I texted was Lindsey, but I didn't tell her where we were." Realization hit and Cass felt the blood drain from her face. "I, uh, did send her a couple pics. But I didn't say where we were. I swear."

Gran sighed. "No need for swearing. But this does complicate things. Stay here." She walked into one of the bedrooms, and Cass could hear her talking to someone, but she couldn't make out the words.

A chill ran down her arms and she rubbed them. Unless she misunderstood, someone had traced them through the pictures she'd sent Lindsey.

This was bad. Very bad.

26

FLORENCE

After Hank finally lost the incredibly persistent black SUV, the team grabbed their things from the hotel and moved to an Airbnb on the outskirts of the city, complete with a garage to hide their car. A quick stop for groceries and a local map and they settled around the dining table, laptops in hand.

"This Caesar Gallo guy is a piece of work." Camille had her laptop open and was reading from the info Cass had e-mailed earlier. "He lives and works in Milan but owns real estate all over, plus a shipping company, several wineries, and apparently has definite Mafia connections. Anytime anyone complains about him or the police bring charges, the witnesses disappear, never to be seen or heard from again. *Yikes.*"

She opened another page, stopped. "Oooooh. Nice."

"What?" Hank leaned closer.

Camille spun her laptop so they could all see. "Caesar will be presiding over the tree-lighting ceremony in Piazza del Duomo tomorrow night. The Duomo is the largest church in Florence, and tomorrow is the eve of the Feast of the Immaculate Conception, when they'll light the tree for the season."

"Despite the rumors, I don't think he's found the book yet. I think he's here searching for it." Sophie peered over the top of her laptop.

Mercy nodded. "I agree. If he'd already gotten his hands on it, I think he'd be long gone, trying to find the rest of the treasure." She held up one of the documents they'd found in the statue. "This appears to be a document listing properties owned by Fontana family descendants, but here's the interesting part. One of them has a *G* next to the address."

They traded excited glances.

"That has to be it," Camille said.

"Read me that address." Sophie's fingers flew over her keys. "We know several of Gallo's ancestors lived in Florence, but only one had shipping connections. Ah. Here we go. The address is for the family villa, which was sold a few decades ago and is now an exclusive rental property. They say it's like stepping back in time since everything has been kept completely authentic." Sophie grinned. "Guess where Gallo is staying?"

"Read that address again?" Camille typed, then enlarged a photo and beckoned them over. "Check it out. The website says this is one of the oldest villas in this area. The brick tower dates way back to the 1400s."

"Zoom out, would you, Camille?" Mercy pointed to the vineyards spreading out in every direction. "Are these part of it, too?"

"Yes."

Sophie had stood up to pace, but now she stopped and turned toward them. "I have an idea. Two, actually."

Hank crossed her arms over her chest. "I recognize that gleam in your eye, but go ahead."

"We search the villa for the Book of Days while he's lighting the tree."

Camille grinned. "I like it."

"Do we know where in the villa the book would be?" Mercy wanted to know.

Sophie cocked her head, thinking. "My gut says the old tower."

"I agree," Camille said.

"What's the other idea?" Hank asked.

"What if we put the word out to him—and possibly others—that we have a clue to the rest of the treasure that we'd be willing to sell . . . for a price?" Sophie eyed the team. "Then we also put another post on Cass's Instagram saying she gave the diary to an expert in New Orleans who suspects it's a fake."

"That would definitely send all the treasure hunters away from Cass." Camille drummed her fingers on the desk, thinking through all the angles.

"It would also transfer the bull's-eye onto us," Mercy pointed out.

"We can handle it. Plus, that'll help us narrow down who's after us," Camille said.

"Does that matter?" Hank turned to Camille. "I get protecting Cass. But why bring them all here? And who cares who they are?"

"I'm with Camille. Knowledge is power." Sophie pulled up another folder on her laptop. "Even though we don't have Picasso on this mission, Cass is doing a great job." Sophie pointed to the list of files Cass had sent them. "The more we know about who we're up against, the better we can prepare. And get around and ahead of them."

Hank checked the battered watch on her wrist. "Then we'd better get busy."

FLORENCE, ITALY—THE NEXT EVENING

"I'm at the edge of the vineyard," Sophie said into Camille's earpiece. "Place is dark except for the security lights around the perimeter."

Camille, also dressed all in black, hurried toward the house, keeping well back in the shadows of the trees that lined the driveway leading to the massive stone villa. "This place is a lot bigger than it seemed in the photos."

"Tree lighting starts in ten minutes," Hank said. "Mercy, you in place?"

Silence.

"Sister? Check in." Worry threaded Hank's voice.

"Yes, sorry, got delayed by the crowd, but I'm here." Mercy lowered her voice. "The proprietor of the wine shop didn't want me anywhere near his famous wine window unless I agreed to a, quote, 'date' with him." She snorted. "Changed his tune fast when I played the nun card."

Camille listened to the chatter with half an ear, all her focus on her surroundings. She and Sophie had spent hours yesterday staking out the villa, checking for guard dogs, and locating security lights.

Hank and Mercy had sent the bait to Caesar Gallo, offering to sell a page of the Book of Days that contained a clue to the treasure. For good measure, they also logged into Cass's Instagram account and added the "too bad the diary is a fake" post.

According to their research, two security guards were stationed outside the villa, but they patrolled the grounds on a nice, predictable one-hour schedule. The housekeeper had left right after the family climbed into a big black SUV and headed to Florence, where Hank would keep an eye on them.

According to Cass's research, Caesar didn't like technology. He carried a cell phone for business only, he'd said in an interview. But for the rest, he preferred dealing with people directly. He probably didn't like the electronic trail either. When the interviewer asked about his personal security, he was quoted as saying he had good people working for him.

Camille hoped the house didn't have an alarm system. But they couldn't be sure. A little zip of adrenaline spiked through her veins.

The team's research had turned up pictures of the spectacular library, with custom shelves built into the walls of the round tower by Antonio Gallo in the 1600s. She and Sophie were betting the Book of Days was somewhere in that room.

They both figured it would be hidden well since no one had found it in all these years, so they'd spent significant time researching secret compartments and various hiding techniques used over the centuries. Hopefully they'd know it when they saw it.

Camille stopped at the edge of the trees, checked her watch. Two minutes until the guard came by. Then not again for thirty minutes. Piece of cake. She tugged the ski mask more tightly over her features, checked the straps on her backpack, and ran across the yard to the outside staircase at the rear corner.

No motion lights sprang on, so she breathed a sigh of relief as she raced along the stone balcony.

Once she reached the outside door to the tower, she crouched on one knee and made short work of the lock. She held the knob in a gloved hand and slowly turned it, poised to run if an alarm screeched, but nothing happened.

Footsteps pounded from the other direction, and she let out a breath when Sophie rushed around the corner.

They slipped inside, pulled the door closed, and Camille took out her penlight, keeping the beam low. "We're in."

"Countdown for the tree lighting is about to start." Hank's voice was barely discernible with the crowds in the background.

"Surprisingly long queue at the wine window," Mercy muttered. "Here you are, sir. *Grazie.*"

Camille swung her light around the room. First, they quickly checked the obvious spots behind the paintings, but there was no handy safe. Gallo would have checked that first. Camille pulled out the desk drawers, ran her hands along the edges, checked behind them, then got down on her knees and looked up, while Sophie did the same. It was amazing how often people taped keys under drawers. Their eyes met. Nothing.

"Let's check the shelves." Camille stood and ran her free hand along the bookshelves, pulling books out, pushing them in, searching for a hidden mechanism. Across the room, Sophie did the same.

"You're six minutes in, ladies." Hank's tone implied the need to hurry things along.

"Moving as fast as we can." Camille stopped, took a breath, then scanned the room again, looking for anything that didn't belong or seemed out of place in some way. The bookshelves had been built to hug the curved walls, so there couldn't be a hidden compartment between the wall and a shelf.

Where could it be?

Hank's voice burst into her earpiece. "Camera feed shows a dark SUV racing up the road. Get out of there now!"

They couldn't leave yet. Not without the book. Or at least a clue.

Camille's eyes landed on the two club chairs by the fireplace, and she rushed over. She got on the floor and shone her light underneath. Nothing.

She turned toward the fireplace.

One of the thick stone tiles in the floor beside it was slightly uneven.

Sophie joined her as she dropped beside it, pulled out her knife. They spent precious seconds trying to pry it up.

Sweat trickled down Camille's neck by the time they managed to slide the heavy tile aside. Their eyes met, and her own excitement was reflected in Sophie's expression. They brushed at the cobwebs and uncovered what appeared to be a simple, old-fashioned combination lock.

Except the numbers were made of wood and spun above what she hoped was some kind of early combination safe, 1600s edition.

"Where are you two?"

"Found something. Two minutes." Camille pulled a scrap of paper from her pocket and started reading combinations to Sophie: Antonio Gallo's birthday, anniversary, two daughters, one son.

Sophie entered each one in rapid succession.

Nothing.

"The SUV just turned up the driveway," Hank muttered into their earpieces.

"Almost there." Camille's mind raced. "Try Countess Alonza's date of birth. That kind of audacity would be just like a Gallo."

Sophie spun the dial, the numbers lined up, but nothing happened.

"Push down, hard."

Sophie pressed down with all her strength, and the tumblers dropped into place with a clatter. They high-fived and she lifted the box out.

When Sophie opened the lid and pulled back the tattered silk, Camille's breath caught. It had to be the Book of Days, and it was gorgeous. It was also smaller than she'd expected, about the size of a drugstore paperback novel. Temptation whispered to flip through the pages, to admire every beautiful illustration, but they didn't have time. "I bet Gallo doesn't have any idea it's right here."

"If he did, he'd have it secured in a high-tech vault. At least that's what I would do."

Camille grinned. "I kind of like the irony of snatching it out from under his nose." She quickly tucked the book back into the box and replaced the silk. Then she wrapped the box in sheepskin she'd brought along and secured it in her backpack.

"Agreed." Sophie returned the grin as she closed the safe. "Let's get out of here."

They slid the tile back into place, then sprinted for the door.

As Sophie disappeared around the corner, Camille pulled the door closed behind her and raced along the balcony in the opposite direction. She flattened herself against the stone wall when headlights passed her location.

She was about to rush down the back stairs when two Dobermans appeared around the corner of the house. They stopped directly below her hiding spot and started barking their heads off.

This was not good.

Camille spun back toward the tower, glad she hadn't taken time to lock the door. She bolted across the room and flung open the door to the small Juliet balcony. She reached into her backpack and yanked out her grappling hook. She swung it a few times, then sent it sailing over the courtyard—and the barking dogs—where it gripped the roof of the covered pergola.

With quick motions, she switched the backpack to her front, then hauled herself along the cable, hand over hand, legs crossed in front of her.

Once to the roof of the pergola, she scrambled along the thick vines covering it to the opposite edge.

She stopped. The gap between the pergola and the stone wall was too wide. She didn't have space for a running start. And the dogs were getting closer.

With a quick prayer for help, she leaped out as far as she could go.

She almost made it.

27

The man locked his office door behind him, then reached under his desk and pushed a hidden button. It always amazed him how gullible people were. They saw what they wanted to see and, at the same time, thought they were invisible, their sins concealed from the world. He shook his head. Soon, several more would learn differently.

Those who thought their "good deeds" would cancel out their sins had to be punished. Liars could not be allowed to continue wreaking havoc.

One of the wide bookshelves on the opposite wall swung out, revealing a secondary shelving unit. He took out his state-of-the-art laptop, a much newer one than what his employer had issued him, and sat behind his desk.

A few keystrokes and his encrypted e-mail account appeared. He read the first report. His man in New Orleans had followed Miss High-and-Mighty Benoit to their apparent safe house and settled in to watch. He scrolled through the photos and stopped at the picture of the SUV leaving the property. The old lady must have spotted his man or been tipped off somehow. He'd bet his favorite knife the granddaughter was hiding in the backseat. He gave the old lady points for trying to protect her.

Too bad it wouldn't make a difference.

He gritted his teeth as he struggled through the atrocious grammar littering the report from his secondary team in Europe. Even if you were from some inconsequential former Soviet country, you should know how to speak and write proper English. He ignored the request for a better vehicle, despite his lackey's claim that he couldn't keep up with the team's vehicle. He reminded them he was paying them to get the job done, no matter what.

Failure was not a part of his plan. He'd better have the diary and the Book of Days by this time tomorrow. Clearly he deserved the "untold riches" everyone was yammering about. Just think how much that money would benefit his mission to purge the world of evildoers. If he was the tiniest bit concerned about the "judging motives" part of the legend, he'd deal with that when the time came.

He hit Send, then pulled up a spreadsheet from an encrypted folder hidden in his laptop. He smiled as he read over the list of names, all liars and cheaters and hypocrites who were no longer polluting this world.

For good measure, he added several names to the "pending" column just as the phone on his desk buzzed.

The receptionist's heavily accented voice said, "The staff meeting starts in ten minutes. Kindly do not be late."

He bristled at her officious tone but smoothed his features as he saved the file, then hid the laptop and closed the bookshelves. He took his notebook and trotted off to the conference room, just another worker bee, doing what was expected.

A quick check of his watch confirmed he had plenty of time before his flight.

Time to put the next phase of his plan in place.

And show these meddling women exactly who they were dealing with.

28

PIAZZA DEL DUOMO, FLORENCE

This was a terrible idea. Someone else should be doing this part.

Mercy was used to blending into the background, being invisible, especially when she wore her habit. Nobody noticed nuns, and that let her move about freely and observe without being noticed. This was different. She felt exposed, uncertain.

And her scalp itched under the Tara-look-alike wig, but she couldn't risk scratching her head and setting it askew. No matter how awkward and conspicuous the disguise made her feel, she had to put her discomfort aside. She had a job to do.

Never mind that her heart hammered as though there were a flashing neon sign pointing to the fake page of the Book of Days she had hidden under the counter.

She forced herself to think about something else. The wine-window idea was actually very clever. And frankly, Mercy loved it. Started in Florence by wealthy artisans and nobles who made their own wine, the little windows, about one foot wide and eight inches tall with a curved top, were a way for them to sell their surplus vino. Historians claimed they also came in handy during the bubonic plague, as a way for shopkeepers to serve their customers wine, which they believed had medicinal powers, without getting too close.

A quick peek at the crowd milling about the narrow street and Mercy spotted their quarry. Caesar Gallo moved like a man who knew his place in the world and expected others to know it, too. He also hadn't missed many meals. The crowd automatically parted for his large frame, and he swept toward her like Moses parting the Red Sea.

Mercy ducked her head when his hard gaze speared her. Don't be memorable, don't be memorable. "*Buona sera, signore.* What can I get for you?"

His eyes narrowed. "Hand it over and be quick about it."

"We require payment in advance, *signore.*" Mercy forced herself to shrug carelessly, buying time. Where was Hank? "I'm sure you understand."

"Do you know who I am?" His chest puffed out as he straightened to his full height.

Mercy shrugged again, held her palms up. "I am sorry, *signore*. I mean no offense. I am new in town and these are the rules."

"I see him. Almost there."

Mercy nearly let the tension in her shoulders drop at the sound of Hank's voice, but she couldn't do that. Hadn't Sophie drilled the need to stay in character over and over? Mercy held out her hand, then glanced behind him as if to get him to hurry up. "If you would give me the payment, *signore*, I can get you your wine."

"I will speak to the owner about you. This will be your last night working here."

"*Scusi, signore.* I mean no offense. I am just trying to do my job." She waited expectantly.

He nodded to a man Mercy had not even registered behind him. The big hulk of a man pulled an envelope out of his jacket pocket and handed it to Mercy.

She nodded to each man in turn. *"Grazie, signore e signore."* Hopefully that would let Hank know there were two of them. She reached under the counter and grabbed the envelope containing the fake manuscript page and then slowly passed it and a glass of wine through the small opening and into Caesar Gallo's waiting hands.

Behind him, his bodyguard reached into his jacket and his weapon slid into view.

"Gun!" Mercy yelped, and slammed the window closed. She whirled back into the small room she'd been serving from and headed for the door. "Bodyguard just pulled a gun!"

"On it!" Hank shouted. "Head for the car, Sister!"

Camille had jumped as far as she could, stretching her body and arms out, desperate to make it across the gap. She'd known she wouldn't get there, but she'd had no choice. She landed hard on the bricks in the narrow strip between the pergola and the eight-foot courtyard wall.

She scrambled to her feet, desperate to escape before the dogs—and their teeth—got to her. She shuddered at the sound of their claws scrabbling over the bricks as they raced her way. Just as they rounded the edge of the pergola, Camille jumped up as high as she could, one foot braced on the wall, the other on the pergola's corner post.

One of the dogs leaped up and scraped her ankle, teeth drawing blood. She yelped and used her arms to brace herself and plant her feet farther up the walls. She gathered her strength and hopped up again. And again. This had been a lot more fun when she was a kid, climbing up the wall in a friend's hallway.

The dogs barked louder and leaped higher and higher, desperate to reach her.

Camille's arms and legs shook as she worked her way up the wall, one jump at a time.

Finally, she used every bit of her remaining strength and threw both arms over the top. She swung her legs up and over, then perched on top for half a second, trying to catch her breath.

"I'll take that," a calm male voice said from behind her.

29

Camille heard her teammates in her ear and knew they were trying to get there to help her, but nobody except maybe Sophie could reach her before it was too late. Camille kept her focus squarely on the masked man standing on the stone wall behind her, his gun pointed at her chest.

"Who are you and what do you want?"

He laughed. "Who am I?" The sound sent a chill over her skin. "Who I am doesn't matter." Tall and lean, he had a runner's build. "And if I were a betting man, I'd say you know perfectly well what I want. The same thing you came here to get. Thanks for saving me the trouble, by the way." He gestured with his free hand. "Hand it over. Now."

"Almost there," Camille heard Hank say just as the sound of a car engine reached her.

Out of the corner of her eye, Camille saw a car skidding around the corner, racing alongside the wall toward where she and the masked man stood.

When she glimpsed Lucien—not Hank—behind the wheel, she

froze for a split second, then shook her head to clear it. She'd think about that later.

She counted off the seconds in her head.

Three.

She slipped the backpack off her shoulders like she was going to give it to him.

Two.

Strap tight in her left hand, she braced her feet.

One.

Lucien barreled toward her.

Camille spun and swung the backpack with all her might, knocking the gun out of the man's hand.

As she completed the spin, she shoved him toward the courtyard below and leaped over the opposite side of the wall.

She landed on the car's roof with a thump and a yelp.

Lucien never slowed, just yelled, "Hang on," and sped away.

Camille flattened herself on the roof, gripping one of the doorframes in each hand so she wouldn't slide off. Thankfully, Lucien had opened the windows. She did love a practical man.

"Stay with me, Princess. I'll get us clear."

A bullet sprayed dirt up on the left side of the car.

Lucien started zigzagging as more dirt spit on the right side of the car.

Camille slid back and forth on the roof with every sharp swerve. She tucked her head down and prayed she could hang on until they got to safety.

30

Lucien hung a hard left and raced toward the vineyards that surrounded the villa.

"Slow down and let me go on foot. You distract them." Camille's voice was barely discernible, but Lucien heard her clearly enough.

"I said I'll get us out of here."

"No. Let me off here." Before he realized what she planned to do, Camille swung the backpack through the open window and bashed him in the head. He automatically grabbed the bag, tossed it into the passenger seat. "Ouch. Geez. A little warning next time."

"Desperate times and all that. Slow down."

Lucien bit back his fury. Foolish, reckless woman was going to get herself killed, and then where would they be?

One eye on the SUV now chasing them, Lucien swung around a stand of trees and slowed to a stop. "Get in the car, Camille," he barked. Then added, "Please."

"Well, since you asked so nicely." Camille slid off the roof, leaped inside, and pulled the door shut as Lucien sped away. It tried to swing open again, but she yanked hard with both hands and managed to get it closed.

The back windshield shattered.

31

"Get down!" Lucien shouted and pushed the pedal to the floor.

Beside him, Camille hunched down in the passenger seat, phone out, a map up on the screen. "Turn left down the next road. There's an old barn up ahead. Sister? You headed this way?"

It took him a minute to realize she was wearing an earbud, talking to one of the other women he'd seen her with in Florence earlier.

He ignored her and kept going, eyes on the rearview mirror. He raced out of the vineyard and into the surrounding woods, headlights too close behind.

She pulled off the ski mask and turned to him, still breathing hard, her black hair a mess and annoyance all over her pretty face. "You missed the turn."

He spun the wheel to the right, satisfied when the headlights started to fall behind. "Not going that way."

"While I appreciate you showing up—by the way, how *did* you know to come here?"

He gripped the wheel harder, made another sharp turn. "Stop. Talking."

She grabbed the dash when he whipped the car around another tree and deeper into the forest. "What is wrong with you?"

Jaw clenched, he took them deeper and deeper into the trees.

Finally, when he hadn't seen the taillights for several minutes, he hit the brakes and brought the car to a rocking stop. He was out of the vehicle and striding into the woods in a flash, determined to get his emotions under control before he did something they'd both regret.

He hadn't taken more than a dozen steps when she grabbed his arm and jerked him around.

"What?" she demanded.

He stopped, gripped her upper arms, the need to shake some sense into her pushing him hard. "Do you realize if I'd gotten there three seconds later you'd be dead?!"

She reared back in his hold, eyes wide. "But you didn't. You were right—"

He released her so suddenly she stumbled back a step. "I wouldn't be able to live with myself if something happened to you, too." He huffed out a breath, met her eyes. "Do you not get that?"

Before she could respond, he turned away, kept walking, his heart slamming against his ribs as he put distance between them.

"I do now," she said quietly from behind him.

He stopped, took a deep breath, turned to face her.

"But I'm not J. T. It was never your job to keep him safe. And it isn't yours to keep me safe, either."

The utter absurdity of that statement crashed through his self-control, and he yanked her into his arms. Then held her tight against his chest as his mouth came down on hers and he kissed her with all the fury and fear and relief ricocheting around inside him. She'd come so close to dying.

She froze for a split second and then kissed him back, her own anger a sharp blade against his tongue. Hearts pounding, they battled each other, too many emotions for words arcing between them as the kiss went deep, then deeper still.

Slowly, gradually, the anger burned itself out, the icy fear melted away. He cupped her cheeks in his hands and gentled the kiss. Her hands came up to cover his, and she relaxed against him, the fight gradually leaving them both.

Until something terrifyingly close to tenderness reached in and grabbed him.

He placed a gentle kiss on her forehead. "I'm glad you're okay."

She blinked at him, her beautiful brown eyes dazed, and reality slapped him, hard.

He eased back. *Get your head on straight, Broussard.* Camille was as out of reach now as she had been in high school. Even if they could get past their loyalty to J. T., they literally lived half a world apart.

And he had a promise to Pops to keep.

He let her go and started toward the car. "Your friends will be wondering where you are."

The Speranza team gathered in the kitchen of the Airbnb for late-night coffee and sandwiches. Camille poured a cup and sat at the table. She couldn't get that kiss—or the tender look in Lucien's eyes—out of her mind. But she had to, and fast. Her number-one priority was keeping Cass safe. And that meant leading the team as Willa expected her to. She didn't have time for an old schoolgirl crush on Lucien Broussard.

Camille took a sip of her coffee and eyed the team. "I know Willa's not available for the usual debrief, so I'll just say it: Y'all did good tonight. Wow."

"All in a day's work," Hank mumbled around a bite of her sandwich.

"Mercy, you're a far better actress than you've let on." Camille saluted her with her coffee cup.

"It was terrifying." Mercy paused. "But I kind of liked it."

"You were great." Sophie nodded. "Truly."

"Your leg okay?" Camille saw Mercy massaging her thigh above the prosthesis.

"Yes. It lets me know when I push too hard. Just like the rest of you, I imagine." Her eyes swept the table, daring anyone to argue with her.

Just like Picasso's scars, the story behind Mercy's prosthetic leg was hers to share. Or not. Camille wouldn't push. She rolled her shoulders. "I'll be sore tomorrow, for sure."

"Who tried to take the book from you guys?" Hank folded her elbows on the table. "Camille, did you recognize him?"

"No. But it could be anyone who heard the rumor that Caesar Gallo had the Book of Days. The local news mentioned the tree lighting. And where he was staying. Perfect opportunity."

Mercy took a sip of her coffee. "Except he's going to be after you now. And maybe Sophie, too, if his people are the ones following us."

"Right. But we expected that." Camille shrugged. "At least it takes the attention off Cass."

Hank turned to Camille. "Speaking of Cass. How did Lucien know where you'd be tonight? Though my money's on Marcel. No offense."

Camille sighed. "None taken, especially since you're probably right. Cass talked to Marcel recently. She wouldn't have thought twice about telling him what was going on since he's family."

"It wouldn't be right to tell her to keep things from her uncle." Mercy took another sip of her coffee, expression thoughtful.

"Maybe not, but it would sure make things easier."

No one disagreed with Hank's assessment.

"Have you spoken to Marcel?"

"No answer when I called. Shocking, I know. Lucien claims they're not working together, but he admitted Marcel sold him a copy of the diary. He said it was either that or steal it from me, but he was grinning when he said it." Camille scanned the team, saw their curious expressions, and debated her response. "The Broussards have a reputation for dealing in antiquities of dubious lineage, leading all the way back to some ruthless pirate ancestors. Lucien was raised by his grandfather Claude, who is currently in rehab with a broken hip. Lucien said Claude wants him to find the Book of Days."

"Do they have experience treasure hunting? And stealing?" Mercy asked.

"Yes to treasure hunting. J. T. told me years ago that Lucien and Claude spent summer vacations and school holidays searching for treasure. But nothing I've found online suggests they've made any significant finds. Or stolen anything." She shrugged again. "I just did a quick search."

Sophie nodded. "Loyalty to family combined with the value of the Book of Days are strong motivations. I don't see Lucien backing off."

"Me, either." Heat flooded Camille's face as she thought of their kiss.

"What's the deal with you two, anyway? There's . . . something." Mercy raised an eyebrow.

"We went to high school together. He was my husband J. T.'s best friend, who convinced him they should join the Army together." Camille paused. "I admit I wasn't happy about that."

"Only Lucien came back," Mercy said quietly.

"Survivor's guilt," Hank muttered.

Camille's heart stuttered as she remembered Lucien's words. *"I wouldn't be able to live with myself if something happened to you, too."* Why had she never considered that?

"Or maybe he cares for you. And Cass." Mercy tilted her head. "You didn't stay in touch?"

"No. I . . ." Camille stopped, decided to take a risk. "At first I blamed him for J. T.'s death, but then I realized it was God I had to make peace with. And I had a daughter I was solely responsible for. There was no time for what-ifs." There was more to it, but she couldn't delve into her complicated feelings for Lucien right now. Not until she knew Cass was safe. Maybe not even then.

"Hate to interrupt but we need to go." Hank stood by the window, watching the street. "If we're right and Gallo's Mafia types drive a dark SUV, they just drove past."

32

Caesar Gallo knocked on the door of the small cottage on the outskirts of town. His Cadillac Escalade idled at the curb, his driver at the wheel. Some things a man didn't need an audience for.

He knocked again, louder, and a light clicked on in the back of the house. He had his hand raised to knock again when an old man eased the door open a crack. "What do you mean—?" The man stopped mid-scold as he realized who his visitor was. "*Scusi, signore.* Please come in. How may I be of service?" He smoothed a quick hand over his wispy white hair and belted his robe more securely after he closed the door. "May I get you some refreshment? To what do I owe this honor?"

Caesar took a seat in the small living room, folded his hands across his belly, and regarded the man in front of him, said to be the best art forger in all of Italy. "What do you know about the Fontana family's Book of Days?"

The man gasped. "Everyone has heard of it in this area, but no one has ever seen it." He gripped his paint-stained fingers, voice thick with anticipation. "There have been rumors that it is now safely in your possession, *signore*. Would that it be so."

Caesar reached into his jacket and produced the envelope he'd purchased earlier. He set it on the coffee table, then slid a piece of parchment out for the man to see.

The old man's eyes widened, and he reached out a hand but paused halfway. "May I?"

Caesar nodded.

The man stood and went to a worktable in the corner, where he turned on a light and picked up a jeweler's loupe. He slipped cotton gloves over his gnarled fingers and carefully set the parchment on the table. He aimed the light, sank down on a stool, and spent long minutes studying the brightly colored, gilt-edged page of an illuminated manuscript.

An ornate clock ticked, which was the only sound in the room. Finally, the man turned to Caesar, who kept all expression from his face.

"Is this a page from the Fontana Book of Days, *signore*?"

"That is why I am here. To confirm its authenticity. I was told it holds the key to discovering the location of the Portable Altar of Countess Alonza, which is part of the Liar's Treasure."

The man swallowed hard. Then again. He stood, wrung his hands, took a step back. "I regret that I must tell you, *signore*, that this is a forgery."

"What?" Caesar sprang from his seat, fists clenched as fury pounded through him. No one double-crossed Caesar Gallo. No one.

The man paled and put his hands out in supplication. "*Sì.* It is true. I am sorry. But I cannot lie. It is an exceptional forgery. One of the best I have ever seen." He swallowed hard again. "But it is a forgery nonetheless."

Gallo stormed past the old man, knocking him down as he left.

NEW ORLEANS—THE NEXT DAY

Gran walked into the kitchen of the carriage house where they had gone to hide after the other place was "compromised," as Gran called it, and Cass almost spewed her mouthful of soda. She made horrible gagging noises while trying not to cough up a lung.

"Good morning, Cassandra." Gran bussed her cheek on her way to the coffee maker and poured herself a cup. She added her usual teaspoon of sugar and splash of cream and then studied Cass as she took a sip, perfectly sculpted eyebrows raised.

"I'm sorry. Who are you and what have you done with my grandmother?"

"Don't be cheeky, young lady." But Gran looked like she was trying to hide a smile. Maybe. It was hard to tell with Gran.

"Bu-but you're wearing jeans. And a denim shirt. And—and a ball cap!" Cass leaned sideways in her chair. "And are those tennis shoes? Has the rapture happened and you're some impostor pretending to be my grandmother?"

This time, one side of Gran's mouth definitely curved up in a half smile. "You have your grandfather's sense of humor, I'll give you that." She wagged a finger. "But don't get carried away."

Cass swallowed hard at the mention of Gramps and fiddled with the shoelace bracelet. "I miss him." Everything had felt off-kilter in her world since he died. Even worse, she hadn't quite realized how much he was a part of every bit of her life—until he was gone.

"I do too, darling. I do, too."

"But you guys hardly ever spent any time together," Cass blurted. She wanted to call the words back the second they left her mouth, especially when Gran flinched.

Gran took another sip of coffee, then met Cass's eyes head-on. "That's true. We were very different people and lived fairly separate lives. But that didn't lessen our love for each other. Or our devotion." She set her cup down. "Gramps adored you, you know."

Cass blinked back unexpected tears. "Yeah, he did. I loved him, too." Why on earth hadn't she told him that more often?

"Of course you did." Gran set her cup in the sink, her crisp tone declaring the emotional portion of the morning concluded. "Now then. We have work to do today."

"What kind of work?"

"We're going to Tulane to do some research at Jones Hall, where the special collections are housed."

Cass cocked her head. "Aren't those libraries only for students? How do we get in?"

"We have an appointment, arranged by a friend of a friend who works there."

"Dressed like that?"

"Yes, dressed exactly like that." Gran raised an eyebrow. "People see what they expect to see. If we're keeping a low profile, this will help."

Cass was impressed despite herself. Sometimes she forgot that Gran ran a big company and that nothing got past her. Like this carriage house they were currently staying in. It was above the three-car garage of a dilapidated estate in a run-down neighborhood. Gran said it belonged to a friend. She had also come up with a rusted compact car in an ugly beige. Cass figured that wasn't an accident either. Realizing Gran had a definite plan loosened some of the tightness in her chest, kept her from freaking out with worry.

Gran leaned forward to open the ancient dishwasher and Cass sucked in a breath. "You have one, too. Your necklace. It has the same emblem as the tattoo inside Mom's wrist."

If Gran heard the statement, she didn't respond. "Are you ready to go? I have other things to do today, including a conference call later on."

"Sophie wears a necklace like yours, too." Cass's eyes narrowed. "What does it mean? Does everyone Mom works with have one?"

Gran closed the dishwasher and studied Cass for a moment. "That is a question best left for your mother." She grabbed a battered tote Cass had never seen and pulled it over her shoulder. "Bring your laptop or however you take notes, and let's see what we can find out about this Book of Days the entire world is yammering about."

33

ROME—THE NEXT DAY

Camille couldn't remember the last time she'd been this tired.

They'd decided it was best to get out of Florence before Caesar Gallo or anyone else suspected they had the Book of Days, so they'd snuck out of their Airbnb and Hank had driven them back to Rome. With all the backtracking and watching for tails, the three-plus-hour trip had taken close to five. If only Hank could have commandeered a helicopter. After a short nap, the team had spent the morning poring over photocopies of the diary Sophie had created before they left New Orleans.

"If there's another clue in here to the other pieces of the Liar's Treasure, I sure can't find one." Camille bent forward, touching her toes, trying to work out the kinks in her back.

Sophie stood as well. "Yeah, I need a break, too."

Three sharp knocks on the door signaled Hank's return, the yeasty smell of fresh pizza following her inside. Camille's stomach let out an unladylike growl as she opened the box, started handing out slices cut-to-go or *al taglio*, which was Italy's answer to fast food. "Everything okay out there?"

"Far as I could tell." Hank pulled out a bunch of carrots, their green tops sticking out the top of the bag. Then she removed a sheaf of papers hidden under the produce, and finally, the carefully wrapped Book of Days. "You guys find anything in the diary?"

Mercy yawned as she approached the table. "Nothing." She grabbed napkins from the small kitchen. "But this smells fantastic."

Hank pointed to the photocopied pages of the Book of Days. "I made two sets, just in case. Maybe the info we need is in there."

"Here's hoping." Sophie scooped up a huge slice of pizza, folded it in half, and took a bite. She closed her eyes and made a humming sound deep in her throat as she chewed. "This is so good."

Camille had barely taken three bites when her cell phone rang. She put it on speaker. "Hey, Jolie. What's up?"

They heard the sound of a door closing, then Jolie's quiet voice. "I think I know why Tara was killed. Maybe. If she found out. I'm not sure. I thought . . . but then . . ."

"Take a breath, Jolie, then tell us."

The other woman cleared her throat. "Right. So, the Beckers are on a rampage and I can't blame them. The police said that when they interviewed the women in the artisan village, they mentioned a man who had been asking questions before Tara died. He wanted to know if the villagers would sell him their land. Turns out he works for a developer who wants to build a resort there. They said no. Apparently, he wasn't happy and made veiled references to the artisans' regretting their decisions."

Hank propped her hands on her hips. "And suddenly, the well is poisoned."

"That seems rather convenient, doesn't it?" Mercy asked.

"It gets worse. Magda, the older woman artisan, died last night from the poison."

Silence filled the room, broken only by several frustrated exclamations. Mercy crossed herself, and Camille whispered a prayer for the woman's family.

"We just got back to Rome," Camille said. "Who is your contact with the local police? I'd like to view the security footage from where Tara was attacked. See if we recognize anyone."

"Recognize anyone? You mean you've been followed?"

"A time or two. We'd like to know if it's the same people."

"I'll forward the name to you right away. Please be careful, Camille."

"Same goes. Have you found out anything about Mr. Sanele's death?"

"No. I keep running into brick walls trying to get information. It's incredibly frustrating. I get the feeling the people are afraid to talk to me. And the numbers on the well project aren't adding up, no matter what I do. I think Tara had seen the same thing, but I can't figure out a pattern or what's going on."

Jolie lowered her voice. "But my biggest worry is that I think Nelson may be losing his grip on reality. He has done almost nothing but pore over the diary since I gave it to him. Every time I see him, he quizzes me about the Book of Days and *how exactly* it's supposed to judge motives. Like he totally believes the legend. Today he said they're adding a 'test' to the activities next week."

"What does that mean? What kind of test?"

"He wouldn't elaborate. Just said he knows you have the Book of Days and expects me to send it to him—today." Jolie drew in another breath. "And then he added that he expects you to find the entire Liar's Treasure by the summit next week."

"What? That's crazy!"

"Right. When I told him that wasn't even remotely possible, he said he needs it for the trial. Said I'd better make sure I get it for him."

The team exchanged glances.

"What trial? Did he say what that means? Is that different from the test he mentioned?"

"I don't know. He just kept saying he needs the whole Liar's Treasure."

"How did you leave things with him?" Camille asked.

"I told him what he wants is completely impossible, but I would talk to you. If anyone could find it, you could."

"We appreciate the info, Jolie. Keep doing what you're doing, but be careful. And next time Nelson asks about the Book of Days or the Liar's Treasure, tell him we're doing our best to find them."

Camille hung up, turned to the team, the next steps running through her mind. "I'll have Cass try to find the developer sniffing around the artisan village, see if that will help us figure out why the well was poisoned." She stopped. "But it doesn't explain why Tara was killed, especially here in Rome."

Hank folded her arms. "Or why another board member is suddenly dead and if any of it is connected to this developer."

"Right." Camille scrubbed a hand over the back of her neck. "This test or trial or whatever it is Nelson is planning really worries me. Sounds like he's gone off the rails, which makes him dangerous. The summit is next week. We need to know what he's planning and how—or if—it connects to the well or the other deaths." She checked the time, then sent Cass a text to call her when she woke up, since it was still early in New Orleans. "In the meantime, let's each take some of the pages of the Book of Days, see if anything pops about where to search for the rest of the treasure."

The Ghost was not a happy man. He still couldn't believe the woman had managed to evade him, with the Book of Days in hand, no less. It was untenable. She would pay for her arrogance. No one bested The Ghost. She and her merry band of women thought they were so clever. They were under the mistaken notion that they were invincible, that they could somehow outsmart him.

He tipped his head back and laughed. They had no idea who they were dealing with.

Feet propped up on the desk, he leaned back in his expensive leather chair and studied the priceless artwork lining the walls. So many delightful works of art. All his.

Of course, the most magnificent works were stored in his underground viewing room, carefully climate-controlled at all times.

His business was all about timing, about lining things up just so to suit his purposes. Very soon, he would add every piece in the Liar's Treasure to his collection. His fingers itched in anticipation of stroking the ancient pieces.

These women were simply a minor irritation, easily outsmarted by someone with his skills. He turned his attention to the monitors in front of him. It had been child's play to hack into the traffic cameras around Florence to see where they went last night. He sent a text with their location to Nadia. She would keep an eye on the women for him.

Also, his man in New Orleans had confirmed that the grandmother and granddaughter had not left the city.

Satisfied for now, he went back to studying the ship captain's diary he'd purchased online.

34

FLORENCE

Lucien sat at a small café, his laptop open beside him, frustration humming under his skin. Camille and her friends had snatched the Book of Days right out from under him last night, and the knowledge chafed worse than wet socks in combat boots. He'd been on his way to Gallo's villa when he'd seen her on the roof. And realized she'd beaten him to the book.

Never mind saving her fool neck. His heart skipped a beat just thinking about that guy pulling a gun on her—and the desperate kiss that came after.

He'd kept Camille safe, but she was no less off-limits than she'd ever been. And maybe if he kept telling himself that, it would eventually sink in.

The issue right now was the Book of Days. He couldn't go back to NOLA without it. Pops not only needed the money it would bring—which could be in the millions, based on a similar book Sotheby's had auctioned off recently—but Lucien owed Pops the satisfaction of finding it. If he told Pops Octavia's granddaughter snatched it out from under him, it would only pour salt in an old wound.

Which left him with two choices: 1) Take the book from Camille, or 2) Find the rest of the pieces and then make a deal with her for the Book of Days.

Dollars to donuts, as Claude liked to say, Camille and her friends had hightailed it out of Florence with the book last night. It's certainly what he would have done.

So option 2: Figure out where the other pieces of the Liar's Treasure were hidden, *without* benefit of the Book of Days, which supposedly contained the necessary clues.

He huffed out a breath, grinned. He'd been in tougher situations.

First he checked all the news sites again, which merely rehashed what he already knew. The treasure supposedly consisted of three parts. The Book of Days and an ornate portable altar, commissioned back in the 1300s, of which he'd been able to find zero pictures online. Then there was the altar set. Which actually meant several pieces, often some kind of bejeweled cross, a couple chalices, maybe candlesticks. Possibly a few other pieces, too. No idea how to figure out what this particular altar set consisted of.

Every piece was incredibly valuable in its own right, but the more Lucien dug into it, the more convinced he became that the fascination went much deeper than that.

Legend said the treasure could discern motives. He drummed his fingers on the table. He'd read about this part before he left NOLA and dismissed it as silly rumor.

But what if it wasn't? What if the book really could judge the human heart?

More important, did the legend contain any clues to help him find the treasure?

One article mentioned the biblical story of Ananias and Sapphira, which he'd heard when J. T. dragged him to vacation Bible school when they were kids. He reread the story online. A couple sold a piece of property and donated part of the money to the church, but they kept some of it for themselves. No problem.

But when the husband lied and said he'd given the church all of the money, he dropped dead on the spot.

Several hours later, his wife showed up and told the same lie. She, too, keeled over dead.

The Fontana lady who started the legend was a marketing genius, in Lucien's opinion. When her husband—reportedly an arrogant, unscrupulous businessman and abuser—tried to steal the family treasure from her, he died and she let it be known it was because of his motives.

What better way to keep people far away from the treasure? He grinned. The whole idea was straight out of a Hollywood blockbuster.

But was the legend true? Or had the wife come up with a way to murder her no-good husband and keep others from going after her family's fortune at the same time?

Either way, how could that help Lucien?

He was still pondering that when the chair opposite slid back and Marcel plopped down. "Hey, Lucien, what's shaking, man?"

Lucien hid his surprise at the other man's appearance. He leaned back in his chair, casually closed his laptop. "Didn't you have some unfinished business to take care of in New Orleans?"

Marcel shrugged but couldn't quite hide the wince.

"Bruises still healing?"

Marcel beamed. "Almost back to normal."

"Hope you made enough from selling the original diary to solve your money issues."

The other man's expression turned wary. "Who told you about that? Camille?"

Lucien raised an eyebrow. "We both know New Orleans is just a gossipy small town."

Marcel laughed. "True." He paused. "Did you find the Book of Days?"

"Would I be sitting here if I had?"

Checking to be sure no one could overhear, Marcel leaned closer. "I don't think we need it to find the next piece."

"There is no 'we,' Marcel." Lucien kept the disinterested tone. "Besides, everything I've read says you can't find the rest of the treasure without the Book of Days."

"They're wrong." His voice dropped even lower. "I think I know where the portable altar is. The one they say is covered in precious gems and gold."

"How did you find what everyone has been searching for the last couple hundred years?"

Marcel pulled a folded sheaf of papers from his backpack and made sure no one was paying attention before he started flipping through them. He turned one page around so it faced Lucien, tapped it with his finger. "Here, right here."

The photocopied pages were written in the same loopy, old-fashioned French script Lucien had been squinting at for days. He followed Marcel's pointing finger and read aloud from the diary. "'The woman warned me to leave her be, as she belonged to God.'"

Marcel snatched the page back. "You see?" He tucked the pages away. "My offer stands, Lucien. Help me find the treasure and we'll split the profits."

"If you know where to look, what do you need me for? Why not just go find it yourself?"

Marcel shrugged like it didn't matter. "Because you've done this before."

There was something the other man wasn't saying.

"And?" Lucien prompted.

"And you've got a good reason to want it."

Lucien kept his expression blank. "What do you know about my reasons?"

Marcel squirmed in his chair and wouldn't meet his gaze. "I heard your pops may have entered into a partnership he'd rather not be in."

Lucien kept his tone even, barely interested. "What else?"

The silence lengthened while Marcel fiddled with a napkin. Finally, he blurted, "Your motives are pure."

It took a second for his words to register, and then Lucien threw back his head and laughed. "You think I won't die if I touch it, but you might? Even though everyone thinks the Broussards are a bunch of lying, cheating pirates?"

Marcel smiled, shrugged. "It is not a risk I want to take, eh?"

Lucien reached for his wallet and threw several bills on the table. He tucked his laptop into his backpack as he stood. "Sorry, Marcel, no can do. I work alone. But good luck."

Still, as he turned and left the café, his thoughts whirled.

Time to find out more about this ship's captain and where he went during this time period. Did he have any connections to religious institutions, or go ashore near any? Was it possible Marcel had stumbled onto an important clue?

35

NEW ORLEANS, TULANE UNIVERSITY SPECIAL COLLECTIONS

Cass was a total history and book nerd, and she wasn't ashamed to admit it. Okay, sometimes she was, like when people at school were jerks about it. But right now, Cass was happier than a pig in slop, as Gramps would say. Four or five research books lay open on the table in a semicircle, her laptop in front of her to take notes. She was also snapping pictures with her phone every other page.

This whole Fontana family was made up of a bunch of really tough ladies. Especially Countess Alonza Marino, the one who had the Book of Days commissioned. From what Cass had read, the more money you had, the better the artist you could hire to illuminate your book. And since the countess seemed to be pretty wealthy, her book was fancy. Cass about peed her pants when she found a record of a Book of Days that had been sold at auction for over four million dollars. Four. Freaking. Million!

Cass pulled her attention back. Her mom had said to focus on the genealogy aspect of the Fontana family. She didn't think she'd have wanted to live in Florence during the 1500s. Several sources said the countess might have been part of a group of ladies who dealt in poison. One article said there were as many as seven hundred women who were part of this loose affiliation. If you had a mean dog of a husband, you went to see one of these ladies and they'd sell you a potion that would make the problem go away. As in permanently.

She shuddered. One website even said things got so bad for a while that anytime a prominent politician or businessman died, it was immediately assumed that poison was involved.

Whoa.

Gran had slipped out to make some phone calls, and now she slid into the seat beside Cass. "Making any progress?"

"You won't even believe some of this stuff." She started to tell Gran all about what she'd learned when Gran interrupted.

"Cass, dear, tell me about that part later. It sounds fascinating, truly, but we don't have much more time. What have you learned about the other Fontana women?"

"Right. Sorry. So I've also been digging into the genealogy. From what I can tell, the countess and her two daughters eventually went to the Vendée region in western France, which is where the countess died. Then there are some gaps, but during the religious wars and some famine and stuff during the early 1600s to 1700s, some of her descendants went to L'Acadie, which was part of Samuel de Champlain's colony in what is now Nova Scotia."

"I'm impressed, Cassandra. You found all this out today?"

Cass grinned at the high praise. Gran wasn't one to smother you with compliments, so this was a big deal.

"After that, like in the 1700s, there was what the Acadians called the Le Grande Dérangement, where some of the Acadians wouldn't pledge allegiance to Britain so they went to Louisiana. From what I can tell, some of the countess's descendants were part of that." Cass drew a deep breath, fairly bursting with excitement. "Here's the best part. Some of her descendants settled here in New Orleans. But one sailed off to the Caribbean and founded a convent there. Maybe that's where the portable—"

"Keep your voice down, my dear."

Cass snapped her mouth shut, embarrassed. She always got louder the more excited she got. "Sorry."

Gran patted her hand. "We don't want to attract undue attention."

There was a rustling behind them, and as Cass turned around, she locked eyes with a man wearing a hoodie who was staring right at her from between two shelves of books.

Gran saw him, too, and before Cass could say anything, the man turned and hurried down the row. She and Gran watched him rush out the door.

"I'm sorry, Gran."

Gran scanned the library, then said quietly, "How about you tell me the rest in the car, all right?"

Cass closed all the research books, tucked her laptop in her bag, and followed Gran out of the library.

Once they were in the ugly beige car, Gran at the wheel, Cass asked, "Do you think he was listening?"

Gran didn't take her eyes off the rearview mirror as she tilted her head from side to side. "Maybe, maybe not. But let's not take any chances. Tell me the rest of it."

"Like I said, if I've been following the right lineage, some of Countess Alonza's female relatives ended up in New Orleans. And one of them went to an island in the Bahamas called Roberts Island, named after a pirate, and founded a convent there."

"Good work, Cass." Gran sped up and whipped around a corner just as the light turned red. Then she turned left and then left again. "You're thinking this woman took the portable altar there?"

Cass thought about it, then nodded. "It's a long shot, for sure, but it seems like that would be the logical thing, wouldn't it, for a nun to have the portable altar?"

Gran didn't say anything for several minutes as she wound through the city, but then a smile spread across her lips. "I think it makes perfect sense. Well done, Cassandra, well done."

Gran's eyes darted to the side mirror, and she grimaced. "And as soon as we lose this pesky tail, we'll call your mother and you can tell her all about what you discovered. By the way, did you find anything about the developer nosing around the Romanian village?"

Cass grimaced. "Sorry, Gran. I got so excited about the other stuff, I totally forgot." She reached for her phone. "I'll do it right now."

The car behind them inched closer and closer until Gran said, "Later. Right now, hold on, my dear. It's going to get a bit dicey."

Cass gripped the dashboard as her normally calm, collected Gran took off like an Indy-car driver. She stomped the gas and took the next corner practically on two wheels. The car behind them turned the corner, too, and Cass could see the hoodie guy from the library driving.

"That's the same guy!"

"I see him." Gran turned the wheel hard, then shot down the alley, dodging garbage cans and recycling bins as she went. She crossed oncoming traffic at the next cross street, horns blaring, then barreled down another alley. She hung a hard right, then a left, and shot through two more alleys before she slowed enough to make the turn into an open garage. The minute the car came to a rocking stop, Gran hopped out and mashed the button.

The door rumbled down. Cass slipped out of the car and saw Gran peering out the high windows in the door.

"Where are we?"

"A friend's place. We're just borrowing her garage for a few minutes." They waited, not talking as the car passed by. "He kept going."

Several minutes later, Gran turned from the window and put an arm around Cass. "Let me call Camille before we head back to the carriage house."

36

ROBERTS ISLAND, THE CARIBBEAN—THE NEXT DAY

"We're reasonably sure this is the right island?" Sophie asked.

Camille had a white-knuckle grip on the armrest of the small six-seater plane that brought them from Nassau, her eyes closed, studiously ignoring the aquamarine water far, far below. "Reasonably sure."

"By the way, I turn that same shade of terrified whenever I'm in a helicopter."

Camille ignored the teasing grin in Sophie's voice. "Yeah, I don't love small planes. Or big ones, for that matter." She should never have agreed to come, not after Gran's call telling her she and Cass were followed from the Tulane library.

But this plan made sense. Even though Mercy was a nun, which could come in handy here, the conditions in Rome should be slightly less hard on Mercy physically. Hopefully. She and Hank would still be chasing down clues in churches.

Camille took several deep breaths and forcibly peeled her fingers free and laced them together as though she were fine. The queasy pitch and roll of her stomach claimed otherwise. But the need to find the next piece of the treasure overrode everything else. Whatever it took to ensure Cass's safety.

"You didn't seem to have a problem on the commercial jets between Rome and here."

"That would be thanks to my good friend Dramamine, whose impact has sadly worn off now." It was the only way she knew to deal with it.

"Ah, that explains how you slept through all the turbulence."

Camille stiffened. "There was turbulence?"

"You didn't miss anything exciting, don't worry. So, back to my question."

"Right." Camille took a deep breath. "You went over the copy of Cass's research I e-mailed you?"

"I did. But there doesn't seem to be a lot of hard evidence."

"True. No convenient *X* marking the spot, either," Camille teased.

"I like a little more certainty, is all. When I retrieve a painting or a piece of artwork, I'm 99.9 percent sure it's been stolen, or I won't do it." Sophie let out a sigh. "This really feels like a shot in the dark."

"That's because it is. Though we do know a few things." Camille ticked them off on her fingers. "One, we know from his diary that Captain Talon did some of his best privateering and pirating in these islands. Two, we have that line in his diary about another feisty girl, maybe Cira's sister, Maura, telling the sailors to leave her alone because 'she belonged to God.' And three, if we connect that with what Cass found out about a female Fontana descendant starting a convent here in the 1700s, I'd say we've got a good starting place."

Camille braced herself when the captain announced their preparation for landing. She closed her eyes and gripped the armrests as the plane touched down hard, bounced twice, and finally came to a screeching stop between two jagged volcanoes.

"Welcome to Roberts Island, and thanks for flying Roberts Air, where all of our pilots were trained on aircraft carriers."

Camille heard the chuckles around her and finally opened her eyes, reassured by the palm trees outside the windows. "That explains a lot."

They were outside the terminal, searching for a taxi, when Camille's phone rang. She put it on speaker. "Good morning, Reverend Mother. We've just arrived and are headed your way."

"I am afraid I need to reschedule our meeting until tomorrow. We've had an unfortunate incident here today. The police—"

"We'll be right there."

ROME

"We won't find the altar pieces here," Hank snapped irritably, hands on her hips as she surveyed what had once been Santa Evelina's Church a few hundred years ago.

After they dropped Camille and Sophie at the airport yesterday, she and Mercy had scoured their copy of the Book of Days, searching for clues to the location of the altar pieces. When the delightful Captain Jacques Talon questioned his dying wife about the treasure, she'd only said, "Santa Evelina will protect what is hers." Their genealogical research had uncovered a Countess Evelina Romano who had lived in Rome.

It wasn't much to go on.

The large church had clearly burned at some point in its history, given that in places the roof had caved in. One side had been left to decay, the inside now filled with plants and paths, creating a quiet green space within the city.

"You may be right." Mercy turned in a slow circle as she took it all in. "I wonder why they didn't rebuild or repurpose it, like they do everything else?"

"Too busy digging up more old stuff," Hank muttered, and Mercy raised an eyebrow at her tone. As they'd driven around, they had seen more than one archaeological dig right in the middle of the city and even spotted an old temple where the spaces between the columns had been filled in with bricks to create apartments.

"You okay?" Mercy asked. "You've been edgy since before we left New Orleans."

Hank bit back a snarl. Took a deep breath. "I will be." She wasn't angry at Mercy. Or her caring. "Let's just say that I'd gotten a little overconfident, a little too complacent, thinking my need for a drink was a thing of the past." She scowled at the street littered with cafés. That served alcohol.

"I think most hard things in life aren't one and done, much as we'd like them to be. They try to sneak back in. Then we have to fight again."

Hank raised an eyebrow. "Speaking from experience?" Mercy didn't talk about her past.

The silence lengthened. "You don't watch your family mowed down by rebels and not have to battle the need for revenge."

Hank absorbed the words, images from her military days flashing behind her eyes. "No, I don't suppose you do." She huffed out a breath. "One day at a time, right?"

"And distraction helps." Mercy smiled and hitched a thumb toward the opposite side of the old church, where the outside wall had become part of a library of some kind. "Let's try there."

They rang the bell on a heavy wooden door. And again.

They were ready to give up when a fragile wisp of a man opened it, leaning heavily on a cane, peering at them from behind thick glasses.

"Buongiorno, signore," Mercy greeted. "We were curious about Santa Evelina's Church. Could you tell us more?"

He scrutinized them before motioning for them to follow. He led the way through a large room crammed with books, to a small office where he sank behind a cluttered desk. He folded his hands and eyed Mercy. "How may I be of assistance, Sister?"

"What year did the church burn down?"

"Sometime around 1720, but there are conflicting reports." He studied them. "You could have found that information in any guidebook for sale in the city."

Time to cut to the chase. "Does the name Countess Evelina Romano mean anything to you?" Hank caught a flicker of recognition at the name.

"No, sorry. Is she a friend of yours?"

Hank shrugged. "She lived a long time ago. We wanted to learn more about her."

The man fiddled with his tie, chin down. "Have you checked those ancestry sites on the computer? Supposedly you can find anyone that way."

They stood and Mercy extended her hand. "Thank you for your time." She turned to go, then stopped. "What about the relics and artwork from the original church? Did any of them survive the fire?"

He blinked several times. "I'm not sure." He considered for a moment, then grabbed a piece of paper and jotted down a name and address. "The museum curator is a friend of mine and may be able to shed more light on your search."

They thanked him again and left. Hank waited until they were well away from the building before she said, "Was it me, or was he acting squirrelly? Like he knows something."

"Definitely squirrelly."

Hank glimpsed the older man standing in the doorway, a scowl on his face and a cell phone pressed to his ear.

37

ROBERTS ISLAND

There were no official taxis at the tiny two-gate airport but plenty of private jitneys, aka old beater cars. Thankfully, Camille and Sophie's French was close enough to one driver's Haitian Creole for them to negotiate a ride. They held on for dear life as the jitney raced around switchbacks with no guardrails, sliding in the dirt at the edge of the road, climbing higher and higher toward the top of one of the volcanoes. All on the left side of the road. Behind them and far below, several other islands shimmered in the distance. It really was beautiful here.

While Sophie chattered away with the driver, Camille thought through their upcoming meeting. If she wanted to help Cass, she had to stay focused.

When the driver skidded to a stop in front of a plain white-washed building, she and Sophie took in the two police cars parked in front. Apparently the Reverend Mother hadn't exaggerated the "unfortunate incident."

Camille paid the driver and turned to Sophie, hands clasped in front of her. "Ready?"

At Mercy's suggestion, they were both dressed as nuns today. No one would question—or remember—a couple of nuns headed toward a convent.

As they started up the walk, Sophie whispered, "Glide, Sister Camille. Don't stride like you're late for a plane."

"Right." Camille grimaced and slowed her steps. *Head in the game.* She knew how to play a part.

At the door, a tiny nun with a wrinkled face smiled wanly when she saw them. "Welcome, Sisters. Your friend Sister Mercy told us you were coming, but as the Reverend Mother told you"—she glanced over her shoulder—"this isn't really a good time."

"We just need a few minutes."

Camille leaned in closer to the tiny woman. "The police always make me a bit nervous, even though I haven't done anything wrong." When the other woman nodded in agreement, she asked, "Is everyone all right? Is there anything we can do?"

"It's such a tragedy." The woman sniffed and her blue eyes filled with tears. She lifted her chin as she pulled a handkerchief from a pocket of her robe and wiped her eyes. "I shouldn't grieve because I know she's with God." She paused and made the sign of the cross. "But I will miss her. We were friends for over thirty years."

Camille and Sophie's eyes met over the woman's head.

"It is always hard to lose a good friend, even when we know they are eternally secure and safe." Camille gave her a gentle hug.

The tiny woman returned the hug fiercely, then stepped back and blew her nose.

"Can you tell us what happened? Was she ill?"

"No—no. She was healthy and spry. The police think it was a robbery, though what anyone thought was worth stealing in our library, I have no idea. Sister Inez was on the ladder reshelving books when someone came in through the French doors, knocked her off the ladder, and then proceeded to tear our library apart." More tears filled her eyes. "Inez hit her head on the stone floor. And the books, so many irreplaceable books, were absolutely destroyed."

Camille hugged the woman again, making soothing noises as she sobbed.

"Sister Mary Magdalene, kindly pull yourself together," a stern voice commanded.

Camille turned toward the tall, thin woman and started to extend her hand before she caught herself, tucked her hands into her robe, and nodded. "Good morning, Reverend Mother. We are—"

"I know who you are, and I told you not to come."

Camille nodded, eyes down. "We mean no harm. We merely thought we might be able to offer some assistance in your time of need."

"And what kind of assistance, pray tell, could you two possibly provide?"

Camille started to pull back her sleeve and show the woman her tattoo, when she caught a sharp headshake from Sophie, who slid her Speranza medallion out from under her robes. Right, a tattoo was probably not going to garner the response they sought.

The Mother Superior took in the emblem, then her eyes flicked between Camille and Sophie before she nodded. "Come with me."

38

He sat behind his desk, research materials spread all across the mahogany surface. He had extracted every single secret the pirate's diary had to offer, but it still wasn't enough. He needed the Book of Days. That's where the real info was hidden, the clues he needed. He couldn't believe those women thought they could outsmart him.

He needed that book! He thumped a fist on the desk. He not only needed it, he deserved it. It should have been his decades ago. And would have been, if not for—no, he wouldn't think about that right now.

He stood and paced, determined to focus on the task at hand. He went to his bookshelf and took down the Bible, opened it, and reread the story of Ananias and Sapphira out loud, to be sure he hadn't missed anything.

Just like in the book of Acts, the truth must come out. The liars had to pay the price. Their sins had to be exposed, their motives shown for the hypocrisy they were. The Liar's Treasure—brought together at long last—would guarantee it.

Gathering the treasure pieces, however, was proving more difficult than he'd expected.

His conscience twinged at what he was about to do, but he shoved the guilt away. Sometimes one had to make hard choices—for the greater good.

From the bottom drawer of his desk, he plucked out his new burner phone and dialed a number he'd located and carefully programmed into the phone, just in case.

It rang three times before an annoyed voice demanded, "Who is this?"

He placed his handkerchief over the phone to make sure his voice couldn't be recognized. "That doesn't matter. What matters is that you do exactly what I tell you."

He outlined what he wanted, and the coward immediately started sputtering in outrage.

"Absolutely not! I can't do that. No. I don't know who you are, but I won't do it."

He waited until the other man ran out of steam. "How else will you pay off your debt?" he asked quietly, and was rewarded with a quick indrawn breath.

A long pause followed.

"You're saying if I do this, you'll take care of the debt?"

"Paid in full. Guaranteed."

Another pause. Then a sigh. "Tell me what I have to do."

39

ROBERTS ISLAND

Camille and Sophie followed the Reverend Mother down a long hallway. She did not so much as hesitate at the open doorway of what was clearly the library. Police milled around and Camille quickly catalogued the destruction, pausing for a split second at the covered body lying on the floor. She and Sophie made the sign of the cross, then hurried to catch up to the Reverend Mother, who marched along with the sure stride of a much younger woman.

She led the way into a sparsely furnished office at the end of the hallway and sat behind her desk, indicating the two straight-backed chairs across from her.

Camille took the lead. "We are very sorry for your loss. Can you tell us what happened to the sister?"

"Sister Mary Magdalene told you all that we know. Someone broke in, knocked Sister Inez off the ladder, and she hit her head as she fell."

"Do you know what they were searching for?"

"What makes you think they were searching for anything?"

"Libraries are not usually ransacked for no reason. Especially one in a convent."

The Reverend Mother's dark eyes flicked from Camille to Sophie and back, missing nothing. "What do you think they were after?"

"Do you know anything about the Fontana family's Book of Days?" Sophie reached into the folds of her robe and pulled out a picture of one of the pages. "It is an illuminated manuscript from the 1500s."

The Reverend Mother pulled up the glasses on a chain around her neck and perched them on her nose. "It's lovely." She peered at them over the tops of the glasses. "And no doubt worth a fortune."

"Yes. Actually, a very large fortune."

"That would explain why someone might search a library. But it does not explain why they would search for this book *here*."

Camille nodded to Sophie before she said, "According to the research we've uncovered, a pirate by the name of Captain Talon claimed to have had this book and two teen girls who were carrying it aboard his ship hundreds of years ago. One of the girls claimed that anyone who touched the book with impure motives would die. He reported that happening to one of his crewmen before she leaped over the side of the ship and disappeared."

"And you think she and her book somehow ended up here?"

"Not her, necessarily, but possibly a descendant. Did she?" Camille kept her eyes steady on the older woman's face, but she didn't show any sign of recognition.

"She did not."

Sophie leaned forward in her chair. "What about the Portable Altar of Countess Alonza? Is that familiar to you at all?"

This time, the Reverend Mother dropped her gaze, fiddled with the letter opener on her desk. "No. That is not familiar to me, either."

"With all due respect, Reverend Mother," Camille said quietly, "now is not the time for prevaricating."

"Prevaricating?" She arched an eyebrow. "So much less accusatory than asking if I'm lying, isn't it?" She studied the crucifix on the wall for a long moment, then sighed. "Do you honestly believe that someone trying to find this Book of Days caused Sister Inez to fall from the ladder?"

"Or she was pushed when she refused to cooperate." Camille wouldn't add to the woman's grief by telling her they'd already found the Book of Days.

The older woman drew in a harsh breath, then let it out slowly. She picked up the letter opener again, set it down. "What is your interest in this book?"

"The Fontana family's Book of Days is part of a larger group of valuable objects known collectively as the Liar's Treasure. The legend is that if you try to steal it or even touch it with impure motives or a desire to deceive, you will die. Similar to the biblical story of—"

"Ananias and Sapphira in Acts," the Reverend Mother finished. "Is it true?"

"We don't know for sure."

"You still haven't explained your interest in this Book of Days or the Liar's Treasure."

Camille thought fast, trying to decide how much to say.

"It is twofold," Camille said. "In the long term, we want to be sure the pieces are found and returned to their rightful owners. But in the near term, besides Sister Inez, another woman has already died and my daughter has been targeted. We need to find the treasure, and quickly, before anyone else dies. Can you help us?"

The Reverend Mother raised an eyebrow at the word *daughter* but didn't comment. "You truly believe Sister Inez's death is related to this book?"

"We do."

The Reverend Mother opened the top drawer of her desk, pulled out a sheet of her personal stationery, and wrote several lines. She slipped it into an envelope, sealed it, then handed it to Camille. "There is another, older convent, on Lesser Roberts Island. What you seek is not here. But it is possible it found a home there. Give this to the Reverend Mother. She may be able to assist you."

A knock sounded on the door and another nun poked her head

in. "Pardon the interruption, but the police would like to speak with you, Reverend Mother."

The Mother Superior stood. "Thank you, Sister. I will be along shortly." She turned to Camille and Sophie, indicating that they should proceed her. "I wish you Godspeed."

40

NEW ORLEANS

Octavia Benoit pulled the phone from the pocket of her jeans and frowned at the unfamiliar number. Her frown deepened as she read the text message: **I have information on the Book of Days that will help keep your granddaughter safe. Meet me at this address. One hour.**

After the address it simply said, **A friend.**

She tapped a finger on the steering wheel. Was this a legitimate offer or some scoundrel wanting to get near Cassandra? She stuck her hand in the tote bag on the seat beside her, the feel of her gun a steady reassurance in case this person had nefarious motives.

She debated dropping Cassandra off somewhere to keep her safe, but where? No, they'd be safer together.

Still, if the offer of help was genuine, she had to check it out. She plugged the address into the GPS. It took them west, out of the city and into farm country.

Cassandra finally looked up from her phone. "What are we doing way out here?"

"Hopefully gathering some information."

Before they got close to their destination, Octavia pulled in behind an abandoned farmhouse and turned to Cassandra. "I need you to get into the backseat again, under a blanket. I have a meeting, but I'll leave the keys in the car so if something goes wrong, you can get out of there."

"What? No. What's going on? You're scaring me."

"That's not my intention. I'm trying to protect you. Everything should be fine, but in case it isn't, you take off and get to the nearest police station, all right?"

"But what about you?"

"Promise me, Cassandra." She waited until Cassandra met her eyes and nodded. She had to be strong, couldn't let the girl see her own fear.

Once Cassandra was safely hidden, Octavia got back on the road. She turned onto the gravel road the GPS indicated, then the dirt track, and finally pulled into a wooded area. The farther they got from civilization, the more alarm bells sounded. Were they walking into a trap?

She stopped in front of a sagging cottage from the 1930s, turned off the ignition, and tucked the keys into the cupholder. "Stay hidden, no matter what," she whispered as she climbed out of the car.

Father, protect us both.

The front door of the cottage stood open. She surveyed the area as she slowly climbed up the sagging steps. Weapon in hand, she poked her head inside the living room, poised to run. "Hello? Is anyone here?"

A shiver of foreboding slid over her skin and she spun around, ready to run back to the car.

Too late. A hand clapped over her mouth and nose and another grabbed her around her waist.

She twisted and fought, trying to breathe, trying to break free, but the edges of her vision started to dim.

Her last thought was, *Dear God, save Cassandra!*

ROME

Hank and Mercy picked up a tail as soon as they walked away from the burned church. Tall and lanky, he wore a black watch cap, hiking boots, and a peacoat that no doubt hid a weapon.

Hank steered them around the crowds clogging the sidewalks and down several narrow cobblestone streets, hoping to shake him. "Not one of the usual tails."

Mercy glanced in a shop window as they hurried past. "I don't see him anymore."

"Good. Car is just over here. Can you plug that museum address into the GPS?" Hank slid behind the wheel and they pulled away from the curb. "Do you remember where Tara was found?"

"I should have that somewhere." Mercy scrolled through her phone. "Oh, we missed a text from Camille. Jolie said the police won't give us access to the security footage from where Tara died since it's part of an active investigation."

"Disappointing, but not unexpected. Did you find the address?"

"Right. Okay, got it. Go left at the next intersection." Mercy enlarged the map with two fingers. "The ATM should be on the northwest corner of the street."

Hank sped through a yellow light, bouncing over the cobblestones, expression intent.

"Should be just ahead." Mercy paused. "Now that's interesting. The museum is just around the corner from the ATM."

Hank narrowed her eyes. "I don't believe in coincidences."

"Me, either. Let's see what this curator has to say."

"Or whatever the guy from the church told the curator to say when he called him."

Mercy sighed. "Or that. Yeah, something was off about all of it."

Hank slipped into a parking spot two blocks away, and they walked toward the museum.

"See if anything jumps out at you," Hank said as they drifted around the corner and toward the ATM.

"Like what?" Mercy peered at the buildings and scanned the sidewalk.

"Anything—or anyone—who doesn't belong."

"I don't—oh wait. Watch-Cap Guy who's been tailing us just turned onto this block."

"Then we'll come back later."

They reversed direction and walked into the small museum halfway down the block. Inside, it had that slightly musty smell peculiar to history museums.

"*Buongiorno*, and welcome. How may I be of assistance?" The voice came from an older gentleman, round and bald, who resembled everyone's favorite grandfather.

Hank nodded and let Mercy take the lead.

"Thank you. We were sent by a friend of yours." Mercy said the man's name and then added, "I think he called to tell you we were coming?"

The curator cleared his throat and wouldn't quite meet their eyes. "Just so. He said you were interested in the history of Santa Evelina's Church."

"Yes. We know it burned down in the mid-1700s. Was there any warning? How did it start?"

"Come with me." He led them to a small display in the back of the high-ceilinged room. Several placards described the church's history and showed before-and-after illustrations of the church. "The fire started during Sunday-morning mass, behind the altar. A candle in one of the candelabras tilted and set one of the heavy draperies on fire. The fabric was very old and the fire spread quickly." He indicated one of the panels that described the fire.

"Was anyone hurt?" Mercy asked.

"Fortunately, and by God's grace, no. Someone saw the flames and shouted a warning. The priest immediately told the parishioners to run out the back doors to safety. Which they did."

"What about the artwork and other relics?" Mercy indicated one of the artist renderings of the original church. "It had gorgeous artwork everywhere."

"The priest snuffed the candles, wrapped the altar pieces in the altar cloth, and told the altar boys and priests to grab what they could carry and follow him."

"Wow. That takes a lot of presence of mind. Did they get all the important things?"

The curator shrugged. "It depends on how you define 'important.' Certainly, he saved the altar set, but there were other relics of saints and statues that were lost in the fire, mainly because they were not easily transportable."

Hank stayed quiet, reading the posters, letting Mercy do the talking.

"Thank goodness everything wasn't destroyed. I'm curious, though. Why didn't they rebuild the church?"

The curator smiled. "It's a long story, but in short, politics."

"Politics?"

"The church leaders couldn't agree on a new location, so they divided the parish and absorbed it into others in the city."

Hank caught Mercy's eyes, tapped her watch. *Move it along, Sister.*

"What happened to the altar set and other relics the priest saved?" Mercy asked.

The curator's eyes flicked from one to the other. "Interesting. You are the second person in the last week to make the same inquiry."

"Who else asked about it? A woman, perchance?"

His bushy eyebrows climbed up his forehead. "How did you know?"

Mercy pulled out her phone and showed him Tara's photo from the Becker Foundation website. "Was this the woman?"

"Yes. Terrible what happened to her." He shuddered. "Did you know her?"

"She's a friend of a friend."

Hank asked, "Can you tell us what happened?"

"She came in and asked me about the old church, like you have. But when she stepped outside, two men tried to rob her. I saw her struggling and rushed to help, but she took off down the street, the men in pursuit. I called the police, but I didn't see her again."

He paused, his eyes sad. "The authorities arrived and I thought all was well. But next thing I heard, she'd been killed just around the corner." He sighed. "Terrible, terrible thing." He wrung his hands. "I wish I could have done more."

"Calling for help was the right thing to do," Mercy soothed.

Hank tried to curb her impatience. "What else did she ask about?"

"The same thing you did. She wanted to know what happened to the altar set."

"What did you tell her?"

"From everything I know, the set was sent to a small church in the Moselle region in Germany, along the Moselle River."

"Do you know which church? Which town?"

He shook his head.

"Have you heard if it's still there?"

Hank barely heard the curator's reply because all of her attention was on the two men marching toward the entrance. Watch-Cap Guy now had a friend along, this one wearing a leather jacket.

Watch Cap pulled the door open, and the other man stepped in and drew his weapon.

Hank grabbed Mercy's arm and propelled them toward the back door, pushing the curator ahead of them. "Guns! Run!"

41

LESSER ROBERTS ISLAND

After they left the convent, Camille and Sophie caught a ride back to the airport with the same taxi driver, only to discover that the last—and only—flight to Lesser Roberts was already gone. Their helpful taxi driver introduced them to a local charter captain who was willing to take them along as he headed home.

It was a choppy ride and Sophie's face had a sickly green tinge by the time they reached Lesser Roberts Island.

"You okay?" Camille asked. "You look like I did after the plane ride."

"Just happy to be back on terra firma," Sophie said weakly from her seat on a nearby bench.

Camille checked her phone. She'd left Gran a voicemail earlier, asking for an update. She fought the urge to leave another message. Gran would call back as soon as she could. She had to trust her.

Captain Thomas said the best way to get up the mountain was by motorcycle, so he introduced them to his cousin who just happened to have a few to rent.

Camille strapped the helmet on and nodded to Sophie. "You know how to ride one of these?"

Sophie laughed. "Of course. You?"

"Been a minute since I raced all over Gramps's farm on a dirt bike, but I'm thinking it'll come back to me."

"It will." Sophie swung a leg over her bike. "Except, you know, we're driving on the wrong side of the road." She grinned. "You good to lead?"

Camille nodded, then took a deep breath. She could do this, *without* her directional dyslexia sending them off a cliff. She pointed toward the volcano that loomed over the lush tropical island. "Basically, we go up until we can't go any higher."

"Which should make it easy to spot our tail." Sophie started her bike.

When they'd arrived, they spotted a guy following them, his black jeans and black button-down making him stand out like flashing neon amongst the colorful locals. But they'd lost sight of him earlier and hadn't seen him again.

Camille checked the address she'd programmed into her phone GPS and muttered, "Left side, left side."

Then she started her bike and accidentally goosed the throttle. It shot forward and jumped a curb so she braked too hard and nearly flew over the handlebars.

Sophie pulled up beside her, flipped her visor up. "You sure you're okay to do this?"

An embarrassed flush crept over Camille's cheeks. "Just had to remember how it all works. I'm good now."

With a grin, Sophie revved her engine, flipped her visor down, and indicated for Camille to lead the way.

Their young captain hadn't been kidding when he said to go up the mountain until they ran out of road. Thirty minutes later they rounded another blind curve and skidded to a stop when the pavement abruptly ended in a gravel drive.

The view was amazing. Blue-green water shimmered in all directions, the town and its marina a tiny speck at the base of the cliff.

The old convent loomed before them, built of rough-hewn sandstone bricks and shrouded in an air of decades-long neglect.

"Huh. This isn't what I expected," Sophie murmured.

"Agreed."

A rusty chain stretched between the two crumbling stone towers on either side of the driveway, blocking the entrance. But the grass poking through the gravel drive had been flattened in two straight lines.

"Someone has obviously driven in recently."

Camille nodded. "Let's check it out."

They left the bikes hidden in a stand of trees but within reach for a quick getaway, then started up the drive.

"They do have electricity, at least." Sophie hitched her chin toward sagging power lines.

As they rounded the bend in the drive, they got a close-up of the convent. At least three stories tall with a chapel to one side, it was impressive and showed much less decay back here than the entrance indicated. The ten-foot-high massive wooden door swung open and an imposing figure in a nun's habit eyed them as they approached.

"May I help you?"

"We are here to see the Mother Superior."

"Who are you?"

Sophie pulled out her Speranza medallion. "We are friends, trying to help a friend."

Camille buried her impatience, kept her voice mild. "Did your friend, the Mother Superior at the Sisters of St. Clement, tell you we were coming?"

"She did. It is tragic what happened to one of the sisters there." She made the sign of the cross. "Please, follow me."

Lit candles flickering in wall sconces guided them down a short hallway and through a large gathering room, past a chapel, and into a small office. The Reverend Mother sat behind her desk and folded her hands on top of it. "What would you like to know?"

"We are trying to track down a sister who we believe served

here a long time ago. Do you keep records of all the nuns in the convent?"

"We do. Why do you want to know?"

"We are trying to locate a portable altar from the descendants of Countess Alonza of the Fontana family."

The Reverend Mother's eyes flicked to the side briefly, then returned to them both. "Countesses do not generally become sisters of charity."

"True, but sometimes their descendants do."

"I do not know what any of this has to do with our small community."

"We want to know if any of the countess's descendants served in this convent."

"How long ago?"

"Probably mid-to-late 1700s."

The Reverend Mother's white eyebrows rose. "That is a long time ago."

"But you have those records," Camille pressed.

"We do. But you haven't told me why you wish to see them."

"We are doing some genealogical research and have traced one of the countess's descendants here. We'd like to confirm our research."

The older woman steepled her fingers as she thought.

Sophie said, "Forgive me for saying so, but the convent seems to be fairly empty. Do sisters still live and work here?"

The Reverend Mother smiled sadly. "There are only a few of us left. So many young women are drawn to a different life these days."

"What kind of work do the sisters do here?"

"Some of them weave baskets from palm fronds and sell them to the tourists to help keep the order alive. We also staff a small medical clinic in town. Many of our sisters trained as nurses."

"Admirable and necessary work."

She eyed them both sternly. "We do not provide access to our records to just anyone." Then her eyes landed on Sophie's medallion again. "I will consider your request and return in a few minutes."

She indicated one of the tall bookcases on the other side of the room. "We house all of our older registers along that wall."

She sent them a meaningful glance, then glided from the room and closed the door behind her.

Camille hopped up from her chair and crossed the room. "Let's see if we can find that book."

"Be careful or they may crumble to dust." Sophie opened one slim volume, replaced it, and pulled out another. "Some of them have the decade written inside the cover."

"At least they're in chronological order." Camille pulled out another volume. "Here we go. 1750s." She scanned the list of names, but nothing jumped out at her. She pulled out her phone, opened the camera. "Let's start with this page. We can study the info later."

"Perfect."

They worked quickly. Sophie held a page open and Camille snapped a photo. Again and again, from the mid-1700s to the early 1800s.

They heard a jangle of keys and Camille quickly snapped one last photo. Sophie slid the volume back on the shelf, and they both leaped into their chairs just as the Reverend Mother opened the door. She studied both of them, then the bookshelves before shaking her head sadly as she took her seat behind her desk.

"I regret to inform you that I cannot allow you to peruse our ledgers. Our sisters have the right to privacy, even those who've gone on before."

Sophie nodded. "We understand, of course. Thank you for your kind consideration."

They stood and moved to the door.

Camille chose her words with care. "If we might issue a warning, Reverend Mother. We believe this particular sister brought a valuable artifact with her, one that some very unscrupulous people would like to get their hands on."

A flicker of alarm passed over the Reverend Mother's face before she assumed her normal calm expression. "Sisters of charity do not own property or valuables."

"No, but if they did prior to taking their vows, they would donate any property they arrived with to the convent, wouldn't they?" Sophie asked.

The Reverend Mother's chin lifted and she nodded. "It is possible."

Camille gestured to a notepad on the Reverend Mother's desk. "May I?" She scribbled her phone number and handed the pad back. "For the safety of the sisters who live and work here, please let us know if anyone else comes around asking about the portable altar."

The Reverend Mother's gaze sharpened suddenly. "You believe someone was searching for the altar at the Sisters of St. Clement when the sister fell?"

"Possibly, or they were trying to find a Book of Days containing clues to the altar. Either way, if we figured out to come here, they will, too." Camille refused to sugarcoat the danger. "If the altar is here, please be sure it is well secured and make sure the sisters are prepared. And if you need us, please call. Anytime. We'll do what we can to help."

The older woman's face paled, and she made the sign of the cross.

42

ROME

"What's happening?" The curator ran ahead of Hank but kept trying to stop and peer over his shoulder.

Hank kept a firm hand on his back. "Don't stop. Just keep moving." The two men hadn't fired . . . *yet*, but Hank was taking no chances.

Mercy pushed through a door in the rear, and they found themselves in a narrow alley. To the left, a white delivery van blocked the exit to the street. "Is there another way out of here?"

The curator waved a hand in the opposite direction, and they took off. Hank looked back just as the two men burst out of the rear door, guns drawn. There was a pop and chunks of brick exploded from the side of the building.

The curator yelped but thankfully picked up the pace.

More bricks exploded.

"Suppressors." *Dang.* Hank brought up the rear while Mercy took point, leading them around dumpsters, past trash cans and cardboard boxes. She might be new to this, but she knew what she was doing.

They raced into the street and Mercy turned left and sped up.

"Taxi!" Hank shouted when one turned onto the busy street.

Mercy's arm shot up and the car slid to a stop.

Hank shoved the curator inside. "Call the police and don't go back to the museum until you know they're on-site." She slammed the door and the taxi lurched away from the curb.

"Alley," Hank shouted and Mercy veered hard right. They ducked behind a dumpster not far from the mouth of the alley. Mercy let out a small sigh of relief when the two gunmen ran past on the street.

They waited several minutes, but there was no sign of the men.

When Mercy started to rise, Hank pulled her back down. "Stay low and let's sneak out the other way."

They turned the opposite direction and sprinted down the alley, then down another, and finally took a roundabout route back to their car.

When they drove past the museum, the area was swarming with police. The curator stood just inside, waving his arms, giving a statement to several officers.

"What in the world?"

Hank turned at Mercy's shocked exclamation.

The leather-jacketed gunman stood outside on the sidewalk, chatting with a police officer as though they were old friends.

The man turned just as they drove by and locked eyes with Hank.

"Who is that?" Mercy asked.

"Snap a pic, quick."

Mercy fumbled for her phone and snapped a picture just as the man turned his back to them.

LESSER ROBERTS ISLAND

Camille and Sophie rode down the mountain, checking for a tail, but thankfully there wasn't one. They parked the motorcycles outside the little beachside cottage—one of a cluster of six—they'd rented from their captain's mother's cousin. On a small island, it seemed everyone was related.

Laptops in hand, they curled up on the wicker furniture on the small porch, which overlooked the beach.

"I just sent you the photos from the monastery," Camille said, "though given the speed of the Internet connection, it may be tomorrow before you get them all."

"At least we have Internet." Sophie opened her laptop, then wandered into the kitchen. She returned with glasses of lemonade and a plate of fruit. Once the pictures transferred, she started scrolling. "That is some seriously small, cramped handwriting, isn't it?"

"Yes. I've enlarged them, but it's still tough to decipher."

They fell silent as they scanned page after page of the ledger.

"Some of these ladies sure didn't have much in the way of personal belongings, did they?" Next to each sister's name was a list of the possessions she'd brought with her to the convent. Camille read out loud. "One dress, one pair of shoes, a bag containing a drawing of her family, a crucifix."

"Wow. Such a contrast to our overstuffed lives."

They fell silent, the only sound the steady ticking of the sailboat-shaped clock on the wall.

"I think I found it." Sophie was grinning widely as she turned her laptop toward Camille and pointed. "There. 1762. A woman named Evelina Gallo Esposito. She became Sister Evangeline."

Camille nodded. "Oh yeah. Caesar Gallo claims the treasure belongs to him since his ancestor was married to the original countess." Camille leaned closer. "What did she bring to the convent?"

Sophie read the list: "One pair of shoes, a dress, a brass candlestick, and a wooden box."

"Does it say what was in the box?"

"Nope. Just lists the box."

"Makes sense. I wouldn't expect they'd list 'priceless gold-encrusted traveling altar containing the relics of saints.'" Camille grinned and stood, excitement thrumming through her veins. "I think we found it. And I think it's still there. The Reverend Mother definitely wanted us to figure that out. But she hedged her bets, too. It doesn't tell us where in the convent they have it stashed."

Sophie sat back on the couch, arms folded. "I think it's probably kept somewhere behind the altar with other valuable artifacts or hidden in a secret compartment or niche somewhere so they can use it on special occasions. They sure wouldn't leave it on display on a regular basis. For them, it's more part of their faith than a piece of art or history."

"I agree." Camille leaned against the wooden railing. "But I'm very concerned that someone ransacked the convent library over on Roberts Island. It's only a matter of time before they show up here. I don't want any more sisters dying."

"Absolutely. I think we need to get it sooner rather than later." Sophie's fingers flew over her keys, then she motioned for Camille to sit beside her. "Here are some photos from a local history website that show the layout of the property. We need to narrow down the list of possible hiding places." She scrolled through the pictures, then grabbed a notebook and pencil and started sketching.

Camille watched the design taking shape, impressed. "I sometimes forget just how talented you are."

Sophie shrugged, adding more details to the sketch. Then she picked up her laptop again. "Okay, some woman posted pictures on her travel blog of the inside of the chapel, the courtyard area, and the library, though she admitted they were asked not to." She frowned. "Not cool, but it works for us."

About thirty minutes later, Sophie held up the drawing of the entire convent she'd created from the photos, including details of each room, with possible locations listed on the side. "This will give us a starting place. And a handy reference for what's where."

"Nice. I found something, too." Camille pulled up a map of the island. "Remember that estate the captain showed us? Big castle-looking thing perched high up the mountainside that belongs to the richest guy in town? I think his name is Rommy Williams?" She grinned at Sophie. "Any relation, by the way?"

Sophie laughed. "Ah, no."

"Bummer. Okay, check this out. We passed his estate on our way to the convent, but all the foliage keeps the entrance hidden from the road." She leaned back. "The property backs right up to the convent."

"Perfect. All we need is a way to get onto the property without setting off alarms or anything."

For a few minutes, the only sounds were keyboards clicking, then Camille said, "Oh yeah, baby. I found our way in." She turned the laptop so Sophie could see.

SOMEWHERE OUTSIDE NEW ORLEANS

"Gran?" Cass tried to keep her voice steady. "Are you here?"

Cass's brain still felt a little fuzzy, and she couldn't remember what had happened exactly, but she figured out that she was sitting on a hard wooden chair, arms tied to the chair arms, feet tied as well. A blindfold covered her eyes, which scared her most of all.

"I am. Are you all right, child?"

Gran's brisk tone sent relief rushing through her tense muscles, and she sagged back in the chair. "I'm trying to be. What's happening? Where are we?"

Gran let out an annoyed huff. "I don't know where exactly, but I suspect we're being held in the same house I foolishly walked into. I'm sorrier than I can say that I brought you with me."

"I'm not sorry. I'd hate for you to be here all alone." Cass fought back her tears. Gran hated displays of emotion.

"You're right. That would surely be even worse. But I hate that I got you into this situation. When I get my hands on whoever perpetrated this evil on us, they will rue the day they were born."

Hearing Gran's fancy language and harsh determination let Cass finally draw a deep breath. Then another. Gran would take care of her. Make sure they were okay. "This is about the treasure, isn't it? Someone thinks Mom and her friends will find the treasure for them if they use me as bait. And maybe you, too."

What felt like four years passed before Gran finally responded. "You are a very smart girl, Cassandra. I think you are absolutely correct in your thinking, much as I wish it weren't so."

Cass debated for several minutes, then dredged up her courage to ask, "Will they let us go . . . if Mom and her friends get them what they want?" She tried to keep her voice from shaking but wasn't sure she pulled it off.

Gran was silent and Cass's fear grew. "Gran?"

"I honestly don't know, child. But I do know that I will do everything in my power to ensure we both get out of here alive."

It helped, but not much. "What do we do now?"

"We pray. And we think and we pay attention and we plan."

43

LESSER ROBERTS ISLAND—THAT EVENING

Lucien unfolded his length from the dilapidated little car, paid the driver, and set his plumed black hat back on his head at a jaunty angle.

"You make a mighty fine pirate, sir," the driver said with a grin and a wave. "Enjoy the party."

Lucien thanked him and fastened the big brass buttons on his red wool coat. Sweat already trickled down his back, but this was the only costume he'd been able to find that would fit him. He had a part to play tonight, humidity or no humidity. He belted the sword around his waist and pulled the black mask over his eyes as he approached the pirate guarding the barely visible entrance to the estate.

"Welcome, sir. Your invitation, please."

Lucien produced the invite from his inside jacket pocket and handed it over. Pops had finagled it from a friend, who knew a guy, who had a brother-in-law, whose son was part of the estate staff. The man studied the white vellum, checked Lucien's name off his list, and indicated the iron gate behind him. "Welcome to the 37th Annual Pirates' Christmas Ball. Enjoy your evening, sir."

Lucien nodded his thanks and slipped through the gate. He nodded to the heavily armed guard, thankful his coat concealed his own weapon.

He followed a walkway lined with thick shrubs until it opened onto a large brick patio lit with tiki torches. It didn't take more than half a second to determine that Camille hadn't arrived. Yet.

French doors stood open and music from a calypso-style band spilled out of the house. Lucien moved in that direction, surprised by the crowd.

Pirates of every rank and women attired as everything from high-society ladies to tavern wenches gathered in little clusters, drinks in hand, masks hiding their faces. There must have been close to two hundred people milling around, which he hadn't expected on this small island.

He accepted a glass from a passing waiter and sipped, scanning the room. Still no Camille. But she was smart. If he'd figured out to come here, so would she.

A striking woman in a low-cut blouse, high heels, and tight skirt sashayed up to him, enveloping him in a cloud of cloying perfume.

"Hey there, handsome. How about a spin around the dance floor?" She batted her lashes. "For starters."

Lucien started to refuse, then set his glass on a passing waiter's tray and led her to the dance floor, where he could watch for Camille without being obvious. The band switched to a slow number, and she plastered herself to him. Lucien eased back and positioned them as if this were a waltz.

"Don't be so unfriendly, Captain Jack." She pouted and tried to snuggle into him again, and he eased her away, again.

A sudden but unmistakable shift in the atmosphere told him Camille had arrived. He turned his dance partner so he could look over her shoulder and nearly swallowed his tongue.

Over the years, he'd seen many pictures in the local paper, online edition, of Camille dressed to the nines for one charity event or another hosted by her grandmother. Tall and elegant, she'd always been heart-stoppingly gorgeous.

But tonight? She was magnificent. Instead of wearing a gown, she was every inch a pirate in a flowing white shirt and slim black pants with knee-high leather boots. A wide black belt cinched her waist, and a sword hung off her left hip. Her dark hair was tucked under a tricorne black hat, and huge gold hoops dangled from her earlobes, highlighting her sculpted cheekbones. Despite the mask, he'd have known her anywhere.

The song ended and he turned to his dance partner. "If you'll excuse me."

"But we was just getting to know each other," she slurred.

He deftly stepped away. "Enjoy the rest of your evening."

When he turned, he came face-to-face with Camille.

"What are you doing here?" She was even more beautiful when she was annoyed.

The band struck up another number, so he pulled her close and guided them into the dance. She tried to put distance between them, but he ignored the maneuver.

"Hello, Camille. You make an impressive pirate captain, if you don't mind my saying so."

Something like appreciation flickered behind her mask, then disappeared. "Answer the question."

"Same thing you are, I imagine." He quirked up one side of his mouth. "Dancing."

She narrowed her eyes behind her mask. "Don't be obnoxious, Lucien."

Their eyes met, held. Interesting that she'd recognized him as easily as he had her. Perhaps she wasn't as immune to him as he'd assumed, their kiss in Florence notwithstanding. That would be dangerous, for both of them.

"What's that line from *Casablanca*?" He grinned. "'Of all the gin joints in all the towns in all the world, she walks into mine.'"

"You followed me. Again." Her eyes shot flame his way. "I'm tired of it."

He shrugged off her irritation. "I was already on the island when you arrived."

"You're not getting the treasure."

"We'll see." His grin widened as he spun her out, then back into his arms, ignoring her muttering.

She suddenly aimed her megawatt pageant smile at him and momentarily blinded him. She ran a long fingernail down his cheek, then leaned close and whispered, "Stop following me or I'll tell the police you ransacked the convent library."

He laughed out loud at her audacity. "Try it and see what happens. Did I tell you the chief of police on Roberts Island is an old friend of my grandfather's?" The fact that the man was as corrupt as they came didn't need mentioning.

They stared each other down, and it took a few seconds for him to realize the music had stopped and people were staring at them.

Another pirate, this one built like a linebacker, tapped Camille on the shoulder. "Dance, mademoiselle?"

Camille bowed regally and allowed the man to sweep her into his arms and away.

Lucien eased through the crowd and filled a plate at the buffet table. He propped a shoulder against the wall as he ate, keeping Camille in his sights.

Which was how he noticed her dance partner steering her toward a doorway in the back, a tight grip on her arm. Camille was trying to ease away, but the man wouldn't let go.

Lucien dumped his food in a trash receptacle and was halfway across the crowded room before he realized he'd decided to follow.

Camille planted her feet, determined to stay in the ballroom. She'd just told Lucien to leave her alone, but a little help right now wouldn't be amiss. "Let. Me. Go."

Instead of answering, something hard and round, like a pistol barrel, poked her in the back. "Move."

The man opened the door and shoved her through, then pulled it closed behind them.

After the noise and color of the ballroom, it took a few seconds to realize they were in a dim hallway lit only by wall sconces.

"Where are you taking me? This is an outrage." Camille jutted her chin and channeled Gran. "Unhand me immediately or I'll be having a serious discussion with your boss."

Another man appeared from the shadows, opened a door along the corridor, and motioned her inside. "You're about to get your wish. Mr. Williams wants to know who you are and how you snuck into his party."

Camille scrambled for a plausible explanation.

"Darling! There you are! I've been searching all over for you."

Camille angled her head and met Lucien's gaze, which clearly said, "Play along."

"Hey, sugar." Camille grinned and tried to turn toward Lucien, but the goon wouldn't let go of her arm. "I was trying to find the ladies' room when these two"—she paused—"gentlemen took me captive. I know it's a pirate-themed ball, but come on."

Lucien marched up to them and clamped a hand on the shoulder of the big goon holding her at gunpoint and tried to shove him away. "Unhand my wife, if you please."

The guy didn't budge.

Lucien stepped beside Camille, eyed the pistol still pointed at her back, and demanded, "What is going on here? Is this how guests are treated?"

The man's partner asked, "She's with you?"

"Of course. She's my wife."

The second man crossed his arms, then nodded to the linebacker, who holstered his weapon. "You didn't arrive together."

So there were cameras, at least at the entrance. Or very observant staff.

"I was so excited, I came in right away." Camille leaned against Lucien, draping herself around him. "I didn't want to wait while he dealt with the whole check-in rigmarole." She waved an airy hand.

"There is only one main gate onto this property, madam."

Camille sent him a sly grin. "Which is why I took the other path and found a side entrance. Such a pretty walk."

The two men visibly stiffened. Guess they hadn't expected that.

Lucien put his arm around her. "Come along, darling. I think this has gone on long enough." He steered her back down the corridor, and they pretended not to notice the men following them.

Once they returned to the ballroom, Lucien took her hand and led her onto the dance floor a second time, turning her so he could scan the room. As he spun her out, she spotted the two men standing against the wall, arms crossed, watching their every move.

"Time to give them a show, wife of mine," Lucien said as she twirled back into his arms. Without warning, his lips came down on hers.

Startled, Camille sucked in a gasp and automatically pulled back, hands on his chest, ready to shove him away. His deep-blue eyes flashed a warning as he gripped her hands.

Play the part.

Right. She pasted on her best pageant smile and wrapped her arms around his neck while he pulled her closer. Suddenly, they were flush against each other, his arms a protective cage around her. Her heart pounded so hard she worried he might hear it. Without meaning to, she inhaled his familiar scent, a mixture of sandalwood and man, and her knees threatened to shake.

He met her gaze for a brief second and instead of the fury that ignited his kiss at Gallo's villa, Camille glimpsed a flash of want so bright she instinctively closed her eyes against it.

But before she could shore up her defenses, he cupped her cheek and took her mouth with the bold confidence of some long-ago pirate ancestor and jolted Camille into kissing him back with equal fervor, balanced again on that knife-edge between safety and want.

She stepped closer. Want was definitely winning.

As though reading her mind, he deepened the kiss and tightened his hold, which finally brought Camille's protective instincts screaming to life. What was she doing?

She forced herself to pull back slowly, despite the urge to run like the frightened teenager she'd once been. J. T. wasn't here for her to hide behind anymore. She would finally have to face her inconvenient, impractical, terrifying longing for Lucien.

But not tonight. She had to protect Cass. And Lucien was after the portable altar, same as she was.

She stepped out of reach. "They've stopped glaring at us." She nodded regally. "Thank you for the dance, kind sir."

A shiver slid over her at the searing heat still burning in Lucien's eyes.

He winked as he swept off his hat and bowed low. "My pleasure, madam."

Sophie's voice whispered in her comm. "Lose the pirate and meet me outside ASAP. The Reverend Mother is in trouble."

Camille let him escort her off the dance floor, then leaned close and hissed, "I meant what I said. Stop following me."

He raised a brow and his rough voice scraped against her ear. "Or what?"

Camille wasn't one to back down from a challenge. "Or I'll run you through with my sword."

He had the nerve to laugh, the sound skittering along her nerve endings. "You are welcome to try, Princess."

In case there were still eyes on them, Camille kissed his cheek—instead of giving in to the urge to slap the smirk away.

Camille wound her way through the ballroom, then slipped out another set of French doors, whispering, "Where are you, Chameleon?"

44

Lucien followed at a safe distance, willing his heart rate to settle. They were playing a dangerous game, he and Camille, and if he wasn't careful, they'd both get burned, badly. He had to keep her at a distance, for both of their sakes.

But that didn't mean he'd let her walk into danger without backup. These were not people you messed around with.

When she had crossed the room and slipped through another set of French doors, the two goons were right on her tail. Lucien was careful not to lose her in the elaborate garden maze, which belonged somewhere in the English countryside, not the middle of the Caribbean.

He followed her around another bend. The thugs were gaining on her. He ducked through a hedge and walked parallel, surprised when another woman appeared next to Camille, also dressed as a pirate, only she wore a vest over her white shirt and a wide sash over one shoulder. She wasn't as tall as Camille's six feet, but she carried herself with the same air of confidence. He peeked through the foliage. The enforcers were closing in fast.

"Darling? Where are you?" He kept his voice light and playful, like a besotted husband. "I can't find you, my sweet."

He stopped and parted the shrubbery and met Camille's annoyed expression. He jerked his head in the direction of the men following them and held up two fingers.

She nodded, then she and her friend disappeared.

Lucien eased around another shrub so he was closer to the goons. "Darling? Is that you?" He stepped through the hedge and stopped. "Oh, you're not my wife." He grinned indulgently. "She loves to play hide-and-seek." He raised his voice again. "Darling?" When there was no answer, he shrugged and turned away. When he was out of view he said, loudly, "There you are. Come here, love."

He stayed hidden in the hedge until the thugs passed him on their way back to the party.

Then he set off after Camille and her friend.

Sophie was right behind Camille as they hurried down the garden path. "Who was that yummy-looking pirate?"

Camille felt a little shiver go through her at the memory of the appreciative gleam in Lucien's eyes as he'd scanned her costume. "Lucien Broussard."

"I thought I recognized him. I knew he was after the treasure." Sophie sent her a grin. "Didn't realize he thought you were one of the prizes." She waggled her eyebrows and Camille stifled a snort of laughter.

But at the remembered feel of his lips on hers, the temptation to linger, to taste, she cleared her throat. "Nope. Just the actual treasure."

The path curved, beginning its return loop toward the mansion, so they stepped off into the dense jungle beyond the manicured grounds. Camille pulled out her phone and set the GPS to night mode but kept her hand cupped around the screen to block light from escaping.

They wove through the trees and shrubs, thankful there was a bit of moon showing tonight. Enough light to help them find their way along a faint path. Not so much that they were standing under a spotlight.

A rustling sound came from the left.

They froze, listening.

It came closer. Paused. Moved toward them again. There was a thud. Leaves rustled and a branch swayed.

The hair on the back of Camille's neck bristled as a pair of yellow eyes flickered in a nearby tree. The clouds shifted and she stopped breathing. The big cat was huge. And had spots. Jaguar or leopard, maybe. Did those even live here? Or did it belong to their so-called host? Camille had no idea except it was beautiful—and terrifying.

She quietly pulled her sword. Sophie did the same, holding hers like the fencing pro she was. Camille mimicked her stance. Even though their swords were flimsy pieces of cheap metal—mere costume props—but better than nothing at this point.

The big cat eyed them lazily from its perch, tail swishing.

"Keep your eyes on his," Camille whispered. "We need to be ready in case he pounces."

Every muscle in her body tensed as the big cat suddenly coiled all its muscles, ready to spring.

A loud crash sounded from behind them and the cat froze, eyes darting back and forth.

In one graceful movement, it turned and leaped into a nearby tree. From there it landed nimbly on the ground, glanced over its shoulder at them, and disappeared into the night.

Camille's heart hammered in her chest. "Let's go before he changes his mind."

"Maybe we can spot who—or what—scared him off."

Sophie was right, of course, but the urge to bolt was strong.

They hurried farther into the jungle, the path climbing steadily higher, the terrain getting steeper, but they saw no one. They held on to foliage to keep from sliding in the soft mud that never dried after the rain. No sunlight ever made it this far under the tree canopy.

A muffled sound came from behind them.

"Guess we still have a tail," Sophie whispered. "Your friend?"

"Better him than the cat." Camille grabbed another branch and bit back a shriek when something on it moved. She snatched her hand back and leaped forward.

"What?" Sophie scrambled to keep up.

"S-s-snake." Shudders raced over her skin, but Camille wouldn't let herself think about that now. She checked the GPS again. "Fence on the property line should be just ahead."

"Do we know if it's electrified?"

Camille's breath came faster as they rushed ever higher. "Couldn't tell. But it wouldn't surprise me."

The moon slid from behind some clouds again, and Camille saw the fence two steps before she would have run headlong into it. She stopped short and Sophie crashed into her back.

"Found the fence."

Behind them, the sounds grew closer. There was no doubt they were being followed. The only question was whether it was man or beast.

Lucien had done enough recon in Afghanistan that following Camille and her friend was child's play. So was keeping an eye on Williams's goons, who also followed them. It was the large cat also keeping pace that gave him pause. He held his weapon at the ready but really hoped he wouldn't have to shoot the magnificent creature. Not only would that be a shame, it would bring every goon on the property running.

The only reason Camille and her friend would head this direction was to gain access to the convent farther up the side of the mountain. But why not just go by road? Why try to sneak in this way?

He paused to listen, smiling as the answer occurred to him.

Why indeed? They thought the Portable Altar of Countess Alonza was hidden inside this smaller convent—not the one on Roberts Island—and they were planning to snatch it.

Except, of course, he couldn't let that happen.

If anyone nabbed the altar tonight, it would be him.

Behind him, the cat let out a growl that raised the hair on the back of his neck.

Unless the big cat had other ideas.

45

Camille froze as the big cat screamed somewhere behind them.

Sophie nudged her back. "Don't stop now, Eagle Eye."

With a quick nod, Camille grabbed the eight-foot chain-link fence, relieved when no jolt of electricity shot through her, and started climbing. Sophie hopped up beside her and did the same.

Camille swung one leg over the top, but as she shifted, she snagged her sleeve and almost fell headfirst down the other side. She yanked. Nothing happened.

Sophie clambered over and landed nimbly on the ground. "Hurry up." Then she muttered, "This is why I work alone."

Determined not to slow them down, Camille gave another tug and ignored the tearing sound as she broke free. She scrambled down and jumped to the ground, desperate to catch up.

She'd just spotted Sophie through the thick foliage when the ground by her feet exploded. She stifled a yelp and sped up.

Williams's goons had found them.

She kept running.

"Hard left. Hard left," Sophie said in her ear.

Camille turned and crashed into the trunk of a tree. She bounced off with a muffled "Ow."

"Other left." Sophie's tone held definite laughter.

Camille changed directions, rubbing her forehead. "Not funny."

"No, but kinda." Sophie's breath came in short pants.

They were running almost straight uphill now, grasping branches as handholds.

"Don't stop now, girl. Not much farther." Sophie kept up a running commentary as they climbed.

Camille felt like her lungs were trying to pull air through a wet blanket, the humidity was so thick. She didn't check to see if anyone was still following. All her concentration was on putting one foot in front of the other. She'd been a fool to stop running regularly the last few months.

"Stop. Moving. The. Cheese," she panted.

Sophie's chuckle sounded in her ear. "It's just up ahead. Promise."

True to her word, lights appeared through the shrubbery. The steep climb leveled off, and the vines that kept tripping them up gave way to neatly clipped hedges.

"This way," Camille whispered. They took off, staying in the shadows.

The back entrance to the convent was on the opposite side of the brick courtyard. There were neat paths bordered by plants, with ground lighting every few feet.

Somewhere a door opened and a male voice said, "I will not ask again."

A muffled female voice begged, "Please. Don't do this."

"Hand over the altar. Now."

A gunshot reverberated, and several women screamed just as the door closed.

Sophie pulled her sword from its scabbard, and Camille reached into the small pouch at her waist as they raced toward the door.

They stepped into a dimly lit hallway. Ahead, the space opened up into the convent chapel. Candles flickered in the high-ceilinged room.

A strong hand grabbed Camille's arm from behind and she twisted away, pulling her sword to defend herself.

The Reverend Mother sucked in a breath and drew her hand back, clutching the box to her chest. She jerked her head down the hall. They hurried to keep up.

She slipped into a small office and closed the door behind them. "Please. You were right. Take it and keep it safe. It can't end up in the wrong hands. It would be too dangerous."

"You're worried someone will reassemble the Liar's Treasure?" Camille asked.

"Right now I'm more concerned about what someone might do to get their hands on the altar. We know it is a crucial piece. Please, keep it safe and return it to us when the danger has passed. I pray it isn't too late."

The distant sound of another gunshot filtered through the heavy door.

"What about the sisters?" Camille jerked her head toward the hallway.

The Reverend Mother made the sign of the cross. "All the sisters have sworn to protect the altar, with their lives, if necessary."

"Let's see if we can't avoid that." Camille took the box, which was both smaller and heavier than she expected, and quickly slipped it into the small, padded backpack Sophie had pulled from under her pirate vest.

"Trade me." Sophie slipped off the wide sash she'd been wearing diagonally across her chest and tossed it to Camille.

"Why?" Camille slipped the sash over her head. "I can take the backpack." They'd secreted the Book of Days inside the sash, secured in a double layer of waterproof pouches. They couldn't risk leaving it inside their cottage. But they didn't want to be too obvious about carrying it, either.

Sophie shrugged and started for the door. "I'm used to carrying a backpack. You're used to carrying your camera bag in front of you."

"Makes sense. Let's go."

In case one of them was caught, they'd decided to keep the pieces separate.

"Go with God," the Reverend Mother whispered as they slipped out the door. "Follow this corridor, then turn right and you will find the back entrance to the chapel."

Lucien watched Camille and her friend slip inside the convent. He hurried after them and had just stepped inside the corridor when he heard shouting and a gunshot. He took off in that direction.

He reached the chapel and stood flat against the wall, then leaned around the corner for a quick peek. A tall man dressed all in black, including the ski mask over his face, held a nun at gunpoint in front of the simple altar. Eight nuns sat huddled together in the front pew.

The man tightened his grip on the terrified-looking, heavyset sister standing in front of him and jabbed the barrel of the gun against her temple. "I am out of patience. Unless you tell me where it is, right now, I'll put a bullet in her head."

The sisters let out alarmed protests, making the sign of the cross.

Lucien scanned the cavernous room and eased along the side wall, keeping one eye on the gunman while searching for something to use as a distraction.

He spotted a freestanding candelabra and stepped up next to it, wrapping his left hand around the stand. The candles were lit, so that should help.

But before he could toss it, he caught movement from the front of the chapel, behind the gunman.

Camille tiptoed silently toward the altar while her friend approached from the other direction. The lighter in Camille's hand flickered as she lit a fuse. She tossed something toward the gunman.

It hissed for half a second and then exploded, sending a shower of sparks and thick smoke through the room. The nuns screamed.

Lucien didn't hesitate. He launched himself toward the row of nuns just as Camille barreled through the smoke and grabbed the man's hand. She yanked the weapon free and tossed it away before she twisted his hand up behind his back.

"This way, Sisters," Lucien shouted, waving his arm to indicate the side exit while keeping himself between them and the gunman, just in case. Though Camille and her friend were tying him up like a steer at a rodeo.

Lucien and the nuns were almost to the side door when Williams's goons from the party burst in from the rear, guns drawn.

"Duck and run, Sisters!" He pivoted and grabbed the candelabra, then tossed it at the two men, hitting the first one square in the chest with the cluster of lit candles.

The man screamed as his jacket caught fire. He yanked it off and stomped on it, but when he realized his shirt was still burning, he stopped, dropped, and rolled.

His cohort didn't offer help, just leaped over him and ran for Lucien.

Lucien ducked behind a thick column and stuck out his foot, surprised when the guy went sprawling.

He made sure the fire was out before he took off. The idea was to slow them down. Not burn down the chapel.

The nuns had disappeared, so he hurried after Camille and her friend, sliding around the corner in time to see them slip out a back door. Williams's two goons burst out another door, saw them, and took off at a sprint.

"Camille!" He indicated a smaller door cut in the side of the building.

She caught sight of him, shouted, "This way, Sophie!" and both women raced in his direction.

He slammed the door behind them, slid the bar across the opening. He flicked on his phone flashlight, illuminating a stone staircase that spiraled down. Pounding sounded outside the door, then a bang, as if one of the men had put his shoulder into it. They heard a muffled curse, then another bang. The stout wood held. But for how long?

They rushed down the circular stairs. The farther they went, the more damp and slippery the steps became.

"Where are we going?" Camille asked.

"If my research is correct, this leads under the convent and into the cave system inside the mountain."

"But how will we get out?" Camille's friend eyed him over her shoulder, her suspicions clear.

"Again, if everything I read is correct, the caves lead to an underground cove and a way out by water."

"And if you're wrong?" Camille raised an eyebrow.

"Then we're trapped."

"Nice," Sophie muttered.

"You have a better idea?" He switched his phone to his other hand. The light helped, but not much.

"Nope." She shook her head and they kept going.

Down. Down. Down.

He stayed in shape, but even his thighs were protesting after what felt like eighty flights of stairs. He was also starting to get dizzy from going round and round.

He stopped, grinned in triumph. "Hear that?"

They paused, all breathing hard. Sure enough, the unmistakable sound of lapping water reached them.

They hurried down several more flights before the staircase spilled into a large cavern. He held up his phone flashlight and the two women did the same.

"Whoa." Camille turned in a slow circle. "This thing is huge."

The ceiling of the cavern easily reached thirty feet in the air. Water filled the area below them like a giant underground swimming pool.

"Ugh. Bats." Sophie aimed her phone flashlight up high. "Lots. Not a fan."

He shone his light into one of the corners and grinned. "My contact came through, though."

A small wooden boat that had clearly seen better decades had been shoved up out of the water and onto a rock ledge. Even more important, there was a small outboard motor attached.

Just as they reached the boat, they heard pounding feet running down the staircase. Sound was distorted here so Lucien wasn't sure how close they were, but he wasn't taking any chances. "Let's get this thing in the water."

It took all three of them, but they muscled the boat off the ledge and hopped in. Lucien grabbed the tiller and yanked hard on the pull cord.

The engine sputtered to life just as the masked gunman from the chapel burst into view.

46

"Get down and hang on!"

Camille bent forward as far as she could go, gripping the sides of the small boat as Lucien turned them in a circle, sending a spray of water and waves toward the gunman. They bounced over their own wake as the boat shot forward.

Instead of heading toward the lighter area that appeared to be the mouth of the cave, Lucien headed toward a pitch-dark, narrow passageway leading inland.

She made eye contact with Sophie, who wore a similar expression.

Then they entered the passage and Camille couldn't see the hand in front of her face. "Do you know where you're going?" she whispered.

"Hopefully."

Her head snapped around. Lucien had one hand on the tiller, night-vision goggles over his eyes. He held his phone in the other hand, GPS in night mode. The sliver of illumination showed one side of his mouth curved up in a lopsided grin. "You can sit up now."

The narrow channel twisted and turned, and Cass's research

suddenly made sense. No wonder the island had been a haven for pirates and privateers. What a perfect way to smuggle cargo in and out with no one the wiser. Apparently, Rommy Williams, the owner of the estate, was a descendant of some of those pirates.

The minimal light from Lucien's phone showed rock walls on either side and a fairly low ceiling, which meant cargo would have to be carefully packaged to get through the channel.

After what felt like ten minutes or so, the passage suddenly opened again and they found themselves in another cavern.

This one made the first appear small by comparison. They shone their lights around as they approached the stone quay at the water's edge.

Camille pointed her flashlight toward the cavern opening. "Some pirate could easily bring his ship inside here and no one would ever know." Her quiet words echoed off the walls.

"I've always found it extremely helpful myself."

The three of them froze as the masked gunman from the convent stepped from the shadows, his weapon pointed directly at Camille.

Camille's eyes flicked from the weapon to the man. He had his flashlight pointed directly in her face as he stepped to the edge. The water was about a foot below him. "Pull your boat up here." His voice confirmed the sinking feeling in her gut. This was the same man who'd appeared atop the stone wall at Caesar Gallo's estate in Florence. He wouldn't be happy that she'd bested him.

But there was no way he was getting the altar.

She stood in the small boat, feet spread to keep her balance, and set her hands on her hips, within easy reach of her sword. Lucien inched closer to the edge.

Several cleats used to tie up boats were spaced at intervals. Camille said, "Toss me a line, would you, Lucien?" She nodded over her shoulder, hand on her sword, hoping he understood what she wanted him to do.

"Tide's rushing out," Lucien said quietly.

Which meant they wouldn't have to fight the current as they headed for the mouth of the cave. The water would sweep them along.

All she had to do was get them away from the gunman.

"Here you go."

She turned toward Lucien as he tossed a coiled line. But he threw it toward Sophie, which was exactly the opening Camille needed. She slid her sword from its scabbard as she whirled around, using her momentum to knock the weapon from the gunman's hand.

It made a satisfying splash as it hit the water.

Lucien shouted, "Hold tight!" as he veered them away from the dock.

The man leaped toward their boat and landed halfway inside, his legs still in the water.

As he scrambled for purchase, Sophie pounded his arms so he couldn't get a solid grip. Camille planted her right boot on his chest and knocked him backward into the water. He thrashed around as the salty liquid closed over his head.

"Waves!" Lucien shouted. He maneuvered the boat like the experienced captain he was, but between the rushing tide and the man's splashing, they bounced on the swells. "Make sure there's nothing in the water." He raised his voice to be heard above the motor.

Camille pointed her phone flashlight ahead of them and Sophie turned hers on, too. It didn't do much to illuminate the cavern, but it was enough for Lucien to navigate.

"There!"

Lucien swerved to avoid the log, then another, as they zigzagged their way down the rock-lined channel.

Suddenly, they heard another boat motor. Behind them, Camille spotted an inflatable Zodiac racing toward them, Williams's goons from the estate inside. "Our earlier escorts are back. Better get the lead out, husband of mine."

Lucien's teeth gleamed in the dim light. "Anything you say, dear." He pushed the throttle and the little motor struggled to keep up.

The closer they got to the mouth of the cave, the faster the water rushed through the narrow opening before it exploded out into the ocean. Boulders on either side peeked from just below the surface as waves crashed over them.

"Hang on tight," Lucien said. "There's a reason they call this the Devil's Cauldron."

A huge wave hit the rocks and burst over them, soaking everyone to the skin.

Before they could shake the water from their eyes, the current grabbed their little craft and shot it toward the opening just as another huge wave barreled toward them.

47

“Don’t let go,” Camille shouted to Sophie as their little johnboat was thrown around like a rubber duck in a bathtub.

Lucien had the tiller in a white-knuckle grip to keep the boat on the backs of the waves so he didn’t stuff the bow under the water.

But the little outboard was no match for the Cauldron.

Camille’s stomach swooped and dropped with each wave. Sophie had turned green. “Keep your eyes on the horizon!” Camille shouted to be heard over the rushing water.

Sophie nodded and tipped her chin up, breathing through her nose.

A quick peek over Lucien’s shoulder showed the Zodiac gaining on them. She hitched her chin toward Lucien. “Bad guys! Incoming!”

Lucien glanced back just as a giant wave lifted their boat up, up, up.

Camille felt the heat leave her face as panic swept over Lucien’s expression.

She met Sophie's eyes and tightened her grip on the gunwales. "Please, God, get us out of here alive!"

Like a giant hand in a bathtub, the wave flung them out of the Cauldron. They sailed over the wave and hit the next trough with enough force that her teeth rattled and she could feel her vertebrae smack together. Camille expected the boat to break apart. Her hands ached and her stomach churned, but she fought to hold on.

They slid over another wave, then another as Lucien maneuvered with everything he had. But the waves just kept coming.

Just when Camille thought she couldn't hold on another second, they rounded the northern edge of Lesser Roberts Island.

She gasped in shock.

They were not getting away that easily. The Ghost stood at the helm of the twenty-four-foot center console, his v-hull cutting through the Cauldron with an ease that the little wooden johnboat couldn't dream of. Not that handling the Cauldron would ever be easy. But a boat designed to handle it was definitely a plus. He was glad he'd followed his instincts and hidden his vessel in a side cavern, just in case. He always had a plan B.

Ahead of him, the tiny wooden craft slammed into wave after wave, like a child's toy. He sliced through the water, one eye on the wooden boat and the other on the idiots in the Zodiac also in hot pursuit.

Not happening.

There was no way they were getting their hands on that altar.

He reached into the glove box and withdrew his spare weapon, then tucked it at the small of his back as he nudged the throttle.

The guy at the tiller of the wooden boat had skills. He'd give him that. A lesser captain would have flipped it ten seconds into the Cauldron.

But that would have seriously messed with his plan.

He kept the bow up and rode the backs of the waves until he cleared the Cauldron. Then he eased the throttle forward and gradually picked up speed.

No need to hurry. That little boat wasn't getting very far ahead of him.

But first, time to remove the competition.

He angled his boat to intercept the Zodiac and pulled out his weapon.

A crack of thunder startled Lucien. A squall line was approaching fast, lightning splitting the sky. He hadn't expected that, not in December, when it was usually dry. Thunderstorms were more of a summer thing.

But expected or not, it was blowing in quick, pushing more water and waves ahead of it. They couldn't seem to catch a break. Williams's goons in the Zodiac were gaining on them.

Worse, a center console had just burst out of the Cauldron and was also aimed in their direction. If he was not mistaken, the masked gunman from the caves manned the helm.

He wouldn't be happy they'd escaped.

Lucien frowned. Cave Guy also obviously had skills and experience at boat handling.

Worse, his boat had enough power to intercept them in a matter of minutes.

Priority one was protecting Camille and Sophie.

But he also had no intention of letting this guy take off with the altar. Neither woman had mentioned it, but the bulky shape and weight of the item in Sophie's backpack could be nothing else.

He considered several scenarios to outwit Cave Guy. He'd always subscribed to the theory that the best defense was a good offense.

Lucien whipped the boat around and headed back the way they'd come.

Camille's eyes went round with horror as she glared at Lucien over her shoulder. "What are you doing?"

"You still as good at throwing a baseball as you were in high school?"

"Yes, but what does that have to do—?"

"Reach into my right coat pocket." He shouted to be heard above the wind and waves.

Camille swiveled around on the narrow wooden bench seat and met his eyes, ignoring the intensity in them. Now was not the time to be thinking about that kiss and her long-standing and ridiculous attraction to the man.

She leaned forward and her fingers brushed over several objects in his coat pocket. She pulled a handful out. They were a lot heavier than she expected. "What are these?"

"Musket balls. I found a pile of them next to the quay. Figured they might come in handy."

"What do you want me to—?" She broke off as he grinned. "I can't hit those guys from here."

"That's why we're going to get closer. You throw the musket balls." He nodded to Sophie as he handed her his knife. "You poke a hole in their boat."

The only similarity between a baseball and a musket ball was that they were both round. The weight difference was insane, but Camille smiled. Yeah, she could absolutely make this work.

She dipped back into his pocket until she'd transferred all twelve musket balls to her own pocket, testing their weight as she transferred them, calculating the distance they'd have to travel.

When she glanced at Lucien, their eyes met, held for a beat too long.

"You got this, Princess."

She studied the waves, ignoring Sophie's raised eyebrow. She grabbed one of the musket balls and blocked everything from her mind but the Zodiac speeding toward them. Lucien had set them on a direct collision course, starting a deadly game of chicken.

"Get ready!"

Her heart raced as the other vessel headed closer.

And closer.

And closer still.

The goon in the bow of the Zodiac raised his arm.

Camille tightened her fingers around the musket ball, pretending his arm was the catcher's mitt and she was standing on the pitcher's mound.

By the time Lucien shouted, "Now!" she was already in motion. With the chop, she couldn't risk standing, so she twisted on the hard bench, pulled her arm back, and sent her game-winning fastball into the hand holding the weapon.

Direct hit. The gun went flying as the guy cried out and grabbed his hand, his curses echoing over the waves.

The goon at the tiller hit the throttle, and the Zodiac picked up speed.

Camille stifled the urge to close her eyes. She'd never been good at playing chicken. Certainly not on the water, during a storm.

"Keep throwing!" Lucien shouted even as Camille wound up for another pitch.

This one dropped into the water short of its target.

She grabbed another, nailing the gunman in the shoulder as he tried to stand up. He slumped onto the seat and disappeared from view.

Camille fished another musket ball out of her pocket and aimed straight at the goon's hand on the tiller. It bounced off and he yelped and let go for just a second.

It was enough to send the boat out of control.

The Zodiac whipped around, sending a wall of water straight toward their little boat.

Just then, another wave caught their vessel.

They rode the swell higher as the Zodiac dropped into the trough in front of them.

Camille's stomach dipped sharply. This was not going to end well.

"Get ready, Sophie!" Lucien shouted.

Camille dropped onto the seat, gripping the gunwale as the swell pushed their boat higher.

Sophie was on her knees, eyes glued to the Zodiac as the waves pushed it closer and closer.

As their boat slid down the front of the wave, the Zodiac's bow rose.

Sophie gripped the wooden bench seat with her left hand, knife held in her right, her entire focus on the inflatable boat. She'd only have one chance, and Camille whispered a prayer that she would make it count.

When the Zodiac's bow slid under their craft, Sophie leaned forward and jabbed her knife into the side.

It bounced off the vinyl.

"No!" Sophie gripped the knife in both hands and stabbed the side of the boat with every ounce of her strength.

Camille let out a relieved breath at the sharp hiss of air.

But in the next heartbeat, Lucien's boat came up out of the water and all three of them were tossed into the churning sea.

"Swim for the boat!" Camille shouted to Sophie, who struggled to stay afloat while keeping her grip on the backpack. She muttered a quick prayer that the weight of the portable altar wouldn't pull her friend to the bottom of the sea.

48

"Over here!"

Camille turned in a circle, one hand on the sash that wanted to float up in front of her face. Thankfully, she hadn't lost it as she fell. She could only hope the waterproof bag was keeping the Book of Days dry. Taking it with them tonight suddenly seemed like a terrible idea.

She spotted Lucien hanging onto the side of their boat, waving his other arm in her direction.

The sky chose that moment to open up, and rain poured down as if God had dumped a wash bucket. She sputtered and spun around again. "Sophie!"

"Here!"

Relief flooded Camille when Sophie's head appeared above the other side of the boat.

She started swimming toward them, fighting the waves.

The sound of another boat's motor reached her just before the center console they'd seen earlier slipped between her and Lucien and Sophie.

Had the driver not seen her?

Camille swam along the opposite side of the center console, out of view, and headed toward the stern of the boat. She approached the motor with extreme caution. One unexpected wave could slam her right into the still-spinning propeller.

She sighed with relief when she spotted the swim ladder. She held on with one hand, slid the rungs down with the other, and then pulled herself up out of the water.

In a crouch, she swung her legs into the boat and started toward Florence, aka the guy with the gun.

"I'm tired of this. Hand over the portable altar or I start shooting."

"I don't have it anymore." Sophie's voice carried over the rain from where she was treading water. "I lost it when I went overboard."

The sudden crack of a gunshot made Camille flinch. *Please, God, no.*

"Get over here. Now."

Camille's knees went weak with relief.

"Okay, okay. Stop shooting." Sophie sounded annoyed.

Camille inched closer to the man, ready to spring into action.

"Toss it up here."

"Can't. It's too heavy."

Florence muttered but grabbed the boat hook and leaned over the side of the boat, his gun hand wrapped around the console post for balance.

Camille didn't hesitate. She leaped toward him, ready to shove him overboard.

She must have made some small noise because he swung Sophie's backpack onto the deck and took aim at her with his other hand.

Camille ducked as a bullet split the air.

She popped back up and shoved him backward, taking them both into the water.

The second she surfaced, she tried to grab him, but he was already swimming for the boat, Lucien and Sophie swimming hard after him.

Camille fought the wind and waves, but he was moving fast.

They had to stop him before he got on board.

More important, they had to get the altar back.

The guy beat them by inches, grabbing the ladder and flinging himself back onto the boat, then scrambling for the helm.

Lucien sprang up the ladder, Sophie right behind him.

Sophie reached down and grabbed Camille's arm. "Quick!"

Camille had one foot on the bottom rung when the guy hit the throttle. She flung herself up the ladder and dove into the boat headfirst. She banged her shoulder and hit her head hard, but she made it. It all happened so fast.

She blinked away the dizziness and scrambled to her feet.

Lucien was trying to wrestle the gun away from Florence.

Sophie leaped at his back. Florence twisted around and ducked. Sophie lost her grip, and before Camille or Lucien could react, he tossed her overboard.

Lucien dove for the guy's throat, his muscles bulging with the effort. Florence tried to break his hold, clawing at Lucien's hands. They grunted, bouncing off the gunwales, neither giving an inch.

Camille raced to the bow, grabbed a life jacket, and hurled it toward Sophie with as much power as she could muster.

The boat was moving too fast for it to land anywhere near Sophie, but hopefully she could swim to it and hang on. At least until Camille could turn the boat around and go pick her up.

Camille dodged the two struggling men and grabbed the wheel. She hadn't been at the helm since Gramps died two years ago, but she'd been piloting boats since she was a kid. She spun the wheel left to turn them around but turned too sharply. The boat leaned hard to port and she was afraid it would flip over. She quickly turned the wheel back the other way, but the damage was done.

When the boat's angle shifted, Florence maneuvered Lucien toward the rail. He bent him back farther and farther and threw him overboard, too.

"No!" Camille pulled the throttle back so fast she slammed into the steering wheel.

The force knocked the breath out of her and she fought to draw air, trying to calm down enough to think.

She had to get to them. She had to save them. And the altar.

One hand on the wheel, she was reaching for the throttle when something slammed down on the back of her head and everything went black.

49

Lucien's heart almost stopped when he saw Cave Guy smash something down on Camille's head. She disappeared from sight as he stepped behind the helm, hit the throttle, and took off.

Lucien had to go after her. Which meant swimming back to their boat. He'd never be able to catch up, not with their tiny motor, but he had to try.

But where was Sophie?

He whipped around and breathed a sigh of relief when he saw her reach for the life jacket Camille had tossed. Good thinking on Camille's part.

They started swimming toward their little boat, which bobbed in the distance like a child's bath toy.

The rain was still pounding down, and they were both exhausted when sirens suddenly split the air as some kind of official vessel turned on a spotlight and illuminated the scene. "Are you folks okay? We got a distress call about people in the water."

Oh, he'd just bet they did.

The second man tossed a life ring into the water. "Let's get both of you aboard, make sure you're okay before we take you back to port."

"Just take us back to our vessel. Thanks." Lucien pointed over his shoulder toward their boat.

"Sorry. We need to check you out first."

The first officer, who seemed to be in charge, couldn't have been more than twenty-one and was clearly very proud of his position of authority. He tilted his chin up, pointed. "Grab the life ring. Now."

Lucien debated knocking the arrogance off this young pup's face and taking off with their vessel, but ending up in a local prison wouldn't get Camille back.

He nodded to Sophie. She grabbed the ring and let them pull her in while Lucien swam to the vessel.

Once they were aboard, the first officer pulled out a small notebook. "We need you to tell us what happened."

"We got caught in the storm, got tossed out. That's it." He shrugged.

"But we appreciate you coming to our rescue." Sophie sent each man a blinding smile.

After a barrage of questions about exactly nothing, Lucien was ready to toss both men overboard. But he refrained, and finally the officers slid the vessel alongside their little craft.

Lucien climbed down the ladder and hopped into their small boat. Thankfully, the motor caught on the first try, so he motioned Sophie aboard.

He waited until the official vessel turned toward Lesser Roberts Island, then turned in the opposite direction and pushed the throttle as far as it would go. "Hang on."

Sophie gripped the seat as they bounced over the waves. "Why aren't you going after Camille?"

"I am. I think Cave Guy circled around this smaller island and is headed for Roberts Island. I want to catch him before he gets there."

She studied his face for a moment. "What if you're wrong?"

Lucien's jaw tightened. He didn't want to consider the possibility. "Then we come up with plan B."

Sophie nodded and kept her chin up, eyes on the horizon as they rattled and bounced their way over the choppy sea.

Camille came to with a groan and slowly moved her head from side to side, trying to get her bearings. She was lying on the deck at the stern. She started to get up and realized her hands were tied behind her back, her feet tied together at the ankles. Her head throbbed and her stomach roiled and she was shivering in her wet clothes. It was all she could do to fight the nausea.

She raised her head just far enough to see Florence at the helm, totally at ease, as though boat handling—and kidnapping—were everyday things.

Her eyes didn't want to focus, which meant she probably had a concussion. Still, she scanned the vessel. Sophie's backpack with the altar was nowhere in sight, so he'd probably tucked it under one of the seats. Which was what she would have done, too, but that didn't help.

Focus, girl. There had to be a way out of this. Would he take her back to one of the islands? Or would he toss her overboard instead?

A shudder raced over her at the thought of sinking into the water, hands and feet tied. She shoved the image away. Drowning was not an option. Cass needed her. And Gran. And maybe the team needed her, too. Lucien's grin when he handed her high heels back to her filled her head, but she shoved the image away.

Survive.

She studied the small deck. No matter how hard she focused or how much she willed it, a weapon wasn't going to magically appear.

God of the impossible, please help.

The Ghost eyed his unwelcome passenger and sighed. Now he had another problem to deal with. Although this one was relatively easy, all things considered.

The storm had cleared out as fast as it blew in, and the moon was shining brightly, like a touristy postcard.

He slowed the engine, then set it at an idle before he turned to get the woman.

Pain exploded in his midsection as she kicked him in the stomach. She'd slithered onto the seat to get enough leverage, and the force knocked him back, bouncing him off the thigh-high railing. He'd have bruises tomorrow and that did not make him happy.

With a growl, he grabbed her by the hair and hauled her to her feet. Feisty thing wouldn't stop twisting and trying to kick him.

"Enough!" he roared. He should have taken care of her on that rooftop in Florence.

She didn't stop fighting.

He heard the sound of an engine and spotted an official boat rounding Lesser Roberts Island, heading straight toward him.

Time to go.

He grabbed the squirming, kicking, biting dervish with both hands and tossed her overboard.

Leaning over the side, he waited while she sank.

Then he hurried back to the helm, shoved the throttle forward, and took off toward Roberts Island.

Camille sucked in a lungful of air before she hit the water. As she sank down, down, down into the clear blue sea, panic reared up inside her. Her heart raced and she struggled against the rope around her wrists. But it held fast.

She finally sank all the way to the bottom and expected her feet to hit sand. Instead, they hit rock. No, not rock, coral. She'd landed on a reef.

It took her a second before that registered. *Thank You, Jesus.*

She dropped into a crouch and pushed off the bottom with every bit of strength she could muster, apologizing to the sea creatures that lived there for disturbing their home.

Her head popped up to the surface and she gasped. Then she rolled onto her back and used her legs to try to keep herself afloat. But without her arms to help, she kept sinking. Not enough to drop all the way back down, but enough that she couldn't keep her head above the water. Every time she sank, she had to kick hard to raise her face high enough to take another breath.

After the fifth time, she was starting to tire.

After the seventh, it was a struggle just to get that next breath.

Dear God, please don't let me die out here.

She started sinking again, and this time she couldn't stop herself. Couldn't kick hard enough.

Down. Down. Down.

Several colorful fish swam by, and she realized they might be the last things she ever saw.

She wanted to cry. Would Cass ever understand just how much Camille loved her?

Her feet hit the coral again. Slid off the edge. Camille kicked to regain her footing, then mustered all her remaining strength and propelled herself to the surface one more time.

50

"There!" Sophie pointed, scrambling to her knees on the seat as Lucien raced to the spot they'd last seen Camille. He'd given Sophie the headlamp he'd hidden in his costume and she was using it like a spotlight.

As soon as they got close enough, he killed the engine and jumped overboard. Where was she? Even though the water was clear, there were shadows telling him there was coral below. He swam down, searching left and right.

Come on, Camille. Where are you?

Between the weight of her pirate costume and the fact that Lucien saw the guy hit her in the head, she might have sunk like a stone.

He dove deeper, swimming parallel to the reef. There were deep chasms between the coral and he checked those, panic rising as his supply of air rapidly ran out. Where was she?

Another scan of this section and he pushed off the bottom and shot to the surface to gasp for air. "Has she surfaced?"

"Not yet. But I think I see a darker shadow over there." Sophie pointed about five yards away.

He filled his lungs and dove. *Please, God.* It was all the prayer he could muster.

He'd begun to think he still wasn't in the right place when he spotted her white shirt, a circle of red staining the water near her head. Her body floated just above the coral, her arms and legs tied.

Fury shot him through the water like a missile. *Absolutely not.*

Using every bit of strength he had, he scooped her into his arms and put his whole body into pushing off the bottom, desperate to get her to the surface, to much-needed oxygen.

Their combined weight stopped his upward momentum about a foot short of the surface. He kicked harder, then circled her from behind and raised both of their heads above the water. He dragged in a breath, but she didn't. "Breathe, Princess. Breathe."

A splash and Sophie appeared beside him. They dragged Camille back to their little boat. Lucien scrambled in and Sophie held Camille next to the boat so he could haul her over the side.

When he reached a hand back for Sophie she said, "I've got this. Take care of Camille."

He laid Camille on her side in the bottom of the small craft, careful of her head wound, and checked her breathing.

Nothing.

He slashed the ropes around her wrists and ankles, rolled her onto her back, and started CPR.

"Come on, Princess. Breathe."

He kept all of his focus on counting compressions, gave two breaths, checked again. Panic kicked, hard, when there was no response. *Please, God.*

Another round of compressions and she finally started gagging. He rolled her to her side and heaved out a relieved breath when she coughed up what seemed like gallons of water.

He yanked off his shirt and wrapped it around her head before he restarted the motor.

When he turned back, she was blinking up at him, expression dazed.

Dropping beside her, he pushed the hair back from her face and smiled. "Welcome back, Princess."

"Thanks for saving me." She smiled weakly, then rolled over and puked in his lap.

Lucien threw back his head and laughed. *Thank You, God.*

LESSER ROBERTS ISLAND—LATER THAT DAY

When Camille woke up, she winced at the sunlight peeking through the blinds. And the pain at the back of her head. She gingerly poked it, felt the bandage. She turned her head slowly, trying to remember where she was. *Right. Island. Beach cottage.*

More bits and pieces of the night before slammed through her aching head. Masquerade ball and Lucien's kiss. The portable altar and boat chase. Abject terror when she was tossed overboard. Then Lucien yelling at her to breathe, and her shock at the horrible scars on his back.

She sat up in bed, only to flop back down when a wave of dizziness hit her. She groaned, breathing through her nose until the pain in her head subsided and the nausea passed.

Easing up, she checked her phone and frowned, trying to clear the cobwebs from her brain. Still nothing from Gran or Cass. Alarm shivered through her when she called and it immediately rolled to voicemail. She kept her voice calm as she left a message. "Hey, Cass, call or text me and let me know how things are going, okay? And I'll fill you in on the pirates' ball I attended last night. Love you, baby girl."

She hung up, then dialed again, the knot in her gut tightening. "Hello, Gran. Please check in and let me know how you and Cassandra are doing. Thank you." Camille wanted to believe they were fine and they'd call when they could, but every instinct was screaming that something was wrong.

She forced herself to take several more calming breaths before she slid her legs over the side of the bed, then risked standing. *Whoa.*

She grabbed the wall, waited. A few more breaths and she walked a couple steps, feeling a bit stronger with every minute, despite the pounding headache.

She eased open the door, and the smell of coffee wafted into the room.

Sophie sat on the rattan sofa, her laptop open. She guided Camille to a stool at the counter. "How are you feeling?"

"Truth? My head hurts, I'm dizzy, and not a little queasy."

"Yeah. Not surprised. Lucien has a lot of first-aid training, and he thinks you have a concussion. You refused to go to the ER, but he thought you would be okay."

She suddenly remembered someone telling her to open her eyes. "Wait. Did you check on me all night?"

Sophie shrugged. "It's what friends do, right?"

"Yes. Thank you." Camille sighed. "I really messed up last night. I was trying to help."

Sophie handed Camille a mug of coffee and took a sip of her own. "You didn't screw up. I did. That guy escaped with the portable altar."

Camille met her friend's eyes. "It's the same guy from Florence, so he followed us somehow."

"That's my guess. Now we have to figure out how to get it back. Fast."

Her stomach took another spin. "I still haven't heard from Cass or Gran. When I called, it went right to voicemail." She took a breath. "Again."

Sophie stilled. "Have you checked with your gran's housekeeper? Maybe she's heard from them? Cell signal isn't great here."

"I didn't even think of that." She called Mrs. H., but the housekeeper hadn't heard from Gran either.

"Let's give it a little more time before we panic, okay?"

Camille nodded, but she saw her own worry reflected back at her.

"The good news is we still have the Book of Days." Camille set down her coffee and walked into her room as fast as her aching head would allow. She grabbed the heavy sash and opened the zipper.

She pulled out the plastic case, opened it, and froze. She blinked, trying to get her brain and eyes to work together. She slowly shook her head, focused again.

Her heart started galloping as panic slid through her veins.

The Book of Days was gone.

51

"Sounds like you two had a wee bit more excitement than we did." Mercy eyed them from the screen.

Camille and Sophie were huddled on the couch of their little cottage in front of Camille's laptop, video chatting with Mercy and Hank, who were in their Airbnb in Rome, recounting the last twenty-four hours.

"Yeah. Glad you're not dead," Hank said.

Camille burst out laughing, then winced. "I can always count on you to keep things in perspective, Hank."

The other woman shrugged. "Just saying. By the way, you both look like you've been keelhauled."

Sophie chuckled. "Bet you've been waiting to use that term, haven't you?"

"Oh, I've got lots more, but they'll keep. So, to make sure we're all on the same page, Williams's two goons chased you from the masquerade ball, Camille's high-school crush showed up to complicate things, the Reverend Mother gave you the portable altar for safekeeping, some other guy showed up with a gun, you escaped through some caves in the mountain, took off in boats, ended up in the water in a storm. Camille was kidnapped, hit in the head, thrown overboard, and almost drowned, but Lucien and Sophie rescued you and got you both back to Roberts Island." Hank sat back and grinned. "You can't make this stuff up."

Camille grimaced while Sophie let out a frustrated sigh.

"Oh no. What else?" Mercy glanced from one face on the screen to the other.

Sophie hung her head.

"Don't you do that," Camille said sternly. "It wasn't your fault."

"What wasn't?" Hank demanded. "Come on, spill it."

Sophie lifted her chin. "It is my fault. Cave Guy—who is actually the same guy from Florence who tried to steal the Book of Days—escaped with the portable altar."

Hank said something under her breath.

Mercy gasped. "How?"

"He took it from me at gunpoint and put it on his boat."

"I climbed aboard trying to get it back," Camille added.

Sophie crossed her arms and glared at Camille. "And got a concussion for your trouble."

A moment of silence passed before Hank asked, "Any idea where he went?"

"No. He called the authorities to check on us to buy himself time to get away. He was long gone before Lucien dropped us off."

Camille cleared her throat, ducked her head. "So about the Book of Days—"

"Say it isn't so." Hank studied her face. "But it obviously is. What happened?"

"Sophie hid the Book of Days in an old-fashioned-type sash for the party. We wrapped it in several waterproof layers and made the bag part of her costume."

Sophie picked up the story. "When the Reverend Mother gave me the portable altar, we figured it was safer to each take one piece of the treasure, so Camille took the book and I took the altar since I'm used to wearing a backpack."

"Should never have given it to me," Camille muttered.

"You both need to stop this, right now."

Camille and Sophie both stared at Mercy in open-mouthed astonishment. The soft-spoken nun rarely raised her voice. "The fault, as you put it, lies squarely with the thieves who stole the items from you. I know you both. You did everything in your power to protect the treasure. Beating yourselves up helps nothing."

"She's right." Hank nodded. "We need to focus on getting them back." She eyed Camille. "Who has the Book of Days? Florence?"

Camille shrugged, but Sophie said, "I think Lucien took it after we fished Camille out of the water. Though he did do CPR first, by the way."

Camille froze in shock. *He did?*

On-screen, Mercy made the sign of the cross.

"Like I said, glad you're not dead, Camille," Hank said.

"After she coughed up several gallons of water, we took the sash off and Lucien wrapped her in an old tarp to keep the wind off her. He must have taken it as we headed back to the island."

Mercy cocked her head. "Isn't it equally possible that Florence took it when Camille was unconscious on his boat?"

Camille hadn't even considered that. "Yeah, absolutely. I'm not sure how long I was out."

Hank considered it. "Then our next step is to figure out who has the Book of Days. And then figure out how to get it and the portable altar back."

"Without knowing who this guy is, where do we even start searching?"

"I think Camille should ask Lucien if he took the book."

Everyone gaped at Mercy, again.

"What? He's got a thing for her. Why wouldn't he admit he has it?"

Sophie seemed intrigued. "I agree with Mercy. You should straight-up ask him."

"And if he admits he does?"

"Then we figure out how to take it back, of course."

"Like you did in Cologne, Sophie." Mercy grinned. "That kiss with Mac provided the distraction we needed to get the painting back from him." She paused. "How is Mac, by the way?"

Sophie waved that away, though everyone saw the color race over her cheeks. "It was a means to an end. We need to do something similar if Lucien has it. Or, Camille should."

Hank drummed her fingers, and they could see her shuffling possibilities. "Either way, we need to bait a trap. This Florence guy will go to ground until the interest surrounding the portable altar dies down. He won't surface unless he has a compelling reason to. Same thing if he—or Lucien—has the Book of Days." Hank aimed her question at Camille and Sophie. "What can we do to lure them out of hiding to get both pieces back?"

Camille cleared her throat. "Before we get to that, I can't get ahold of Gran or Cass." She watched the concern bloom in their faces. She needed their perspectives to make sure she wasn't overreacting.

"How long since you've heard from them?" Mercy asked.

"Not since yesterday. Mrs. H. hasn't heard from Gran, either."

"I said we should give them a bit more time. Cell service can be sketchy here," Sophie added.

"I agree with Sophie," Hank said. "Let's wait a bit in case it's something simple. In the meantime, we need a plan."

Camille took a deep breath, acknowledging the wisdom of their thinking, trying to quiet the panic and instead trust. "Okay, we'll circle back to that. Right now, I think we're missing another important step," Camille said. "We still don't have the altar pieces. Did you two make any progress there?"

"We weren't just sitting around drinking coffee, in case you wondered. Though that might have been more helpful." Hank shot them a rueful smile.

"What happened?" Camille yawned, then gingerly touched the back of her head. "Sorry. Still have a headache." She took another careful sip of coffee.

Hank and Mercy took turns outlining their trip to the museum and chat with the curator, ending with the guys with guns chasing the three of them down the street.

"Here's where it gets most interesting," Hank said. "When we drove past, the curator was inside talking with police and one of the gunmen was outside chatting with a police officer like they were old friends." She paused. "We think we have a good idea of where to find the altar pieces."

Camille held up a hand like a traffic cop. "Before we get into that, did you figure out who this gunman is?"

Mercy scrolled through her phone, then held up a photo. "I was able to snap a quick pic before he turned around. Does he look familiar?"

Camille shook her head, winced. "Ouch." Then she examined the photo again. "Actually, now that I'm thinking about it, I'm pretty sure I've seen him somewhere before. . . ." Her fingers flew over her phone, then she held it up so Sophie and Hank and Mercy could see.

A stunned pause followed, then Hank blurted out what they were all thinking.

"This is not good."

52

The man Hank and Mercy had seen was listed on the board of directors of the Becker Foundation.

Camille dialed, waited through several rings. "Hey, Jolie. Got a question. Is Jamie Lawson still part of the Foundation's board of directors?" She put the call on speaker.

Jolie paused, cleared her throat. "He was. A retired professor from Scotland, very personable. I think he had a crush on Tara."

The team traded glances.

"They were dating?" Sophie asked.

"I don't think so. Tara said they'd gone out a few times but she wasn't interested so she started politely declining his invitations. Why?"

"You said he *was* on the board. He's not anymore?" Camille asked.

"They told us at the staff meeting this morning that he died overnight. They think he had a heart attack or something while he was driving. We're all very shaken up. I liked him." She drew a shuddery breath.

It appeared that the trail of bodies connected to the Foundation was growing.

Camille typed with her thumbs. "I'm texting you a picture. Is this him?"

A few seconds later Jolie said, "Yes. Why do you have a picture of him?"

"It's a long story. Did they say where he died?"

"He lived in Amsterdam. Police said he was heading home from the airport. One-car accident on an icy road."

"Nobody said where he was coming home from?"

"No. Why?" They heard a shocked gasp. "Oh my goodness. You think someone killed him, too?"

Camille ignored the question. "How are things going for the summit? Anything new we need to know about?"

"Nothing except Jamie dying. And Nelson muttering in his office and then demanding an update on your search every hour or so." Jolie sighed, but there was an edge to her voice.

"Let us know if you hear anything else, especially about Professor Lawson and how he died."

"Wait. What about the treasure? Do you have the Book of Days?"

"We're working on it."

"Where are you? I need something to tell Nelson. He keeps saying, 'We need answers.'"

"Tell him we're in the Caribbean, getting close. Just . . . just string him along and stay out of trouble. We'll keep in touch. You do the same, okay? And seriously, be careful." Camille hung up before Jolie could ask more questions.

After a few moments, Hank said, "Interesting. The same guy chases us in Rome and suddenly he's dead? It begs the question why."

"And also, who was he working for?" Mercy added.

Sophie nodded to Hank and Mercy. "You said you had a lead on the altar pieces?"

Mercy picked up the story. "Since the museum curator mentioned a church in the Moselle region of Germany, we started going through the copy of the Book of Days, looking for churches. We found a beautiful rendering of an altar in the book."

"Yikes. There's an altar in every church. How do we narrow it down?"

Camille noticed Hank's smug expression. "You found the church?"

"Maybe. We think we found the church pictured in the book, and it's in the Moselle region. Whether the altar pieces are there now is another question entirely," Hank said.

Sophie made a "hurry-up" motion. "So? Spill. Where is it?"

"Based on the drawing and the name 'Friedrich' mentioned several lines above the drawing, we think some of the altar pieces may be at Heidelberg Castle in Germany, in the chapel of Friedrich's Wing."

Sophie's fingers flew and she held up a photo. "This it?" At Mercy's nod, she expanded the picture. "Okay, I can see it. Those candlesticks appear to be the ones in the book. But I don't see the jeweled cross or chalices anywhere."

"They wouldn't leave those out where hordes of tourists traipse through every day. Too dangerous." Mercy's voice held authority. "I'd expect those to be safely tucked away somewhere. But still nearby to use for mass."

"Like the portable altar," Camille said.

"Exactly." Mercy nodded. "We did find one more thing, though. The legend says the Liar's Treasure can discern motives, like Ananias and Sapphira, right? Well, we found this phrase in the Book of Days: 'The chain of connection will light the way, burning away lies to uncover the truth.' Next to it is a painting of the portable altar with flames behind it."

"'Chain of connection' is interesting," Sophie said. "Maybe the pieces link together in some way?"

"Definitely something to check on as soon as we find them," Camille said. "Good work, guys."

"Mercy and I are heading to Heidelberg as soon as we hang up. How long will it take you two to get here?" Hank asked.

"We'll be there as soon as we can. But don't wait for us. We need to get our hands on that treasure, quick." What Camille didn't say was that if she didn't hear from Cass or Gran soon, she'd be on the next flight to New Orleans to find them. There was trust . . . and there was a mother's instinct. And right now, everything in her said something wasn't right.

She ended the Zoom call and turned to Sophie. "Could you—?"

"I'm already checking flights. You call Lucien."

Oh, I'll call him, all right. Camille opened her contacts and dialed his cell.

"Broussard." Lucien held the phone to his ear and covered the other one so he could hear despite the constant PA-system flight announcements.

"Did you steal the Book of Days while I was lying in the bottom of a boat, half dead?"

He grinned. "Glad to hear you're feeling better, Princess. I was going to call you in a few hours."

"Don't mess with me, Lucien. Yes or no?"

He sighed. "You know I need that book. Same as you."

"Are you back in New Orleans?"

"Yes. Miss me already?"

"Like a rash." She paused. "I'm furious that you stole the book from me. But I hear you did CPR after I almost drowned. And bandaged my head." She cleared her throat. "So thank you."

He'd bet she about choked on the words. "You're welcome. One had nothing to do with the other, by the way. But let's call it even."

"Absolutely not. We're so not even. I need it back, Lucien."

"I just left the hospital. Pops had another heart attack so I caught the first flight back." He heard a boarding announcement for his flight and checked his watch. He still had a few minutes.

"I'm sorry. Is he going to be okay?"

Lucien rubbed the back of his neck. "The doctors are cautiously optimistic, but it'll be a long road."

She paused again. "I need that book, Lucien. You had no right to take it."

He ignored that. "You should have seen Pops's face when he held it for the first time. He's been trying to find it for years. That book is what's keeping him going right now. I can't take that away from him."

"I understand that. But I need it, too. I have to keep my daughter safe."

His stomach clenched at the reminder. Her daughter. Who was also J. T.'s daughter. That was the crux of his dilemma, the one gnawing a hole in his gut. Pops versus Cass. "Tell you what, I'll put the word out everywhere that I have the book so all the crazies chasing her will chase me instead." It sounded lame, even to his own ears.

Camille sighed. "Lucien, you know that isn't—"

Another flight announcement blared. He had to go if he wanted to make his flight to Frankfurt. "We'll figure it out, Princess." He paused. "Promise."

He hurried to the gate and spent the flight poring over the copies he'd made of the Book of Days and trying to figure out how he was going to keep that promise.

Octavia Benoit tried not to let her fear for Cassandra get the best of her. How were they going to get out of here? Cassandra had gone quiet some time ago, and Octavia prayed she'd fallen asleep. Anything for a few moments of escape. Her own bladder was screaming for relief, and she was getting lightheaded from lack of food, so she knew Cassandra was no doubt suffering with the same.

She heard footsteps in the hall and Cassandra roused. "Gran?"

"Shh. Someone is coming. Let me do the talking, all right?"

"Okay."

The fearful quaver in her great-granddaughter's voice made Octavia see red.

The second she heard the door open, Gran started in. "I demand that you release us. Immediately. Do you know who I am?"

No response. But she felt someone step closer. She braced for an attack. "You won't get away with this, you know."

"Do what I say and you'll be fine." The voice was mechanically altered and sent gooseflesh rippling over her arms.

"If I don't check in with Cassandra's mother right this minute, she will move heaven and earth to find us. She may already have called the authorities to track us down. And when she does, you'll wish you'd never been born. I will make absolutely sure of it."

"You do not make the rules here. Or make demands. Do what I say or I can't guarantee your great-granddaughter's safety."

That horrible mechanical voice sent chills down her spine and made Octavia want to rage with fury. The coward, hiding behind his technology. But this wasn't about her. She had to protect Cassandra. She kept her voice calm but firm. "I'll do whatever you want. Just don't hurt my great-granddaughter."

"Stay where you are until you hear the door close."

Octavia flinched when a gloved hand touched her arm. But miraculously, the strap holding her in the chair loosened slightly. Then the other. She held her breath, let it out when the bindings on her legs loosened as well.

The footsteps moved away, toward where she believed Cassandra sat. Then she heard the click of the door closing behind him and the dead bolt turning.

Octavia yanked at her bonds, trying to free her hands and feet. "I think he cut the ropes. Try to get free."

"Working on it." Then Cassandra's voice was right next to her chair. "Here. Let me help."

The blindfold came off, then the bonds, and Cassandra hugged her so tight Octavia feared she'd break a rib. But nothing had ever felt so good. "We're okay, child, we're okay."

"They took our cell phones," Cassandra said.

"Not surprising." Octavia scanned what appeared to be a small bedroom. It was almost completely dark, the only window boarded up from the outside. Two rusting twin-bed frames with musty-smelling mattresses and a thin blanket and pillow on each, plus the chairs they'd been tied to, were the only furnishings. A rusting sink stood in the corner, a chamber pot beside it.

Cassandra tried the light switch, but nothing happened. A small wobbly end table by the door held a flashlight, two sandwiches, and two bottles of water.

Octavia turned on the flashlight and yanked hard on the doorknob, not surprised to find it locked from the outside.

"What do we do now, Gran?"

She kept her voice upbeat. "We eat. And get some sleep. And we keep praying and planning."

Please, God, save us.

53

NEW ORLEANS

"We need to go, Camille," Sophie said for what felt like the fourteenth time.

They were sitting at the departure gate at Louis Armstrong New Orleans International Airport for their flight to New York.

Camille ignored her—again—finger poised over the app to call an Uber to take her home.

She could not, would not, board the plane until she heard from Cass and Gran and knew they were safe.

"Final boarding call for Flight 555 to New York. All confirmed passengers should now be on board." The gate agent faced them as she spoke into the microphone.

Sophie had wanted to book flights from the Bahamas direct to JFK in New York and then on to Frankfurt, but Camille had flatly refused. Not before she heard from Cass or Gran.

Why hadn't they responded? Worry gnawed at her nerves, and she fingered Gramps's shoelace where it was tied to her camera bag. *Please, God.*

Camille sent Cass another text: **I need to know you're okay, baby girl. I can't leave for New York until I hear from you. Text me. Please.**

Sophie stood. "If we don't board right now, we'll miss the flight."

Camille took a deep breath, as much to reach for patience as to calm her pounding heart. "I told you, Sophie. I won't leave until I know Cass and Gran are okay. They still haven't checked in."

"Which could mean nothing." Sophie slipped her laptop case over her shoulder, sighed. "I understand. I do. But Cass will never be completely safe until we get this done."

"She could be in danger *right now*." Camille's voice carried over the empty space, and the gate agent propped her hands on her hips, silently asking if they were coming. "Just go. I'll catch the next flight."

"No." Sophie plopped back down in her seat. "We stay together."

"Last call, ladies," the gate agent said.

Camille checked her phone again. Still no response. "I've called and texted, multiple times. Something's wrong."

"You don't know that."

"I don't know they're safe, either!" Camille hissed.

The gate agent had turned away and was preparing to close the door.

Sophie saw her too, turned to Camille. "We don't know where Gran took them to hide out. If we stay, how will we find them?"

"I don't know! But I will figure it out, if I have to turn over every rock and hiding place in this city."

They eyed each other.

"Ladies, I can't wait."

The agent was slowly closing the door when Camille's phone buzzed. *Cass.*

We're fine, Mom. Geez. Stop worrying already.

Camille held the phone to her chest for a moment, let out a breath. "They're okay. Let's go."

Sophie sprinted for the door, Camille right behind her. They scanned their boarding passes and ran down the Jetway.

The cabin door closed behind them.

Curious eyes followed their progress down the aisle.

The minute they were seated, Camille texted back: **Thank you, baby girl. I'll call you once I'm on the ground.**

"Ma'am, you need to turn off your cell phone in preparation for takeoff."

Camille buckled in, taking deep breaths to slow her frantic pulse. "Thank You, Father," she whispered, throat clogged with tears.

Once they were airborne, she leaned back, popped a Dramamine, then tucked her jacket around her shoulders as a blanket and slept the entire flight.

He clenched his fist around Cassandra's phone, eyeing the text he'd just sent, furious that he'd been put in this position. He pulled out the other phone, finger poised as he debated sending an additional text, but he decided this was enough to keep Camille doing what she needed to do.

The temptation to toss both phones into the nearest trash can and leave town pushed hard, but that would be a foolish play. This was his ace in the hole, his access to information he needed.

A neon sign flashed in the distance, and he marched down the block and slumped into a booth at the back of the diner and drummed his fingers on the table. If Camille was headed for New York, that would buy him some time to get a handle on the other players, figure out his next move, and turn this hand to his advantage.

The game wasn't over until the very last card had been played. And he was absolutely determined to win.

HEIDELBERG, GERMANY

After their call with Camille and Sophie, Hank and Mercy caught a flight from Rome to Frankfurt, then rented a car for the hour-long drive to Heidelberg. Once there, they checked into an Airbnb in the heart of Altstadt, or Old Town, and then went out to hunt up dinner and scope out the town.

Heidelberg, whose university was founded in the fourteenth century, was also famous for its Renaissance architecture, especially the red-sandstone Heidelberg Castle ruins high above Old Town on Königstuhl hill. The rest of the city perched along the banks of the Neckar River and was a popular stop for river cruise ships.

Hank and Mercy strolled through the Christmas Market in the center of Old Town and wandered into several churches, including the well-known Gothic Heiliggeistkirche, to check out the altars and make sure the pieces weren't sitting in plain view somewhere.

They weren't.

Hank was itching to get this done. Get the pieces and get out of Dodge. This waiting around nonsense did a number on her nerves—and made it harder to ignore her craving for a drink. Which annoyed her to no end. But this late in the day, the castle was closed. It would be foolish to try to go there now. Much too conspicuous.

Instead, they found a little restaurant with white walls and dark beams. Hank ordered *Wiener schnitzel* with *spätzle*, and they ate buttered dark bread while waiting for their food.

Hank nodded to Mercy. "Our escorts have arrived."

They pulled the menus up to cover their faces as Ponytail and Scarface, who had been on their tail since Oradea, Romania, strolled past the restaurant.

"Wonder when the rest of our tails will show up?" Mercy speared another bite of her *Rouladen*, rolled-up beef covered in dark gravy.

"Only a matter of time." Hank took another bite. "Anything from Camille or Sophie? They should have landed in Frankfurt by now."

"Patience, grasshopper," Mercy teased.

Hank growled in response.

54

HEIDELBERG—THE NEXT DAY

It was a clear, crisp winter morning in the picturesque town of Heidelberg. Smoke rose from chimneys and clouds hovered over the top of the hillside, shrouding Heidelberg Castle in a beautiful mist.

The team was gathered in the kitchen of the small flat they'd rented, hammering out a game plan.

Camille sipped her coffee, struggling with that weird combination of jet lag and the buzz of anticipation before any mission. Plus the lingering headache. So much was at stake today. If she thought too much about that, or about her desire to have this over for Cass's sake, she wouldn't be able to function. Instead, she compartmentalized, narrowing her focus to the task at hand.

Hank had spread a map of Heidelberg on the table. Sophie had her laptop open, checking times and schedules for not only the castle but also tours within the castle.

"What time does the cable car start operating?" Mercy asked.

Sophie's fingers clacked over her keyboard. "Actually, in case anyone is interested, it's called a funicular. Basically, it's a car that runs on railroad tracks and is pulled up the side of the mountain by a cable."

"Huh." Hank walked around behind Sophie's chair. "Show me a close-up. Couldn't tell last night." She leaned closer. "Interesting. Does it go all the way up the mountainside?"

Sophie pulled up another picture, pointed. "The castle is halfway up, then the funicular keeps going all the way to the top of the mountain. Two stops, basically."

"Send those pics to my phone, will you?"

"I just sent them to all of you." Phones buzzed around the table.

Hank turned to Camille. "What about the river cruise ships? When do their castle tours start? Do you know?"

Camille also had her laptop out. "Hang on. Yes. From what I can figure, they do their castle tours in the morning, then end up at the Tun for a wine tasting."

"What's the Tun?"

Camille turned her laptop so they could see and grinned. "Only the largest wine barrel ever. Like big enough that there used to be a dance floor on top of it. Certainly the largest in Europe, though there are those who would argue."

"Why is it so huge?" Mercy asked.

Camille laughed, fascinated by the whole thing. Cass would love this story. "Basically, it was a way the local winemakers thumbed their noses at the tax collectors way back when. They were told they had to give a percentage of the wine they made to the government, so they took their required shares and dumped them all into one barrel."

Sophie made a face. "Ewww. That would taste horrible."

"It did. That was the whole point. Nobody wanted it, so it was given to the soldiers to drink."

Hank sat back and laughed. "I feel sorry for the soldiers, but that was pretty clever."

Mercy studied the staircase that went up one side of the barrel and came down around the other side. The photo showed the stairs crammed with tourists. "Are we thinking the chalices are somewhere near there?"

Her question brought everyone back to the task at hand.

Camille's phone buzzed with a text from Cass. She smiled as she opened the message app, then sucked in a horrified breath, gripped a hand over her heart. "No. No. No. Please, God, no," she whispered. "Cass!"

"Camille?" Mercy appeared behind her, the rest of the team crowding in.

"What's wrong?" Sophie asked.

She couldn't force the words out, just turned the phone so they could see the picture of Cass and Gran, blindfolded and tied to chairs. The caption read: **Your daughter in exchange for the Liar's Treasure.**

"Oh, dear Jesus, help us." Mercy made the sign of the cross. Beside her, Hank said something under her breath and Sophie rubbed Camille's shoulders.

Her worst fears had come true.

Camille wrapped her arms around her middle, rocking back and forth, trying to keep it together, to hold the terror at bay. "I was right. I should have followed my gut and never boarded that plane." This was the thing she'd feared the most from the very beginning. That someone would hurt her baby and she wouldn't be there to protect her.

She swiped at the tears she couldn't stop. "Somebody kidnapped my baby. And Gran. How do we get them back?" She jumped up, started pacing, then pivoted and grabbed her laptop. "I need to get on the next plane home."

Silence filled the room until Sophie stepped in front of her. "I don't think that's the answer, Camille."

"She's my baby." Camille felt her heart breaking, and fear immediately shot into all the cracks.

Mercy took both of Camille's hands in hers and started praying. "Dear Father, keep Cassandra and Octavia safe and give Camille the kind of peace only You can give. You said if we ask for wisdom, You will give it. We're asking. Help us get them back safely. Please." She squeezed Camille's hands again and murmured, "Amen."

"Amen," the team echoed.

Another pause, then Hank said, "I agree with Sophie. If we want to get them back, I think we'd better figure out how to get those altar pieces. Today. That's our bargaining chip. That's how we keep them safe and then get them back."

"But first, we need to ask for details." Sophie grabbed Camille's phone and spoke as she sent a text. "Tell me when and where. But if you hurt my kid, you'll get nothing."

Camille's breath heaved as they waited for a response. Time dragged. Then finally . . .

Becker Foundation Summit. Don't be late.

Camille wiped her tears, took a deep breath, then another. *Okay, God, I'm doing my part to put feet to my faith even though I'm terrified, but I need You to do what I can't. Protect my girl. Please.*

Within two hours, the team headed to the funicular that would take them to Heidelberg Castle. And, if the clues were right, the altar pieces.

There were only two ways to get to the castle. You could ride the funicular or you could walk. To make Mercy's life a bit easier with her prosthetic leg, she and Sophie were at the front of the very long line for the cable car, Mercy wearing her nun's habit and Sophie dressed as a nobleman, sword at her side. People assumed they were part of the castle tours, which was exactly the point.

Camille and Hank walked up the steep path single file, each wearing a nun's habit and carrying a backpack.

There were no new texts from whoever held Gran and Cass. All Camille could think was, *God, please. Protect my baby. Protect Gran.*

Those words repeated with every beat of her heart. *God, please.*

Once they reached the halfway point to the castle, Camille

deliberately pushed her fear for her daughter out of her mind. Otherwise, she wouldn't be able to function.

The Old Town lay directly below them and the Neckar River sparkled in the distance, a picturesque bridge spanning the water.

Directly below the castle, buses disgorged throngs of cruise-ship passengers who clustered around guides holding up identifying pennants and speaking to their groups via headsets. It was controlled chaos and Camille nodded approvingly.

This was exactly what they needed.

She and Hank exchanged a look and kept walking.

Once they entered the castle grounds, Camille stopped and took a moment to gain her bearings. The pictures had not done it justice. The brick courtyard was huge. Over the years, different rulers had built their own palaces along the perimeter, creating a mishmash of architectural styles and time periods.

Camille headed directly toward the chapel in Friedrich's Wing while Sophie strode toward the entrance to the wine cellar in another building, where the Tun was displayed. Hank and Mercy would keep watch from the courtyard and provide backup as needed.

Head down, Camille tucked her hands in the front of her robe and slipped inside the chapel, her footsteps echoing on the stone floor. She paused to genuflect, then glided down the center aisle and stepped into a pew two rows from the altar. She knelt, hands folded in prayer, and studied the candlesticks on the altar.

"The lights are exactly where we thought," she whispered into her comms.

"Any sign of the others?" Mercy asked.

Camille sat up, then walked down the pew and out to the side aisle. "Checking."

She heard voices and peered over her shoulder as a tour group entered the chapel, whispering quietly and snapping pictures.

She kept her back to them, but no one seemed to pay her

any attention as she stepped into the shadows beside the altar. She stopped behind a pillar and studied the walls, artwork, and statuary.

Beautiful, but not what she was after.

Another quick peek over her shoulder and she ducked behind another column, scanning, always scanning. Several niches were carved into the walls, but none of them held the jewel-encrusted cross.

She cut across the chapel behind the altar to the left side, aiming for the door through which the priest entered. Hand on the door, she stopped, turned back.

There.

A small niche in the wall was covered by a wooden door, no more than two feet by two feet.

She hurried back to it and whispered, "Maybe," as she tugged on the iron handle. It didn't budge. She pulled harder. Still nothing.

The voice of the tour guide got louder. They were getting closer.

"Got company." Hank's calm voice through the comms helped steady Camille's hands, though her heart still picked up speed.

She risked another glance over her shoulder, saw the group approaching down the center aisle. She ran one hand over the top of the curved little door and the other along the bottom edge, tugging, pushing, trying to figure out how it opened.

Just when she wanted to pound the door in frustration, her fingers slid over a tiny round button along the top. She smiled and pushed down on it. She heard a quiet click and the door swung open on silent hinges.

The golden cross stood on its base, rubies and emeralds and sapphires glowing in the dim lighting as though they were lit from within.

Camille's hands trembled as she slowly lifted the cross from its hiding place. It was far more beautiful than the pictures indicated.

It was also a lot heavier.

She felt the movement behind her a split second before a male voice said, "I'll take that, thanks."

Camille pivoted and smacked the man in the side of the head with the cross.

He let out a yelp as he stumbled backward. *Scarface.*

Camille turned to run in the opposite direction, tripped over the hem of her habit, and landed in a heap. Before she could get both legs under her, he lunged.

She tucked the cross against her chest and rolled over, protecting it with her body. "Help! This man is trying to attack me!" Her voice echoed in the high-ceilinged room.

The sound of running feet charged in their direction.

"Headed your way!" Hank sounded like she was sprinting.

"This is not the end," the man muttered in a thick Slavic accent, then kicked her in the ribs and took off out the back door.

Ignoring her aching side, Camille braced one hand against the wall and climbed to her feet. She shoved the cross inside the front of her habit and turned as footsteps approached.

"Are you all right, Sister?" The man was older, tall and thin, and he put a steadying hand on her arm. "Did he hurt you? Should we call the police?"

The rest of the tour group gathered behind him, concern on their faces.

That was the last thing they needed. "Thank you. I'm fine. Just a bit rattled." She inclined her head. "Enjoy your tour. Go with God."

Then she turned and slowly walked out of the chapel, the heavy cross carefully hidden in the front of her habit, clutched in both hands.

Outside, Camille scanned every tour group pouring onto the castle grounds and milling around the courtyard, but she didn't see her attacker anywhere. "He's hiding behind a ball cap and sunglasses, but it's Scarface," she said into her comms. "Anything, Hank?"

"Not yet."

"Haven't seen him," Mercy said when Camille reached her.

They stepped behind a half wall and Camille turned her back to the courtyard before sliding the cross into Mercy's hands.

"Oooh," Mercy breathed. "It's beautiful."

Camille wrapped the cross in a soft cloth, tucked it inside the backpack Mercy handed her. "It is also heavier than we thought. You good with carrying this?"

Mercy rolled her eyes and slipped it over her shoulders. "Yes, Camille. I can carry a backpack."

"That wasn't what I—" Camille sighed. "Thank you. I meant no offense."

"I know." Mercy nodded and started walking. "Headed to the funicular," she said into her earpiece.

It was early yet, so most of the people were still coming to the castle, not leaving. Which worked to their advantage. Enough people for cover. Not so many that they'd get trapped.

The funicular arrived and disgorged its crowd of tourists.

Mercy moved forward to step aboard.

55

Careful not to draw attention to herself, Camille walked back inside the chapel and slipped past a tour group gathered around their guide. She hurried up the left-hand stairs to the balcony. She hoped there was another way down at the other end. She was also counting on no one questioning her religious garb.

She hurried forward until she was above the altar that held the two candlesticks they were after. The replicas Sophie had constructed out of wood and gold spray paint were secured inside a special pocket she'd sewn into Camille's robe. Camille leaned over the stone balcony, deciding on the best approach.

Climbing or jumping would attract far too much attention. She'd have to walk right up to the altar and do a quick switch-and-go.

Just as she turned to head back the way she'd come, a priest stepped into view below, head down as he approached the altar. She leaned over the railing to get a better look at him. Something about the way he moved . . .

Without hesitation, he grabbed one of the candlesticks in each hand, tucked them into his robes, and turned to go.

"Hey!" she shouted.

His head shot up at her shout, then he ran for the back door of the chapel.

Furious, Camille raced along the balcony, flew down the stairs. "Lucien has the lights."

"On it," Hank said, and Camille heard pounding feet as she gave chase.

He was not getting away with another piece of the treasure.

Camille burst into the courtyard, breath heaving, and stopped, trying to spot Lucien.

He was gone. But as she turned, her heart rate kicked into high gear and she took off running for the wine cellar.

"Chameleon. Florence is headed your way. Sword on his costume. Be there ASAP."

Camille raced across the courtyard and down a long corridor adjacent to the wine cellar, ducking into a rarely used alcove at the end. She yanked off the nun's habit and stuffed it into her backpack, then pulled a waistcoat over her white shirt and pantaloons, slung a small bag over her shoulder. Then she grabbed the sword she'd stashed there earlier and fastened it around her waist. Sophie's quick sword-fighting lesson wouldn't help Camille against an expert, but hopefully she could put on enough of a show to draw attention away from Sophie.

"Headed in," she whispered as she walked into the wine cellar, surprised at how large it was. Whitewashed arches supported the high ceiling, and the stone walls helped keep the wine chilled. People lined up to take pictures in front of the Tun, the humongous wine barrel that had made the castle famous. She stopped, studied it and the area around it, but did not see Sophie—or the chalices they were after.

She headed into the tasting room, shocked to see people seated at tables and standing around wine barrels with wineglasses in their hands at—she checked her watch—ten in the morning. Apparently, tours waited for no man. She scanned the perimeter, noting the coats of arms, swords on display, but no chalices.

To her right, a line was forming to climb up and over the Tun. Camille's research said the barrel, built in 1751, was seven meters high and eight and a half meters wide and could hold fifty-eight thousand gallons of wine. The staircase was only wide enough for one person, and she joined the line that snaked up past the carved statue of Perkeo, a court jester known for his ability to hold his liquor. He held a carved chalice, but unfortunately, that wasn't one of the ones they were after, either.

Camille supposed if they were that easy to find, someone would have snatched them long ago.

Once she reached the top of the wine barrel and its famous dance floor, she checked every corner. A quick peek over her shoulder and she spotted Sophie below, her eyes also scanning every possible hiding place.

What if they had gotten it all wrong? What if the chalices were hidden somewhere else inside this ginormous collection of ruins and they were in the completely wrong place?

No time for doubt or second-guessing.

Camille hurried down the stairs behind the Tun and returned to the tasting room. She forced herself to take a breath and focus.

They had to find the chalices, and fast.

Her eyes landed on a flag hung on the wall above the tasting counter. It rippled slightly, and when it did, she caught sight of something attached to a horizontal board on the wall below it. Dark wood, about three feet wide and eight feet long, it displayed a lovely sword. But that wasn't what caught her eye. Just above the sword, someone had fastened a small wooden box with mesh covering the two openings. Two chalices stood inside.

Excitement sizzled up her spine. Every instinct she possessed told her these were the chalices they needed. It was the perfect way to hide them in plain sight. Tucked inside the box, they were in shadow and appeared to be common drinking vessels. She pulled out her phone and zoomed in.

When she caught a shimmer from one of the jewels, she almost let out a "Yes!"

Almost.

She looked across the room and met Sophie's equally excited expression. Sophie nodded once and hitched her chin toward the high shelves stocked with wine bottles.

Camille calculated the distance. If Sophie scaled the shelves below the sword, she could reach the box. Switching the chalices for the copies in her bag and making her escape would be a bit trickier.

"Found. Retrieval could get dicey," Sophie whispered into her comm.

"Distraction ready," Camille responded.

They met in front of the tasting counter, Sophie loosening the drawstring bag draped over her costume while Camille approached one of the workers behind the counter. They were pouring wine as fast as they could while servers circulated with trays, trying to keep up with the hundreds of people who crowded the room, expecting a glass.

Camille leaned close and said, "My friend and I were hired to provide a bit of entertainment, so don't be alarmed."

Without giving the woman a chance to respond, they both leaped up onto the counter. Camille walked to the end opposite Sophie and raised her voice. "*Guten Morgen, meine Damen und Herren. Willkommen* to the wine cellar at Schloss Heidelberg."

Behind her, Sophie started climbing up the shelves. Excited murmurs rumbled from the crowd below. When she reached the top shelf, she rotated so her back faced the crowd.

"You have seen the Tun, *ja*?" Camille grabbed their attention while Sophie opened the compartment and deftly switched the chalices, tucking the originals safely into her bag.

"Ja!" the crowd shouted.

Sophie turned around, one of the fake chalices in her hand,

and raised her arm in a toast. "I will tell you what we think of this absurd wine tax. Bah!"

The crowd laughed.

Camille grinned and spread her hands. "You like our answer, *nein*? The prince wants some of our wine as a tax? We tossed it all into one barrel! Let the prince drink that swill himself!"

Once the cheers died down, Sophie called, "Here's to good wine—from a bottle, not the Tun! *Prost!*" She pretended to take a sip, then stuck the fake chalice into the compartment, closed it, turned to the crowd, and bowed from the waist.

As Sophie started her downward climb, Camille caught sight of Florence headed their way, mask in place, sword at his side. A spurt of adrenaline hit her system and she grinned in anticipation. Time to practice her new skills. "Florence headed our way."

"Lose him and get out of there," Hank responded.

"That's the plan."

While Sophie quickly climbed off the shelves and landed on the serving counter, Camille drew her sword, watching as Florence elbowed his way through the crowd toward them.

"Pay your tribute to the prince!" he shouted, and Camille raised an eyebrow.

He wanted to give the crowd a show, too? Oh, they could totally do that.

She and Sophie shared a look, then nimbly leaped off the counter and landed near him. Camille pointed her sword at him while Sophie started backing toward the exit.

All around, the guests backed up and gave them room, enjoying the show.

Florence stepped closer and tried to prevent Sophie's exit.

Camille got between them, grinning, eyebrow raised as she blocked his path.

He thrust, she parried, then stepped out of reach. "You will not get more! We have paid our tribute!"

The crowd cheered as their swords clanged.

Camille narrowed her eyes as the impact vibrated up her arm.

He was good—more than good, actually. She wouldn't underestimate him again.

Camille backed her way across the room, keeping him busy while Sophie steadily worked her way toward the exit.

Sophie had almost reached the door when Florence suddenly leaped up on a chair, pivoted, and landed behind Camille.

"Oh no you don't," Camille muttered, whirling around, desperate to get between him and Sophie again. "Stand your ground, you miserable tax collector!" She lunged and slit the back of his waistcoat with her sword.

When he glanced over his shoulder, outraged, Sophie took her opportunity and sprinted toward the stairs leading to the top of the Tun. "Make way! Make way!" Thankfully, the crowd parted to let her through.

Camille sheathed her sword and raced after them, elbowing past the people squeezed to one side to let her by. She reached into her bag as she ran.

Ahead of her, the crowd tried to stop Florence's progress, but he muscled his way past them shouting, "You won't get away with this!"

Sophie whirled to face him when she reached the top of the Tun. The cluster of tourists already there quickly stepped to the edge of the former dance floor to give them room. All around, cameras flashed and people hit the record icons on their phones.

Camille was right on Florence's heels as he burst up the last step and lunged toward Sophie.

Sophie swung her sword up under his, forcing him back a step.

They circled each other, the sharp clang of metal echoing off the stone walls as they fought.

Camille lit the smoke canister and rolled it onto the dance floor. There was a hiss and a clunk just before a burst of pink smoke filled the air.

The crowd gasped as Sophie disappeared in the smoke.

Camille leaped in the opposite direction. She hopped on the banister and slid down, shouting, "Bit of room, *bitte schön*."

People inched aside and she picked up speed. At the bottom, she hopped off and ran from the wine cellar as the crowd cheered.

A quick peek over her shoulder showed Florence fighting his way through the crowd. They were laughing and blocking his path, thinking it was part of the show.

Camille raced down the stone steps and burst into the courtyard.

"Head east, Eagle Eye," Hank said.

She turned, picked up her pace.

"Other way."

Camille would have howled in frustration, but she didn't have time.

"Backpack halfway down in a little niche," Hank added.

She sped through a long hallway that led to a promenade atop the castle wall. Midway, she scooped up the backpack and kept running. "Got it, thanks."

She peeked over the edge to the town of Heidelberg far below.

Wait. Was that . . . ? "No, sir," she muttered and pulled her grappling hook from the backpack and secured it to the wall.

Lucien had shed his priest's robes somewhere along the way, secured his own grappling hook, and had almost reached the bottom of the castle wall.

"Going after the pirate." She swung a leg over the side and began a quick descent. By the time she dropped to the ground below, Florence had his leg over the wall, preparing to follow her down.

"Halt!" a deep voice shouted.

She didn't wait to see if that command was meant for her or Florence, just took off running.

She yelped when a shot rang out and rocks exploded at her feet.

56

Camille's foot hit a rock and she tripped, stumbling forward and skidding on her palms before she banged into a boulder. She stopped to catch her breath, rubbing her sore elbow. Where was Florence? There weren't many places to hide.

She scrambled to her feet when she saw Lucien stop just below her, scanning the steep trail behind them, too. She took off running again. He was not getting away with those candlesticks.

Hank's voice came through her comms. "Sister, Ponytail and Scarface, our two friends from Romania, boarded behind you."

Camille glanced back toward the castle's funicular station as she ran. People were streaming into the cars in droves. She tried to find Mercy, but the sun on the glass made it impossible to see inside.

"Head toward me, Sister," Sophie said. "I'm in the front."

Camille let out a sigh of relief. Good. Mercy wasn't alone.

She held on to her sword and picked up speed. Lucien was getting farther ahead.

Hank said, "I can't get on. Too crowded. Meet you at the bottom."

Camille saw her sprinting down the other path toward the main funicular station at street level.

"Eagle Eye, duck!" Sophie shouted.

Camille dropped behind a bush as more shots splintered the vegetation around her. Had to be Florence, but where was he? Unable to spot him, she took off again. Better than being a sitting duck.

Ahead of her, Lucien ran into the main funicular station.

Camille followed, elbowing people out of her way. "Sorry, excuse me, sorry, very sorry."

He disappeared around a corner and she picked up speed.

She stopped, scanned the busy station. There. Across the street. He'd swung a leg over a black motorcycle and fired it up.

Ignoring the blaring horns, Camille darted through the traffic, grabbed his arm, and hopped on behind him, gripping him around the waist. When he whipped around, she tightened her grip and growled, "Drive."

He hesitated only a moment before one side of his mouth curled up. "Then hang on, Princess. It's going to be a bumpy ride."

Lucien spun the bike in a one-eighty, and as they raced past the station, Camille saw Hank hop on another motorcycle.

"Straight ahead, ladies, keep coming," Hank said.

Behind them, Camille glimpsed Mercy and Sophie sprinting toward Hank, Ponytail and Scarface muscling their way through the crowd in hot pursuit.

Camille heard another motorcycle and spotted Florence racing toward them from the side street. She gripped Lucien's waist tighter as he hit the throttle and bullets ate up the pavement around them.

She yelped and ducked when one of those bullets grazed her arm.

The scenery flew by as Lucien dodged and weaved through the narrow streets of Heidelberg as though street racing were his day job. Camille was impressed despite her fury. He had put his backpack on his chest, and she could feel the weight of the candlesticks against her arms, taunting her. He was not getting away with them.

They'd finally lost Florence several miles back when two police cars darted out of a side street and boxed him in. Lucien kept going, leaving the town behind. When traffic thinned to almost nothing, Camille finally loosened her death grip on his waist.

Another little town appeared. He slowed and wound his way through the streets before pulling up at a small park along the riverbank. He turned off the motor, removed his helmet, and dismounted, the backpack firmly in his grip. She ignored the hand he held out and climbed off the bike, frustration and fury raging through her.

They faced off, both breathing hard.

"Are you okay?" He stepped closer and nodded toward her torn sleeve.

She waved him away and checked her upper arm. "I'm fine." Thankfully, it was barely a scratch.

"Look, Camille—"

She held up a hand to stop him. "Cass has been kidnapped."

He flinched as though he'd been gut punched. His jaw clenched and he rammed a hand through his short dark hair. "By whom?"

"Don't know. Doesn't really matter. Except that they want to trade her for the treasure."

He took a deep breath as though getting his emotions under control. "Tell me what happened."

Camille pulled out her phone. When he saw the picture of Cass and Gran, his face drained of color and he turned away, hands on his hips, jaw working.

"You and your friends have a plan?" He kept his back to her.

"We're going to make sure we have all the pieces of the treasure and use them to get her back." She told him about the Becker Foundation and the upcoming summit. "I need those candlesticks, Lucien. And the Book of Days." She paused. "Please."

He turned back to face her, his expression hard. "They're yours to use—on one condition."

"What?"

"I work with you. I'm part of the team."

She raised an eyebrow. "How do I know you won't just take off with the treasure?"

He clenched his jaw. "You know me better than that."

"Do I?" She stepped closer and jabbed a finger in his chest. "You just nabbed the candlesticks, never mind the Book of Days."

He leaned in until they were nose to nose. "That was different! That was for Pops."

"How is it different? He wants the whole treasure, doesn't he?"

"Yes."

"Then how am I supposed to trust you?"

He scrubbed a hand over the back of his neck, then met her eyes, trapping her in their clear blue depths. "I would do anything for Cass," he said, and Camille didn't doubt the steely determination in every syllable. "She's J. T.'s daughter."

"What about the treasure?"

He abruptly stepped back, his voice a low growl. "It isn't about the treasure anymore. It stopped being about that when you showed me the picture of Cass."

Camille studied him, suddenly saw anguish in his eyes. "What aren't you saying?"

He folded his arms, idly rubbing the dog-tag tattoo, then met her eyes squarely. "It's my fault J. T. is dead."

Survivor's guilt, Hank had called it.

"Your convoy was ambushed. How is that your fault?" A sudden memory flashed, the scars she'd seen on his back after he'd pulled her into the boat. "You tried to protect him by covering him with your body."

He hadn't been at J. T.'s funeral. Someone had told her he was in the hospital, but she'd been too shocked and grief-stricken to ask why.

"Yes," he ground out. "But he should never have been in that godforsaken corner of the world to begin with. He should have been at that fancy college he had a scholarship to, planning his future with you. I convinced him to go." He turned away, fists clenched.

Camille was stunned that he'd been carrying this guilt all these years. She stepped in front of him. "No. This was not your fault. It never was. Frankly, you don't have that much power."

After a shocked moment, one corner of his mouth lifted. "You never were one to pull your punches, were you, Princess?"

"J. T. might have been easygoing, but he also had a will of iron. He stood up to his father, told him he wasn't interested in working for the family firm right then. He decided he wanted to join the military, and nothing you or I or anybody else said, for or against, would have changed his mind. Took me a while to accept that." She touched his arm. "Let it go, Lucien. It's not yours to carry."

He paused, studied her. "You ever wonder what would have happened if—?"

Camille held up both palms like a traffic cop. "Don't go there." Conviction stiffened her spine as they stared at each other, memories and unspoken longings suspended between them. Had she played what-if over the years? Of course. But if she hadn't kissed Lucien on prom night and hadn't let that guilt send her straight back to apologize to J. T., she and J. T. wouldn't have gone too far that night and there would be no Cass. Though the circumstances hadn't been ideal, she and J. T. loved each other, their short marriage was real, and she'd never trade Cass for anything in the world.

The silence lengthened.

"I still miss him," Lucien said quietly.

Camille nodded. "Me, too. I see him in Cass. The way she cocks her head. She has his laugh."

"Let me help get them back. I won't cheat you—or let you down, Camille. You can trust me."

She thought she could, probably. But she subscribed to the Speranza motto of *Trust, but verify.* Especially when it involved Cass. "I'll talk to my friends."

"It's all going to be okay, you know."

That made her laugh. "I don't remember you being such a pie-in-the-sky optimist."

"That's not optimism. It's confidence. I'm smart. So are you.

We're going to get your daughter and your grandmother back." He raised two fingers. "Scout's honor."

Camille snorted. "You were never a Boy Scout."

"Pirate's honor, then."

She was still chuckling when he turned back toward the bike.

"Talk to your friends and let me know how I can help. We need to find those two."

57

Lucien dropped Camille off at the Airbnb. Two hours later, the team was gathered around the dining table dressed in comfy clothes, sipping coffee. They'd all wandered around the city for a while to be sure they didn't have a tail before finally taking a convoluted route back here.

The altar set—both chalices, the two candlesticks, and the bejeweled cross—sat on the small dining table.

"I still can't believe Lucien just gave you the candlesticks," Mercy said.

Camille nodded. "I think it was his way of showing that his offer to help find Cass and Gran is genuine."

"These really are impressive." Hank picked up the cross, hefting its weight and studying the bright stones embedded in the gold.

Camille looked up from her laptop. "They're worth a whole lot of money, even separate from the rest of the treasure. And with good reason."

Hank picked up a chalice, then the other, studied the back. Then did the same with the cross and the two candlesticks. "They all have a very small notch in the back. Maybe that's how they attach. We'll have to see once we have all the pieces."

"Can we trust Lucien to bring the Book of Days to the summit?" Hank asked Camille.

"I think so, yes." Camille had told him about the summit in Florence and the mysterious trial Nelson Becker kept talking about. "He was headed to the airport to catch a flight home and check on Pops. He didn't want to risk mailing the Book of Days, so he'll get it from Claude and meet us there."

"He's a good guy." Mercy smiled.

"Sexy, too." Sophie mimed fanning herself and brought a much-needed chuckle. Her phone buzzed with a text and a blush rose in her cheeks as she responded.

"Speaking of swoony men, be sure to tell Mac we said hello," Hank drawled.

Sophie's blush deepened and she tucked the phone away.

Mercy grinned, then propped her hands on her hips. "Meanwhile, how are we going to get our hands on the portable altar by the day after tomorrow?"

"Good question." Camille's cell phone buzzed. "Marcel. Didn't expect to hear from you."

"I don't want you to panic, Cuz, but—"

Camille stabbed the speaker button. "Do not start a sentence that way. What's wrong?" She kept her voice calm but her heart flapped like a moth in a jar, slamming against the walls of her chest.

"Gran called me. Couple hours ago. I was, ah, asleep when the call came in."

Meaning he'd been drinking and had passed out. "What did she say? Wait. How did they escape? Where are they?" she demanded, rapid-fire. A female voice sounded over a PA system. "And where are you right now?"

Marcel huffed out a breath. "So here's the thing. She said to tell you she was sorry. And for me to get Cass."

There was a moment of stunned silence.

"Get Cass?" Camille's hands started to shake. This made no

sense. Cass and Gran were being held together somewhere. "Where is my daughter?"

"I don't know."

Camille shoved out of her chair. "Tell me what's happening, Marcel. Right. Now."

He blew out another breath, and Camille could almost hear him trying to figure out some way to spin his story. "Straight up, no chaser. I don't have time for your tall tales."

Another pause, longer this time, and Camille forced herself not to consider even more worst-case scenarios than the ones she'd already been imagining. Facts first.

"Okay, fine. I woke up a little while ago, saw a message from Gran that said she was sorry and to get Cass. She'd left an address about an hour outside New Orleans, but when I got there—" He paused, and Camille wanted to reach through the phone and yank the words out of his mouth. "When I got there—" his voice shook—"I found Gran on the floor in the kitchen of a small house. She's alive, but she'd been badly beaten."

"And Cass?" Camille rubbed the ache in her chest. She wanted to be wrong, but in her heart, she knew what he was going to say.

"I don't know. She was gone when I got there."

"What did the house look like?" Hank demanded.

"Who is that?" Marcel demanded.

"A friend."

"Yeah, the place was trashed. No sign of Cass. I went to call 911, but Gran woke up and made me promise I wouldn't tell the police about Cass. She said to call you instead. I told her I'd only go along with that if she let me call EMS."

"She agreed?"

"Yes. Which tells you how bad she's hurt." He waited through another announcement over the PA. "I'm at the hospital and they just took her back for X-rays. They think she has a few broken ribs. They want to be sure it isn't worse than that."

Camille's heart clenched and she forced words past the lump in her throat. "I need the truth, Marcel. Do you have any part of this treasure?"

"Aw, Camille. You know I only have the diary." He paused again. "Actually, I have a copy. I, ah, sold the original."

"I'm sure you did. Time to man up, Cousin Mine. You're going to do what you promised and find Cass."

"I'm, ah, not really very good at that sort of thing."

"What sort of thing? Taking responsibility? You're in New Orleans. I'm in Germany." She hesitated, desperate to get through to him. "Your niece's life is literally hanging in the balance. Do you still not get that?"

The silence lengthened. "Tell me what you need me to do."

58

Camille sank down in her chair, arms wrapped around her middle, trying to keep it together while the team talked with Marcel.

She tried to block out mental pictures of Gran, battered and bruised in a hospital bed. Of Cass being hauled off somewhere and held prisoner, all alone. She sucked in a breath, rubbed a hand over her heart.

"This doesn't make any sense."

All eyes turned to her.

"Someone already had both of them. Why would they suddenly beat up Gran and take Cass somewhere else?"

"If they're using Cass to get you to bring the treasure to the summit, which we believe is true, then they don't need your gran." Hank shrugged. "I'm just glad she's alive, frankly."

Camille shivered and rubbed her arms.

"I agree," Mercy said. "Whoever has Cass will take very good care of her until they get what they want."

Camille sincerely hoped that wasn't just wishful thinking.

"So our job right now is to figure out who has the portable

altar," Sophie said. "I reached out to Picasso." She held up a hand. "I know she needs to recover. But she texted that she was going crazy with nothing to do. Several people recorded my sword fight with Florence and posted videos online. I managed to grab a screenshot and sent it to her. She's been running it through facial rec."

"Anything?" Hank asked.

"Nothing. Which makes me even more curious. I know most of the players in the, shall we say, art-retrieval world." Sophie made air quotes. "But this guy is a blank." She drummed her fingers on the desk. "Though there are rumors of a masked thief who slips in and out with priceless treasures unseen. The media has dubbed him The Ghost." Her laptop dinged and her fingers flew over her keyboard. "Oh, hello! Picasso just matched the footage with a screenshot from Interpol. Even the masks match. Florence is The Ghost."

"I'm not sure if that's good news or bad, if Interpol can't find him." Camille's phone rang and she put it on speaker. "What's up, Jolie?"

"I just wanted you to know Nelson is getting really demanding and sounding more off his rocker every time I talk to him. Dot hasn't come out of her office in days. Meanwhile, Nelson is rarely here, and when he does show up, he keeps demanding I give him the treasure, as though I have it stashed in the file cabinet and am holding out on him."

Jolie drew a deep breath. "Sorry. But he's really scaring me. He just left my office, saying since I've not kept my end of the bargain—I don't remember making a bargain, but whatever—he's made additional arrangements to guarantee he gets what he wants."

Everyone on the team froze, all eyes on Camille. She shook her head. She wouldn't mention what was happening with Cass.

Was Nelson behind the kidnapping?

"I don't suppose he told you what he meant by that?"

"No, though I asked, several times. I don't know what's happening."

"You're doing great, Jolie. All the info you've been giving us is super helpful. Do you by chance have the agenda for this summit?"

"Sending it now. I'll also attach the summit location. What else can I do?"

"You're doing it. Keep your ear to the ground and let us know about anything you hear." Camille paused. "And stay safe."

Not two minutes later, Camille's phone buzzed again. "Unknown number." She opened the text and her breath hitched at another picture of Cass, again tied to a chair, blindfolded. The text was only two words: **Tick. Tock.**

Mercy laid a hand on Camille's shoulder. "She's okay. There's no sign of injury."

"My baby's tied up. And alone and scared." Camille fought against the tears that wanted to escape. But if she let herself start crying, she was afraid she'd never stop. She had to stay focused.

"We're going to find her, Camille." Sophie took the phone from her hands and sent the picture to everyone, then enlarged it on her laptop. "It appears she's being held in some kind of warehouse." She tapped the screen. "See the metal beams and roof?"

"It doesn't look too old, either." Hank pointed.

Mercy nodded. "I'm sending it to Marcel. See if he recognizes it."

Sophie stood up, met Camille's eyes. "I have an idea that may help us. But it's risky. Really risky."

The Ghost sat in his elegantly appointed hotel room and sipped coffee, nibbling at a croissant from his room-service tray. Outwardly, he presented his usual calm. Inwardly, he was seething. He'd had enough of these women getting in his way.

His phone dinged with several notifications. He'd set them up to tell him anytime the Liar's Treasure or any piece of it was mentioned in the news.

He'd also done his homework and discovered that one of the women he'd been chasing across Europe was none other than Sophie Williams, business manager of the Fortier Gallery in Munich, which had recently garnered worldwide attention over the reappearance of a long-missing royal portrait. She was considered an art expert.

She was apparently also an expert swordsman. Interesting.

He'd scrolled through various social-media sites and found video clips of himself dueling with her earlier. Luckily, his mask hid his face, but it was a chance he shouldn't have taken. She'd goaded him into acting impulsively, which annoyed him. He was never impulsive. He hadn't gotten where he was by being careless.

The taller woman, a Camille Abernathy of New Orleans, photographer and sometimes-fashion-model, was worthless with a sword, but given her performance in Florence, she could rappel down buildings like they were nothing.

And handle a boat.

He drummed his fingers on the desk, irritated. Too bad she hadn't drowned like she was supposed to. These annoying amateurs no doubt believed they could beat him to the rest of the treasure.

His slow smile could have chilled wine.

He already had the portable altar. The rest of the Liar's Treasure was as good as his.

His phone chimed again, alerting him to a notice on one of the message boards he frequented on the dark web.

To my dueling partner at the castle. Bring your trinket to the summit the day after tomorrow for the chance to try again. To the winner go the spoils, but only if your motives are pure, of course. Do you dare take the chance?

He grinned as he hit Reply and typed a single sentence: **Winner takes all.**

Anticipation hummed through his veins, especially after another notification popped up. He scrolled to the update, now making headlines worldwide, that the Becker Foundation had just announced that anyone with a piece of the Liar's Treasure was invited to join them for a special event as part of their annual summit, scheduled for the day after tomorrow near Florence, Italy. A piece guaranteed entrance to the Liar's Trial. Or—and he found this fascinating—you could bring one million dollars as your admission fee to be part of the trial.

He scanned the rest of the article and sat back, chuckling. He didn't believe a word of that nonsense about the pieces judging motives, of course, but he'd just found the perfect way to ensure that he ended up with all the pieces. This would be child's play for someone with his skills.

Treasure beyond imagining. That was the kind of trial he could get behind.

He punched the address of the summit's location into his laptop and mapped out a plan.

Afterward, he sat back and raised his cup in a toast. "To Liars and their Treasure."

59

Marcel made sure Gran was safely tucked into her hospital bed with a dose of pain medication before he climbed into his car. Seeing her bruised and battered face had torn something inside him. She'd fought whoever had taken Cass, tried to protect her great-granddaughter.

He had kissed her on the forehead. "Rest well, Gran. I'll be back after I find Cass." He'd paused, then added, "Love you."

She had patted his hand without a word.

Once in his BMW SUV, he slammed a hand on the steering wheel as he raced out of the parking lot. He had always known that one day, his bad decisions would come back to bite him in the butt. He'd accepted that as the cost of the risky lifestyle he lived and had always been okay with it. So far, the reward had been worth it.

But this was different. This was Gran. Who'd taken him in and tried to force him to walk the straight and narrow, to no avail.

And Cass. Beautiful, funny, whip-smart Cass, the closest thing to a daughter he'd ever have.

Somehow, by involving her in all of this, however innocently it had started, he'd put her life in danger. And Gran's.

Which meant it was up to him to find his niece. And fast. To somehow make it right.

One of Camille's friends had sent him the picture of the warehouse. He pulled into a drive-through for coffee to clear the cobwebs in his mind and studied the photo as he waited.

From the angle of the shot, he could see a window behind Cass. He enlarged it and grinned. The lighting was terrible, but the silhouette of the St. Claude Avenue Bridge was instantly recognizable.

He pulled up his maps app and zeroed in on the four-lane drawbridge. He'd always thought the early-1900s design was cool, allowing it to rise and lower as part of the industrial lock system. It became well-known via Hurricane Katrina news footage, when many folks in the Lower Ninth Ward used it to escape the rising floodwaters. For a while after the storm, it was one of the only ways to reach that part of the city.

He rotated the map until the bridge was in line with the warehouse, like it was in the photo. He paid for his coffee and headed in that direction.

It was a long shot, but it was the best lead he had.

He drove slowly, one eye on the map, the other on his surroundings, noting the figures huddled in dark corners. Streetlights were mostly out, and many of the warehouses had been abandoned, slowly caving in after years of neglect.

His expensive car stood out like a neon sign reading, "Go ahead. Rob me." He reached into the glove box for his Glock, checked the magazine, and tucked it under the front seat. Just in case.

The moonlight glinted off the river as he approached the line of warehouses. He cut his lights and slowly rolled down the street. When he saw headlights approaching from the opposite direction, he backed up between two buildings, rolled down his window, then killed the motor and waited.

A black Cadillac SUV pulled to the curb and two men got out, one from the passenger seat, one from the back. They rolled ski masks over their faces and approached the warehouse, weapons in hand. The driver stayed in the vehicle.

Marcel's pulse sped up. The fact that they were wearing masks was a good thing, right? If Cass couldn't see their faces, she couldn't identify them.

He turned off the dome light and had just opened his door when the two men reappeared, one carrying a rolled-up blanket over his shoulder. He wasn't sure it was Cass until the bundle started squirming and fighting.

"That's my girl," he muttered. He slipped across the street, preparing to intercept them when his cell phone rang. Panicked, he ducked behind a dumpster, yanked the phone from his pocket, and stabbed it off, then turned off the ringer. *Idiot.*

He peered around the edge of the dumpster in time to see the men toss Cass into the back of the SUV and take off, tires squealing, headed back the way they'd come.

A few long strides brought him back to his SUV. He hopped inside and sped after them.

Cass was not only terrified, she was furious. Who were these guys? When she was with Gran, the guy who talked through the mechanical-voice thingy had untied them, given them food. So who were these losers? Did someone *else* kidnap her? Or was this some kind of terrifying handoff?

Mom would totally lose it once she knew what had happened.

But the worst had been seeing Gran lying on the floor as the masked bullies dragged Cass away. Gran's eyes had been closed and there was blood.

Cass's breath hitched. She didn't look like Cass's tough, no-nonsense Gran. She just looked old.

Tears filled Cass's eyes, but she blinked them back. She couldn't cry, not with this stupid tape over her mouth. She had to stay strong. For Mom. And for Gran.

The good news, if there was any, was that they wouldn't kill her if they got what they wanted.

Probably.

No. Mom and her friends would find her. She had to believe that.

She thought of Gramps's shoelace, still tied around her wrist. *"You've got to put feet to your faith, Cass, my girl. Faith is easy when you're standing on familiar ground."*

Please, God, help.

She kept it together until the SUV started slowing down and she heard the unmistakable sound of jet engines firing.

Marcel checked his map and cut down a side street so he could slip in behind the Cadillac without attracting attention. As they raced through the quiet streets, Marcel zoomed out on the map. Where were they going?

Several minutes later, he had his answer.

A private airstrip.

If he stayed behind them, they'd see him and that would put Cass in more danger. Every instinct told him to ram the car and try to rescue Cass, but reality said that there were three of them and if he did anything stupid, Cass would pay for it.

Reluctantly, he turned off a side street and pulled to the curb. He scanned the map, found an access road, and jotted their license plate number on the back of his hand so he wouldn't forget it.

Five minutes later, he pulled up on the opposite side of the airport.

His phone buzzed, Camille's name on the display. He ignored it.

The SUV pulled up beside the lone hangar, where a jet waited, engines running. He used his phone to snap pictures of the vehicle, the plane, and its tail number.

Fear bloomed in his chest when one of the goons pulled Cass out of the back of the SUV, climbed the steps into the jet, and disappeared. He came back without her, then got in the SUV.

The door to the plane closed, somebody pulled back the stairs, and the jet eased onto the runway and took flight. It all happened so fast.

"I love you, Cass. Stay strong, sweetheart." He wiped at tears he hadn't known he'd cried and drove back around to the access road. Once the SUV passed where he sat hunched in his seat, he drove to the hangar.

He stepped inside and found a young woman in coveralls pushing the stairs against the wall. "Hello?"

She pivoted, gun in her hand.

He shoved his hands in the air, grinning. "Whoa, whoa. I come in peace."

"What are you doing here? This is private property."

He grimaced and studied her from under his lashes. "I was hoping you could help me." He hitched a thumb in the direction the plane took off. "That's my girlfriend on that plane." He glanced away, then back, expression chagrined. "Her daddy doesn't like me much"—he shrugged—"but I couldn't seem to stay away. Never thought he'd go this far, though."

She holstered the weapon, shook her head.

His smile widened, every bit the lovesick fool. "I love her, you know? I'm just trying to figure out where her daddy sent her, that's all."

"I can't give out that information. I'd lose my job." She propped her hands on her hips.

"What if you didn't give it to me? What if you took a bathroom break and the flight plan just happened to be sitting on your desk?" His eyes pleaded with her.

She didn't say anything, just marched past him to a small office in the corner. He followed her in, saw her put a piece of paper on the desk. "I'll be right back. There's a vending machine in the corner if you're thirsty."

"Thank you so much."

She rolled her eyes and left.

Marcel scanned the paper, snapped a photo, then ran back to his SUV.

60

Camille kept her eyes on Sophie, who sat in front of her laptop, waiting. Their plan was audacious. They also knew it could go utterly and completely wrong, but none of them had been able to come up with a better idea.

A notification chimed and Sophie huffed out a breath. She rotated her laptop and showed the team The Ghost's response on the dark-web message board.

Winner takes all.

"Game on, then." Hank rolled her shoulders.

Sophie's phone buzzed with a text. "It's from Picasso, a link to a news article." She read the article and muttered, "Oh, shoot."

Camille rushed over. "What?"

Sophie read the article out loud, which rehashed everything previously reported about the treasure, and then added new information: The Beckers had invited anyone with a piece of the Liar's Treasure—or a million-dollar entrance fee—to join them for a Liar's Trial at their upcoming summit the day after tomorrow in Florence.

Camille tried to absorb this as the team traded glances.

"So The Ghost will be there with the portable altar." Mercy scanned their faces. "Between Lucien and us, we have the other pieces. Plus, anyone with a spare million. Won't every treasure hunter in the entire world show up, too, thinking they'll steal all or part of the treasure?"

Heads nodded all around as that sank in. It was going to be a logistical nightmare.

"Why would the Beckers do something so stupid?" Mercy asked.

"I think they're desperate," Sophie said.

"For what?"

"The treasure. Jolie said Nelson is always buying some rare artifacts. They obviously don't come cheap. Maybe they need the money."

Camille stood and paced. "Right now, I don't care why they're doing this. I just want to figure out how to stop it and get Cass back."

"Right. We need to figure out where she is." Hank chewed the inside of her lip, thinking. "I'm guessing they'll keep her hidden in New Orleans."

"Or they'll take her to the summit location," Mercy said.

Camille turned, pacing the opposite direction. She dialed Marcel again, got voicemail. "Why hasn't he called?" Her hands clenched around her phone to keep from screaming in frustration.

"Camille. You know he'll call when he can." Sophie grabbed the copy of the diary and her laptop. "In the meantime, I've been wondering why the Beckers chose this particular location in Florence instead of a convention center as usual. Picasso is checking."

Camille stopped as a thought occurred to her. "What about the treasure itself? If we're reading the Book of Days correctly, 'the chain of connection will light the way' means the pieces fit together, right? And 'burning away lies to uncover the truth' refers to its judging motives. If your motives are pure, you gain untold riches." She tapped her chin. "So are the pieces the 'untold riches,' or do the pieces *lead* to 'untold riches,' aka another treasure?"

Everyone stared at her in shock.

Sophie recovered first. "I can't believe we never considered that."

"And do the pieces have to connect in a particular sequence?" Mercy asked.

"Now we're asking the right questions." Camille sat down and her fingers flew over her laptop. "Sophie and Hank, go through the diary again while you wait to hear from Picasso. Find any clues to the treasure. Right now, it seems the diary only points to the pieces of the collection. Let's make sure we didn't miss anything." She nodded to Mercy. "You and I will go over the copy of the Book of Days as that seems to point to the treasure itself. Let's see if either tells us what we need to know."

She forced herself to focus as she and Mercy read passages aloud, time ticking like a metronome in her head.

"This confirms what Hank found earlier." Mercy turned the copy of the Book of Days around and showed them a beautifully illustrated page. It showed all of the altar pieces, facing away, displaying the notches in the back. Chalice, candlestick, cross, chalice, candlestick. "Check out the order in which they're lined up."

"I've got something, too." Sophie tapped a page. "Our lovely friend Jacques Talon wrote that when his wife was near death from the fever, she kept muttering about the treasure, saying it was 'somewhere no one would ever think to look. It belongs to Speranza and no one but Speranza will ever find it.'"

Mercy rubbed her arms. "I just got chills. What a long history of strong women Speranza has in its ranks."

"It really is awesome." Camille held up the copy of the Book of Days so they could see the impossibly small Speranza emblem on the next-to-last page. She flipped through several pages. "Here's the illustration from earlier, with flames behind the portable altar and the bit about the 'chain of connection.'"

Hank took the book from her. "I think I saw something, too." She flipped through more pages. "There it is." She turned the book around and pointed. The painting showed a pair of gloved hands holding the portable altar. The open top showed the Book of Days resting inside it. A gold chain circled the altar.

"That means a chain connects the pieces, in a certain order, but where's the chain and how do we find it?" Camille shook her head in frustration.

"Hold that thought." Sophie held up one finger. "Picasso did a deep dive and found out that the property where the summit will be held was once owned by Countess Alonza's family. And that she supposedly died there, as well."

"The Beckers must have found out, too."

"But we still have no idea if there's another treasure or how the Liar's Treasure will lead to it, right?" Mercy asked.

"Wait. Hold on." Sophie frantically flipped pages. "There." The page she indicated showed an open drawer and a gloved hand holding a piece of metal with the Speranza medallion. In the background, the setting sun glinted off a stone arch.

"I think that glove confirms what we've suspected about poison, since so many ladies back then resorted to it to rid themselves of unwanted husbands," Mercy said.

"Maybe the Speranza medallion is the key to all of it." Camille looked from one to the other. "Since Countess Alonza lived where the summit will be, maybe the medallion will lead to the treasure somewhere on the property."

They stopped, stared at each other.

"We are so close. Keep digging." Sophie's fingers flew over her keyboard as Hank and Mercy pored over the book and diary, desperate for clues.

Camille kept reading, too, trying to focus, but it was hard. When her phone finally rang, she snatched it up on the first ring. "Did you find her?"

"I have both good news and bad news," Marcel said. "Which do you want first?"

Camille put the call on speaker. "I don't have time for games. Just tell me. Is she alive?"

"Absolutely, she's alive." He told them how he'd found her based on the St. Claude Avenue Bridge in the background and said they'd put Cass in the back of an SUV, driven her to the private airfield, and taken off.

"What do you mean they took off? You just let her go?" Camille's voice rose with every syllable.

"I didn't want to risk her getting hurt. They were all wearing masks, which is good. She can't identify them. She was blindfolded, too, so that's another layer of protection for Cass. And after they left, I finagled a peek at the flight plan. And I got the SUV's license plate and the plane's tail numbers. I'm texting them now."

When Camille read the flight plan, she dropped into a chair. "She's on her way to Florence."

61

OUTSIDE FLORENCE—TWO DAYS LATER

Camille watched Jolie walk across the terra-cotta tile floor of the enormous ballroom and step onto the dais at one end. This year's Becker Foundation Summit was being held at a historic villa about twenty-five miles northeast of Florence that had been converted into a corporate retreat center. The sprawling estate easily accommodated their group of just over two hundred people.

The ballroom boasted several huge chandeliers and a balcony that ran the perimeter of the entire room. Padded chairs for the attendees had been set up in rows on the ballroom floor and in the balcony. Sunlight streamed through the French doors that overlooked the rolling hills beyond.

Jolie had managed to stay calm throughout the morning as she'd introduced speakers from various countries to give updates on their work. All those long-ago pageants were coming in handy, because if she was nervous, it didn't show, which was exactly what they needed. Jolie beautifully described the Becker Foundation's work and how they were making a difference in the lives of people within their home countries. It was impressive and Camille could see why Jolie had joined the Foundation.

Now, as the afternoon session began, Camille sat in the third row, professional smile in place, relying on that same long-ago pageant poise. Anxiety and dread made her stomach cramp, and her hands badly wanted to shake.

They still didn't know where Cass was being held, though Camille and the team had searched the property from top to bottom. Multiple texts and calls to the unknown number had not been answered or responded to.

Jolie's smile was a little wobbly as she stepped behind the podium. "Welcome back, ladies and gentlemen. I hope you enjoyed the delicious lunch the chef and his staff prepared for us." She led the applause, then waited for it to die down.

Camille assumed the pasta, salads, breads, and slew of decadent desserts had been top-notch. She hadn't been able to choke down a single bite. The atmosphere in the room had definitely gotten more tense so she figured she wasn't the only one on edge.

The team was in place, along with several people Nelson told Jolie had paid the million-dollar entry fee for the event. Hank was in the balcony, a last-minute replacement for a sound tech who'd suddenly fallen ill, courtesy of a hefty payoff. Mercy was seated at the back of the room, filling in for a pregnant member of the resort's medical team whose doctor suddenly wanted to see her.

Camille sent Jolie a bland smile as the other woman scanned the assembled guests. She'd told Jolie the less she knew, the less anyone could force out of her.

"This afternoon, the Beckers have something special planned," Jolie continued. "Most of you have read a bit about it in the news, but I'll let Nelson tell you more."

The whole idea of a Liar's Trial was the craziest thing Camille had ever heard, but she made sure none of that showed on her face.

Nelson Becker appeared from the side of the room and stepped onto the stage, his wife, Dot, by his side.

"Thank you all for coming, especially those who've traveled

great distances to be here. I believe you will find it was worth the trip." He started with a brief genealogy of the Fontana family and added that Countess Alonza's parents had originally owned the villa, a little-known fact that Camille and her friends had already unearthed.

Nelson described the Book of Days, the portable altar, and the set of altar pieces, then moved on to the legend, and ended with the biblical story of Ananias and Sapphira.

"Now it's time to put the legend to the test." Nelson smiled benignly.

As he spoke, four men strode up the center aisle and positioned themselves around the stage. They were all wearing black suits and holstered weapons under their jackets.

"These gentlemen are here to ensure nobody does anything out of order or unexpected."

Camille glanced around, shocked that people weren't running for the exits. Did they think this was some sort of joke, part of the conference entertainment? Surely the million-dollar entry fee would have told them differently. She could understand treasure hunters waiting it out, hoping to snag a piece of the treasure, but she couldn't fathom anyone else agreeing to be part of this craziness. Not when the legend said you could die if your motives weren't pure.

"Let's get started, shall we? First, I'd like anyone who brought one of the pieces of the Liar's Treasure to bring it up to the dais and place it on the table."

Showtime.

Father, help.

Camille took a deep breath as she stood and worked her way past the others in the third row, ignoring the looks aimed her way. Some seemed impressed, others excited, a few appeared green with envy. She wore a white blouse, blue pantsuit, and low-heeled pumps she could run in, along with a polymer knife strapped to her calf, which she'd snuck past security. She tightened her grip on the thick briefcase.

Lucien, dressed in an immaculately tailored gray suit, stood from where he sat four rows behind Camille and also exited the row. He glanced her way as they met in the aisle and winked. She'd never admit to her relief when he arrived at the villa last night exactly as he'd said he would. Knowing he was part of the plan to rescue Cass helped control the worry gnawing her insides. They could do this.

Camille walked straight up onto the stage, calm and confident, as though this were a pageant. She nodded regally to Nelson and briefly met Jolie's eyes. Lucien strode up beside her, wooden box in his hand.

She held up the briefcase. "This case contains the altar pieces that once belonged to Countess Evelina Romano." She scanned the room, desperate for some glimpse of Cass, but her daughter was not here.

"Open it, please," Nelson commanded.

Camille set the case on the table and slowly and carefully unwrapped the set of candlesticks. She held them up one at a time, then set them on the table to the oohs and aahs of the crowd. Next came the jeweled chalices, to appreciative murmurs, and finally, she used both hands to show everyone the bejeweled cross, which glinted in the overhead light. She made sure to display the pieces in the order depicted in the Book of Days.

The crowd applauded softly.

Camille bent to close the case and whispered, "Caesar Gallo, back of the room."

"Got him," Hank whispered from her spot in the balcony.

Nelson took an eager step toward the table, hand out as though to touch the pieces, but Dot stuck out her arm to hold him back and whispered something Camille couldn't hear. He nodded.

"Sir, you are next." He pointed at Lucien.

Lucien nodded and set the wooden box on the table, opened the lid. Without touching the actual book, he held up the box. "This is the Fontana family's Book of Days." The crowd gasped at the beautifully illuminated cover.

Once the applause died down, Nelson scanned the room, eyes glittering with excitement. "Now then, where is the third and final piece of our little trio?" He indicated the table in front of him, then faced the crowd.

A well-dressed man of about fifty, bald with a paunch, started down the center aisle from somewhere toward the back, a cloth-covered bundle in his hands.

"That's not The Ghost," Sophie whispered through Camille's earpiece. She was also seated in the balcony, the plus-one of an elderly, wealthy Foundation donor.

"Then who is he?" Hank asked.

"Decoy. I'll keep looking."

Every attendee had gone through a metal detector and been checked for weapons before entering the ballroom, but that didn't make Camille feel any better. She and each of the Speranza members had various items secreted either on their person or hidden under a nearby bench by Jolie, so she assumed others were equally prepared.

But Camille's biggest concern was Cass. They still didn't know where she was being held, despite hours of prowling the conference center.

The decoy stepped onto the stage beside Camille and Lucien.

"Unwrap the treasure, please," Nelson instructed.

He set the Portable Altar of Countess Alonza on the white tablecloth and unwrapped the soft fabric covering it. Gilt and jewels caught the light, and this time the crowd burst into thunderous applause.

"Open the box, sir."

He opened the lid to reveal little cloth bags said to contain the relics of saints.

"And the drawer."

He pulled it open, revealing a beautiful dagger inside.

The crowd whispered approval.

All Camille could hear was Cass's frightened voice in her head, pleading for her mother to come find her. Her fists clenched.

"Play the part, Eagle Eye," Sophie cautioned softly in her earpiece, and Camille loosened her fists and pasted a neutral expression on her face.

"Thank you. You may be seated." Nelson indicated the front row, and Camille, Lucien, and the impostor took their seats.

Nelson turned to the crowd and smiled, anticipation shining from his features like a kid on Christmas morning. "Now then, it is time to begin the trial. The court calls Dr. Garcia of the Becker Foundation to the stand."

An attractive older man stood and buttoned his suit jacket as he approached the stage. "I'm not sure what this is all about, but it should be interesting. I'm told this trial will help fund another water project." He shrugged and smiled at the assembled guests. "Anything for a good cause."

The crowd chuckled uneasily.

Nelson waited until Dr. Garcia stood beside him. "We'll start with an easy question first." Nelson paused, scanned the room. "Be aware, sir, that the treasure will judge your words and motives."

Garcia turned to the crowd again and chuckled. "Sure. Whatever you say."

Nelson ignored his mocking tone. "Kindly pick up the Book of Days." When he reached for it, Nelson snapped, "There are gloves inside. Don't touch it with your bare hands. The oils from your skin could ruin it."

"Okay." Garcia slipped the leather gloves on and picked up the book.

"It's beautiful, isn't it?" Nelson asked. "Go ahead, flip through the pages, show everyone. *Carefully.*"

Dr. Garcia did as he was told, holding the book aloft every few pages so people could see the beautiful illumination. Many of the pages were works of art in their own right.

"Now then, Dr. Garcia, did you or did you not poison the well in the small town of Mărgău, Romania, causing the death of at least one person?"

"What?" He laughed. "That's absurd. Why would I do that? I'm a doctor. I helped make the water project happen."

"So you didn't poison the well."

"I did not."

"Very well. Next question. Are you or are you not part owner of a development company that wants to turn that small town into an upscale resort, displacing all the artisans who live there?"

This time, Garcia's face paled slightly and he lost some of his bluster. "This is crazy. Where are you coming up with this stuff?"

"Do you deny ownership?" Nelson nodded to Dot, who pressed a button on a remote. A curtain slid open, revealing a large screen. An image appeared showing several corporate documents with Dr. Garcia's name clearly listed as an owner.

"Okay, fine. I may have made some investments. But that doesn't mean I killed anyone."

"So you had nothing to do with Dr. Tara Jameson's death in Rome?"

In the front row, Jolie let out a choked sound. Whispered murmurs of confusion and anger filled the room. All around, Foundation members muttered angrily.

"No, I did not. This is madness." He yanked off the gloves and tossed them onto the table. "I'm leaving."

When he turned to step off the stage, he had the portable altar tucked under one arm as if to take it with him, the dagger in his other hand, daring anyone to stop him.

The guards closed ranks as he hurried down the steps.

Garcia had one foot on the bottom step when he suddenly froze, a surprised expression on his face.

Before anyone could react, he collapsed in a heap on the floor.

One of the guards knelt beside him, ear to his chest. "He's not breathing. Get help." Then he bent forward and started CPR. Mercy rushed down the aisle holding an automated external defibrillator.

The assembled crowd watched in astonishment as Mercy and the guard worked to revive him.

Several minutes later, the doors burst open and another guard led a team of medics into the room. They checked the man's vitals and shook their heads.

Dr. Garcia was dead.

62

The crowd erupted in horrified gasps and muttering. Several people hurried from the room while others gestured and pointed, as though still unsure if this was some sort of performance for their amusement.

Camille leaned forward and caught Jolie's eyes. The other woman trembled, hands over her mouth as though to hold in her screams. Camille signaled her to breathe deeply. She had to keep it together.

Jolie nodded and squeezed her eyes shut, breathing through her nose.

The medics covered the doctor with a sheet and wheeled him out of the room, with Mercy following.

Maybe he didn't kill Tara, but had Dr. Garcia poisoned the well, causing the older woman's death?

Nelson's voice suddenly barked through the speakers and the microphone squealed. He paused for quiet. "I trust that you all are now believers in the legend of the Liar's Treasure. Just like in the biblical story of Ananias and Sapphira, you lie at your own peril."

Nelson nodded to Dot, who carefully set the portable altar back on the table, then pulled on gloves before she picked up the dagger and tucked it back inside the drawer.

Nelson scanned the room. "Next, the court calls Mr. Payne Martin. For those who don't know, he handles donations and other financial matters for the Becker Foundation."

Nobody moved. The crowd murmured uneasily.

"Mr. Martin, please come forward," Nelson said firmly.

Camille swiveled in her seat and saw a man stand from his place in the middle of the room and signal to two men in the back. They moved to the rear doors while he headed for the podium. A chill slid down her spine when she saw them close the doors and take up positions in front of them. Where had Mercy gone?

"I'm in the balcony with Hank," Mercy whispered in her earpiece.

Nelson waited until the tall, distinguished-looking man stood in front of him. "Now then, Mr. Martin, did you—?"

"I do believe I'll be asking the questions from now on." As he spoke in a clipped British accent, Martin slid a weapon from behind his sport coat and pointed it at Nelson.

A collective gasp went up in the room.

A suppressor was attached to the barrel of the gun. Camille leaned forward as though adjusting her shoe and whispered, "Be ready."

"Stand next to your husband, Dot." When the older woman didn't move from her place at the side of the dais, Martin barked, "Now."

Dot hurried to her husband's side.

"What are you doing, Payne? This is not what we planned." Nelson's earlier excitement had turned to confusion.

"Slide your gun across the floor to me."

"What? No. How dare you!" Nelson flicked his eyes toward the back of the ballroom. "Guards! Remove this man at once."

They didn't move.

Martin glanced toward the men, then faced Nelson and chuckled. "*Tsk. Tsk.* You should have hired people who aren't so easily bought off. Those gentlemen now work for me." He waved his gun at Nelson. "The gun. Now."

Nelson glanced at Dot, then slowly slid his weapon from the holster at his back and set it on the floor. He slid it to Martin, who scooped it up and pocketed it.

Martin smiled at Nelson. "You wanted a trial? Well then, let me accommodate you. The court calls Dot Becker to the stand."

Dot's face paled and she took a slight step back. "Absolutely not. This is outrageous."

Martin's voice turned mocking. "But if you have nothing to hide, you have nothing to fear from the treasure, correct?" He waited until Dot nodded. "Let's continue then, shall we? Put on the gloves and pick up the Book of Days." He turned to the guests. "As Nelson said, we don't want to ruin this beautiful book with oily hands." He waited until she slid her hands into the gloves.

"Dot Becker, did you or did you not embezzle two hundred thousand dollars from the Becker Foundation over the last two years?"

The room went deathly quiet.

Dot's chin came up. "I did not."

"Wrong answer."

There was a muffled sound, and Dot collapsed with a scream of pain, blood pooling around her leg.

Nelson leaped forward. "Dot!"

"Stay where you are," Martin warned.

"Tell me he's lying!" Nelson pleaded, eyes glued to his wife.

"Where did you expect me to get the money for these ridiculously expensive manuscripts you keep buying?" Her tone said she thought her husband was an idiot.

"But you told me we had the money!" Nelson appeared completely baffled.

Dot huffed out a breath and tried to climb to her feet, but it was awkward in the leather gloves. She finally stood, turned her outrage toward Martin. "I can't believe you shot me!" Her voice rang out over the crowd.

Martin raised his gun, but before he fired again, Dot suddenly swayed, then crumpled to the floor.

A shocked gasp filled the room.

Nelson dropped to his knees beside his wife, sobbing Dot's name.

Martin turned to the crowd, smiled an evil smile. "I do believe the treasure has spoken again."

People leaped from their seats and Martin shouted, "Sit down!" He aimed his gun at one of the chandeliers and pulled the trigger, sending shards of glass flying.

Nelson glared over his shoulder at Martin, shouted, "I trusted you! I asked you to help me find the treasure and set up the trial, to find the traitor in our organization!"

"I am helping you." Martin turned his back on the couple and faced the room. "Those who steal—and then lie about it—will be punished. Just like all the rest who claim to be good people and then sin under cover of darkness. People like them are not"—he made air quotes—"'making the world a better place.' Be sure your sins will find you out, isn't that what the Bible says, Nelson?" Disgust dripped from his words.

Camille froze. *What sins?* Had Nelson kidnapped Cass?

Nelson paled and clambered to his feet. He visibly pulled himself together, jaw tight with grim determination. "You killed Tara. Why?"

The crowd murmured uncomfortably.

Martin stiffened, eyes flashing with fury. "She had an affair with a married man."

"Was her affair with Jamie Lawson?"

He nodded. "Lawson was also involved in the development scheme with Garcia."

Nelson folded his arms. "So you arranged his accident in Amsterdam."

Martin grinned, very proud of himself, and Camille glimpsed the fanatical light in his eyes he'd no doubt kept carefully hidden. "I did what needed to be done. I am committed to making the world a better place."

He paused and scanned the room. "Next, the court calls Jolie Ward to the stand."

At the sound of Jolie's name, Camille's heart started thumping like a jackhammer.

Nelson turned toward Jolie, shoulders slumped in defeat. He glanced at Dot and swallowed hard before he met Martin's gaze. "When I asked you to help me get the treasure for the trial, this is not what I expected. I wanted to flush out the traitor in our midst, the one behind the deaths. I never dreamed *you're* the one I was trying to find." His eyes filled with anguish. "Please, end this now. Let Jolie go. Let all of them go."

Martin cocked his head, studied the man. "Nelson Becker, you have not led your organization with integrity, nor surrounded yourself with honorable people. You have acted selfishly while proclaiming your righteousness. The punishment is death."

He raised the gun again and fired. Jolie screamed as Nelson crumpled to the floor. More shouts erupted as people leaped up, ready to run.

"Sit!" Martin fired another round at the chandelier. "Step up to the front, Jolie. You are next." He walked over and slid the gloves from Dot's hands, set them back on the table.

Camille's mind raced as Jolie stepped onto the stage. When Jolie glanced back, Camille nodded. *Play your part.*

"Mercy and I are headed to disarm the guards at the back," Hank whispered in Camille's ear.

Good. But how would Camille keep Martin from killing Jolie? They had to take him down and find Cass. She glanced at Lucien, who was also scanning the room, seeking an opportunity.

"Isn't punishment God's job?" Jolie demanded once the crowd quieted.

"Sometimes even the Almighty needs a hand," Martin said briskly. "Now then. Let's begin. Put the gloves on and pick up the book."

Jolie squared her shoulders. "No."

"What do you mean, no?"

Jolie lifted her chin. "I won't stand trial." She turned to step off the stage.

"Will you let a child die due to your cowardice?"

A remote clicked and an image suddenly filled the screen. The crowd gasped. Jolie glanced over her shoulder and paused midstride.

Camille's heart stopped, then started again at a thunderous pace. The screen showed Cass tied to a chair, gagged, and blindfolded. But that wasn't the worst of it. She was being held in a deep, dark, round pit, like an old stone cistern. Water flowed into it from a spigot shaped like a fish several feet above Cass's head. The water lapped at Cass's knees. She wouldn't drown—yet—but the implication was clear.

It took every single ounce of Camille's self-control not to leap from her seat. Only the knowledge that Martin would shoot Jolie before Camille reached her kept her seated.

Lucien leaned forward, met Camille's gaze. *Patience*, his look said. *We'll find Cass.*

No question, but they had to save Jolie, too. Camille couldn't stand by and let her die.

Martin turned back to the crowd as more people rushed from their seats, crowding the aisles. Two guards stepped forward. "Please return to your seats. No one will enter or exit the ballroom until the trial is completed."

Anxious murmurs filled the air.

"One guard down. Searching the property," Hank whispered.

"Okay. I'll do it," Jolie said, her voice quavering.

She looked over her shoulder and Camille surreptitiously wiggled her fingers. If what she suspected was true, the gloves that accompanied the Book of Days were laced with a fast-acting poison.

"Second guard down, still searching," Mercy said in her ear.

Onstage, Jolie pulled a pair of white gloves out of her pocket, still in their plastic wrapper. "I'd like to, ah, wear my own gloves. I just bought these. I'd hate to damage the fragile pages in any way." She slipped the gloves on and picked up the Book of Days.

"Jolie Ward, while you were in high school, did you or did you not stab your father, multiple times, with a kitchen knife?"

Camille sucked in a breath. *Oh, Jolie. I'm sorry I wasn't there for you.*

Jolie nodded, her chin high. "I did."

"Why would you do such a thing?"

"I-I—" She stopped, tried again. "He'd beaten my mother, badly. I couldn't let him hurt her—or me—anymore." Tears streamed down her face.

Camille slid forward in her seat, hand reaching for the knife under her pant leg. Nearby, Lucien moved forward too.

"Jolie Ward, you are guilty of murder and must pay the price."

"I didn't kill him!" Jolie shouted. "He was alive when my mother and I escaped."

"That doesn't excuse what you did!" Martin lifted the gun.

63

Camille leaped to her feet. "Don't shoot!"

Martin turned the gun in her direction, then addressed the assembled crowd, his smile smug. "There you are. Let me introduce Camille, Cassandra's mother."

He jerked a thumb at the live feed of Cass on the big screen, where the water now reached her waist.

Camille braced against the panic. "Let Jolie—and my daughter—go, and I'll put the treasure together."

His voice hardened. "You do not make the rules here."

"Unless I connect the pieces, the legend won't work."

Martin laughed, waving a hand toward Dot's still form. "It clearly works without your assistance. I don't need you."

He raised his weapon.

Camille scrambled for a response, a way to buy time. Then the truth dawned. "Ah, I get it. You judge people's motives and are content to let the treasure judge them, too. But you're afraid to have *your* motives put on trial. In case the legend is true." She kept her focus on his face. "Either way, I think you want the 'untold riches' part of the legend. And for that, you need me."

The slight twitch in his expression told her she was right. The lowering of his weapon confirmed it.

"The Ghost, on the move, left side of the aisle." Sophie's voice came through their comms.

Martin canted his head to the left, considering. "You don't think my motives are pure? Or do you think yours are?"

"Release my daughter." Her eyes swung briefly to Jolie. "And my friend. Let them go and any untold treasure is yours."

"Picasso is trying to locate any cisterns on the property," Sophie whispered in her earpiece.

Martin studied Camille. "Connect the pieces. Then I'll let them go."

Camille folded her arms. "No. Release them first."

He raised his gun again, but this time he aimed it squarely at Jolie's chest. "You might want to rethink your position."

Camille met his eyes, saw the darkness there, the lack of emotion of any kind. She nodded once. "All right."

"Still looking. Buy time." Hank's voice was a mere thread of sound through her earpiece.

Camille forced herself to ignore Cass's picture on the screen and instead turn all of her focus to the task at hand. The team had spent last night poring over the clues in the Book of Days again and again, making sure they understood what it was telling them.

Please, God, let us have guessed correctly.

Camille stepped over to the table and nodded to the two guards. "Help me remove the tablecloth."

They turned to Martin for permission. He nodded.

Once the cloth had been removed, Camille reached into her pocket and pulled out a pair of gloves just like Jolie's. She slipped them on, nodded to Jolie, then moved the pieces closer together.

Praying that she remembered everything, Camille opened the lid on the portable altar. Then she opened the wooden box containing the Book of Days and gently lifted the book out and set it inside the portable altar before slowly closing the lid. There was an almost inaudible click and she let out a small sigh of relief.

Step one, done.

Next, she ran her hands over the scrollwork that wrapped around the sides of the portable altar, hoping her gloves were thin enough to feel what she was searching for.

There?

She pressed. Nothing.

She slid her fingers farther along.

Here? She applied a bit of pressure and slid what felt like a tiny lever to one side as she lifted the altar off the table. Her breath whooshed out in relief when the compartment opened, revealing what looked like a gaudy costume-jewelry necklace with several gold charms.

The crowd shifted expectantly.

"Connect them clockwise," Sophie whispered.

The room went silent. Camille glanced over her shoulder and realized that her every move was being broadcast on the big screen behind her.

Her hands wanted to shake. She picked up the necklace and opened the clasp. Then she carefully inserted the end of the clasp into the front of the altar. It clicked into place.

"Very good," Martin said. "Keep going."

She picked up one of the candlesticks.

"No. Chalice next," Sophie whispered.

Camille froze, her blood pounding in her ears. She'd almost made a deadly mistake. She forced herself to slow her breathing as she set the candlestick back down. She slowly reached for one of the chalices, waiting, but Sophie didn't say anything, so she inserted the charm on the next section of the necklace into the back of it.

"Now the candlestick," Sophie said.

Camille nodded and connected it. Then came the bejeweled cross.

She used her arm to wipe the sweat off her forehead, glanced at Jolie, who nodded encouragement.

Martin had lowered the weapon as he watched Camille with single-minded focus.

Would they be able to take advantage of the opportunity?

"We're waiting," he prodded.

Camille looked down, blocked all else from her mind.

The next charm connected to the second chalice.

The one after that tethered the candlestick to the chain she was creating.

Her chest tightened.

There was only one connection left to make.

64

Camille tried to slow her breathing. She flexed her fingers once, twice. If she and the team were right, connecting the pieces would somehow reveal the location of the treasure.

But if the legend was true and the treasure decided her motives weren't pure, she would die. She wanted her daughter and Jolie safe. That had to count as a pure motive, right?

She took a deep breath and then eased the end of the necklace into the back of the portable altar.

She stepped back.

Waited.

Nothing happened.

The crowd shifted uncomfortably.

Martin frowned. He raised his weapon and stepped closer to Jolie.

Camille wanted to grab him by the throat and toss him across the room. She glanced over her shoulder at Sophie. What had she done wrong? Why didn't anything happen?

"Flames," Sophie whispered in Camille's comm. "It has to do with fire. That's the part we couldn't figure out. What could burn?"

Frantic, Camille studied the pieces. All gold. Unless they were put into a forge, none of them would melt easily. What was she missing?

"String? Gunpowder? Anything?" Sophie whispered.

"Why isn't anything happening?" Martin demanded.

"Not sure." Camille crouched down to study the altar.

"If this is some elaborate ruse to—"

Camille ignored him while she considered what would happen if she was wrong.

She checked again.

She didn't think she was wrong.

Prayed she wasn't wrong.

She pulled the lighter from her jacket pocket and flicked the flame to life.

The guards tensed, prepared to spring into action.

"Enough!" Martin shouted. "This is nothing but fiction!"

The side door opened and Ponytail and Scarface, who'd been on their tail since Romania, came in pushing a cart, a small hibachi barbecue sitting on top. Ponytail flicked his lighter and large flames sprang up.

"He's going to destroy the Book of Days the minute he gets the treasure!" Sophie whispered. "He's afraid of it."

"Buy time, Camille." Mercy's voice was adamant. "Picasso, Hank, and I are still trying to find Cass."

Camille registered the words, but all of her focus stayed on what she was doing. She touched the lighter to the spot where the chain connected to the back of the altar, melting the tiny layer of wax she'd almost missed.

Head down, she whispered, "Get ready."

Lighter in one hand, she shifted position to block the camera. With her other, she pulled a fistful of firecrackers she'd snuck past security from her other pocket and tossed them onto the hibachi.

The moment they started exploding, people screamed and ran for the exits, desperate to escape whatever was happening.

Camille reached for the smoke bomb Jolie had taped under the table and set it off, too. Then she waited, ignoring the noise and smoke, focused on the altar.

When the final compartment sprang open, she didn't hesitate. She scooped up the Speranza medallion inside, shoved it into her pocket, and leaped toward Jolie, who stood frozen, unmoving.

Martin yelled, "Stop them!" and started shooting.

65

Camille tackled Jolie as bullets carved up the wooden dais where they'd been standing.

"Little help!" she shouted into her earpiece.

Sophie rappelled down from the balcony and made it to the stage just as the decoy reached for the portable altar. She tackled him and they skidded across the floor. She must have been taking lessons from Mercy because she had him on his stomach in seconds, hands and feet bound with rope from her pocket.

Camille whirled around. Through the smoke, she saw some guy heading toward the Book of Days. She kicked him with all her might, sending him sprawling across the stage. His head hit a stone column and he slid to the floor.

She turned and saw Lucien punch Caesar Gallo in the face, then snatch the gold cross from his hands.

Mercy charged into the ballroom and snapped her whip with deadly precision. Another guest screamed.

Camille charged a heavyset guard struggling to his feet. Head to his midsection, she rammed him backward into another column.

She glanced back to see Jolie shove her hand into another guard's face with enough power to break his nose.

Hank rappelled down from the balcony, jumped into the fray. "Haven't found Cass. Yet. Picasso's still digging."

Sophie was grabbing the treasure pieces and stuffing them into a bag while Lucien fought off more guards.

Hank and Mercy fought off all the people swarming the stage to grab a piece of the treasure for themselves. Through the billowing smoke, Mercy's whip cracked, bringing screams every time it connected.

Hank had a knife in her hand and was slicing the air to keep people at bay with more skill than Camille had been aware of. Not that she was complaining.

To her left, she saw Sophie fight with a man, go down hard, then scramble to her feet and give chase.

"The Ghost has the altar, heading out the side door," Sophie panted as she rushed after him, hands gripping her ribs.

"Where's Payne Martin?" Camille shouted, scanning the smoky room.

"Lost sight of him," Mercy said. "Still looking."

Camille spotted Lucien, knife in hand, rushing a shell-shocked Jolie down a long hallway toward an emergency exit. He rammed the door open with his hip, clicked a key fob, and the lights on a car parked at the curb flashed.

"No sign of Martin. And Gallo got away from me," Hank muttered. She paused, then shouted, "Sophie, no!"

Camille twisted around looking for Sophie when she spotted Martin running down a hallway in the opposite direction. "Found Martin! I'm going after him!"

"Camille!" Lucien caught the door before it closed and started toward her. "Wait!"

She didn't have time. She had to catch Martin.

No way would she let her daughter drown.

Camille rushed down the hallway. She had to fight her way through two more guards, but they barely slowed her down. All of her focus was on Martin. She burst through doorways, startling staff, muttering apologies, and kept going.

Where had he gone?

She raced down another long hallway and saw him turn the corner at the end. "Martin!"

He tossed a glare over his shoulder that had her running faster than she ever had in her life.

"Where's my daughter, you miserable excuse for a human being?" she shouted as she ran. The stitch in her side was getting worse, but it meant nothing.

Cass. She had to find out where he was holding Cass.

His laughter echoed against the stone corridor.

Camille chased him out a door and across the manicured grounds, leaping over flower beds and running through hedges.

He'd vanished.

She stopped in the middle of the lawn, hands on her hips, breathing hard. She turned in a circle, forcing herself to concentrate.

There.

She caught a glimpse of his suit jacket as he rounded another corner of the building.

With every bit of speed she had left, she sprinted around the corner.

She was too late.

A black BMW sped out of the lot and turned toward Florence.

66

"Camille!" Hank shouted.

She and Mercy, with a furious Sophie in tow, rounded the corner of the building.

"He got away! Now we'll never find Cass!" Camille scoured the area, arms wrapped around her waist, defeat threatening to take her under.

"We're not done yet, grasshopper," Hank said.

Camille rounded on her. "What does that even mean?"

"We need to search the villa." Mercy's tone brooked no argument.

"Agreed. Maybe we'll get lucky and find The Ghost hiding out somewhere." Sophie glared at Hank. "You should have let me go after him."

"Right, because the altar is so much more important than your life. That car almost flattened you."

Camille paced, mind racing, barely listening as Hank and Sophie bickered.

"Camille!"

Her head snapped up. "What?"

"What was in the hidden compartment in the altar?" Mercy held her hand out, waiting.

"Oh. Right." She yanked the metal piece out of her pocket and held her palm out.

"We were right." Sophie shook her head, grinning.

The familiar Speranza emblem—the anchor with a feather diagonally across it—had been pressed into the center of the rectangular piece of metal, about one inch wide by two inches long. Like an oversize domino.

Hank picked it up, examined the notched edges. "What are these?"

Sophie snapped pics from every angle. "I think it fits into something. Picasso?" she said into her comm. "Can you check?"

"On it." Picasso's keyboard clattered in the background.

"I don't care what it fits!" Camille shouted. "It still doesn't tell us where he's hiding Cass! The water keeps rising!"

Everyone stopped, looked at her.

"Let's take a second and see if this can help us find her," Mercy said gently.

Hank took the piece and turned it over. "What's this on the back?"

Sophie turned on her flashlight, illuminating another symbol, this one fainter than the other. "I'd say it's a family crest. There's a shield."

"That's a fountain." Mercy pointed. "Fontana means 'fountain.'"

"What's this wavelike thing?" Hank asked.

"Countess Alonza's surname was Marino, meaning 'of the sea,'" Sophie said. "Maybe?"

"That could work." Hank pointed. "What's it say under it?"

Mercy read it out loud. "*Riposa sotto al mare.* It means, 'Rest beneath the sea.'"

Camille stopped pacing and studied the rest of the team. "That sounds like a graveyard of some kind."

"Wait." Sophie frantically scrolled through her phone. "I took a pic. Yes!" She'd enlarged part of the picture of Cass. Above her head was the same crest.

"Picasso, is there a family graveyard near here? Maybe by some water?" Camille's voice shook.

"I've been checking while you talk and . . ." Keys clattered at a furious pace. "It looks like it. But I can't find anything that shows a cistern. The two might have nothing to do with each other. I did find a reference to passageways beneath the villa, though."

"I'll start there! Let's go!"

Camille raced back into the villa with the rest of the team hot on her heels. "I'm betting Martin hid her close by. Maybe there's a crypt in the passageway near the cistern."

"Try to find either of the symbols, anywhere and everywhere," Picasso said into their comms. "I'll keep searching online."

"I'll take the kitchens and staff areas belowstairs." Sophie turned off in that direction.

"I'll check the main guest areas and ask the staff." Mercy gripped the stethoscope around her neck as she ran.

"I'll cover the grounds and outbuildings. Meet in the basement in"—Hank checked her watch—"fifteen minutes. Or less."

Camille wasn't listening. She was racing down the hall toward the basement stairs she'd seen earlier.

Hang on, Cass. I'm coming.

She burst through the door and pounded down the stairs, eyes scanning—always scanning—the stone walls. *Come on, come on, where are the symbols?*

At the end of yet another endless hallway, the corridor took a sharp turn to the right. Camille raced around the corner and suddenly, there it was. "Speranza symbol, on the wall."

"Sweet. Staff says they've only seen them in the basement," Mercy confirmed. "Heading your way, Camille."

"Nothing in the old barn or stable. Nothing in the gardener's shed either." Hank sounded like she was running. "Got two more outbuildings to check."

"Nothing in the kitchen or staff rooms," Sophie said. "Heading to intercept you, Eagle Eye."

Camille didn't slow down, just kept running full tilt.

She heard footsteps behind her and peeked around another corner to see Mercy headed her way.

A few minutes later, Sophie appeared from the opposite direction.

The three of them kept running, following the Speranza symbols.

"Headed down," Hank said. "Where are you?"

Sophie grabbed her phone. "Compass says we've been heading east."

"You should be near the back of the villa that faces the lake," Picasso said.

Camille's phone buzzed with a text. She read it as she ran. "Lucien sent Jolie away from here with the treasure. He got the chalice from Gallo, too. He's headed to meet up with us. I'll let him know which way we're going."

They turned down another bend in the hallway and stopped. It was blocked by a heavy wooden door.

"Look." Mercy pointed. Both the family crest and the Speranza symbol had been painted above the door, hidden amongst the painted vines.

Hank and Lucien arrived just as Sophie was trying to open a heavy padlock without much luck.

"It's too massive. My picks can't budge it."

Lucien pulled a small screwdriver from a backpack he must have had stashed somewhere on the property. "Try this."

Sophie grinned and went back to work. The lock clicked, she removed the padlock, and they wrestled the heavy door open.

A dark tunnel loomed before them.

Five phone flashlights flicked to life.

"Let's go!" Camille led the way.

Several minutes later, they rounded another bend and stopped. The tunnel suddenly split off in two directions.

Camille shined her light on the walls. The rest of the team did the same.

The Speranza symbol continued in the right-hand tunnel.

The Fontana family crest appeared on the left side.

"The crest was in the photo of Cass." Camille took off in that direction.

She heard Lucien and the rest of the team running behind her, but she was focused ahead. "Cass! Can you hear me? We're coming!"

When the tunnel ended at another wooden door, Camille reached out and pulled with all her might.

Just like the other one, it didn't budge.

She rammed her shoulder into it. "Cass!"

Lucien nudged her aside. "Easy. Let Sophie get it open."

Sophie crouched before the lock and used the screwdriver again with lightning speed.

Lucien and Hank hauled the door open and Camille burst inside.

She almost fell headlong into the cistern, but quick hands yanked her back.

Horror burst through Camille as she looked down.

Cass's panicked face was turned up toward her, water lapping over the tape covering her mouth.

"Hang on, baby, we're coming."

Camille prepared to leap over the side, but Lucien pulled her back a second time. "Wait. Let's get a rope around you first. We need a way to pull her up."

Her focus solely on Cass, it took a second for his words to register.

Lucien pulled a grappling hook from his backpack, attached it to the ledge, then fastened a rope around Camille's waist and ran it through her legs. "Ready?"

Camille nodded, then blinked several times to clear the panic from her mind.

Mercy pulled a sheathed polymer knife from her ankle holster and handed it to Camille. "To cut the ropes around her."

She remembered her own knife, but this was quicker. She tucked

Mercy's knife in her pocket, then swung a leg over. "I'm coming, baby. Just hang on."

Once she reached Cass, Camille dove down and cut the ropes, then yanked Cass up by her arms so she was standing on the arms of the chair. Camille ripped off the tape covering her mouth and pulled her close while Cass gasped for air. "I've got you, baby, I've got you."

A sobbing Cass wrapped her arms around Camille so tightly she couldn't breathe.

"Send her up, Camille," Hank ordered.

Camille eased back, then took off her makeshift harness and fastened it around Cass. "Put your feet against the wall, lean back, and start climbing. They'll help from above."

Cass's eyes were round with fear but she nodded, once. "I'll try."

"You can do this. I'll be right behind you."

It seemed like it took forever before Lucien, Hank, and Sophie pulled Cass to safety, and another eternity before the rope came back down and Camille climbed up.

Lucien helped her strip off the rope before she pulled Cass into her arms for another long hug. "You're safe, baby girl. Thank You, Jesus. You're safe."

"Touching as this little scene is, you haven't given me the untold riches I came for."

Camille froze, her back to Payne Martin, Cass quivering in her arms. She met Mercy's eyes and pushed Cass into her arms before she whipped toward Martin, knife at the ready. Beside her, Lucien also gripped a knife.

Martin grinned from his spot in the doorway, gun trained on them. "In a game of rock, paper, scissors, my gun trumps your knives. Too bad." He shrugged, then his expression hardened.

Camille exchanged a questioning glance with Lucien. Martin held the Book of Days in his other hand, but Lucien had said he'd sent the treasure off with Jolie. So how had Martin gotten the book? Had he hurt her? Lucien's pained expression said he didn't know.

"Take me to the rest of the treasure." Martin waved the gun.

"We don't know where it is."

"Then you're going to help me find it."

Mercy's hand reached under her scrub top for the whip she'd wrapped around her waist.

"I wouldn't do that if I were you." He nodded behind him and three of the armed guards appeared in the small room. "Hand over those knives." He pointed to Mercy. "And whatever that is."

Camille met Lucien's eyes as they handed their weapons to one of the guards. He mouthed, *Be ready.*

She nodded. At least she still had her knife strapped to her calf.

"Let's get moving. I haven't got all day." Martin waved Camille, Cass, and Lucien in front of him, while each of his guards walked beside another team member, firm grip on their arms.

67

Camille kept her eyes on the walls as they retraced their steps, praying they were right about the Speranza emblem, too. She fingered the metal "key" in her pocket and asked for wisdom. They hadn't come this far to die now.

In her ear, she barely heard Picasso's whisper, "Help on the way."

Camille pretended to stumble, then stopped, leaned against the wall, buying time.

"Keep moving." Martin prodded her with his gun.

"I'm feeling dizzy. Just give me a second."

She made eye contact with Sophie, knew she and the rest of the team had heard Picasso, too.

"Move. Now."

She slowly stood upright and kept walking. Cass's eyes were full of questions, but Camille gave the slightest shake of her head. *Keep walking.*

Lucien was coiled like a spring, and Camille knew he was also waiting for an opportunity.

In far less time than she'd hoped, they reached the intersection. Camille started down the right-hand tunnel this time.

Their group marched in silence, no sound except their shoes on the brick floor.

The tunnel ended at another wooden door, similar to the one guarding the cistern room.

"Open it." Martin waved his weapon at Camille.

She felt a bead of sweat trickle down her neck, tension thick in the air.

"We can't." Lucien shrugged. "Lockpick broke."

Camille blinked, then realized he'd palmed the screwdriver to use as a weapon.

Martin nodded to one of his men. "Open the door."

The man raised his weapon. "Back up and turn your faces away."

As soon as they did, he fired at the lock and pieces of metal flew everywhere. Cass yelped when a piece hit her arm.

But it worked. The guard pushed the door open and shined his flashlight into the dark interior.

Impatient, Martin shoved him aside and stepped into a dank storage room. He turned in a circle, flashlight in hand.

"Where is it?" His outraged bellow echoed off the stone wall as he aimed his weapon at Camille.

She pushed Cass behind her. "I-I don't know."

"Wrong answer."

In a blur of motion, Lucien spun on the balls of his feet and jabbed the screwdriver into Martin's thigh just as Camille bent over, yanked the knife from her sheath, and caught him in the back.

He screamed and raised his weapon, the Book of Days clutched in his other hand as blood ran from his wounds. "Tell me right now or you all die!"

Camille pushed Cass farther behind her, knife ready to strike again.

Lucien held the screwdriver at the ready, too.

They advanced on Martin, whose face had suddenly gone pale. He backed farther into the room, stumbling slightly. His arm wavered as he fired, hitting the wall behind Lucien and sending chunks of brick flying.

Beads of sweat formed on Martin's face, and he suddenly started foaming at the mouth. Camille realized he was clutching the Book of Days with bare hands.

He stumbled back one more step and the book slid from his grasp. The floorboards gave with a crash and he disappeared through a gaping hole.

A muffled scream echoed in the room. Then silence.

"Police! Hands in the air!" a female voice shouted.

Camille's hands shot up and she turned to see none other than Eloise Cuvier of Interpol standing in the doorway, weapon held in both hands. They'd last seen Eloise in Germany during their previous mission. A team of officers spilled into the room behind her.

Camille tipped her head toward the hole in the floor.

Eloise and her officers inched forward. "Careful." Another flashlight clicked on.

"Ouch. That had to hurt," one of the officers muttered.

"Stay here, Cass," Camille said.

She and the team stepped up beside Eloise and saw the hole where Martin had fallen through the rotting floorboards. He'd landed on the spikes of some sort of rusted farm implement twenty feet down.

"I guess the fall finished what the poison started," Hank observed.

"Good thing we all wore gloves whenever we touched the Book of Days. Guess it wasn't just the old leather gloves that had poison on them." Mercy rubbed her arms, shivering.

Camille hurried back to Cass, wrapped her in her arms and held tight.

Above her head, Camille met Lucien's eyes. *Thank you,* she mouthed.

He nodded once, then winked as one of Eloise's officers led him away for questioning.

Art investigator Mac McKenzie stepped into the room, eyes searching for Sophie.

She rolled her eyes when she spotted him, then grinned. "Took you long enough to bring the cavalry."

He sent her a lopsided grin. "Flight got delayed. Sorry."

Camille smiled at the lovestruck expression that passed between them. *Guess what they started in Germany is still a thing.*

Eloise gave her men instructions, then turned to Mercy, pulled out a pad and paper. "Start at the beginning."

Camille figured they were going to be here awhile.

68

Several hours later, Eloise and her team had rounded up all of the suspects and finished interviewing Camille and the Speranza team. They found out Martin had run Jolie off the road and stolen the treasure, but she was fine. Eloise's team had recovered the treasure from the trunk of his car.

Lucien had gotten a call from the hospital letting him know that Pops had fallen again, so he was heading for the airport. Before he left, he gave Cass a hug.

"Glad you're okay, kiddo. You're one tough cookie."

Cass sent him a cheeky grin. "You're pretty tough yourself . . . for an old guy."

He laughed and mimed being stabbed in the heart, then turned to Camille.

Without hesitation, she stepped toward him and wrapped her arms around his neck as he pulled her close.

"Glad you're okay, too, Princess," he said so quietly that only she could hear.

She smiled at the nickname and eased back so she could see his face. "Thank you for being here, Lucien. For all of it."

His blue gaze never wavered. "I'll always be here. As long as you want me to be."

Before she could respond, he winked and turned away, wishing the team safe travels before he hurried to catch his flight.

"Well now," Sophie said, fanning herself.

Camille ignored the team's teasing as they stood on the sloping lawn that led to the lake.

"It's a beautiful sunset," Mercy said.

"I'm glad you're okay." Hank fist-bumped Cass.

Cass grinned. "Except for the part where I was scared to death I was going to die, it was pretty cool, the way you guys showed up." Her gaze encompassed each of them in turn. "Thank you."

Camille pulled her close, whispered a prayer of thanks, then kissed the top of Cass's head.

"Um, guys?" Sophie's voice held a definite smile. "Look."

They followed her pointing finger down the slope and around the small lake to the neighboring family's crypt. The setting sun lit up the huge stone arch that guarded it.

Mercy shaded her eyes with her hand. "What are we—?"

"Holy smokes!" Hank laughed and took off running in that direction.

It took Camille a second, then she laughed, too. "The arch in the Book of Days." She grabbed Cass's hand. "Come on!"

The team raced down the hill.

By the time they reached the arch and the crypt behind it, the light was almost gone. Camille pulled out a flashlight and illuminated the padlock on the heavy wooden door.

Hank pulled out her screwdriver and Sophie opened the lock, grinning. "Glad you are always prepared, Hank." They tugged the door open.

Dust motes swirled in the air as Camille shined her flashlight over the ancient sarcophagi arranged on stone shelves like bunk beds.

Sophie moved closer to the nearest sarcophagus. Then the next. And another. "We need to find the Speranza emblem."

"You think it's here?" Mercy asked.

"Picasso, any chance the property next to Countess Alonza's was owned by her no-good husband's family?" Camille asked.

"Checking." Her voice was muffled.

Hank ducked and shined her light under each stone shelf but found nothing.

Camille circled the large room, probably ten feet by twenty, checking the walls. "Yes! That's it. Hank, I need that screwdriver again." Since Camille's knife was in an evidence bag somewhere.

Sure enough, there was the faintest outline of a doorway in the stone. She ran the screwdriver along the edge, again and again.

Mercy pulled out a handkerchief and rubbed it over a dark spot on the door, revealing another Speranza emblem, this one with a vertical slot in the middle.

The team gathered round. Was it possible?

Camille fished the metal piece she'd pulled from the portable altar out of her pocket and carefully slid it into the slot.

Nothing happened.

She pushed on it and something clicked. She pulled the metal ring.

The door wouldn't budge.

"Why won't it open?" Cass asked.

"I don't know."

"Turn it," Hank suggested.

Camille gripped the edge of the metal piece and turned it clockwise.

There was another click.

This time when she pulled the handle, the door shifted slightly. Hank stepped closer and together they managed to pull it open.

Camille stepped inside and her jaw dropped open in shock.

"Wow!" Cass whispered.

Beyond the opening lay a room the size of a large garden shed. Every nook and cranny was filled with gold and valuables. Sturdy wooden chests held hundreds of gold coins while necklaces, rings, chalices, and other priceless treasures littered every available space.

Camille struggled to take in what she was seeing.

"We found it!" Sophie whispered, grinning as she filtered gold coins through her fingers.

Picasso's voice came through their comms. "You were right, Sophie. The property next door was the countess's no-good husband's family estate."

Hank started laughing and the rest of the team joined in. "She was quite the lady, our countess. After she buried him, she buried her treasure in *his* family's crypt."

"No wonder Cira said the treasure was somewhere no one would ever think to look."

Camille hugged Cass. "What was the quote? 'It belongs to Speranza and no one but Speranza will ever find it.'"

"What's Speranza?" Cass searched their faces.

They fell silent as all eyes turned to Camille. "A really cool ancient society of women that I'll tell you all about someday. But today isn't that day."

When Cass opened her mouth to ask questions, Mercy wrapped an arm around her. "I don't know about you, but I'm starving. How about we eat?"

Cass's eyes got round as saucers. "We're just going to leave all this here?"

"For now," Sophie said briskly. She turned to Cass. "This is our secret, okay? No telling anyone. I mean it."

"But what about Uncle—?"

"No one," Hank added sternly. "Ever."

Cass finally nodded, though her eyes were still full of questions.

After they carefully closed the vault door, Camille tucked the metal key into her pocket for safekeeping.

She pulled her daughter close as they started up the hill. "I'm so glad you're okay, baby."

Cass laid her head on Camille's shoulder. "Me, too. I knew you'd come."

"Always, baby girl. Always."

EPILOGUE

NEW ORLEANS—TWO WEEKS LATER

Though the sun was out this afternoon, there was a definite chill in the air, but Camille didn't mind. She stood at the helm of Gramps's beloved *Easy Does It* and fired up the engines, smiling at the familiar rumble. While they warmed up, she wrapped her gloved hands around the wheel and took a deep breath, watching several gulls fly overhead.

"We found Cass, Gramps, and she's okay," Camille said, though she figured he already knew. But she'd always felt closest to him when they were on the boat. "She's actually become a bit of a celebrity at her school after the media got hold of the story." She laughed, then paused. "Gran's doing well, too. She's amazing."

"Ahoy! Permission to come aboard, Captain?"

Camille turned to see Lucien standing on the dock, hands tucked in the pockets of his leather jacket. Dark sunglasses hid his eyes, but his smile was all warm invitation.

"What brings you here?"

"Thought maybe you could use a first mate for the trip to the farm."

Camille smiled. "That I could. Welcome aboard."

He untied the lines, hopped aboard, and Camille backed out of the slip, then headed out of the marina toward Gramps's farm.

"You look very comfortable at the helm, Skipper."

Camille laughed. "I hadn't realized how much I missed this until right now."

"I think your gramps would like knowing you're taking her out."

"I think you're right." She smiled. "How's Claude? Is he able to drive yet?" Camille asked as they motored along.

Lucien quirked his lips. "Nope, and it's making him cranky. But apparently Octavia said she'd pick him up for today's shindig."

"You're kidding. Really? Those two?"

He shrugged, winked. "Pops said something about catching up on old times."

"Is that what they're calling it these days?" Camille chuckled.

"Hey, whatever works."

Camille shaded her eyes and pointed to an osprey flying overhead, fish gripped in its talons. The motion pulled up the sleeve of her jacket and Lucien stepped closer, lightly touched the Speranza tattoo on her wrist. "I like this. What does it mean?"

She flashed him a smile. "Hope."

He propped his shades on his head, met her eyes, curiosity in his. "I've seen it before."

Camille stilled, glanced away, kept her voice casual. "Oh yeah?"

"Twice, actually. Once in the Book of Days, so small you might miss it." He paused. "And once in my grandmother's diary."

She kept her eyes on the horizon. "Huh. How interesting."

He put a gentle finger under her chin and turned her head to face him. "You going to tell me more?"

She shrugged. "Maybe someday." But she smiled to take the sting out of the words.

Thankfully, he didn't press. Now that Pops was in physical therapy and steadily improving, Lucien was headed back to Africa for a couple of months, just long enough to find someone to take his place so he could come back home for good, be closer to Pops. Camille had to admit she liked the sound of that. In the meantime, he'd invited Camille—and Cass—to come to Africa, see what he did. Camille thought she just might take him up on it.

The ride went by too quickly, but she couldn't be sorry as all of her favorite people were milling around Gramps's dock when they pulled up. Lucien hopped off to tie the lines and put the ramp in place.

"'Bout time you got here. Thought the food was going to get cold," Mrs. H. grumbled as Lucien maneuvered a ginormous pot of her mouthwatering gumbo aboard. "Cass, honey, bring the bread, would you, dear?"

Cass held up a tote with loaves of bread sticking out of it, Lindsey carrying the paper goods. "Hey, Lucien." Cass gave him a side hug. "Meet my friend Lindsey."

Camille hurried toward Gran as she made her way slowly toward the boat, leaning on the cane she despised as a "necessary nuisance." Her broken ribs were healing well and her hip, which thankfully hadn't been broken, was healing, too. Gran scanned the length of *Easy Does It*, then glanced back at Camille and nodded, both their eyes just a little misty. Gramps would be happy to know that his boat was back at the farm. At least for today.

"Gran!" Cass ran toward her, then slowed and wrapped her in a gentle hug. "I love this look on you!" Gran was resplendent in her grandmother's vintage fur coat and, surprisingly, a pair of jeans. She gripped Cass's hand as though she never wanted to let her go.

Lucien's grandfather was right behind Gran. He was still using a walker, which he also deemed a nuisance, but he rolled aboard with ease.

"Welcome aboard, Mr. Broussard."

He leaned in to kiss Camille on the cheek. "Just call me Pops, ya hear?"

"Aye, aye, sir," she said, and he laughed, eyes twinkling. Just like his grandson's.

Hank and Mercy boarded next, both loaded down with various desserts.

"I may never leave," Mercy said. "Mrs. H., you have spoiled us rotten."

"Anything for you, sugar," Mrs. H. said. "You're always welcome here."

Camille raised an eyebrow as Sophie and Mac came aboard together, both toting extra folding chairs. Sophie just grinned. She hadn't said anything about it, but she and Mac had disappeared the day after they rescued Cass. They had come back with the portable altar, which had then been returned to the Fontana family along with the other pieces. The family said they would make sure the altar was returned to the convent.

Eloise Cuvier at Interpol was still piecing things together, but apparently, Payne Martin had taken it upon himself to rid the world of anyone he deemed dishonest. Picasso's research said his mother committed suicide after being lured into an affair with their priest when Martin was young. His father never got over it and died several years later. Shortly thereafter, so did the priest. When Nelson asked for his help finding the treasure, that had apparently been a two-for-one opportunity Payne Martin couldn't refuse. Meting out justice *and* gaining "untold riches." Apparently Martin had also put the extra money in Tara's account to confuse police.

The official Fontana family descendants and rightful owners of the Liar's Treasure had been identified and had shown their appreciation for the return of their family legacy through a substantial finder's fee, which had been divided between Lucien and the team. Speranza's share would fund quite a few missions.

Meanwhile, Jolie had been unanimously appointed the acting CEO of the Becker Foundation and was continuing to work with Interpol to get everything sorted out.

Marcel had checked himself into rehab as soon as he heard Cass was safe, and according to Gran, he was doing well. Camille still couldn't wrap her head around the fact that he'd kidnapped Cass and Gran. She'd been ready to tear him limb from limb for putting

Cass and Gran in that kind of danger. Eventually, Gran had helped her calm down enough to see the convoluted logic behind his reasoning. He said he agreed because he needed the money to pay his debts, but he also knew he could keep them safe. Well, until he couldn't, and Martin's henchmen beat up Gran and transported Cass to Florence. Camille was slowly working her way through all of that, but she was glad her cousin was getting the help he needed for the gambling and the drinking. Gran had mentioned that she and Marcel had developed a restitution plan going forward.

In no time at all, their group was gathered in chairs on the boat's aft deck, eating gumbo, laughing, and talking. Lucien caught Camille's eye from where he sat beside Pops, nodded toward the empty chair beside him.

Just as she headed in his direction, Gran asked for her help, and someone needed another helping of gumbo and then Hank wanted to talk about a helicopter she was working on.

By the time they'd polished off the last of Mrs. H.'s beignets, it was dark.

Camille had just started toward Lucien for a second time when Cass stood and clapped her hands. "Don't go anywhere, everybody. It's time for the best part."

Grinning, she and Camille stepped off the boat and headed to the open area behind the barn, where they'd staged the fireworks display earlier. Cass had been wanting to learn, and Camille felt she was finally ready. "Time for the last check."

Cass nodded and they ran through the safety checks one more time. "I wish Gramps was here," Cass said.

"Me, too. He'd be so proud of you, baby girl." Camille hugged her, then said, "Ready?"

Cass nodded and together they lit the fuses, then ran back to the boat, laughing as the first burst of color exploded overhead.

As everyone oohed and aahed, Camille stepped up beside Lucien, who leaned on the rail, smiling as she approached. He wrapped an arm around her shoulders and pulled her close, placing a kiss on her temple.

They stayed that way for a few minutes, enjoying the show. Then he leaned in and murmured, "So what do you think, Princess? Can you put up with a pirate in your life?"

She eased back and saw that the shadowy weight of guilt and sorrow he'd carried was finally gone. For him, and maybe for her, too. Instead, she saw a future filled with love and laughter reflected in the mischievous glint in his blue eyes. She could almost feel J. T. smiling, too.

Eyebrow raised, she sent Lucien a cheeky grin. "Planning to steal my heart, are you, Broussard?"

He winked, his face lit with a grin brighter than the fireworks overhead. "Working on it, Ms. Abernathy."

Camille threw her head back and laughed, then leaned in and whispered, "Glad to hear it."

She rested her head on his shoulder and smiled at all her people gathered round, safe and sound. Contentment filled her. This was all the treasure she needed.

Thanks for this place, Gramps—and for reminding me to put feet to my faith.

A Note from the Author

I hope you've enjoyed *The Liar's Treasure* and spending time with the Speranza team. I think today, more than ever, we need stories that center around strong, courageous, flawed women who help other women and are making the world a better place.

People often ask how I develop my stories. For *The Liar's Treasure*, my curiosity about priceless treasures led to research into the legends surrounding them and the creative ways people have tried to hide and protect them. That got me thinking about the biblical story of Ananias and Sapphira, which has always fascinated me because they died for lying. I wondered, *What if a legendary treasure could judge motives?* From there, the plot took off.

But beyond providing a fun adventure, my hope is that *The Liar's Treasure* encourages you to take a leap of faith, like Camille and the team did, even when it's scary. To step out of your comfort zone and take risks, especially on behalf of others.

Bravo to those who have told me the Speranza team's courage has inspired you to do exactly that. Don't stop! We need your voice. Your compassion. Your strength and wisdom and kindness. Keep looking around and seeking out where you can help. No small act of kindness is ever wasted.

My hope is that together, we will spread *speranza*—hope—around the world.

Connie Mann

Acknowledgments

Thank you to every single person who has purchased a copy of *The Liar's Treasure*, told a friend about it, written a review, or recommended it to your book club. Your excitement and support for this series and your desire to embrace the Speranza spirit in your own lives is an inspiration to me!

My heart overflows with gratitude for the amazing folks at Tyndale House Fiction who worked so hard to bring this story to life. Associate publisher Stephanie J. Broene has championed this series from the beginning and I couldn't be more thankful. Her keen story insight, together with eagle-eyed line editor Julee Schwarzburg and the whole copyediting team, helped make this story all I hoped it could be. Major kudos to art director Dean H. Renninger for designing this amazing cover and huge thanks to Andrea Martin, Wendie Connors, Stephanie Abrassart, Shelley Bacote, Elizabeth Jackson, and every single person at Tyndale who has worked so hard to get this book into the hands of readers.

Boundless thanks to Leslie Santamaria, my amazing critique partner, children's author, heart-sister, and cheerleader, without whose steadfast encouragement this book could not have been written.

Huge thanks to my fabulous agent, Ali Herring, who is always there to offer advice, answer questions, and help me navigate the business side of things with skill and grace.

A big hug to Tammy Karasek, whose encouragement, launch team leadership and social media savvy make things run so smoothly.

So thankful for my fabulous hubby, who has been my biggest cheerleader for thirty years! And to my children and extended family for their encouragement over the years.

Thanks also to writer friends Caro Carson and Teresa Elliott Brown, my fabulous book club friends, and my fellow early morning beach-walkers who've offered endless encouragement along the way.

And, as always, bottomless thanks to the Great Creator Himself, who gives the gift of stories and invites us to share them with the world.

Discussion Questions

1. If you could become one of the Speranza team members for a day, who would you choose? What about that character appeals to you? How would you spend the day? Are there traits you see in her that you'd like to cultivate in your own life?

2. Camille wants to be seen as strong and capable, but sometimes her directional dyslexia makes her feel dumb. Lucien is a good guy, but he's dismissed as a no-good Broussard because of his family's pirate ancestors. Have you ever had to work to make others' perceptions of you match your internal self? Do people's opinions affect you? How?

3. Gramps's Vietnam combat boots reminded him that "we have to put feet to our faith." Camille also recalls him saying, "Faith is easy when you're standing on familiar ground." What does it mean to put feet to your faith? Do you agree that faith is easy when you're standing on familiar ground? Why or why not?

4. When Lucien admits to Camille that he feels guilty for J. T.'s death, Camille tells him, "You don't have that much power" because Lucien didn't cause his friend's death. Have you ever struggled with guilt and responsibility for something that, in your head, you knew wasn't your fault? How did you wrestle it down and make peace with it? How would you encourage someone else going through this?

5. Camille has to make a tough choice early in the story: Should she stay home to protect her daughter in the short term, or leave her daughter with Gran to protect her in the long term? Do you agree or disagree with her choice? What would you have done? How would trust, faith, and logic play out in making your decision?

6. In this story, the team travels to Italy, Germany, and the Bahamas. Which location is your favorite? Have you been there? If you could go anywhere, where would it be and why?

7. Lucien finds himself caught between a rock and a hard place. He is torn between his loyalty to his grandfather and to Camille, his best friend's widow, who are both after the same thing. How would you have handled his dilemma?

8. The Speranza team is ready to help at a moment's notice. Do you have your own team of friends or family members that can spring into action when needed? Are the people you call when *you* need help different from the ones you call to help someone else? Do you find it easier to help than to ask for help? Why or why not?

About the Author

Connie Mann loves taking readers on heart-pounding, suspense-filled adventures featuring strong, determined women who fight for what they believe—and for those they love. When those stories take place in exciting locales and include a tempting hero, so much the better. Her Speranza Team novels center around a modern-day secret society of resourceful, talented women who travel the globe helping other women, especially those trying to make the world a better place. Connie is also the author of the Florida Wildlife Warriors series, the Safe Harbor series, *Angel Falls*, and *Trapped*. She has won several writing awards, and Amazon declared *Beyond Risk* an Editors' Pick. Through mentoring and teaching writing workshops, Connie is delighted to encourage other writers on their journey.

Connie has been a USCG-licensed boat captain for almost twenty years, and when she's not writing, "Captain Connie" gets to introduce Florida visitors to dolphins, manatees, and other coastal creatures, which is as much fun as it sounds. She is also passionate about helping women and children in developing countries break the poverty cycle through education and entrepreneurship so they can build a better future for themselves and their families.

She and her husband love spending time with family and friends and heading off to explore new places, especially if they involve water and boats. Visit Connie online at conniemann.com and sign up for her newsletter for all the latest news.

CONNECT WITH CONNIE ONLINE AT

conniemann.com

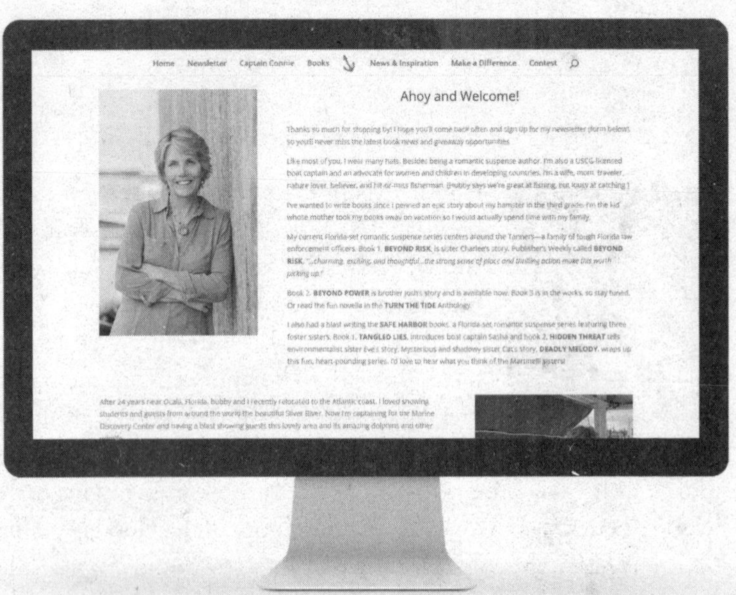

OR FOLLOW HER ON

 ConnieMannAuthor

 captconniemann

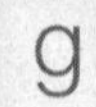 Connie_Mann

 ConnieMann

CP1966